CW00449157

Praise for Elizabe[
The Winds
myBook.to/TheWindsofFate

The Winds of Fate Reviews:

The Winds of Fate "...captivating romance that takes us to the world of seventeenth-century London...Sexual tension and legal and familial intrigue ensue with the reader cheering on the lovely pair."
<u>—Publishers Weekly</u>

The Winds of Fate "has everything...full of passion, betrayal, mystery and all the good stuff readers love."
<u>—ABNA Reviewer</u>

"Original...strong-willed heroine...I love all of it...the unlikely premise of a female member of the aristocracy visiting a man who is condemned to die and asking him to marry her."
<u>—ABNA Reviewer</u>

Surrender the Wind

Elizabeth St. Michel

Library of Congress Catalog Number: 2016905728
ISBN: 0997482400
ISBN: 9780997482409

For my father,
Eugene Dollard
An ordinary man turned extraordinary...
and from whom the well-spring of my creativity has sprung.

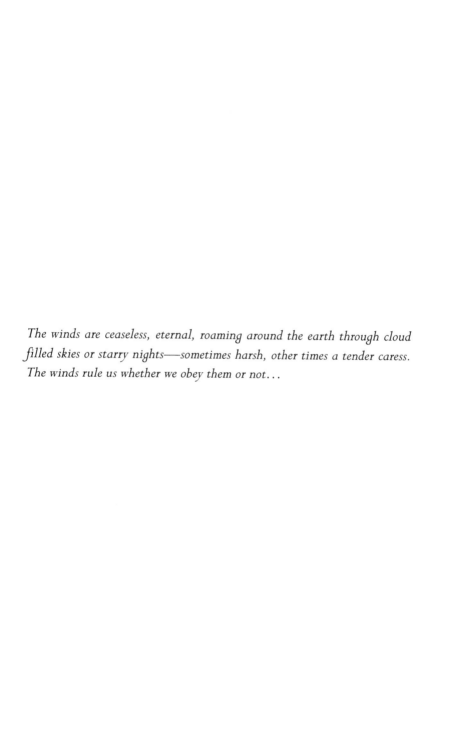

The winds are ceaseless, eternal, roaming around the earth through cloud filled skies or starry nights—sometimes harsh, other times a tender caress. The winds rule us whether we obey them or not...

Chapter 1

Pleasant Valley, New York
May 1864

"This Reb's dead."

A Union soldier dragged a body to the dark mouth of a boxcar and lifted a lantern.

"Throw him out before he stinks anymore," his sergeant ordered.

Catherine gasped and ducked farther into the shadow of the woods, her evening walk to the back part of her farm barred by a train, stopped for the switching yards farther down the track.

The sergeant jerked around. "Did you hear something?"

"No Sir, just these Rebs moaning with sickness. They reek worse than a bunch of polecats and I don't desire to catch a contagion."

"Rebs rot a lot quicker than regular folk." The sergeant yanked his neckerchief over his nose and heaved himself up. With no regard, the Reb soldier's body was swung from the train and rolled to the bottom of the railroad bed, stopping at Catherine Callahan Fitzgerald's feet.

The lack of respect for the dead, Yank or Reb, shocked her. She waited in the gathering darkness until the train hissed and clumped into the night. Wind gusted and lifted her skirts. The air pitched with heavy vapors and piles of dark sullen clouds towered in the heavens. The storm that had dragged its ragged coattails from the south now boomed across the heavens. Rain pattered on her face.

To have escaped Francis Mallory, her hands shook with impotence. What a critical walk. One misstep…if Francis found her… no way would she marry the monster.

Six more months to hide…

Catherine shivered, tried not to look at the body in the ditch. To elude Mallory's thugs, Jimmy O'Hara, an orphan boy, had helped her escape New York City. Her uncle, Father Callahan, a priest in Pleasant Valley, had stepped in and secured her a position as the schoolmarm far away from her home and had provided the small farm, two miles from town—away from prying eyes.

Her arrival was ahead of time and her uncle was out of town. She could not enlist his help and didn't dare ask any of the townsfolk. No, she couldn't afford any notice, not now. Asking someone to bury a dead Confederate soldier whose body was thrown off a train would put her, the new schoolmistress, under too much scrutiny.

At the very least, the poor soul deserved the dignity of a Christian burial. A blast of wind lifted the corpse's hair…the same dark color as her brother's. Her insides twisted with the thought of her dear brother. She glanced about, and once decided, she traversed a quarter mile to her barn, collected a shovel, returned, and then stabbed the blade into the silt, averting her eyes from the body with each shovelful. Not accustomed to manual labor, the task took a long time to dig some semblance of a grave. Her skirts were soaked and muddy, her hair plastered to her face as she attacked the earth. She couldn't help but laugh. What madness was this? Two weeks ago she was dining at the fashionable Delmonico's. Today she was a mud-splattered gravedigger. *How far had she fallen?*

Oh yes, Francis Mallory was charming and witty, charismatic and clever. He was also a madman and killer. Her sides trickled with perspiration as her mind reeled with the hushed whispers and guarded warnings of Mallory's unspeakable crimes to support his lust for power and wealth. Growing up among the roughest gangs in New York, he'd robbed, cheated and murdered, eliminating everyone in his path and emerging as the top Irish Mob Kingpin, ruling the Five Points district and maintaining his power through an alliance with the Tammany Hall political machine.

She threw down the shovel upon finishing the soldier's grave. In heavy sheets, the rain came slanting down, whipsawing against her. Steeling herself, she crooked her arms beneath the man's dead weight and dragged him. Good lord, he was heavy. She stumbled, tripped on her skirts and dropped the Reb's head on the ground.

"I hope you appreciate what I'm doing for you." She rested a moment, hands on her hips. "But you can't appreciate it, can you. You're dead." And she was talking to a dead man. She shook her head, then laid his feet in first then lowered the upper part of his body, wiped her muddy hands on her skirts and spoke a few relevant words, something appropriate for the occasion. The eulogy was not as good as her uncle, Father Callahan, would have offered, but she remained satisfied with a pretty good imitation. The soldier's family would appreciate it if they knew.

She picked up the shovel again, ready to spoon in the rain-soaked earth, then stopped. Of course, she must get his personal effects to notify his family of his passing. Her gaze went to the dark, wet hole in the ground. No. She was not going into the grave with the corpse. The storm raged, tearing and screaming its wrath upon the earth. She shuddered, more from her grisly decision than from the icy rain. Wasn't it the decent thing to do? A family deserved to know.

She swallowed the sour taste in her mouth and scrambled into the shallow grave straddling his body to search his pockets. Lightning flashes ripped through the skies again and again. He was a poor common soldier, with no ornamentation to depict a rank. Her hands trembled as she searched his pants pockets. *Nothing.*

The grave, filled up fast with water. Drat. No documents in his outer coat pockets. Bending further to explore his inner pockets, she heard the wind moan. *It was the wind, wasn't it?* Hurrying, she touched the man's breast pocket and felt…heat. Oh, God. She snatched her hand back. The corpse's body was still warm.

A hand shot out, grabbing her by the neck. She tore at iron-tight fingers circling her throat, her air passage cut off. Dizzy. In the ooze, she tore at his hands, her fingers slipping from his knuckles. Sheer black fright swept through her and she brought both fists down hard on his chest. Her heart thumping madly, she kicked and flailed, her life flashing before her eyes. His hand dropped.

Sweet oxygen poured down her throat, filling her lungs. Catherine pushed to her feet and dragged herself from the grave. Rising, her legs wobbled, the mud shifted under her feet. She teetered, lost her balance and toppled back onto the corpse. Images of the Reb cadaver pulling her to the fiery gates of hell flashed through her head. Hampered by the weight of her soaked skirts, she hitched them up over her knees then kicked, clawed, and once again pushed from the ditch.

She ran as if the devil incarnate charged after her. Reaching her home, she dashed inside, slammed and bolted the door, behind her. Her back against the rough wood, she sucked in long gulps of air. She had read that a corpse could have a final reflex, but to what degree? For a dead man, the Reb exhibited unbelievable strength.

Hands shaking, she placed her mud-spattered spectacles on a shelf. With certainty, the Reb was alive. Had he reached to her for help? She squeezed her eyes shut, remembered his harsh grip on her neck. No, not help.

But what if he was drowning in the flooded grave? She would be responsible for his death. She would be a murderer. Surely God would never forgive her. She touched her throat, felt the raw skin where she'd scratched to get him to release her while her mind warred with moral reason. What if it had been her brother, Shawn, missing for eight months after a skirmish with the Rebels, injured and suffering the elements? Wouldn't she want someone to help him?

Sighing, she unlocked the door and stepped out into the darkness. Light spilled onto her porch from her lantern. The wind gusted in violent blasts and the thunder rolled and attacked as the storm vibrated the heavens with its superior force. Nature had declared war. No doubt she was mad.

She ducked her head and stepped from the roof's protection, staggering as her long skirts plastered against her legs, the hems flapping violently behind her. Reaching the ditch, she peered over the edge. Empty! She gasped. She swung around, her lantern creating fearsome shadows.

A chill black unease raced up her spine. What was she thinking? She yanked a strand of wet hair from her eyes and slogged her way across the mud-slicked path back, struggling to keep her balance, watching her footing lest she slip and fall. Good. He wasn't her problem anymore. She couldn't wait to strip off her wet clothes and submerge in a hot bath.

Once inside, in case the Reb decided to pay her a call, Catherine bolted the door. She leaned her forehead against the door, almost feeling sorry for him, injured and braving the storm. Unlike her, warm and cozy in her own home. Her gaze wandered to a heart-shaped locket she wore, pictures of her parent's closed safe inside, and then to the...footprints.

Her nerves pulled tight. A mish-mash of muddy footprints peppered the floor—footprints larger than hers. She whipped around. *The Reb.* Did she grab a knife from the sideboard or throw the bolt and run?

Instead of doing either, she froze. Even with his leanness, he dwarfed her. Tall, threatening and dangerous, his steel-blue eyes held her, compelling, magnetic. The clear-cut lines of his profile, unhidden by the shadow of his beard, gave him a rakish look. Encrusted with mud, it was too hard to tell the color of his hair. Despite his ill state, he exuded an air of confidence and intelligence, and beneath the filth and dark beard, a rugged flesh and blood man radiated strength, masculinity, and power.

His calm did not fool her. Face flushed, he shivered and sweated with fever. Was he trying to gather a sense of time and place, or recognition of her with her mud-laden dress and long wet hair? Or worse, maybe he was assessing other plans for her. She could not tell. She dared not move. Still she remained, mesmerized, fascinated, and drawn into those steel-blue orbs.

He raised his hand to touch her. She stepped back.

"Don't leave me," he said, and crashed to the floor.

Long seconds passed. She drew a deep breath, forcing herself to relax. He was wounded, but if she tried to help, would he wake and do her harm? The slow tick of the parlor clock beat incongruous to the man's labored raspy breathing.

His mud-caked coat had fallen open revealing a once-white shirt sopped with black-crusted blood and fresh red blood. She stepped back, then forward again, reached out, then drew her hand away. In her entire existence nothing had prepared her for this. He needed a doctor. No. He needed a miracle.

His chest rose and fell—barely. He had lost a great deal of blood and would probably die. She cursed the dispassionate nature of Union doctors. Why had they not treated an injured man?

And wasn't she just as dispassionate if she didn't do something to help. If she left him to bleed to death without lifting a finger. There was another issue…the impropriety of attending a man alone. She snorted. A feeble excuse. She'd never been one to bow to conventionality.

His steel-blue eyes flashed in her mind, wounded eyes, like those of a child reaching out to her for solace, shadowed with sincerity.

"Don't leave me." Her heart lurched. How could she abandon anyone with such a plea?

Girding herself with resolve, she recalled every single surgery Dr. Parks had performed at MacDougall Hospital in Fort Schuyler on the city's edge where she volunteered assisting him throughout the war. After washing her hands, she grabbed a pair of scissors, cut off the Rebel's clothes, and then covered the lower part of his body with a sheet. Except for a minor knee abrasion, he was fine there. But his head was hot to her touch. Would she lose him to a fever? Twice as many soldiers, North and South, died from illness than from actual battle. Sickness and death held no discrimination.

She filled a basin with water from the kettle on the stove. Dr. Parks had warned her to keep everything clean so the patient would not fall ill from the treatment. She sponged and rinsed off blood, mud and filth. Blackish-purple mottled the side of his abdomen. He moaned when she rolled him to check for an exit wound. None. The bullet was lodged inside. As she washed away the last fragments of clotted blood, the coppery smell of fresh blood wafted. New blood was a good sign, wasn't it?

Could she get the ball out? She procured a knife, needle, thread and clean cotton cloth. Alcohol was needed for sterilization. Remembering a bottle of whiskey left in the cupboard by the former schoolmaster, Catherine retrieved it, pouring liberal amounts over her hands, instruments and his wound. She gritted her teeth and began to probe, praying he'd remain unconscious and that no internal organs were damaged. Her fingers slid stickily through his muscle. Bile rose in her throat. She exhaled when she felt the ball.

Doing the deed was not as easy as it had been watching Dr. Parks. The ball eluded her grasp. The Reb thrashed and screamed. She scrunched her eyes shut, pushed down, seized the ball with her fingertips and pulled it out. She threw the ball aside, cleaned him up, again, and bound his wounds.

Fire! Fire! God he was hot. Fever clouded Rourke's dreams and numbed his brain. Attack! Attack! Everywhere attack. Do not let the enemy rest. General John Daniel Rourke knew the importance of first assault. General Robert E. Lee had ordered the Confederate Army of Northern Virginia to attack Grant's Union Army first. John scrutinized the unyielding terrain swallowing up his Rebel brigade, the Seventh and Twelfth Virginia Infantry.

A light fog nestled in the hollows and streams...and the rising sun bathed the woods in a haunting gray mist. General Rourke halted his column to see what was ahead of him. Canteens clanged against other accoutrements, officers shouted commands, tree branches crunched, underfoot in rhythmic pattern. A Union infantry line advanced toward his front. Not yet. Giving a hand signal, so as not to alert the Yanks of their position, the Rebs disappeared around trees like specters in the ground fog.

"Fire!" John roared. Rising en masse, the Confederates volleyed point-blank. The Yanks recoiled under the blast firing, rallying, closing ranks, loading again and returning fire. An asphyxiating pall of burnt powder hung low in the pines and blooming dogwoods, making it difficult to tell friend from foe. Ear-splitting shouts rang from the bush in front of them. Yankees...regiments of Yankees.

"Retreat!" John ordered. Minie balls whistled and hummed about them like swarming bees. His men dodged and darted around trees and bounded

over logs. John staggered under the impact of a spent ball that glanced off the knee flap of his heavy boot. Around him, several of his men cried out and toppled to the earth, mortally wounded.

Between shouts and curses, a furious Yankee commander, shrieked, "Throw down your guns! Drop your colors! Surrender!"

Never would he surrender! An exploding bullet seared into his side, sending a shower of his blood over the forest floor. His men scattered and disappeared in a melee over the ridge. Another volley of shots cracked from behind. A bullet burned against his skull, knocking him beneath dense undergrowth.

Pungent smells of earth, blood and sulfur assailed John's nostrils. His own blood dripped from his head wound, salty on his lips. Distant cries of the wounded wailed around him. His men would have been back for him if they could. It must have been a serious rout. Glancing to his left, he found under his hand a grinning skull; and beneath that, bleached bones with weather-stained clothing. This was a fallen hero of last year's Battle of the Wilderness. Ironic, his parting company, a smirking, grisly ghost. No matter if he was Reb or Yank. He would be joining his boney friend soon.

General John Daniel Rourke's vision cleared to a blurred fuzziness. He strived to ignore the searing pain in his side, struggled to get a bearing on his surroundings. A woman sat in a chair, her head lying on the bed and facing him. Asleep. John studied her in repose. Cascades of long thick gold hair, the color of sunlight and honey, hung in graceful curves over her shoulders and down her back. Sooty lashes dusted delicate ivory cheeks. Her nose was straight, short and charming, and her lips, full and rosy.

Where was he? John shook the cobwebs cluttering his mind. Out a single window soared a high sloping green mountain. Was he a prisoner? In a hospital? He stretched. His side burned like hell. He'd been shot—and he was still alive. *Escape.*

Dusk approached the western sky and cast a glowing mixture of vermilion, orange and gold throughout the room's interior. Even the woman was swathed in gold. Who was she? A northerner or southern sympathizer? Nothing made sense, especially the beautiful woman at his side. And John had grown cynical toward beautiful women.

He did not wake her. She stretched, her hand entwined in his, as if it were a natural thing to do. Her fingers felt cool, soft, stroking against his warm palm in a possessive gesture, as if she owned him. John had never been a man to be owned by a woman. Yet, somehow he favored her gentle touch.

The room had standard appointments. An armoire stood against the wall, and to the right, a matching dresser with mirror on top. Next to the bed, a round top table with an oil lamp, pitcher and washbasin. No weapons. A photograph caught his attention, the confident pose of a young man clad in a Union Colonel's uniform. The sheet strained across his tightened knuckles. What was he to the woman? A husband? A beau? A lover?

Keep your priorities in check. John relaxed his grip. He had to get back to General Lee, to let him know he had survived. He had to get back to the war.

The woman stirred. John closed his eyes. His senses heightened, he perceived she stared at him. Her scent ensnared him... lilac. He heard her rise, her bare feet padding across the floor, and the click of armoire doors. He opened his eyes. She had her back to him, unaware of his conscious state. Unbuttoning her blue dress, she let it fall in a faint swish. The gentlemanly thing to do would be to make his condition known. *To hell with chivalry.* Clad in her undergarments, she bent to pick up her dress, and then reached high to hang it on a hook. Her entire profile stretched before him, her slender white neck to her firm high breasts that strained against the soft silk of her lace-edged chemise. She had a slim waist, small enough to span his hands around, flaring to rounded hips, and long lithe legs. John swallowed. He had been in battle too long.

With discretion, she turned her back to him again and donned a long white gown, removing her chemise from underneath. John gritted his teeth, feeling like a schoolboy bartered out of his prize. The woman stood upright, her gown buttoned to the neck for modesty sake. John's throat went dry. The fineness of the gown left nothing to the imagination. She brushed her hair with long, slow strokes. Unable to tear his gaze away, John lay there in raw, agonizing silence. She placed her silver brush on the dresser, leaned back, massaging her fingers in the small of her back, leaving him with a clear view of the soft rounded curves beneath her gown. He was in pain and certainly not from his wound. The woman turned. He closed his eyes.

"I hope you wake soon. I need my bed. The prior schoolmaster stole most of the furniture upon his departure and you occupy the only place I have to sleep. One more night in that chair and my back will be contorted."

John doubted anything about her would ever be contorted. For several seconds, the woman paced back and forth. The armoire doors snapped open again. Pillows were stuffed in the middle of the bed.

"There," she said, "you have your side, and I have mine."

John almost smiled. Would he be sharing the same bed with the local schoolmarm? He was in heaven. No. He had been thrust into everlasting fires.

After turning down the lamp, the woman slipped into the bed. He suppressed a chuckle with her diligence in keeping the pillows as a barrier, her fingers a death grip on the coverlet and held tight to her neck. Seven horses could not have pulled the coverlet away.

In the darkness, he heard a sniffle, then weeping. What caused her sorrow?

"Please Shawn, come back to me. I know you're not dead."

Her sobbing and her call for her lover hurled cold water on John's fervor. A mocking inner voice cut through his thoughts and a mixture of jealousy and compassion stirred in his chest. He did not relish her devotion to her lover and no doubt, he existed in the hereafter. The war cut two ways...North and South. Thousands of men had died, leaving a void in people's lives on the home front.

With certainty, she was a Yank—her accent pure New York. Melodious. Cultured. Years ago he had visited the city while attending West Point. He could encircle her with his arms and offer comfort, but that would shock and alarm her. She was tired, needed rest, and he needed her to help him fully recover—to escape. Instead he wished for a fine Southern cigar, contented with her warmth emanating from the pillows. This was a new experience for him, sleeping with a woman and not doing what came to mind. She shifted...her movements a faint whisper of silk against cotton. She must have given up her sorrow, her breaths coming out against his neck in a feather-like caress. Asleep.

Chapter 2

Catherine stirred and exhaled. She had slept well, given to dreams of better days when Shawn was home and her parents were alive. Life had soared with gaiety and happiness. But they were gone. Her mother died of influenza followed by her father who died in an accident. Shawn had marched off to war, his recklessness a catalyst to his demise. She opened her eyes and stared straight into extraordinary, compelling, steel-blue eyes. A slow smile greeted her. With a gasp, she hurtled back to earth.

"Oh, my goodness." She leaped from the bed, jerking the coverlet around her.

"Good morning," he drawled, his voice deep and dark as she had imagined.

Heat rose from her toes to the roots of her hair, and loathe to know how long he'd been awake. "Never did I expect you to wake so soon. What you must think—"

He grinned. "Not at all. How long have I been here?" He glanced at the pitcher.

She poured a glass of water, helped him to a seated position and tucked pillows behind him. His shoulders seemed broader against the headboard. "For two nights and three days, I have cared for you, changing your bandages and cooling you down to lower your fever. I didn't know——"

"If I would make it." He finished for her, returned the empty glass, and grimaced from the soreness of his injury. "I am in your debt. I'd like to know where I am."

"Pleasant Valley, New York, a mile north of the Pennsylvania border." *And four hundred miles from Francis.*

"Your name?"

She frowned, his request, too authoritative. She chose her mother's surname. "Catherine Callahan."

"It's a pleasure making your acquaintance, Miss Callahan. Am I to assume it was *you* who aided in my recovery?" In pain, he folded his hands behind his head, watched her, his expression making clear his rightful place in the universe. Was he calculating details about her? She moved to her armoire and snatched her dress. He wanted to know if she were alone. She'd never tell.

His facial expression changed to one of amusement. "Miss Callahan, I wish all the North were as transparent as you, for there would have been a decided victory long ago."

Her breath burned in her throat. So he had guessed she lived alone. Finding perverse delight in piercing his enjoyment, she spun to face him. "You are very smug for someone who is my prisoner."

"I consider it a pleasure." He chuckled as though he played a game—the line drawn. "Since I am your prisoner, could you provide some food? I'm famished—and water. I recall that all prisoners of the North receive some kind of succor."

She tripped on the coverlet and hauled it back up over her shoulder. "I will get your food when I'm good and ready. The sooner you get better, the sooner you'll depart." This was madness. To think she had an army of servants to attend her. Today she played nurse-maid to a Reb who was getting above himself.

In her tiny kitchen, she bathed from a chipped porcelain washbasin, plucked her dress off the ladder-back chair, donned it, then stomped across the warm oak-plank floors, scrubbed and cleaned of the Reb's blood. After placing a teakettle on the stove, she opened her front door and stepped out onto the porch, admiring the brick-red sunrise. Her one-story farmhouse had a kitchen, parlor and bedroom, and held a charm like the gingerbread-laced, fisherman cottages that dotted the shores of Long Island. Except there was no drop to the sea, salt air, or waves crashing on the beach. Burrowed in the Allegheny Mountains, her new home brimmed with the piney smell of hemlock, mingling with cinnamon ferns and damp mosses. The harmonious sighs of mourning doves flowed tandem with a gentle breeze that sifted through the maples and oaks.

The teakettle whistled and she returned to the kitchen, brewed tea, and arranged a breakfast platter. She brushed her hair into a tight bun and placed on her spectacles, then moved toward the bedroom.

Catherine plunked a tray in front of him. He looked at her twice, yet remained too much of a gentleman to comment on her appearance. She gave a crisp nod and sat in the chair next to him, aghast to see him drain an entire pitcher of water and empty a bowl of stew as if Armageddon descended upon him. "We chew our food before swallowing."

"Not when you haven't had anything to boast about in your stomach for a month."

"I thought during your army's forays north, you Rebels thieved and robbed enough to supply the South for the next five years."

The Reb frowned. "However, your northern army was not the least hospitable with even less to entertain, making our friendly visit—brief." His tone was irascible, yet tempered.

"I'll return these papers I found on your person." She pulled them off the table and presented them to him. "I took the liberty of reading them. I believe, Mr. Benjamin Benson, that is to say, Private Benson of Confederate Army of South Carolina, that—"

"That thieving son of a bit—" He caught himself before he finished his slur. "I am not Private Benson."

Catherine almost laughed but dared not, after how upset he'd become. "You should not over exert yourself, Mr. Benson. You may have had a head injury. There are such traumas."

His nostrils flared. "I assure you, I have no such trauma, Miss Callahan. As you know yourself, so do I know who I am."

Was he delusional? "Then who do you think you are?"

"Are you going to turn me in?"

His question was guarded, and she shrugged. "Wouldn't I have done so already?"

Silence as thick as mud oozed between them. Why was he hesitant? Couldn't he remember? His gaze raked her, searching for an answer. To have an amnesiac Reb on her hands…how much more complicated could her life become?

"I am General John Daniel Rourke, Army of Northern Virginia."

He was crazy. "But your papers say——"

"I heard you the first time!"

"You don't have to amplify your complaint. I'm sure there is a logical reason." She placated him as if he were a small child. "Perhaps you admire this individual or maybe you have an intrinsic desire to be a general that allows your thoughts to confuse you. It could happen to anyone." The sooner she got rid of the raving lunatic, the better.

"Surely you jest."

"It's not in my nature to joke about a serious topic such as this, Private Benson." She must not reinforce his delusions.

"Do not call me that name again. I am General John Daniel Rourke, and I will not abide any slight to my family's name."

She gave a weary sigh. "Whatever you say. I am sure you have a plausible explanation as to why you were wearing a private's uniform and carrying a private's identification papers. Why it must happen to everyone in the South. Perhaps the town fool wakes up thinking he's your President Jefferson Davis. Or Jefferson Davis is the town fool."

He dropped his fork and it clanged on the empty plate. "There was chaos in the last battle near Spotsylvania. The lines merged in the wilderness. Injured, I was unable to fight the cur who switched my clothes and paper for his, enabling him to be placed in an officer's prisoner of war camp where there is better treatment. Nonetheless, it is why I carry his papers."

"An interesting story with an unfortunate end. I thought rebels were——honorable?"

"Most, but not all. But it appears I have received the better of the deal." His voice lowered, pleasant, potent, tempered and muted by his Southern accent. It was a voice that could woo seductively, or command in such a way as to compel obedience. Indeed, the man's whole character was in that voice of his.

His eyebrows furrowed. "Why have you helped me?"

The intensity of his gaze sucked the air out of her lungs. She jumped, upended her chair, righted it, then met a sudden need to set everything to order. She straightened her leather boots and tucked her cotton gowns inside the armoire, closing the doors with a bang. She glanced over her shoulder. He assessed her again, as if she should come forward with some powerful revelation. How many times had she asked the question? Wasn't he caught in a world upside down as much as she?

You have six months to force Catherine to marry me—before she reaches twenty-four years and can legally inherit her family's assets. You will be well compensated.

Like standing on the precipice of a bottomless abyss…if Francis discovered her whereabouts…of course, her stepmother, Agatha profited by the arrangement. The easy parlay managed by Mallory would gain him control of one of the largest dynasties in the United States.

She sagged against the back of her chair. "I took pity on you. I'm sick of all the death and dying. It has pervaded every avenue of my life."

"I am a rebel—your sworn enemy."

"It is ironic." She moved to the window. The surrounding countryside was green and lovely with the return of spring and the promise of summer. She wrapped her arms around her in an effort to steady her emotions. Her war was on two fronts.

Millions of Irish immigrants had swarmed into New York City, crowded in teaming tenements, poverty, and ghettos. Along with the uncontrolled growth, the criminal members of an Irish underworld flourished. Those who lived by vice and crime preyed upon the misfortune of others by using brute strength for power and money. Francis Mallory was part of this unscrupulous circle and had manipulated more power with the distraction of the war. Born on the wrong side of the blanket, his blue-blooded father ignored the poverty-stricken life of his bastard son. His mother had died drunk and beaten to death in a West Side brothel.

"You're more than angry."

"I am. This war has taken everything dear from me...Shawn."

John lifted a hand then dropped it, discerning she fought for control and would not desire any sign of consolation that might make her lose it. *Shawn—the Lt. Colonel in the photograph.* He turned over the picture of her long dead lover. He refused to be haunted by a ghost.

She pressed her forehead against the windowpane. "My brother, Shawn..."

John coughed. "Shawn is your brother?" When she nodded, he laced his fingers behind his head and relaxed against the pillows. *Interesting.* So the man she mourned was her brother and not her lover.

"If only he would come back. He would make everything right."

She drew a long steadying breath and seeing her pain, an unfamiliar constriction rose in Rourke's chest. Unable to get her despair out of his mind, he said, "And yet you helped a stranger."

"You are lucky not to have proceeded onto Elmira. It is rumored to be a horrible prisoner of war camp, perhaps worse than your Andersonville. Besides…" she whispered, "…it was my Christian duty."

Her voice swayed for a second, too complicated to ascribe to a lone emotion. Guilt? Desperation? Fear? But why? "Somehow you don't strike me as one of those old harridans, sitting on her porch, quoting scripture and verse."

"How do I strike you?" She turned toward him, blinked behind her spectacles.

John grimaced. How he'd like to toss those horrid spectacles out the window and pull the pins from her hair. "I don't know," he said, except he suspected a lot more beneath the surface.

"I must redress your wound." She removed his tray from the room and returned with jars and dressings that she placed on the bedside table. John rather liked the way her fingers twisted together. Was she nervous touching him now that he was conscious? Would he make it easier for her? No.

She licked her lips and turned back the sheet. Her fingers touched his skin, feather light and the jolt he received from her touch caused him to inhale. She drew back.

"Did I hurt you?"

"No." He gruffed out. Her spectacles had fallen down her nose, revealing lovely emerald eyes, agreeable in expression and totally irresistible. An angel had descended from the heavens, dazzling as the first glow of universe and rescued him from a grim demise.

Her fingers lingered a moment at the top of his bandage, as if uncertain. He felt her innocence in her touch. She untied the knot and peeled the bandage back to peek at his wound. His stomach muscles clenched.

"Better. Needs more poultice to draw out any remaining infection."

Keeping her features deceptively composed, Catherine opened a jar of liniment.

"That stuff stinks to high heavens. You are not going to put it on me."

"I certainly am," and with a quick swipe of a cloth, she layered a thick coat on the healing wound. Did he want to strangle her? She refused to shrink from under his intimidating stare.

"Smells like a nest of riled skunks."

"Yes, but very effective." She laughed, wrinkling her nose. "Besides you need a little humbling. Your fever has left you cranky and overbearing."

He stared at her in disbelief. "I'll have you know if any soldier of mine ever countermanded an order like you have just done, he'd be horsewhipped."

"Is that a threat, Mr. Benson?" She used the soldier's name to prick his ire, despite the fact she was beginning to believe he was telling the truth. No common foot soldier could ever be so commanding.

"Are you always so contradictory, Miss Callahan? Tell me, do they breed all ladies of the North with insubordination?" He drawled with distinct mockery then flinched.

"Only when they are threatened with a horsewhip by some scoundrel. Is the salve burning yet?" Her lips twitched from his growing scowl. "That's when it works best."

"What other treatments do you have? Shoving wood-splints up my fingernails?"

Ignoring his sarcasm, Catherine itched to smooth back the crop of dark hair falling over his forehead. He was so churlish and stubborn, like a little boy who'd scraped his knee. "Are you scorning my expert medical care?"

"That stuff isn't fit for my horse."

Catherine burst out laughing. "In truth, that's what it's for."

"You mean to tell me I'm being wrapped in horse liniment?"

His astonishment was priceless. "You should be more enthusiastic about your treatment. After all, it saved your life."

"More likely will end it," he finished.

"It will stop burning in a few minutes," she said, half-apologetic. "But I must wrap clean bandages around you. For that I'll need your help."

Catherine unrolled long strips of cotton cloth. She helped him lean forward again, wrapping the clean cotton strips around his midsection, then around his back, compelled by a latent need to touch him.

She had volunteered at MacDougall Hospital and had bandaged many men but the isolation of her lone country farmhouse and the menacing Reb added an intimacy she had not experienced before.

Curious about his body, she guided the bandage around his lean rippled stomach muscles, admiring his male sort of beauty. He was devastatingly handsome, his body, lean from years on the march, and she assumed, this rugged, vital man who had a monopoly on virility, attracted women like swarms of locusts. With him conscious, her thoughts clouded and erased all of her mirth. Staving off the quick unaccustomed tingling in the pit of her stomach grew impossible. Did he shudder beneath her fingertips? Twice she dropped the cloth and apologized. What did he say? She swallowed, managed a feeble answer, none of which sounded in any way intelligible.

A warning voice in her head told her to finish the task and leave. She looked down. His gaze was drawn to her breasts where they strained against the fabric of the dress she wore. General Rourke was enjoying himself. To strangle him had merit. He opened his mouth to laugh at her but stopped. A pulse beat at the base of his throat. She couldn't see where his eyes traveled next but rather felt his heated appraisal of her waist and hips. When she stretched to wrap the cloth around him, her breast grazed his cheek.

"Hold still!" She jumped from her own command, flushing as he shifted and fisted his hands in the sheets. "I'll never be able to finish."

She continued the process determined to finish and leave. The general groaned and she tied off the bandage. With her free hand, she pushed her spectacles back up the bridge of her nose and swiped at loose tendrils of her hair.

The general jerked his head back, looked at her twice. "You tried to bury me alive."

25

She flinched. "Union soldiers threw your body from the train that crosses my property. I had gone for a walk...seen what they did...they said you were dead," she sniffed. "I wished to give you a proper burial."

"By letting the worms have me before I'm dead?"

"You tried to strangle me." She grabbed the scissors and discarded bandages. A dangling end caught beneath him and she yanked it out.

"You were picking my pockets. You shoveled dirt over me."

She pointed the scissors at him. "I was looking for your personal effects to notify your family. To think this is the thanks I get." She moved to the door, her heels clacking on the floor, her chin raised. "I'll chalk it up to you being cantankerous and needing your rest." How dare he direct the full blast of his hostility toward her when she had done everything in her power to do what was right?

"Cantankerous? That is for doddering old men."

She waved her scissors through the air. "Add complaining and whining."

"Complaining? Whining? That is novel." He patted the bed next to him. "I don't want to be alone, and neither do you. Sit down," he commanded. "I am a gentleman. Arrogant, but a gentleman and I...apologize."

Catherine opened her mouth at first to decline and thank him for his offer, then stopped. It seemed a betrayal to thank her enemy, to pretend that there was no war between them and that they were—well—friends. Shawn was missing or dead, and maybe by this man's bullet.

A lump grew in her throat, and her chest constricted at the thought. Shawn had been so proud to fight for the cause, but she'd wanted to hold him back. Keep him safe. Keep him close. Now she had no one.

One thing was for certain. If this man was who he affirmed he was, then she was in the company of the Confederate Army's most notorious, if not dangerous, commanders. Over the past four years of war, she had read many newspaper articles of General John Daniel Rourke's exploits. To the discredit and frustration of northern commanders, he had immobilized, attacked and out-maneuvered them embarrassingly, and he did it over and over again. He was one of General Lee's favorite fighting sons of the Confederacy, the toast and legend of the South. Clever, cold and defiant. He remained at the forefront, advancing hundreds of his screaming angry Rebs, their blood-cry and lust for battle sending a chill up any Union soldier's spine. It was hard to believe he was in her bed.

Never would it be proper for a woman to entertain a man without a chaperone, let alone her bedroom, and scandalous in the eyes of New York Society. Yet Pleasant Valley was miles away, her present home far from town, and no one was around to check on proper decorum. The general or whoever he assumed to be was offering her friendship. She could see it in the warmth of his eyes, hear it in the gentleness of his deep baritone voice. How could she turn his friendship aside? And hadn't he apologized?

Maybe North and South were fighting, but for just this once, Catherine thought with perfect clarity, peace could be bridged through friendship—a friendship that connected the spirit of honor, dignity, and compassion. Both of them were alone, an island unto themselves, absent from hate and struggle and death.

Having made her decision after a prolonged period of silence, she lifted her chin, accepting his offer of friendship. She sat on the chair facing him.

"Tell me everything there is about you, Miss Callahan."

Her mind fluttered away. *What was she to say? Tell him outright that she was an heiress to one the largest fortunes in the country? Tell him her family's wealth was made from Fitzgerald Rifle Works, rifles manufactured to kill Rebel soldiers?* They had initiated a friendship. If he knew her identity, he would hate her.

"There's not too much to tell. I am the schoolteacher in Pleasant Valley."

He interrupted her. "You are not from here, are you?"

He hadn't gained his reputation by being slow to see and seize— a discrepancy. She flushed. "I'm from New York City. My uncle is the parish priest in this community and offered me the position when the schoolmaster ran off with the wife of the butcher. Since my mother and father died before the war, and with Shawn missing and no real family remaining, I was detached and lonely. So I decided to take my uncle up on his offer. It's all very simple, really, not much to tell." She smoothed her skirts, depicting an ease she didn't feel.

He frowned with only a slight smile to warm his expression. No doubt, after commanding men, he had acquired an uncanny gift of discernment and not for one moment did she think he believed anything about her was as "simple" as she stated. "How is it you came to be so well educated, Miss Callahan?"

She shifted under his direct scrutiny, Catherine crafted an answer. "I read quite a bit. My father was a great lover of books, and as he had a business of modest means, had the funds to acquire them." She didn't dare tell him they had one of the most comprehensive of residential libraries in New York. Neither did she divulge that prominent invited guests to their home included lively debates on the arts, economics, politics, literature and many other subjects. Among them was Horace Greeley, editor of the New York Tribune, William Astor and Admiral David G. Farragut. All and many more had graced the Fitzgerald table on different occasions. "I try to read everything I can get my hands on, General Rourke." She inclined her head, offering him the same formality in which he had addressed her.

He threw back his head and roared with laughter. "Am I to understand that you now believe I am who I say I am? Believe what you will, but I always speak the truth." He stared at her with well-intended meaning.

Sound lodged in her throat along with her heart. Had he guessed she was not telling the whole story? *That she lived in danger.* Catherine shrugged, betraying none of her nervousness from his continued scrutiny. "Lord save me from a man with his illusions."

"Life is a journey down the landscape of illusion." He probed again, his double entendre.

How dare he patronize her? As if he knew so much more than she. "How philosophical you are, not only claiming to be a general but a Greek scholar too. Was it Socrates?" Did she see a challenge met in his eyes? Catherine smiled. Indeed, he'd find her a worthy foe.

"No Plato." His grin was taunting.

"But Plato based his ethical theory on the proposition that all people desire happiness. Is that not so?" She tempted him.

"Yes."

"Of course," she instructed. "People sometimes act in ways that do not yield happiness. But they do this only because they do not know what actions will produce happiness—like your Cause." Her gaze locked on his, she waited for some frivolous answer—some goading, some crossing of swords.

Instead he considered her, letting the moment draw out, then raising his brows. "The touch of your sword wounds me. Plato further claimed that happiness is the natural consequence of a healthy state of the soul. Because moral virtue makes up the health of the soul, all people should desire to be virtuous, therefore States rights are paramount—as my Cause—for they are virtuous."

What a thrill that he thrived on intellectual debate. "Your so-called virtuous States Rights are flawed. For the soul of Plato, the basic problem of ethics is a problem of knowledge. If a person knows that moral virtue leads to happiness, he or she acts with a natural inclination toward virtue. Your Cause fails in this."

"Our Cause does not fail and will not fail. We view the basic problem of ethics as a problem of the will. The South knows what is morally right and we will prevail."

"You have switched from Plato to St. Thomas Aquinas, General." How she savored to point out the flaw in his argument.

He inclined his head in an exaggerated bow. "My shadow is small in the sun of your greater knowledge."

She ignored his mockery. "The Christian philosophers would argue that owning a man is immoral. Those who allow slavery should not have freedom themselves." She remained emphatic on the subject and would not bend. "Do you have slaves?"

He was introspective for a moment, and then spoke. "At one time, yes, but my brothers, parents and I decided to free them. Some remain and we pay them wages. I always believed slavery was a rotten whore of an institution. What about the cold hypocrisy of the North? What about the women and children in the factories and sweatshops? Is that not a form of slavery? And the Negroes, you give them low-paying jobs—they live below poverty. Is this the emancipation you want them to flee to?"

He was right. Catherine did not have an answer for him. It was the sad hypocrisy of the North. Would it haunt society in years to come?

"I think you would do well with the women of the South, in fact, they would admire you."

A blue jay cawed outside and perched on a tree branch, his sharp blue plumage bright in the sun. Hadn't the general moved the conversation onto safer terrain? "How so?" Her interest was pricked. She really had no prior contact with the culture of Southern women other than what she had read.

The General laughed. "Curious like a woman. They'd respect you for your independence, coming to a small town, away from home, holding a profession...living alone.

She had never lived alone, surrounded by a legion of domestics, nannies and Brigid, her ladies maid. Her stepmother, Agatha lived in the house, taking advantage of all the Fitzgerald assets. Her father had left the estate to his two children. The dilemma was a legal intricacy that her father never had imagined. Since Shawn was missing, Agatha gained control of all Fitzgerald assets until Catherine's twenty-fourth birthday. "They would not venture to do so themselves?"

"Hardly. Women of the South depend on their men folk, their husbands to care for them."

"There is no need for a woman to depend on a man. A ridiculous notion." Her hands froze in her lap. She had asked, high-placed friends of the Fitzgerald's to intervene but one by one they withdrew fearful of Francis Mallory's powerful political machine. She had gone to her family's lawyers, and they challenged Mallory. Two of them had been found dead in their front yards, the rest backed away. No more could she risk anyone else's life. In a letter, she poured out her heart to her uncle and both decided that for the time being, disappearing was her only option. The blue jay lifted off the branch and took flight.

"You've never had an attachment?"

"I didn't say that." A smile curved her lips and her thoughts pulled back to Jimmy O'Hara, a scrappy thirteen-year old, orphan who never ceased to amaze her. Found in the alley outside the orphanage her family had built, and shot in the leg, he had begged her not to tell anyone. The boy touched her heart and sympathetic to his cause, Catherine ordered her driver to convey them to her home. She had Jimmy placed in the room next to hers and summoned, Dr. Parks, the family physician and assisted him in removing the bullet. He congratulated Catherine, admired her mettle and disdained the condescension bred in her peers. He encouraged her to assist him in his surgeries at MacDougall Hospital where they were short of hands due to the high influx of wounded soldiers.

Despite Agatha's objection to having Jimmy in the house, Catherine fed, changed bandages, played checkers, bought him new clothes and taught him how to read. He was a quick learner, so she engaged a tutor for him. The orphan grew stronger, more filled out, his eyes a sparkle. Jimmy taught Catherine tricks in the scandalous game of poker, regaled her with tales of his years as a street-rat, and educated her about real-life beyond the protected walls of her world. They had forged a special bond, Jimmy like a little brother. She was saddened when the restless Jimmy chose to return to the freedom of the streets. She made him promise to keep up with his lessons. Jimmy told her he'd look out for her, although she doubted he would have any wherewithal since he was so young.

"Of course not. Was it lacking in your appeal?" John asked.

Lacking in her appeal? That jerked her out of her woolgathering. Her hands balled into fists. "I was the toast of New——"

"Go on," the Reb waited.

Stupid. He was far too clever in drawing her out. She veered to a more cerebral discussion. "I believe the great experiment of democracy our forefathers began must be preserved. Less than a century later, we are fighting against each other. Is all to be lost? The experiment, this idea, must work and must be steeped in form and tradition. The Union cannot be allowed to divide—to diminish the greatness of what it will be—to understand that our United States is part of a larger idea and to be preserved at all costs. The South has never left England with its inherent aristocracy." She would not yield on her opinion of the war. It was more than about war and the cause of morals and humanity than just politics. Those beliefs had become unshakable and ingrained in her heart as well.

"You Northerners with your large cities full of rabble and decay espouses one notion of liberty, yet ignores our plea for freedom to choose the life we wish."

To hear the censure in his tone was music, how stimulating to turn the tables on him, and as stirring as her escape had been from New York. Two days before, Catherine had informed her stepmother, she was shopping for the orphans and climbed into the Brougham Coach. Mallory's thugs followed her. In the city's traffic, a horrendous shouting and screaming pierced the air. Catherine looked behind her. A runaway cart overturned, sprawling fruits and vegetables over the street and blocking the traffic from behind, including Mallory's men. Jimmy O'Hara knew his trade well.

She had entered a store, made purchases of readymade dresses, clear glass spectacles, and items she would need in the next six months. Minutes later, Catherine Fitzgerald, New York's wealthiest heiress, her hair pulled back in a bun, bespectacled, and newly cloaked in nondescript homespun attire, assumed the appearance of a spinsterish schoolteacher. Departing from the back door of the store, she hailed a cab and vanished.

A knock at the back door drew both their attention. John changed...an edge of alertness about him.

"Do not worry. Some of my new students' parents have made social calls. Remain here." She moved to the parlor and glanced out the window and returned. "It is later than I thought. Samuel is here with our dinner. Rest assured, no one other than Samuel and his mother know of your presence and they are sworn to secrecy. They have escaped from South Carolina and I employ Samuel's mother to cook and to do laundry, giving them the money they need to exist. Samuel will be in to assist with your personal needs. Without his help, I could never have lifted you in the bed."

Chapter 3

Over the week, when she wasn't there, John walked back and forth, stretching his muscles to regain his strength. Like a caged lion, he explored the house and grounds. Outside, there was a half-moon privy and a small empty barn. No neighbors. They were sequestered from the rest of the world. In the distance, a train hooted a whistle. Can't risk to be seen. He returned to the house.

In the parlor there was no furniture except a piano in the corner. Beyond that, a kitchen with a sideboard, table, chairs, stove…and the smell of burnt coffee. That was the end of the house tour. Not much. Very tidy. Very modest. The pieces didn't fit.

During the day, John defended his opinions and at night, he watched her garrison her side of the bed with pillows. So far, he had been a gentleman.

"Say what you will, Miss Callahan, but I am a firm believer of States Rights. Each state is entitled to its own separate sovereignty. There is no debate on the subject."

"Aren't you full of virtuous principle and indignation? Won't you ever listen to my reasoning?"

He gave her a speculative glance, saw where her dress parted, where her fingers touched the hollow of her throat. "It's been my experience that reason and ladies never keep close company."

"Oh-h! How dare you make light of my opinions. Our forefathers fought together for this land and paid with their blood for an idea, an idea unlike any other time in history. Don't you understand that anything that's worth fighting for is the whole?"

"We are two parts." He reminded her.

"But two parts make a whole," she protested. "General, allow me this one small favor to tap into your thick head—a house divided will not stand—it will fall."

John clapped his hands. "Bravo! Spoken like a true Republican Lincolnite! When Washington agrees to reconcile—"

"Reconcile! The damn war is almost over."

Noting her swearing, he drawled, "Of the fullness of the heart, the mouth speaketh."

"Don't quote me any Psalms."

"Wrong. Matthew 12:34."

"You're a fine one quoting the Bible—your Rebs doubtless drink the blood of Yankee boys, dig up their graves and pick your teeth with their bones."

He grimaced. "Almost as bad as picking a dead man's pockets."

"I told you I was getting your personal affects to write a letter to your widow. And to think of it, she's well-suited for the likes of you. I can picture her—fat as an elephant, a complexion as ruddy as a washboard, and beady black eyes ringed like a raccoon. Did I ask you if she had a nose like a sausage? No doubt, she keeps you up all night with her snorting like a horse and constipation problems.

Although I can't say I blame her, living with the likes of you would cause anyone indigestion." She tossed her golden head and eyed him with cold triumph.

"Indigestion?" he choked.

"At the very least, I can summon upon her joy at your passing to the devil's own. Too bad to disappoint her."

"I can imagine her great sorrow." He lived to goad her.

"So you are married. Isn't that amazing?"

"My goodness, we are full of spit and fire, aren't we. Just like a woman to establish her outrage at something in order to secure her true endeavor. To answer your question, no woman has me in her clutches as of this late date."

She pulled her glasses down and peered at him over the rims. "In your *September* years, you remained unmarried?"

"I'm not ancient. I still have my teeth." He smiled and displayed his even white teeth.

"Is there something wrong with you? Some affliction? Madness runs in the family?"

John crossed his arms over his chest and leaned back against the headboard. "I'll have you know I was sought and hunted down like hounds after a fox. In my Virginia county, there was no stone left unturned to find me. Girls sent flowers to themselves written with love notes from me that I never wrote. I'd enter a ballroom and they'd all start swooning. Their mamas tempted me with their food and their papas tempted me with their money. Even the girls themselves tried to compromise me."

She gasped. "Compromise you! More likely you—"

"Why on one occasion…" He stroked his neck and looked at the ceiling with thoughtful reflection.

"Save me from your fantasies. Of course, lots of men are bachelors by choice—but in your case—it's a choice girls didn't want to make."

"How you grieve me." He quirked his brow. "Is there no hope?" A safe bet she'd be stoned at the pillars before she'd fall into that trap.

"You deny your conceit, yet, you seem convinced that if you had never been born, people would want to know why."

He sighed with solemnity, and then placed his hand over his heart. "Miss Callahan, you are a very harsh judge. I am wounded. Perhaps if the Yankees put you in the front line, we Confederates would all run from sheer fright. In fact, they would only have to hear of your arrival, setting the South to fire, causing it to tremble with horror."

"How old are you?"

"How old do you think I am?"

Her mouth curved into a smile. "The Cretaceous period?"

John scarcely heard her. He was still attempting to recoup from the staggering effect of the smile she'd just given him.

"Miss Callahan, your sweetness and poetry are a balm to my delicate condition." In pure admiration, he considered the impact she made on him.

Catherine huffed. "Ha, from what I've read about you, you're no more delicate than a snake and as ambitious as Lucifer."

To keep his mind from going awry and his tongue from getting trussed into knots, John feigned injury. The woman held weapons enough to flay his backside. "And to think I could have more peace in a real prisoner of war camp. Instead, my misfortune is to endure your torture. However, I thank you for the compliment."

"I could never consent to pay a man so great a compliment. Men fall so easy for flattery."

How she poured out the honey. "I am humbled by your flattery. A snake? Lucifer? I am overwhelmed with your adulation, Miss Callahan. Indeed, I could aspire to no greater heights." He shifted his position, the effort stabbing his side. He propped himself up on one elbow, then stared at her, his countenance giving nothing.

"Tell me about your home."

She didn't want the conversation to end and neither did he. Energized by the one topic that gave him pleasure, he said, "My home, Miss Callahan, Fairhaven, as it is called, boasts pin oaks in all their glory, and lobelia and violets as plentiful on the lawn as the stars in the sky. Fields and fields of tobacco, wheat, corn, and peanuts grow forever, and the fragrance of the best ham and bacon smoking in the sheds this side of the universe assails the senses. Deer, fox and raccoon roam abundant among beeches, maples and sweet gums. Fairhaven possesses a modest white house which, I dare say I've only slept in a total of fourteen days since the war's commencement and where my parents reside. With fondness I recall slow, sweet days with picnics on the grounds down by the Shenandoah River—where our family and friends sit on spring-time grass, eat fried chicken and sip sweet lemonade with hunks of ice floating in our glasses. I am glad to sing the praises of my fine home. I have many warm memories. But I fear it will be exposed and, without a doubt, suffer the ravages of war."

"Your home sounds lovely. I hope it escapes any ruin." She heard a knock at the door. "Samuel has arrived."

Catherine departed to allow the thirteen-year-old, strapping boy with black curly hair, to help Rourke with his personal needs. Once the former slave moved past his fear of Rourke they had become fast friends. Across her yard, beneath the cool shade of a giant oak, she picked lilies-of-the-valley for the general's tray.

So far she had been successful at keeping the conversation off her. She thought about the orphanage she had built in New York City using her family's money for the orphans of the war. How were they faring? Hours she had spent volunteering with the orphans, and later divided her time working side by side with Dr. Parks with the veterans, marveling in his unorthodox and legendary skill in saving limbs.

Coming from one of the wealthiest families in the city, no one dared to criticize her breach in decorum. Of course, she chastised her detractors and shamed their idleness when so much was needed. From her example, many of her peers were inspired to volunteer.

Then Francis Mallory came into her life. She rubbed her fingers against the rough bark of the oak. To think she had fallen prey to his charms. He had presented a dashing figure with his flashing black eyes, his long curving mustache and impeccably black tailored suits.

How she remembered the day she met Francis, had been knocked down on Madison Avenue, and her reticule ripped from her wrist. Francis had knocked out the thief and returned her reticule, then pulled her to her feet. She had resisted his courtship, but when he appeared at her fundraisers, donating huge sums of money, then donating a carriage full of toys for her orphans, Catherine melted.

Jimmy O'Hara had later explained the snatched purse trick and informed her of Mallory's history. In lieu of what Francis lacked in paternity, he made up for in internal violence. His blue-blooded father met a suspicious death followed by his stepbrother, the authentic, notwithstanding legal heir to Mallory Foundries. With powerful political connections to back him up, Francis was quick to seize the Mallory fortune by declaring his heritage, albeit an illegitimate claim that no one dared to voice opposition.

Mallory had raised his position in New York Society by two notches, still not enough to gain him entry into the high-class world he craved. To get there, he needed the Fitzgerald stamp to wash away the criminal part of his past. He held a fascination for Catherine, and along with his lust for recognition...nothing would get in his way to obtain both of his objectives.

Mallory's grand design included taking over Fitzgerald Rifle Works by destroying its reputation. Deliberate misshapen gun barrels purchased from Mallory Foundries caused the Fitzgerald rifle to explode when fired, killing or maiming the soldier. The Secretary of War had wired complaints to Helmsley, Fitzgerald's Rifle Works manager. Of course, Mallory Foundries claimed no accountability. The responsibility weighed on Fitzgerald Rifle Works and the well-earned and long-acquired distinction as the oldest, largest and reputable rifle manufacturer laid in great danger. Catherine had ordered Mr. Helmsley to have every gun fired and inspected several times before it left the plant.

She tapped her lip. Hadn't the trouble at the Rifle Works coincided with the exact time of her brother's disappearance? Leading the New York Calvary, Lt. Colonel Shawn Fitzgerald had ridden into battle after battle with hardly a scratch. Manassas, Antietam, Fredericksburg, Gettysburg, Boonsboro. The last of his whereabouts reported at Brandy Station where he disappeared without a trace. She had used the Fitzgerald influence in requesting a military investigation. Despite a full inquiry, the military came back empty-handed, and apologized with respect to that area of the country being fully engaged in battle, making it impossible for further exploration.

Jimmy's street-rat existence produced him a master of the shadowy occurrences and personalities of the city's Irish underworld. He had warned her of Mallory, but she couldn't believe it. She had badgered Jimmy to escort her, disguised of course, into one of the most notorious underground gaming rings. To her horror, Francis Mallory crippled a poor immigrant with his bare fists to the wild cheers of gentlemen. Mallory had lifted his head and never was there a more awful face, a beast raised from the bowels of Hell.

To save Fitzgerald Rifle Works, she had Jimmy fence the Fitzgerald jewels. The funds were given to Mr. Helmsley and a secret foundry was built in New Jersey to supply Fitzgerald Rifle Works, freeing them from Mallory's noose.

Then Catherine disappeared. Now she counted the days before she would legally be of age to obtain control of her family's fortune.

She would hire bodyguards and find legal avenues to take Mallory down.

What if Mallory found her? An image of perdition loomed. She laid in a bed, naked, his callous hands groping at her breasts. Dear God. She clutched the lilies and ran into the house. *Why did she feel safe with John?*

John noted the lilies she arranged on the tray with the roast chicken smothered in currant sauce, braised potatoes and carrots, baked bread with fresh butter, and was that apple pie for dessert? She tucked a napkin under his chin and he liked her female pampering without artifice.

John considered many things: The war. The futility of it. But he knew, the South would never surrender. He would never surrender. He had to get back. General Lee had become short of good commanders. Many had been lost—Johnston, Jackson, Armistead. Their names kept slipping through his thoughts. He could not become connected to a woman.

However, the war had taken a toll on him.

So easy to forget...to stay here...to bury the Cause, yet, he would not be able to forget, his duty, his oath.

John rested against the pillows and smiled at her deliberate evasiveness. The very mysterious Miss Callahan did not fool him for one minute. Despite her subtlety, she was a picture to behold, her slender form sheathed in her simple pink dress with a line of tiny pearl buttons fastened just beneath her creamy white throat.

Her emerald eyes were so agreeable in expression and, he found them irresistible, yet a naked intuition warned him from falling under her spell.

He stabbed his fork into the chicken and closed his eyes, savoring the flavors. He took pleasure in her genial sparring. Catherine Callahan was a welcomed respite from the hard life he had lead over the long war years and keeping her engaged in conversation was paramount to him. Never before had he met such a vixen. A woman so provoking—and so tempting. Didn't she dare to sharpen her debate skills upon him like a rapier on a grinding stone?

He had grown bored, even scornful of females that employed all kinds of machinations to entrap him. He was the oldest son of one of Virginia's wealthiest families and an officer in the Confederate Army, reasons that women attached a romantic inclination. Catherine Callahan was immune to the nuances of Southern women. She had no idea of his family's fortune, and he had the distinct impression she would not give a tinker's damn. She remained unaffected, even disproving of his military status and for all intents and purposes, disparaging.

She cut a slice of bread and handed it to him, her fingers sliding next to his like melted butter. He inhaled. Without a doubt, Catherine Callahan was a paradox. Despite her simple dress, she seemed born of aristocracy. Her poise, her voice, the tilt of her chin—all telling gestures—a refinement not cultivated in the lower classes.

With certainty, she was a Northerner and in support of the Union. She was also a woman who lived alone. North or South, women of her class rarely lived alone. John frowned, experiencing difficulty in defining an entire picture of the enigmatic Miss Callahan. It all led back to the same question. *What was she hiding?*

He sipped creamy milk while she picked at her meal. John did not like uncertainty, in fact, he detested it. He thrived on pure, concise calculation and order. Nothing about her seemed to be in order. Before all battles, he spent an inordinate amount of time in planning, training and reconnaissance. He weighed all pros and cons, exercising his instincts in crafting an image of his enemy's thoughts and motives. As a commander, his repeated success in outwitting the enemy was by knowing the nature of his enemy. He did not know Catherine Callahan. He had never engaged in a battle like this. One could not plan or train or do reconnaissance for such a battle as this. He looked forward to the challenge.

When Miss Callahan had gone for her walks, John exercised every day. He had mended well and grew stronger almost enough to steal a horse and ride south. Not yet. He bided his time, hiding in the schoolmarm's house and relishing their discussions. So he attacked his pie with a vengeance, treasuring, the sweet sugary, cinnamon and apples. To surround her was his first mode of strategy, the lovely and confident Miss Callahan would not be able to defy his charms. He chose a topic dear to his heart, and one that would make her comfortable. Wasn't the best path to conquering, the path of least resistance?

"My mother and father are still living and very much in love with each other." John began, circling her with complete guile. Miss Callahan put down her plate, rolled her shoulders and stretched. The suggestion of her soft rounded curves broadened, while the lace at her throat parted, and the hollow of her neck filled with shadows. John swallowed. "Family history has many rumors which prove to be more truth than fiction. My father kidnapped my mother, compromised her, and obtained his objective by forcing her into marriage. I imagine there were fireworks for some time, but in the end they worked it out. After all, my father declares, they have four healthy sons."

John rather liked the unconscious blush that stole across her face as he wrapped his story around her like a warm blanket. He finished his pie. She had toyed with hers and eaten nothing else, fork and knife crossed on her plate. She rose, took his tray to the kitchen then returned. She sat on the bed and faced him, keeping a few inches away as if the barrier for North and South were drawn right there on the coverlet. He acquiesced to the ritual of her checking his wound and succumbed to the bone-melting flames she stoked. He harnessed the fire in his loins— how easy to roll her beneath him, to consume her in seconds.

"I assume you are the oldest?"

John heard the question only vaguely, his gaze drifting to her mouth. She'd taste of cinnamon and sugar.

Realizing she was waiting, he cleared his throat. Nodded. "Uhm, yes. Zachary, Ryan and Lucas are my younger brothers and, as we are all close together in age, have spent some spirited times. However, since this war, we have all gone our separate ways. Zachary, the youngest, didn't agree with North or South and has headed west during the conflict. Ryan is a colonel and serves in our illustrious cavalry under Jeb Stuart while..." He grew quiet for a moment. "The unfortunate part is that Lucas is serving under your Mr. Lincoln as a Colonel in Washington."

When he saw her brow rise in surprise, he continued. "With regret, we left on very bad terms and haven't spoken since the advent of the war."

After seeing how it cut him deeply, Catherine looked down and began drawing imaginary circles on her skirt. "The war has been a terrible tragedy, ripping family's apart—brothers against brothers, fathers against sons."

"It is a tragedy," John said, his voice soft and low.

She raised her head. "How did you become a general?" *Was it family connections or political assignations, as occurred in the North?* No. General Rourke would have earned his rank by sheer prowess and conviction.

"I graduated from West Point with honors. After that, I served as a Captain in the Texan-Mexican War, outflanked some Mexicans when we stormed a mountain pass at Cerro Gordo, saving General Winfield Scott's head—fought on to Mexico City which impressed the higher ups, who promoted me to Lieutenant. When secession came, I enlisted in the Army of Northern Virginia as a Colonel. I impressed my superiors again and, when General Richardson was shot by a Yankee bullet, filled his shoes. I've served all the Stations of the Cross."

Catherine's eyes widened with his rapid ascent. John had saved General Winfield Scott's life? Wouldn't he be surprised to know General Winfield Scott was a close family friend? "So you were of the Union Army and when secession was decided, you resigned to join the enemy?" The idea was mind-boggling. How could he turn against his own country?

"By the time secession came," John began, his tone heavy with regret. "The politicians had exasperated and heated themselves, and the people, into a fever that only bloodletting could ever cure. War stood the inevitable remedy. So, I was a seceder, and I dreaded the future."

"Tell me about when you were a young boy. I'll bet you were a rascal."

John's face split into a wide boyish grin. Raising his chin, he scratched his throat and, in doing so, the sheet slipped down revealing his well-muscled torso. It was hard to look away. In his state of undress, was he always this comfortable with the opposite sex?

"I had a pet crow once, even taught it to talk. All's I could get it to say was, "What fun! What fun!" The crow went everywhere I went and had a particular fondness for the church belfry. When the priest got to sermonizing, spewing fire and damnation, pounding his fist on the pulpit and perspiring with greatness and the sin of mankind with little or no redemption, the crow would call out, "What fun! What fun!' There would be a giggle and then another and another, until the whole congregation began laughing. The priest was so mad that one Sunday he took out his shotgun and shot several holes in the steeple.

"Did he get the crow?" Catherine was enthralled.

"No. But the crow did get even. Every morning he perched himself by the priest's bedroom window and cawed him awake."

Catherine giggled. "Please…" She begged, experiencing a sense of peace and satisfaction and taking pleasure in his company. "…another story." To think she listened to the South's most notorious general reciting his childhood exploits.

"Now, Miss Callahan, how you do give me pause."

Her greed for personal knowledge about him was a diversion from Mallory. "I apologize, General, if I am indiscreet, though I am interested in your stories."

John waved off her concern. "Please don't rein your interest into the confines of proper behavior. Often, I have enjoyed repartee with other commanders on the field, but as of late, there has been little opportunity and over the years, less desire. It's good to talk about events other than war." Then he grinned at her. "Now where was I? Oh yes…as it happened…being schooled at home, my brothers and I went through many tutors."

"You must have been a pack of devils."

"Well, one must understand the combination of sunshiny days and young boys create an awful longing. Upon one occasion we convinced our tutor he was going bald and the only remedy was what Old Cyrus, an employee at Fairhaven who was a self-proclaimed expert on herbal medicines had stored up. We told him that for it to work, he had to plaster it all over his head, roll his remaining hair up in twigs, and sit in the morning sunshine."

"He must have looked a fright," Catherine said

"And then some. He was seated on the veranda pretty as a picture when young Polly, our servant girl happened by, screamed, and dropped in a dead faint.

"You're incorrigible!"

"I think my mother had far worse feelings about us when hundreds of bees started swarming around the poor tutor's head. He ran like lightning for the river. But what was most remarkable was the rancid smell that lingered for days…and mother's insistence that I return the tutor his money. Afterward, she dismissed him, since he was of no use in the schoolroom and had lied about his credentials. Still, I think it was the smell."

They both laughed and their eyes locked, time without end, glorying in the shared moment. Catherine broke away first. "What about your father. Did he have an opinion?"

"He's still laughing. My mother always said I followed in my father's footsteps—the ones he thought he'd covered up." John's eyes sparkled at the memory.

"No wonder you don't have any manners. What else does your mother say?"

"She insisted that I have more appointments with the hickory stick."

Catherine liked John's family. Her chest constricted. It must have been wonderful growing up in a large family with all that boisterous love and joy surrounding them. Cocking her head to the side, she asked, "I would hazard to guess you are about thirty-six years old. Am I right? And yet you have never married?"

John looked out the window. The breeze lifted the curtains and twisted them. "I was married once, came home one afternoon and discovered my dear devoted wife in a compromised position with her lover. I was prepared to kill them both right then and there. She begged for mercy while I beat the hell out of the scoundrel. The only factor holding me back from complete murder was the break of a scandal. To save my family from embarrassment, I sent them packing and divorced her. Her lover was heavy handed with the lash and they were both killed during a slave uprising."

Mirrored in his eyes were bitterness, rage, and humiliation. A man of John's stature and discipline would allow no dishonor or deceit. She could well understand his scornful view toward women. He was a man of integrity, honesty and loyalty and expected the same from those he loved.

"Enough of me. I want to know about you." John commanded, his form dominating the room.

The breathing space grew hot, and in an unconscious gesture, Catherine pulled her heavy mass of hair up off the back of her neck. "Not much more to tell than I've already told you. I've an older brother who died during the war, although in my heart, I still refuse to believe it. My mother died in a flu epidemic. My father's heart was broken as they were deeply in love with one another. He died in an accident. Father Callahan, my uncle provided me the schoolmarm position and this home. So, I'm here. All quite mundane you see."

"That's all you have to tell?" He drummed his fingers on the bed sheets.

"I-I don't want to bore you with trivialities." She averted her eyes.

"Catherine?"

His quiet voice made her head jerk up. She gasped when he took her spectacles from her, then took a lock of her hair, running its silky length through his fingers. "I assure you Miss Callahan, there is nothing boring about you." He caught her hand before she had any notion of taking flight, his flesh warm against hers...and a vague, sensuous light passed between them. "And I assure you, there is nothing trivial about you either."

Her wariness stood no chance against his allure. With some sensual fascination, he drew and captured her awareness, until the room, the walls, the ceiling, the world itself, faded around them. His hand glided up and down her arm, her body felt heavy and warm, and her heartbeat raced at the mere impact of his gentle touch.

"I give you my word that you will be safe," he said.

His nearness made her senses spin. His gaze roved over her in lazy regard, appraising her, and leaving her exposed. Reason warred with caution—such an attraction would be perilous. She drew an uneven breath.

"Do you question my word, Catherine?"

She shook her head. "You don't understand." Her own pulses leapt with excitement. She could feel the heat from his body— so close. It wasn't him. Too revealing, too much vulnerability... her helplessness...her weakness over him. Her safety, security, her family fortune were at stake. "I can't explain." She tugged. Tears grew in her eyes.

"Catherine—"

"No." She jerked her arm away and bolted off the bed. She stared at him, rubbed her arm where it burned from his touch. She turned in the doorway, then spoke again, her voice even and without a shred of doubt. "This cannot happen. We are two parts. North and South."

The clomping of horses and the rumble of a wagon diverted her attention. "I'm not expecting anyone. Stay here." She closed the door and swore she heard John use her words.

"But two parts make a whole."

Chapter 4

Catherine accepted a handmade quilt from the mother of one of her prospective students. Mrs. Jensen, a nice woman, gave an account of her many stillborns until the Lord blessed her with Thomas. She turned her wagon around and bid good-bye, inviting Catherine to share dinner with her family. Catherine ran her hands over the rainbow colored quilt, touched by Mrs. Jensen's kindness. Her bed at home in the city was covered with silk damask imported from France, but the quilt made by a humble woman who had suffered so much, meant the world to her. How comforting to blend into her new life. Yet, she must not forget Francis Mallory... and the Reb.

With certainty, John waited for some explanation of her visitor. She delayed, taking in the last few rays of the evening sun, a dusky pale of slate blue sending off a streaky glimpse of ivory and vermillion. The Reb raised so many fears and uncertainties—a warmth...wanting.

When two souls touch?

Every fiber of her body warned her against him. *What was happening to her?* She had been courted by all kinds of men and at all times, proper and circumspect. But neither had she encountered a man like John, and her mind burned with the memory of his simple touch.

Falling under the spell of the enemy?

But there was no room in her life for romance. Self-preservation told her she had to keep away from him. He must leave…and soon.

But how? Having saved his life, she held responsibility for his safety. If he went to a prisoner of war camp, he would die. Conditions in Northern and Southern camps were deplorable. He was too far north and too injured to ride a horse back from where he came. And even if he was able to do so, there was a probability he'd end up dead, or, an even worse probability—he'd kill more Union soldiers.

This dreadful war had to stop.

What a dilemma. She sighed with her inability to come up with a solution, placed the quilt over the porch railing, and lingered with a long walk. She circled the house and strolled into the barn, her nose twitching with the dust. The rafters were cluttered with cobwebs and in the descending gloom, she lifted her face into the rays of light that poured between the sideboards…and inspiration blossomed. Hadn't John mentioned a brother in Washington? Lucas. Tomorrow she'd wire Colonel Lucas Rourke in Washington and ask for his assistance. He would take his brother off her hands, wouldn't he?

A gentle breeze blew, and with it, all her fears evaporated. Quite pleased with her ingenious decision, she marched into her bedroom and tossed the quilt on the bed.

"General Rourke," she began, using his formal title. "You have to get rest and I have to get mine. Since I have only one bed, we have to share. Under the circumstances, I expect you to be honorable. You will continue to conduct yourself in a proper manner?"

"Proper is my middle name, Miss Callahan."

She didn't like the trace of sarcasm. Things had to end her own way. They just had to. After turning down the lantern, and grabbing a bunch of pillows, she stuffed a barrier between them. "Everything is appropriate. You stay on your side. And that's an order."

She lay on her side of the bed. "General?"

"Yes, Miss Callahan?"

"You do know how to follow orders?"

"Only when they come from a higher command." He answered with imperturbable masculine logic.

"Good, then think of me as your superior." She turned on her side, presenting her back to him.

"General?"

"Yes, Miss Callahan?"

"Are you still awake?"

"Are you?"

"Don't be ridiculous." She tugged at the quilt, turned over again, facing him in the dark. "Your mother was right."

He let out a long sigh. "About what, Miss Callahan?"

"You should have had more appointments with the hickory stick."

She felt a rumble of laughter then he turned toward her, serious and with stealth.

Silence loomed like a heavy mist.

In the shadowed moonlight, the general's eyes fixed upon her, predatory, a physical threat. She had not the slightest wish to embrace that threat, or to cultivate it. His wound did not bother him? No pain?

He raised a hand and tipped her face up to meet his. "I promise to be 'proper' if you give me one kiss. You owe me."

Had he been out of bed when she wasn't there? How strong was he? His touch was firm and persuasive. "How is it that I owe you?" She pretended not to be affected, her pulse beating wildly like the wings of a sparrow trapped in a cage.

John tensed to break away, told himself he should, that he was obliged to. Her face expectant, radiant in the moonlight, captivated him. "You saved my life."

Her gaze lowered from his eyes to his lips. "That's ludicrous," she whispered. "How did you come to that conclusion?"

John was through with a conversation that was leading nowhere when he had a specific direction in mind. He lowered his head, giving her sufficient time to pull back if she was inclined.

She didn't. She tipped up her face. His lips stroked hers, and then settled in the most proper kiss of his life. Her lips trembled under his. He sensed her innocence in his bones. The urge to consume was formidable, but he bridled his hunger, took only what she offered, and returned no more than that. It was a compromise, an exchange of something more tangible, more potent, than Rourke was prepared to admit...and he knew...she wasn't prepared to admit it was something more tangible too.

Ending the kiss took all the restraint John could muster. He could feel her warmth along his body through the pillow barrier. Slowly, deliberately, he forced himself to withdraw, the insinuation of what they had done drugging him with possibilities.

"This won't do. I apologize for my indiscretion—I mean your indiscretion. Oh, dear..." She placed her hands on her burning cheeks.

He bowed his head. "The fault is mine."

"This is lust. It must not happen again." She pushed away and fled the room.

John folded his hands behind his head and stared at the ceiling. He was playing with fire, ought to leave, head south, catch up with his troops and regain his command.

But he'd never been afraid of fire.

Sometime later, he heard her listening at the door. Assuming he was asleep, she tiptoed in the room then, lay far to her side of the bed, fortifying the pillow defenses and covering them with the new quilt. Years of war had made him practiced, vigilant of his surroundings. He was even more aware of her. He listened to her breathing slow into a gentle rhythm of sleep. Tearing apart the silly barrier, he tossed the pillows on the floor and gathered up her slumbering form in his arms. Before returning to the Cause, he would appeal to his greater inclination. The war would not rob him of this one small pleasure.

Chapter 5

*C*atherine had walked two miles to the town of Pleasant Valley. After forwarding a telegram from the telegraph office to John's brother in Washington, she headed to the dry-goods store. She took two steps back. On a bench was a discarded newspaper, bannered with another headline of the war's progress.

The tone of the day's events contrasted to what Catherine remembered back in 1861, at the advent of the war. *"To overcome the wicked Rebellion to destroy the Union,"* the northern papers had trumpeted and inspired. *"We must combat the lawlessness and treason of Southern leaders as now fully manifested."*

From the battle cry, marched the patriot sons of blood in zealous numbers with their bright uniforms and shiny rifles to conquer their tyrannical and oppressive brethren of the Southern States. Throngs of New York's electrified populace in perfect ovation to the soldiers' line of march, filled the sidewalks with drowning huzzahs for the Union accompanied with many touching scenes of farewell.

She had begged her brother, Shawn, not to go. With their parents dead, he had no opposition. Who will manage the Rifle

Works? Despite her great criticism, Shawn, enamored with war fever, responded to the call.

Catherine walked the block of stores, the wood planks, creaking beneath her feet. She lifted her nose from the smell of horse dung piled against the blacksmith's shop then stepped into Dinkle's Mercantile and Dry Goods, adjusting her eyes to the dim interior.

"Miss Callahan, a pleasure seeing you again," Elias Dinkle gushed, his Adam's apple bobbing up and down. He ushered her to a milk can, slapped his apron over it to knock off the dust and offered her a seat. "Goodness gracious, you make the sun come out on a rainy day." With his fingers, he combed a few remaining strands of hair over his balding pate, and to Catherine's horror, blew a steady stream from his bulbous nose.

Catherine moved away from her admirer, fingering the bolts of calico. "I'm in a hurry, Mr. Dinkle. Would you be so kind as to help me with some of my purchases?" she said, hoping to remove him to behind the counter. She rattled off a list of her requirements.

"Miss Callahan, why on earth do you need a straight razor and men's clothes?"

She pointed with her gloved finger. "And boots…those black ones on the shelf."

"What does a schoolteacher need with men's boots?" Did his nose glow brighter?

Mesmerized by the rapid motion of his Adam's apple, Catherine prevaricated. "I'm expecting a visit from a dear sweet cousin and wish to have a few gifts set aside. He's poor and in need of a few essentials."

If only the poor cousin excuse was enough to abate Dinkle's wagging tongue. With certainty, Father Callahan would get wind of it when he returned. No way did she desire to invite that drama. Her uncle and his Irish temper made an angry grizzly look tame. She fidgeted with the licorice jar and leaned forward. "This is all hush-hush. He's a simple soul, dull-witted, you see." And then burgeoning with inspiration, she added, "It wasn't his fault, dropped on his head as a baby."

Dinkle beamed with delight. The new schoolmarm who he held a snowballing romantic fascination, had taken him into her confidence.

Catherine added a few jars of peaches to her purchases, picked up as many of the wrapped parcels she could carry, and received Dinkle's proud assurance that he would have Samuel deliver the remainder later in the day.

Catherine returned to her home, listening to strains of Mozart played over the piano. She moved beside John watching his long fingers perform magic on the keys. "Your talents never cease to amaze me, General Rourke. Besides holding a gun and mounting cannons against Yankees you can engage in the classics?" Her eyes dipped with disapproval to the sheet wrapped around his midsection.

"I'll remedy the situation as soon as you tell me the whereabouts of my uniform." He drawled, and then ceremoniously stood as if he were in truth a king, given divine right.

Catherine gaped, staring at the heavy musculature of his chest and torso. *Had he no shame?* Lifting her chin in a bold attempt to end his intimidation, she squeaked, "I had it burned."

"What!"

His roar rocked the beams of the tiny house. She nodded. Even when he was flat on his back, John was the most formidable foe she'd ever confronted. And when he was angry, towering over her, like he was now, he was terrifying.

"Without my uniform, I'll be hung as a spy!"

She bit her lip. Never had he been so incensed. "I hadn't thought of that. I've made a few purchases for you." She presented a blue shirt, pants and black boots.

"That will do me real good when I'm swinging from the nearest tree."

"It's better than your current attire. You should be grateful."

"What for? To be fashionable at my execution."

"They didn't exactly have a sale on Reb uniforms at the dry goods." She shot him a withering glance, turned on her heel, and walked into the kitchen.

His footsteps thundered behind her. Predictable. She unpacked the jars of peaches and held one up. The delectable fruit glowed amber in the light. Did she hear his stomach rumble?

"Miss Callahan, you have brought me gold."

He made a grab for the jars, but she lunged, withholding them. "Not until you shave and get dressed. I doubt you array yourself at home in such a state. I'm sure your mother would have something to say about it."

"You wound me, Miss Callahan." He took the proffered clothes and shaving materials.

Did he growl beneath his breath? Catherine smiled. She would command him through his stomach.

When he finished shaving, he returned to the kitchen and seated her. "Thank you," she said, and then stared, startled from his transformation. She handed him a bowl of peaches.

Without a shadow of a beard, the clear-cut lines and angles of his face revealed much more of his character. He had a face in which dwelled a great coolness, inspired confidence, and when relaxed like he was now, an accompaniment of merriment.

"Pardon me, Miss Callahan." He smiled an easy devastating smile, disarming her. "If you are not going to eat your peaches, I'd—"

"Of course," Catherine said, her mortification burning in her cheeks, caught staring again. What was the matter with her? She pushed the bowl toward him. He looked marvelous. The blue shirt clung to his wide shoulders and the pants fit snugly, outlining his long, lean frame.

"I suppose it would be good for you to take some fresh air." She offered. The kitchen was getting a little too warm.

"I'm unsteady and not sure of my endurance."

Catherine reached for her fringed shawl. He was still as weak as a kitten.

John took a deeper view of her home than he had on his prior jaunts. Columbine, clematis, and early daisies scattered around, and far off the porch was a white picket fence with rhubarb growing wild. Hardwoods followed up the mountains, a family of robins chattered away in a nest in a nearby oak and fresh springtime air, scented with sweet honeysuckle, cooled the sunlight pouring down on them.

Everything at peace.

Once past the barn, John without invitation, commandeered the use of Catherine's arm, and with shrewd resourcefulness, exaggerated his injury. "What shall we discuss today, Miss Callahan?"

"Tell me about the other commanders with whom you have served."

He did nothing to hide his surprise. "Such a delicate topic. Most ladies——"

"I'm beyond petticoats and parasols. Do continue——"

How attractive she looked in her blue dress and——how he loved to fence with the charming, Miss Callahan. Lilacs and sunshine, her warm feminine scent spiraled around him.

"Let's start with your General Lee. Surely you think he is a model to which our Union officers fail. Meanwhile, he recruits and furnishes himself in the farmlands of Virginia, Maryland and Pennsylvania."

"Our General Lee is a mighty commander. The South's finest and most revered." John enjoyed the advantage of his height that offered him an alluring display of smooth flesh, exposed by the neckline of her gown. "The South has had the edge because we use West Pointers as our military leaders. Lincoln, for political reasons, has not picked West Pointers, and the generals he chooses have no more military sense than an old woman. Your General Burnside at Fredericksburg? What folly. Ranks and ranks of Yankees went down like snow, melting as they hit the ground. The entire Irish brigade mowed down against the heights, thirteen thousand men, slaughtered. Your General McClellan or *Young Napoleon?* How about his disaster at Bull Run? Mr. Lincoln would be well-advised to leave McClellan in charge with his apparent unwillingness to engage in battle—would make the security and fortunes of the South absolute."

"Tell me, was it foolish of General Lee to invade the North when he was outgunned and outmanned...and knowing the Union would come looking for you? Tell me, General Rourke, did Lee learn a lesson at Gettysburg?" Her eyes flashed. "How about General Ulysses Grant?"

"General Grant?" John grew pensive. Grant had thrown Yankee forces at the Confederates in the Wilderness. Since his capture, he had no news of the outcome. Grant was new. He had not figured him out yet. Frowning, he said, "You Yanks call him, "Unconditional Surrender" Grant. He's an enigma although his western campaigns show he is a fighter and that surprises me. Lowest in rank in his class at West Point, and rumors abound he favors the fermented flavor of wheat and barley too much."

"We shall see, General Rourke. The mongrel dog is always stronger than the thoroughbred."

"But Grant hasn't met Bobby Lee." He touched his forehead in a mock salute.

"Your Bobby Lee is as useful as a milk pail under a bull," she snapped.

"I see you've been sharpening your sword early today. However, time will tell on your General Grant, your supposed hero of the

North." He caressed her cheek with the knuckle of his forehead. He wanted to touch her and keep on touching her.

"What about Jackson? Pickett? Longstreet? Hill?"

"Slow down, Miss Callahan, my mind's dizzy with all you require. Are you asking for yourself—or for Mr. Lincoln?" He quirked a speculative brow.

"I doubt very much if you are ever addled, General Rourke."

His breath whistled out. When she looked up and offered him a beguiling smile that lit the heavens, his knees went weak. "Another compliment? How can I refuse such a delightful woman on a picturesque day? General Jackson—Stonewall that is, now deceased, God rest his soul. Now there was a man who knew how to fight. Did you know he was superstitious? Wouldn't eat pepper. Felt it made his left leg stiff."

"Eccentric," she huffed.

With her cheeks rosy from the sun, her hair curling in thick golden waves about her shoulders, and that bare dip between her breasts—was there any defense? "A little eccentricity isn't bad in a general. It helps with newspapers and women. Southern women are crazy over our generals who are both pious and a little crazy themselves."

"Spare me."

He laughed at her. "There's General A.P. Hill—Texan through and through, but a Southerner first. Always wears a red shirt going into battle, and boy, can those Texans fight. General Pickett—perfume and all. General Longstreet, dark and gloomy at times, but can be humorous. Hell of a fighter and strategist."

He stopped, picked several, yellow, bell-shaped flowers and presented them to her, his fingers warming as they brushed across her hand. "Trout Lilies." He bowed gallantly.

"Why thank you, General Rourke." She extended a slight curtsey then singled out a lily for inspection. Her finger traced the subtle shape of each dip and turn, then rubbed against the thick ridge of the stem. An arrow of liquid heat went straight to his groin.

"You may find this contradictory, but Lincoln never desired war."

"If Lincoln had any clear idea of the nature of war and politics, he showed a delicate art of concealing it." Images of her stroking him like the lily passed hot, raw and carnal.

A slow condemnation grew in her wide emerald eyes. "It seems hard to digest you delivering opinions on Lincoln. We should admire his genius. What he does is for the greater good. President Lincoln said—he'd rather be assassinated than to see a single star fall from the flag of the United States."

To hell with Lincoln. Despite her spectacles, she was alive, animated...her voice, lilting, musical...her golden hair and her shining countenance almost made him want to jump up and shake Lincoln's hand. God she was a siren, leading him to wreck upon the shoals.

They continued walking, and then circled back toward the house. When they approached the rear of the barn, he dragged his feet. No way did he want the spell broken. He stopped, observed her puzzlement. She took to the shade and leaned against the barn, waiting. John squinted at the sky and then focused on her face.

Shaking his head, he removed her glasses. "That's a hell of a lot better."

"You are quite presumptuous, general."

He placed both his hands against the barn, trapping her in between. He lingered, awareness filled his every pore, even the air he breathed. He remained duty bound for reasons she could not understand. He'd be returning soon. *Who knew if he'd survive the war?* They would never see each other again. He could not make a commitment, the way she deserved. *Honor.* His mind repeated the words but his gaze fell on her lips.

Catherine's wicked heart betrayed her, thundered in her chest. "I believe we should remain formal. I—I think it is safer."

He chuckled, deep and throaty. "Did I ever tell you about Molly? She's one of my loves back home. Gorgeous, long, slender legs, and beautiful red blond hair. Always loyal and willing to—"

Catherine pushed away from him. He didn't budge. "How would you know she has long slender legs?"

"Why she shows them all the time."

"Get away from me." She shoved at him with all her might, having suffered enough of his arrogance to last a hundred lifetimes. "You, General, are obtuse and dim-witted!"

"And you woman talk too much." He flattened her to the barn.

Her mouth went dry. With cast-iron certainty, he faked his injury. Why he could probably lift a horse. "I am sure you make your southern belles swoon with glib flattery by hailing your exploits with other women, and then settling on them like an anaconda and swallowing them whole. Pray save your amorous attentions for your lamentable homeward souls."

"Do I detect a wholehearted spurning? Or jealousy? He touched her hair, streaming it through his hand. "I am only a man."

"That is a most flattering dedication. Perhaps the lowest specimen I have met. To think you graduated from the nation's top military school. Without question, West Point has lowered its standards."

"You humble me."

An instant of pretended offense stole into his expression and she flinched when he caressed the side of her face. Warm. Intimate. His hand moved down her throat, down the side of her breast and withdrew. A jolt of deep female longing shot through her body.

Catherine doubted the general had one humble bone in his body. "Your only desire is to display yourself like some banty rooster with all the conceit you can muster." Again, she pushed against his form, steadfast, unyielding, like dislodging a locomotive. *Impossible.*

A Satanic smile spread across his face. *Dangerous.* He leaned against her, long, lean and hard. The palms of her hands burned where they lay upon his chest. *How many foes had he fought? Who would survive this battle?*

"How you damage my reputation." His voice lulled her. "Here I am, yours to abuse on the altar of sacrifice. Would you miss me when I am gone?"

"I would grieve in the span of time it takes to clap my hands together."

Clasping another tendril of hair, he trailed it over her breast, barely a warm brush, just a whisper. Except this time, his hand did not stop at her breast, but continued down her waist to the round curve of her hip.

"Are you going to kiss me?" she asked, though she knew full well what he intended.

"Do you want me to?"

Just as she said, "You can't," he lowered his head. Waves of excitement rippled through her.

"Why?"

"Because I saved your life."

"You're going to have to do better than that." His fingers slid under her chin, lifting her face to his. "I think I should kiss you all the time. It is the only remedy to keep you quiet." In one forward motion his lips stirred against hers, gentle at first, then challenging...and persistent. If only she could remain stiff, immune. The gentle massage of his kiss sent currents of desire through her. Blood pounded in her brain, leapt from her heart and made her pulses race like quicksilver.

He broke apart only inches from her mouth, his steel-blue gaze, hot like molten rock riveting her to the spot. "Perhaps my years at war have lessened my desirability. Do you think you could try harder?"

Catherine strove to gather her wits. Try harder? The arrogant cad. "Let go of me."

Instead, his body imprisoned her, and his lips came down upon her once more. He devoured her. She moved toward him, pressing into him, impelled by her hunger.

He dragged his lips from hers. "Do you think the war has made its mark on me? Will I be cursed in my..." he paused then deliberately used her words, "...senior years? Do you think the ladies of the South will find my kisses pleasing?"

"Yes." Catherine practically screamed, her lips burning in the aftermath. "They'll find you very pleasing. Now let me go."

He did not release her, tilted his head, as if weighing the matter. An odd twinge of disappointment covered his countenance. "I have a secret which I beg you will keep in strictest confidence?"

Catherine nodded her head. She would do anything to get away from him.

"I don't feel very secure about myself. In fact, I think I am at risk. Do you think if I do more battle it will help me improve?" A flash of humor crossed his face.

"Then go do battle with General Grant!"

He mimed a dubious expression. "That's not what I had in mind. General Grant's charms do not interest me as much as yours do." And before she could protest again, his lips came down on hers, this time hard, searching...a kiss so hot it could fuse metals. Catherine quivered. Her knees weakened. Peaches. She moved her hands up his chest, and without guile, her fingers continued upward until they lightly stroked the dark hair at his nape.

He outlined the tips of her breasts with his fingers and her traitorous nipples grew taut. His other hand splayed across the small of her back and Catherine gasped, felt his hardness through their clothes. He cupped her breast in his hand and kissed her eyes, nose, and hollows of her neck and down...

He demanded everything, her compliance, her surrender...

A loud shout heralded from in front of the house. The screech of wagon wheels braked to a stop. She managed to twist from his embrace. Their breathing came in unison. Time froze.

His hands fell to her waist. Yet, he did not release her. At full attention, battle ready, he focused on the anonymous visitor.

She peeked around the barn and shook her head. "Dinkle, from the dry goods. Samuel was supposed to deliver the rest of my order. Dinkle must not see you."

He held her hand. "It was a mistake...for both of us. It won't happen again. I'm leaving—tonight."

A mistake...leaving...tonight? Catherine stood motionless. "Why?"

He said nothing.

A sob trapped in throat. Before she became a pawn in his game...like his Molly, she grabbed her spectacles and ran for the house.

Chapter 6

*I*t was well past midnight when the wagon pulled up in front of her house. When Elias Dinkle had delivered her purchases earlier in the afternoon, she accepted his invitation to a church dance—anything to get away from General Rourke. Of course, she had insisted it was too much of an inconvenience for Elias to return for her. So startled had been Elias when she climbed into his wagon that he started hiccupping.

The social turned out to be a fiasco with someone spiking the punch, and church revelers falling drunk all over the dance floor. Catherine was spared this humiliation for Elias could not dance. The evening might have had a bite of humor except for Elias's endless bout of hiccupping that matched the movement of his Adam's apple to the rhythm of the band music. After listening to Elias's soapbox standing on the perils of bird watching, she didn't even have to feign a headache and begged to go home.

The house remained dark. Good. No doubt the almighty General John Daniel Rourke of the Confederate Army had taken himself south. She dreamed of spending a peaceful night—alone in her bed.

On her porch, she searched for the key in her reticule and missed the strange forward motion of Elias Dinkle. He locked his arms around her.

"Elias Dinkle! What on earth are you doing?"

"I thought you and I could spend a little time together. You living here all alone...no one to keep you...warm." He hiccupped. His breath reeked with the foul stench of liquor.

"You weasel." Shaking off her surprise at his complete change in disposition, she jerked to the side just as he lunged forward, his wet lips puckered for a drooling kiss. She smacked him with her reticule.

"Please, Miss Callahan, just one smooch. Your perfume does funny things to my mind." His hands were everywhere, her spectacles went flying and her hairpins clinked on the planks.

"Elias, get a hold of yourself and release me this minute." But Catherine had hardly pushed at Elias, before he went flying across the porch, seemingly on his own volition.

Leaning casually against the door frame, his arms folded in front of him, stood John. Was that glowering murderous rage directed at her or Elias? He inclined his head toward Elias and drawled through clenched teeth. "Is that the way you treat a lady?"

Elias's Adam's apple bounced moonbeams in the dark but the liquor fortified his gumption. "She's fair game, the schoolteacher."

Before Elias could get one more word out, John had him picked up by the shirt collar and bent the smaller man back over the porch railing. "You owe, Miss Callahan an apology." A chill hung on the edge of his threat.

"I-I apologize. Who are you?" Elias choked, and appealed to Catherine, then glanced to the man holding him.

Catherine put her hand on John's sleeve, before he said anymore, his strong southern accent forming questions in the storekeeper's mind. Elias could wreak a lot of damage. "He's my cousin...remember the one I told you about."

Elias frowned. "No way does he look simple. He looks plain dangerous. Were you really dropped on your head?"

"Dinkle, you're either stupid or a fool." With one punishing right hook, John dealt a blow that knocked Elias over the porch railing.

Catherine peered over the edge. The store clerk wobbled when he stood, nursed a swelling eye and picked barberry thorns off his scalp and neck.

"Where's he from?" Dinkle demanded and glared at Rourke.

Not desiring to create a worse scenario than was already starting, Catherine warned Dinkle. "You better leave...his condition, gets riled awful easy. Never can tell what will happen."

Thirty paces out, Elias thrust out his chest. "He's as ornery and nasty as a stinking Reb."

John started toward Dinkle.

Dinkle made fast tracks to his wagon, whipping his team around. His carriage tipped on sidewheels, slammed on all fours, and then disappeared in a huff of dust. Fuming, Catherine walked past John.

He blocked her, a broad, unsmiling barrier. "I want some questions answered."

"Let me pass." She hissed, and he took hold of her arm.

"Damn you, Catherine, where were you all evening?"

Lifting her chin, she stared mutinously into his eyes. "I was at a church dance."

"With that pile of..." He shook his head. "I wouldn't even give him the rank of humanity."

"You've been drinking. Apparently you also like the flavor of wheat and barley." She smelled it on his breath, so let the accusation snake around him. "As it stands, I have you to thank for compromising me."

"Looked to me, like your reputation was well on its way. Do you realize...that Elias Dunghill—"

"Dinkle. I had the situation well under control." She jerked her arm. He wouldn't let go.

"I believe, Miss Callahan you would have been in desperate straits had I not intervened. You have thrown yourself in with dangerous company."

She glowered at him. "I don't doubt that for one second." Kicking Rourke with everything she had, she caught him in the shin. Pain reverberated from her toes up her leg. Had she broken her foot? Why he didn't budge. He bent low, catching her in the midriff and throwing her over his shoulder.

"Put me down you son of a cur...you unsired son of a chamberpot maker." To split him open with every curse her Irish maid, Brigid, had ever championed.

"Be quiet woman!" He dipped extra low through the doorway. She slipped, the floor loomed. She screamed, and he chuckled, righted her on his shoulder, his hand smacking her bottom. "This is such a charming position."

"Oh-h-h."

He tossed her on the bed, and she rubbed her behind where it smarted.

"Now, answer my question." He crawled across the bed and chucked her under the chin with his finger. Why did you leave with that harebrained imbecile?"

Catherine sat up, and sniffed, refusing to answer him. His lashes fell with a lazy nonchalance. How she relished challenging him.

"Do you know how many times I looked at that clock concerned over your disappearance? When it came to well past midnight, and you had not returned...one nightmare after another crossed my mind. To my complete frustration and disbelief, you've been tapping your toe at a church social?"

Catherine had no answer for him. When his jaw clenched, a slight tremor traveled up her spine and her misgivings of defying him increased by the second.

"That buffoon assaulted you. Even more ridiculous is your idiotic denial of the incident...had the situation under control. Why did you run away?"

Before he finished his last question, she knew he had guessed her reasons, saw it in the myriad of emotions that crossed his face, and then losing all his fury. He became drowsy, his gaze roving downward to her...lips.

The touch of his lips was a tempting sensation——a kiss as tender and light as a summer breeze. She felt drugged by his earthy scent intermingled with whiskey. John placed both his arms on each side of her, forcing her back upon the pillows with an even more demanding kiss. She opened her mouth to say something, but the words died as his mouth covered hers.

Her vow not to become involved with him was like an old wound that ached on a rainy day. The harder she tried to overlook the truth, the more it refused to go away. Her world whirled and skidded. Too fast. *What had become of her?* There was no future with this Reb. He would go on his merry way, back to war, leaving her with nothing but a broken heart. She would be the loser, for he offered her nothing.

Catherine thought about the very striking and startling sides of the general, and she wasn't at all clear she understood who he actually was. She had nursed him back to health and seen him when he was most vulnerable. He could prick her ire easily, enraging her at times, but always manage to make her laugh. He was intelligent and wise, compassionate and strong. He regaled her with amusing stories of his family and in quiet moments like now, kiss her insensibly with an arousing passion and tenderness she had never before imagined. Despite the gentleness he always showed to her, she suspected that it wasn't always the rule. Tonight she had seen a dangerous side in him when Elias Dinkle had assaulted her, and easily entertained the notion that the general was not a man to be trifled with. She even had a stronger notion that anyone who dared to cross him would create a very dangerous enemy. Pushing hard against his solid chest, she stopped him.

He expected a full explanation. Taking a deep breath, she plunged forward. "I cannot be taken in like other women you have had. I am not like that.

He threw back his head and roared with laughter. "Are you jealous?" He fell back on the bed alongside her, his shoulders shaking.

He didn't seem at all disappointed or concerned by her assertion.

Taken aback by his amusement from her grave confession, she twisted to leap off the bed, but John grabbed her wrist in a vise-like grip. "You think to make fun of me. Well get this in your thick head, general, you are no better than Dinkle. In fact, I'd put him a notch above you, and if you think I am going to put up with the likes of you, you might as well hightail it out of here, for I'll scream to high heavens and have the whole Union Army on your trail."

"Would it help if I told you Molly was my dog?" His sudden lazy grin and the truth of what he said made her pulses leap.

"Your dog?" He had been taunting her. A smile found its way to her lips. "You are incorrigible."

His expression stilled and grew serious. "And as far as other women, there are none that compare to you."

John yanked her down and into his arms before she could waiver again. He laughed richly, triumphant at her gasp of utter astonishment. Before she could protest, he kissed her, this time his mouth covered hers hungrily, demanding, his tongue tracing the soft fullness of her lips. When she sighed, it made him roll her on her back, demanding more as he devoured her sweetness. When she reached up and caressed the sides of his face, his breath caught...and his heart melted.

He steeled himself against the onslaught of emotions. Like when he had her plastered up against the barn, all common sense fled. He moved his hands under her neckline and palmed the fullness of her breasts, stroking the creamy mound of flesh, her nipples hardening from his touch. She groaned softly and his control snapped as she curled into the curve of his body, already rigid with desire.

In a span of a second, she tore her mouth from his, demanding desperately that he stop. And then the last thing he expected, iced him. She began to cry. He sank down on the bed beside her, baffled.

"Shawn. Did you?"

He let out a loud breath, yet understanding the pain of losing her brother. "What battle was he lost in?"

"Battle at Brandy Station. Shawn had gone through the war without as much as a scratch. He was serving with the Seventh Calvary, Army of the Potomac. You see it was supposed to be a slight demonstration…but Shawn was caught in the thick of an ill-advised maneuver and was…." She couldn't bring herself to say it. "Union Cavalry completely exposed to Confederate forces…it was seven months ago."

John clasped his hands behind his head. His instinct reared. Her brother populated an unmarked grave. How to break it to her? "I wasn't there. I was farther south on a detail for Lee."

"Thank you," she said, relief mirrored in her face that he was not the one who possibly killed her brother. "I don't believe he's dead. I'd feel it. He's just missing. It's an eerie, uncanny feeling that I cannot explain. Perhaps some southern woman is caring for him like I've cared for you. There has to be some sense of higher powered justice in the world."

"If you say so." He was suddenly tired. His mind burned with memories of the war. He'd seen too many battles, too many dead men. Bodies were thrown into mass graves or the injured, seeking refuge, crawled under tree falls and died. He didn't want to think about it.

The room became silent, their gazes locked and the tension in the air lay palpable. John's lips twisted into a cynical smile, the force of his voice unleashed his great disgust. "The biggest farce of war is to determine who is right but only too late to realize who is left. However, I have the wisdom to hate war. To genuinely despise it. Only fools crave war. The fools caught in their triumphant majesty manipulate, puppet and design we lesser creatures for their own selfish gain. And afterward the fools are left with their cruel armies—armies of cripples, armies of widows and orphans, armies of thieves and in their horrendous wake, an army of dead."

Observing her assessing him, John understood she was trying to make sense of his assertion. He knew how absurd that assertion would seem to her, knowing his history. He understood her repugnance of the maiming, killing and the aftermath of war. He waited for her chastisement or scorn. He would understand immediately—he intuitively knew her thoughts.

She lingered. "Your logic and your humility have struck an inner chord. Your wisdom, respect for life and for peace are aimed directly at my heart. How contrary? A man of war, a leader of many battles...a man of peace?"

She took his hand, the soft pad of her thumb, smoothing across his knuckles. "I understand the truth and pain of your words, garnered from hard-bitten experience, and lived through your soul."

She placed her hands on the sides of his face, her trembling fingers stroking his cheeks. Softly, and with complete sincerity, she whispered, "I believe you are a great man, General Rourke, noble beyond distinction."

The gentle touch of her fingers, and the look in her eyes cemented his resolve. Just days ago he was fighting for the Confederacy, the Cause, and beyond a world he could only imagine, fortune had brought them together. But it was the warmth and reverence of her words that was his undoing. Cautiously, deliberately slowing his alacrity, John moved her gently, sheltering her intimately in his arms, content with the wild beating of her heart upon his side.

It was the most extraordinary torment. He laid stiffly as she stroked his chest, then grabbed her hand to end her simple exploration before something started that he wouldn't be able to rein in. Glancing down upon her silken head, her hair fanned out across his chest in golden splendor, brought warmth to his heart. The whole world could be damned. She was his.

Yet she was afraid to get involved with a Confederate general who had nothing to offer her except a nebulous future. Looking beyond the war, at the what ifs, John envisioned with perfect clarity, everything he could offer her. Wealth, status, a home—a family. In his mind, he saw her in silks and satins sitting on the porch of his beloved home, Fairhaven, laughing and with several children at her feet. *Their children.* But the dream was a fanciful castle in the sky, far from his reaches.

Her eyelashes swept down upon her cheeks, long and sooty, and he watched the rise and fall of her breasts, warm, full, enticing.

She sighed then, and nestled her face into his chest. He grabbed the blankets, covering them both, reached up and turned down the light. Would he get any sleep? He wasn't a saint.

Chapter 7

The bedroom door banged open with a shot. John shielded Catherine with his body and cursed for he had allowed an intruder into the house unaware. Standing in the doorway stood a man a score older than his father, a wizened complexion and white, wild hair. Looking as if he walked from the high mountains of Donegal, the man's blazingly keen, gray eyes bored holes into John, missing nothing and taking in everything. John might have been wary except for the Roman collar strapped to the man's neck and long black flowing cassock. This was Catherine's uncle.

"What the devil is the meaning of this?" boomed the priest in a thick, commanding Irish brogue.

At the crack of his voice, Catherine pulled the bed sheet up to her neck, although she didn't need to for she was fully dressed. Being found entwined with a strange man in her bed was going to take a lot of explaining. John observed her high color as she swallowed hard trying to squeak out a feeble answer. "It's not what you think, Uncle Charlie." She squirmed beneath the priest's accusing glare.

Her uncle shook his fist at them, his stout body trembling as if shaken by some inner wind. "It is a sorrowful sight laid out before me. Don't you be telling me what to think Catherine. I do believe my very eyes."

John lounged, amused. Fortunately, he had the grace to appear compliant, for in Father Charles Callahan's eyes, he was a fox caught in a henhouse. What was more entertaining as Father Callahan thundered and stormed, was witnessing Catherine on the defensive. Hands down it was easy to discern where she inherited her temper.

"I'll be waging with the Lord Almighty that my dear departed sister, your sweet mother is rolling in her grave! And to think of you carrying on with these shenanigans. And who do I receive the good news from? Why Dinkle himself. He made a beeline for me at the railroad depot this morning when I stepped off the train, sporting his newly acquired shiner." He darted a scathing glance at John. "I'll assume you are the donor."

Without affirmation, he blustered on. "And then Dinkle went on to say my niece had a visit from her mad cousin." He glared at John. "I'll assume you are the mad cousin."

John inclined his head. There was nothing more than to let matters come to a head.

Insultingly enough, Father Callahan inspected him—the man who dared to be in bed with his niece. "Were you really dropped on your head? You don't look as if you were dropped on your head, but Dinkle said you were. I don't know where he got that impression," said Father Callahan.

John glanced at Catherine, and she shrank into the pillows. "I have a good idea where Dinkle got his impression."

"Although come to think of it—" Father Callahan hobbled closer, pointing his cane fashioned from a corkscrew willow.

"—Dinkle certainly looked like he was dropped on his head." And then, half in a language John could not understand, but assumed to be Gaelic, the priest bellowed. "Knowing very well you have no cousins to speak of got me to wondering who the devil Dinkle was sputtering about, so I decided to pay you a little visit before Dinkle had the whole town in an uproar!" His glare blistered Catherine.

Catherine put her hand up again, "But uncle—"

Father Callahan banged his cane down on the floor with a thunderclap, like Moses parting the sea. No way was Father Callahan going to allow his niece to get in one word.

"Well, I'll be telling you here and now, I will never condone such sinful mischief, and this behavior will have to be rectified immediately." He looked at John with well-intended meaning.

Catherine exploded from the bed. "What do you mean *rectified?*"

"Marriage, of course, and the sooner the better."

"Marriage! You can't possibly—"

"Be silent, Catherine." Father Callahan roared and she fell silent.

John took careful note of her immediate silence. He could learn from Father Callahan.

The priest scrutinized him like an insect dissected beneath a magnifying glass. "And who do I have the misfortune to be soon related to?"

John figured most men would shrink from Father Callahan's gray-eyed scrutiny, but he gathered nothing but respect. He liked Father Callahan. After all, Father Callahan, or Uncle Charlie as Catherine called him, had handed John his *castle in the sky*. He almost smiled. Instead he moved from the bed and offered his hand.

"I'm General John Daniel Rourke, Army of Northern Virginia," he drawled and there was no mistaking his southern accent or Father Callahan's sudden gaping mouth.

"And how? Of course, there were several reports in the papers claiming you were captured and held in a New England prisoner of war camp. It was a regular infantryman they had in their possession. Perhaps——" He knitted his thick, white brows together trying to figure it all out. "I've seen lithographs of you...how does a Confederate General...and a little far off the mark I'd say... come into the company of my niece?" He glared at Catherine. "Oh, never mind," Father Callahan said, stamping his cane for emphasis. "When my niece is involved, nothing surprises me."

John heard Catherine clear her throat in an effort to remain calm. "Uncle Charlie, I don't like the look on your face. You are thinking a bit too much. You don't have to marry us. We have done nothing untoward." She waited for John to support her.

Leaning casually against the wall with his arms folded in front of him, John said, "For all intents and purposes, Father Callahan, your niece has been compromised. I take full responsibility."

"You what." She exploded and then looked at Father Callahan. "I am not going to do what you're thinking, Uncle Charlie. I absolutely refuse——"

Her uncle was in no mood to argue and spewed his wrath of God on her. "And to think, if your mother was alive today, what do you believe she'd be saying about her daughter carrying on so?"

"Oh no, you don't. You'll not be putting a guilt trip on me. I've done nothing——"

John stepped forward, abruptly grabbing her by the elbow and firmly escorting her into the parlor. "We're ready when you are Father Callahan." He addressed him with benevolent politeness. John dodged a well-aimed kick and, remembering the dainty kick she had given him the night before, skewered her with a warning.

"Certainly not. I wouldn't marry you if my life depended on it."

John pinched her elbow. *'Your life will depend on it.'*

"I see," said Father Callahan, lifting an insolent brow. "Catherine, you have obvious affection for General Rourke, whether you admit it or not, and finding you in bed together is proof enough for me. You've turned up your nose at too many swains vying for your hand and are well past the marrying age. I've made my decision. I owe this much to my sister."

Her uncle pulled his Holy Book from his cassock. "A few side questions before we begin. "You are Catholic and Irish?" Father Callahan muttered more to himself, pleased that those require-ments were fulfilled. "You are from the Rourke family...that is to say," he emphasized strongly, "the *Rourke* family of Virginia?" It was a statement more than a question.

"The same," John concurred, seeing the old priest was wilier than he thought.

"And by the saints what a general—much to the bane of the North. There will be many a rolled eye in New York over this union," Father Callahan said with glee beneath his breath, then straightened, apparently remembering his audience. "I will marry the North with the South, a hopeful attempt to bridge reconcilia-tion...a peace...to make a turbulent world turned upside down by war a dwelling place in the hearts of a man and a woman."

"My niece will be well cared for?" Father Callahan gauged him. Even though the words were not spoken, it was understood between the two men. It wasn't monetary what Father Callahan was seeking. He was looking for a long and caring relationship.

"You have my word," John promised.

"You'll have many children in the eyes of the church?"

"Numerous," John admitted, straight-faced, glancing sideways at Catherine, noting an angry blush steel across her face.

"And peace?" Father Callahan queried.

From the present look on her face, John concluded, peace was like throwing rocks at a hornet's nest. Didn't his parents have a stormy beginning and a tender, peaceful conclusion? "There will be peace...eventually."

Under her glower, Father Callahan muttered into his open book. "Looks to me like you'll have to cap an active volcano in order to get that peace, but hope is a powerful thing."

"Wait! The Banns!" She bounced on her toes, the happy thought of having three extra weeks to declare the banns. "They haven't been announced."

Brilliant. John had forgotten about the age-old Catholic tradition of waiting a month to allow opposing inquiries to take place before the marriage ceremony. It was her last angle.

Father Callahan had enough. "Under the circumstances, I give special dispensation and waive the banns. Now we will begin." And under the deadening heat of his roar, Catherine withered and leaned against John for protection. And this, he reflected, from a woman who said she would not marry him if her life depended on it.

"Dearly beloved we are gathered here today in matters of Holy Matrimony…"

"You mean to tell me you are going through with this farce?" Catherine said.

Father Callahan glared at his niece, her hair wild and disheveled and her demeanor fighting mad. Then he looked to John and said wryly, "You have my condolences, General Rourke. You do not know the hours, days, and years, I have spent praying for her eternal soul. My knees are downright bruised from the ordeal."

John chuckled.

"You'll have your hands full." Father Callahan reminded him.

"It will be my cross to bear." John bowed his head, penitent while holding his irate bride-to-be in place before she bolted.

"I don't believe my ears. I am in the midst of getting married, and you're joking?"

Father Callahan zoomed ahead. "Do you John Daniel Rourke take Catherine as your lawful wedded wife, to have and to hold, from this day forward, for better, for worse, for richer, for poorer, in sickness and in health, until death do you part?"

Catherine sensed John was extremely serious about the vow he was about to speak, despite his merry tone moments before. She sobered. The look of resolute and unwavering determination manifested on his face assured a rare kind of promise, coupled with an indomitable will to succeed.

John straightened and with intense and complete profoundness said, "I do."

Turning to Catherine, Father Callahan repeated the same litany. "Do you Catherine Callahan Fitzgerald…"

"Fitzgerald?" John's eyebrow furrowed at the addition of her surname.

She winced and her uncle raced on with the vows.

"…take John Daniel Rourke to be your husband. To promise to be true to him in good times and in bad, in sickness and in health, to love, honor and…" Father Callahan paused, "obey," he emphasized, "until death do you part?"

She had read somewhere of the last walk which condemned prisoners are supposed to walk, as they march from their cells to the place of execution. Doom filled the very core of her being. *No. No. No.*

"I've just returned from New York City. I am puzzled by your brother's disappearance…I'm thinking of your safety."

Francis Mallory. Her uncle pierced her with the looming threat. Of course, he would hold that over her head. He felt she would be safe married to the general. Yes…and she should have thought of that, also, to not be forced into an arranged marriage by Mallory. It wasn't like she disliked John. Didn't she like his kisses and the way he held her in his arms?

There was a long pause in silence until John infuriated, pinched her arm.

"I do," she squeaked.

"Done. By the angels in heaven, my sister is smiling down on me now." Father Callahan slapped his book closed, paused to shake hands and congratulate them both. "I have some business to do, so I'll be leaving now, and let you two youngsters get acquainted."

Catherine colored from the innuendo. But it was the rapid departure of her uncle that caused panic to erupt. "You can't leave."

"But I must. I have a christening to perform. Lovely family." He looked to John. "The O'Shaunesseys, God Bless them—their eighteenth child."

"Their eighteenth child," she shrieked. "The father should be taken out and shot."

"A man after my own heart." John laughed.

Catherine shot daggers at him.

She followed her uncle out of the house and onto the porch. He gave her a fatherly kiss good-bye. "Trust in God. He has a special plan for you." To John, he held out his hand and said, "As a man of God, I have a clear idea of all manner of mankind—welcome to the family."

Catherine watched her uncle disappear down the road. Melancholy filled her soul. He was getting older. "He's all I have left now." She whispered more to herself than to John.

"You have a husband now." He stood behind her, his shadow engulfing hers.

"You don't have to stay married to me," she said, stunned by what had occurred. Stooping, she picked up her spectacles from where they had fallen the night before and placed them on her nose. We could seek higher authority on an annulment in this situation."

"Situation?" A vein pulsed in his neck.

"I did not ask for you to be thrown at my doorstep. To think my reward for sparing your life will be married to a rebel General. The irony of it, I'm only beginning to understand. I'd be more fortunate possessing the waxed wings of Icarus and flying into the sun."

John's eyes narrowed. "This rebel is now your husband...one you will honor. And obey. Unless a favored Yankee bullet finds my heart, we will be wed until death do us part. But until fortune smiles adversely upon me, you are, by all rights, my wife. Your compliance, your duties, your submission will be in accordance with this role."

"Honor? You don't even know what the word means. "Obey? I'll never acquiesce to that term. Should I genuflect as you pass, General? Do I kneel on rice and pay homage?"

He folded his arms in front of him. "As Mrs. John Daniel Rourke, you will honor the name in the strictest sense. Do I make myself clear?"

"Your hubris, General Rourke—" she took an abrupt step toward him "...will be your downfall, for you underestimate me. You may ponder your successes with your Southern uprising, but with me it will be a very different matter. I will, as my solemn oath, violate every rule you put before me, resist every command, and create disorder in every decision. I am one Yankee you will regret challenging. I will rebel, subvert, and create chaos and bedlam until you are deranged. You could have all the armies of the world, except I will turn your miserable life upside-down. Do I make myself clear?" She jumped when he reached out and removed her spectacles and peered through them.

"Glass. Plain glass. You don't need these at all. What are you afraid of? And suppose you tell me how you neglected to mention the name Fitzgerald?" He turned on his heel and moved to the end of the porch.

She dragged her palms over her skirts. To come up with a suitable answer? To inform him he married the heir to Fitzgerald Rifle Works? How did she explain the glasses were a disguise to hide from Mallory?

"Since I live alone, I feel more comfortable…" Perspiration trickled down her back. Her gown grew scratchy as if it were wool chafing her skin instead of soft cotton. She hated lying as much as she hated the war. Her illogical heart crossed swords with her logical brain. *Stay the course,* her brain warned. "Where are you going?"

John whipped her spectacles first low then high, flinging them with the graceful arc of a discus thrower. "I'm throwing rocks at a hornet's nest." Her glasses vanished into the infinite rising boughs of oak, caught somewhere in its iron chord branches just this side of the sky.

"Why in the world did you do that? You spawn of Satan. You stinking pile of codpieces." On and on she went, raining down every major curse that came into her mind. Gone was the well-bred, proper young lady and in her place was a snappish, coarsely spoken version of a butcher's wife.

She was mad as a cut badger. She was lovely. His mind raced with the folly of their dilemma. There were many points of contention. They didn't know each other at all. Compared to the disaster of his first marriage and with other women of the South, she was an innocent and a rare jewel. They were oceans apart in political viewpoints. They had a war between them, and they were somehow going to have to solidify that division. They had nothing in common. She had a way, which exasperatingly enough, could rile his normally cool state of mind and snap his temper like kindling on fire. Yet, he needed a woman who could challenge him.

In her growing indignation, he admired her wild beauty and, no doubt, her brazen insults could pale the most hardened of his seasoned soldiers. Above a narrow waist jutted the moist satin of her breasts, heaving with anger, and he savored the satisfaction that this passionate, glorious Yankee woman was now his *wife*.

Like a saint to the pillar, she clung to the porch post, cultivating her pulpit of fire and brimstone. The real reason for her outburst was fear, fear of the magnitude of marriage, fear of being a woman, a wife. She had spent herself and slumped, and John could not imagine more of a picture of misery and desolation.

"Why did you throw away my glasses?" She asked near tears.

"I'm your husband. I will protect you now," John said. "You'll never need them."

"You forget you are in Yankee territory, General Rourke. I have to protect *you*."

"There is that," he conceded. "I believe there is more to your story than you're telling me. If it will reduce your worries, you can tell me in your own good time."

She nodded, mollified with that concession. "Will I be fond of being...married?" She swiped a tear, the epitome of despair.

"I believe so," he said, taking one step at a time so as not to frighten her.

"With absolute certainty?"

"With absolute certainty," he repeated, and then took another step.

Like a small bewildered child caught in a frightful darkness, she turned away from him, her face upon the post.

"Will it be similar to your first marriage?" she asked.

"There is no comparison. You know there isn't." He took another step, giving her time to adjust.

"I will not be considered your property," she sniffed, "that would be a tragedy."

"We are equals," he admitted calmly.

"What does a Rebel General's wife do?" He heard the defeat in her words, revealing to him, her vulnerability. John's heart clenched.

"Be a wife." He smiled at the back of her head, and picking up a long strand of her golden hair, fingered it in his calloused palms.

"Be specific. I mean, will I have to knit sweaters for cannon-balls or polish your rifle?"

"God forbid!" He broke into a laugh, and then added seriously, "I have an orderly for those duties."

"He can knit?"

"Who?" he asked, inhaling her lilac scent.

"Your orderly, he can knit?" She turned toward him and bumped into his chest.

"Of course not. He polishes my rifle."

"Oh." She stared straight at his neck.

"Any more questions?" He lifted her chin until her eyes met his.

"Thousands," she whispered.

He kissed her then, slowly, thoughtfully, senselessly.

"He doesn't crochet, crewel or needlepoint either."

"Who?" She was breathless and he liked that fact.

"My orderly." He swept her up, weightless in his arms, crossing the threshold, he kicked the door shut.

This time he took the precaution of throwing the bolt down.

Catherine remained silent as he stood her in front of the bed. She thought she could speak, that there would be many more words to share. But there were no more words. John reached out to her, the heat and passion forged in his body, so great that she trembled, for she really did not know what to do. This was to be her wedding night, and no one had explained what was expected of her. She tentatively, then mechanically lifted her arms around him, locking herself into his embrace.

John pressed his lips to hers, caressing her mouth more than kissing it. She quivered at the sweet tenderness of his kiss, hoping it would last, but somehow knowing it wouldn't. Then he pulled apart for a moment and studied her. She dropped her hands, then looked up to him half-expecting, half-fearing what was to come next. If only he would explain.

"Catherine," he sighed, "Do you believe in me?"

She nodded. "I'm scared. More scared than I've ever been in my entire life."

John smiled his boyish smile trying to relax her, an expression of satisfaction glowing in his eyes. "What we are about to do is between us, as a husband and wife."

Standing this close made it impossible to remain coherent. She tried to think of other things to occupy her mind…her home in

New York, Jimmy O'Hara, the orphans, Dr. Parks. But none of these commanded anything immediate in her mind, the images, fleeting. And now she stood in front of a tall Rebel General, magnified and real, and her husband.

She stood with her arms at her sides as John's long thick fingers grasped her shoulders, finding an incredible consolation in the gentleness of his grasp and undeniable look in his eyes. The stroking of his fingers sent pleasant jolts through hers. The tiny hooks and buttons of her blue day gown melted away. His hands slipped inside the neckline of her dress, pressing down the soft material from her shoulders, searing a path down her abdomen, over her hips and onto the floor in a soft swish. Lifting the lace-edged strap of her chemise, his lips pressed to the spot where it had been. He caressed and teased the flesh beneath the fine silk, until her breasts budded full and hard against his palm.

Like quicksilver his palm moved, the gentle massage sending currents, spreading like embers on a newly turned fire, spiraling down her stomach and lower, eliciting a trembling between her thighs. Her body craved his hands, his mouth upon her lips, and distinct warmth flooded the area between her legs.

"John."

He removed her chemise and petticoat. *Naked.*

His tongue traced the soft fullness of her lips, his hands glided over her shoulders then down, exploring the hollows of her back, pressing her length to the hard contours of his muscled body and hard thighs. Dragging her mouth from his, she took John's lead, imitating what he had done to her and with shaking hands began to unbutton his shirt. She ran her hands over his chest, tracing his nipples with the light touch of her fingertips. His jaw clenched involuntarily as she moved her hands up and over his shoulders until his shirt fell to the ground. They stared in mute silence, sharing an intense physical awareness of each other.

With one fluid movement John gathered her up into his arms, placing her on the center of the bed, her body hot on the cool sheets. Somewhere in her maidenly musings she had dreamed of her bridal night upon satin sheets with poetic refrains, and vases and vases of roses and soft candlelight.

But none of that mattered.

Instead of candlelight, she had the bright light of the noonday sun bathing the room in all its dazzling glory, the scent of honeysuckle, sweetly drifting in from the open window, and for words, the gaze of her husband, desirous and ravenous which no poetic refrains or flowery phrases could surpass.

John shrugged out of his pants and boots, fully exposed, a demigod from some immortal time and place? His shoulders were broad and bronzed, his chest had a light furring of dark hair, his bold stance emphasized the force of his thighs and slimness of his hips—and something else. And it was that something else that caused her to bite her lip and look away, her embarrassment and admiration evident. She had seen him when she cared for him, but now was the startling proof of his desire. She yanked the sheet up to her chin.

The bed sank beneath his weight. She waited, her breath solidifying in her throat. John tore the sheet from her, cupped her chin in his hand. In a voice like rough velvet and raw hunger, he whispered, "You are the most beautiful woman I have ever known."

His mouth grazed her neck, her earlobe, and then swooped to capture her lips. Coaxing them open, his tongue explored the recesses of her mouth, firm, demanding. Catherine groaned.

His arms encircled her, his hand splayed at the bottom of her spine holding her in intimate contact. She gasped as her bare breasts crushed against the firmness of his chest and the hard intimate contact of his arousal against her stomach. Suddenly his hands were everywhere, her body aching for more. Outlining the tips of her breasts with his fingers, John brought their tips to crested peaks. Slowly, languorously, his hands moved downward, skimming either side of her body to her thighs. He explored her thighs then moved up to her taut stomach then plunged down again searching the warmth that lay hidden intimately between. She gasped, and snapped her legs together, her eyes widening.

In a hushed agonized breath, John whispered, "Catherine, I want it worthy, memorable for your first time."

She allowed his expert touch to drown her in a shower of lush sensuality. She arched against him, wanting more, demanding more, the naked emptiness inside her needing to be fulfilled.

The huskiness of John's voice betrayed his cost of control. "I desire you, Catherine." Then his mouth came down on her neck, trailing a warm wet line to her breast, rousing a melting sweetness, her nipples glistening from his mouth. She grabbed his dark head and held him to her, the feel of his rough skin against her smooth breast, kissed him upon his head, his lips, his mouth, and shoulders. Drugged by his earthy scent and to what he was doing to her, passion inched through her veins like hot honey until she could not tell time or place or reality.

She felt his body with all its inherent tension, felt the intense power of his chest, the rigidity of his thighs. She felt the firm demand of his hips and the unyielding potency of that which lay within his loins. He raised himself above her then, and Catherine shivered where cool air touched her body, wanting him to turn back into her embrace.

"Look at me, Catherine," he commanded.

Dazed, Catherine opened her eyes to meet his steel-blue gaze, dark as lapis...and poised above her was the scourge of the North, the man whose reputation made Yankee Commanders blood turn cold. Yet all he had yielded to her was an aching tenderness and fierce, surrendering desire.

Catherine glanced downward and her eyes widened. No way could it happen...could fit.

John stared at her. "We are man and woman, Catherine. We are made to fit. You must believe in me."

With trembling fingers, she placed her hands on both sides of his face. No words were needed. He shifted upon her. The thrust of his knee parted her thighs, and the weight of his body spread her further. He pressed inside her, but paused when he felt the barrier of her virginity. She was tight and so damp. Hanging on to his control by a thread, John bowed his head, his breathing ragged next to her ear.

"I will not hurt you Catherine. Only a moment will there be pain. I promise."

She clenched his shoulders expectant.

He shifted his hold on her, continued his probing, perspiration beading at his brow. Fighting the need to bury himself in her moist warmth was sweet agony, the last vestiges of his restraint disintegrating.

She pushed at him, scrambling to get away. He had hurt her. He stopped, his mouth came down on hers, and he whispered into her mouth, reassuring her. Grabbing her hips, he plunged hard with one solid, powerful thrust. She cried out, pounded his shoulders, but John held her in place. "No more."

John stayed rock still inside her, waiting for her to adjust before he started moving again. "My love, the worst is over." He hated hurting her. But, she felt so damned good.

In answer, her arms entwined his neck in an aching tenderness that tore at his heart.

John began to move, slowly at first, a whisper of a caress, his manhood deep inside her. He groaned as the dormant sexuality of her lush body burst into full bloom. His control shattered like a million shards of glass, nights of control he had harnessed, now unleashed, his ardor mounted as she rose to meet his searing need, welcoming his entry.

In a mating ritual as old as time, John matched her movements, thrusting his thick fingers into the silkiness of her hair and lifting her hips to meet his rhythm Her fingers dug into his shoulders and John buried his face in the side of her neck and let out a raw groan, the pressure building inside of him unlike anything he had ever experienced. Lush. Exquisite. From the soft core of her body, she abandoned herself to him, clamping iron chains around his heart. The bed gave way with every forceful thrust. In a raw act of the total possession he craved, he was mindless to everything except the indulgence of granting them both complete satisfaction.

She arched, and her body vibrated with liquid fire. John taut above her, poured his seed into her. Breathing labored, he rolled to the side, keeping her intimately joined to him. Reveling in the sensation of her wet warmth and the brush of her lips against his neck, John cradled her in his arms, his hand drifting up and down her spine as she leaned her soft cheek against his chest. His chin nestled upon her head and his fingers buried in the golden waves of her hair. For the moment, he abandoned all the fears of the past and future, basking upon the wonder of the intimacy they had just shared.

"Cold?" John asked, pausing to pull the sheets up over them.

"Mm-m-m." She nestled deeper into him.

"John, did I ..." She was too inhibited to ask him if she pleased him."

John exhaled a long sigh of contentment, basking in male arrogance that she was shaken as much as he. He kissed her head, the soft scent of lilac mixed with the musky scent of their lovemaking permeating the air.

"Perfect," he said.

"Is it like that for everyone? I mean does it feel that wonderful for everyone...the first time?"

She was swimming through a new haze of feelings and desires, and she wanted him to explain what she was experiencing. "Seldom," he said.

Will it always be like this?" She squirmed closer to him. Her innocent movements and conversation put tantalizing thoughts into his head. No woman he'd known had ever ignited this uncontrollable surge of lust. Despite his growing desire for her again, he seemed to enjoy her struggle with future expectations of which he had no doubt.

"Better." His voice husked firm and final.

"I wish you would have told me it wasn't as frightening as I imagined." She smoothed a finger down his neck. "I'm quite certain I would have traveled south and captured you myself."

"Ah. But you have captured me, woman. I am your prisoner, the nights I have lain awake holding you, tortured with wicked thoughts, not being able to touch you the way I desired."

She drew his hand to her lips and kissed the hard lean knuckles. "And for all the times you have tortured me, General Rourke? Shall I call upon the Union Army to rescue a maiden in distress?"

John lifted a dubious brow. "You are a maid no more and my *wife*. If the Union Army appears, I will fight every one of them to keep what is mine."

"Is that a threat?" Her eyes were wide and dared to taunt him.

"No, Catherine my love," he whispered. "Only a vow from your husband." His thoughts slammed into him. In the last week he had been shot, almost died, and then married a woman who he knew nothing about. An enchantress. Had he lost perspective? He had to get back. The soldier who had switched his uniform had been discovered as a fraud according to Father Callahan. They would be looking for General Rourke in the Elmira prison camp. He would not be there. The war, a distant, cloying shadow that called him to return. Before he was considered a deserter. Yet he was rooted. Angrier with himself, John rolled her over onto her back and made swift violent love, more desirous, more demanding than before.

Chapter 8

*A*fter several ideal days of wedded bliss, John had never been happier. The treachery of his first wife, and the fact that he had never loved her, left an irreparable scar and had exacted a toll. Hadn't he buried his bitterness in a military career? All of that seemed like years ago. Enamored with Catherine, his new wife in every way that a man could be in love with a woman, John lingered, content.

Everything about Catherine was honey-gold and warm, as if he were the focal point of the whole world. Even the natural and unassuming way she took his hand in hers, soothing, washing away the cynicism that had been roiling within him for so long. Her passionate nature had taught him to love. It was a new feeling for John. A feeling he welcomed.

Father Callahan had come to visit to see if either of them was still alive, ready to rub his hands with glee at the obvious success of his imposed marriage. He had handed John a package of cigars as a late wedding gift, muttering something about all good Virginia men must have them as a staple. Catherine's uncle worked on a plan to get him south. He knew the old priest delayed to give them a honeymoon. Touched by Father Callahan's generosity, and despite the old priest's gruffness, Rourke considered him family, and therefore, under his protection.

In addition to Father Callahan's visits, Samuel had been a regular visitor. John spent time teaching Samuel how to make fishing lures as well as foolproof snares to catch rabbits. Samuel both admired and adulated him, and as Catherine laughingly pointed out, hung on his every word as if it were a sacred decree handed down from God to Moses.

Today she had planned a picnic, and the both of them traversed the mountainsides. Thick buoyant white clouds scudded across a brilliant blue sky. The warm sun illuminated the landscape, rich and alive with daisies and yellow buttercups. It could not have been a more perfect day, in John's mind, with the inherent promise of so much more.

The call to duty had been strong and nagging like an irksome thorn in his side. His wound had healed, thanks to Catherine's ministrations. To head south? Duty. With certainty, his family worried if the war had made a statistic of him. In her pink day dress with no corset beneath and temptingly low bodice, Catherine made an enticing picture, and he luxuriated in the company of his wife. To part from her for even a minute? He clenched his jaw, unable to work out the logistics of moving her to his family's home. He wanted her there. John cursed the war. She belonged at Fairhaven, but with the war upon Virginia soil? The venture proved too uncertain and too dangerous. To leave her behind until conditions changed was the only logical thing to do, and he hated the very thought of that logic.

Catherine tugged his hand, making a witty comment that broke him out of his reverie. John pushed away his gloomy thoughts, determined to seize the day with his lovely wife.

They came to a shady glen bordering a small spring-fed pond, secluded high above a rampart, verdant green in shadow and amber-gold in light, clinging with mosses, ferns and wildflowers. The rich scent of woodland loam mixed with violets wafted over their private paradise. Warmed from their exercise, they settled down on a blanket spread over soft green grass.

"What kind of husband will you be?" said Catherine still laughing at one of his amusing tales as a Rebel General.

"Ruthless, commanding," he grinned with playful pleasure.

"Really?" She angled her head back, scoffing at his superiority.

"M-m-m," he confirmed, plucking a piece of grass and trailing it down her throat. "And what kind of wife will you be?"

"A nagging, complaining, shrew." She burst out laughing.

"I'll have to deal with that particular behavior with—" Rourke made a lunge, grabbed her and rolled her beneath him. "—a hickory stick."

"The hickory stick is for you. Besides..." She dabbed a pointed finger into his chest, "How many children would we have? I always loved and wanted children but the idea up until now seemed nonexistent."

John exhaled a long sigh of contentment. "Ten to start out with. All boys."

"To spite you, I'll have ten girls. All of them like me," she fenced, watching him with smug delight.

"God forbid. How you do seek your revenge," he growled and bent to kiss her.

She pushed at his chest, unbalancing him and throwing him off, then scrambled to her feet and darted behind a tree. From the safety of her position, she taunted him. "Pray tell, do you always plan your military feats with the same endeavor? I find them lacking, for you cannot hold onto your wife."

John rose, and like a predatory lion, greedy and hungering, he stalked her. "I always plan for predictability. But nothing about you, *Mrs. Rourke*, is predictable."

In a vain attempt to outmaneuver him, she ran to another tree. But he was faster and, with lightening quick ease, grabbed her and backed her up against the tree.

Trapped between his arms, she tilted her head to the side in careful measurement of him. With no room for escape, she crafted a different tact.

"Dear General John D. Rourke," her declaration rang with goading command. "In consideration of all the circumstances governing the present situation of affairs of this station, I propose to the commanding officer of the Rebel forces the appointment of commissioners to agree upon terms of capitulation of the forces under my command. In that view, I suggest an armistice until otherwise indicated. Very respectfully, your obedient servant, General Catherine Rourke, Northern States of America." She met his gaze, elated by her strategy.

No way was he fooled. He had her entirely surrounded and *she* was at his mercy. From his experience in the field of battle, he recognized the ploy as a stall for time.

"Dear Madam General." He began, enjoying the gentle sparring as much as she did. "Yours of this date proposing an armistice in appointment of commissioners to settle terms of capitulation is just received. No terms except unconditional and immediate surrender can be accepted, and I propose to move immediately..." He chucked her under the chin with a strong finger, and her eyes widened, "I am, Madam General, very respectfully, your obedient servant, General John Daniel Rourke, Confederate States."

Catherine slid her hands up around his neck pulling him closer. "Dear General John D. Rourke. I will not retreat a single inch and I will be heard. Due to my immediate ceasefire, I again implore a truce and peace agreement settled by the appointment of commissioners to govern the terms of capitulation. Very respectfully, your 'less' than obedient servant, General Catherine Rourke."

"Dear General Catherine Rourke, U. S. Army. Madam, again, no terms except immediate and unconditional surrender." Enchanted by her wit, he pressed her with complete enjoyment, but grimaced when she tweaked the hairs at the base of his neck.

She cleared her throat, forcing a remote dignity into her declaration, and she had no idea how sensuous her voice sounded to him. "Dear General John D. Rourke, Army of the Confederate States. The distribution of the forces—" She stopped breathless as John pushed up against her, letting her feel the force of his longing, and cleared her throat again. "—under my command, incident to the overwhelming force under your command...compel me to accept the ungenerous and unchivalrous terms which you propose. I am, Sir, your disobedient servant," she emphasized. "General Catherine Rourke, United States Army."

John smiled idly as his fingers slid up her bare arms and buried into her thick lustrous hair. He beamed approval before his lips pressed against hers, covering her mouth in a long exacting kiss that left her speechless. He swept her up and carried her to the blanket where his sweet adorable wife began to undress him.

A rush of pink stained her cheeks, blushing at her own excitement as she tugged his shirt free from his breeches. His skin prickled as her cool fingers trailed down his hot naked flesh, and with boldness, she unbuttoned and removed his breeches. Rourke groaned. Scorching, hungering desire snaked through his veins.

Forever their lovemaking would be branded on his brain, remembering with aching poignancy and clarity, and shaking anew with all he held in his arms. For all the years of loneliness, to have found his one true love, his lifelong soul mate, and the fate that brought them together, far beyond the scope of his imagination.

And she had given him so much in return. Although she had never declared it, he knew in his heart, she loved him. She brushed her fingers against his chest and around his neck, playfully testing every muscle and sinew, then rose against him, the soft curves molded beneath the simple cotton of her dress, pressed against his naked chest, alluring and taunting. With heady persuasion, she captured his lips into a deep soulful kiss, sending his body ablaze with all the passion known to strip a man senseless. With due haste, he removed her gown and laid her down upon the blanket cushioned beneath by soft sweet grass.

Latticed light penetrated the leafy bower high above, and rippled over her full ivory breasts. Her hair splayed over the blanket, and a golden aura encircled her, her beauty exquisite and, regal, and in the glowing light of the forest glade made her more ethereal than ever. He encircled her in his arms, one hand held in the small of her back, locked against her spine. She ran a delicate finger across his lips.

"General, I fear you have not laid out the terms of surrender. Without the terms there can be no surrender." She sighed and stretched provocatively beneath him. He exhaled, aware of her scheme.

"Dear wife. If you seek to deny me surrender, then prepare, and without delay, for a full assault. For you see, my patience is at end and any more tricks will yield to a full offensive and escape will be an exercise in futility."

She tapped an accusing finger into his chest. "If you seek to do battle with the same lust you do me—" her voice was light with humor "—then you will soon exceed Napoleon and conquer the world."

He tightened his arm around her. "Would that my lust be appeased with the scant morsels sent my way—"

She hit his shoulder. "You have kept me in bed night and day since we have been married. You are wicked, allowing me no sleep and laboring me with your every whim."

"I do not think that I act alone. I seem to recall...my shrewish wife with her insatiable lust and I, a prisoner to her every desire."

Before she could say any more, John crushed her to him, taking her mouth with a savage intensity, and she responded with equal fervor, arching her body toward him, caressing the muscles across his back and shoulders. His hands began a lust-arousing exploration over her breasts, and then below, his gut ablaze with need and his male satisfaction swelled with pride for she could not disguise her body's reaction.

Moaning with primal pleasure, she gasped as he took her fully and completely, his impatience exploded, sending them both to throbbing levels of ecstasy.

John kissed the top of her head and rolled to his side. Not to be outdone, Catherine climbed atop of him, enjoying the moment and stared down into his face with warm regard. His skin was seared by the pale peaks of her breasts, a sweet, delightful torment. John folded his arms behind his head and contemplated his impish wife. "What new game are you up to now?"

Catherine teased the hairs on his chest. "I need more terms of surrender."

Rourke feigned exhaustion. "If you seek any more, I will be removed from this world under the weary duty of succumbing to your conditions. "But..." he smiled with easy assurance. "A duty well spent, a heavenly way to depart, and an initiative most inspiring. Yet there is great risk. What would we do if we fell in love with each other? What would be in store for us then?"

Catherine's fingers touched her lips, lost in a wave of confused emotions. To drown in languorous warmth, allowing a contentment and peace to sweetly drain all her thoughts and fears of Mallory. Didn't she savor John's raw act of possession? Could she ever get enough of him? She was shameful.

Did she love John? Or was it a combination of loneliness and lust? She could not answer, because she had no answer. She was fond of him, but in love? Never had she been in love with a man or even mildly attracted before John. The forest rang at a dead silence. The squirrels no longer chattered from the trees. The birds no longer sang their sweet song. No wind stirred. And as he waited for her answer, the stillness could be cut with a knife.

A twig snapped. John jumped to his feet, cursed, and yanked on his pants. He hand signaled her silence then moved like a wraith. Through the underbrush, a doe and her fawn appeared, sniffed the air, and ambled into the far reaches of the forest.

John shrugged, and she laughed, putting her arms through the sleeves of her dress. "A Yankee under every bush? Let's eat. All this surrendering has left me starving."

They feasted on cold fried chicken and slabs of oat bread smoothed with creamy butter and followed by peach pie for dessert...and, for the time being, skirted the point where their relationship had to be resolved. What would it be like to witness him leading his men? Command exuded every corner of his being, and stamped on his face was an air of authority from one who demanded instant obedience. That side she had never seen. With her, he was nothing but tender and gentle.

She asked him many questions about his soldiers, where they might be camped, what he thought Lee's next move would be and how many men did he think Lee had left? From the Battle of the Wilderness, he gave her a speculative synopsis of Colonel Mosby, Longstreet's probable location, Early's encampment and Lee's thinking.

He pointed a fried drumstick at her. "Enough questions about the war. I have not eaten so well during this war. Samuel's mother will have me as big as a fatted bull."

His recovery was remarkable. When she had found him, he had been far too lean, but now had filled out quite well.

He needed more time to recuperate and she had been stalling for time, keeping him in the dark of the war's events, she had refrained from purchasing newspapers. He chomped at the bit to return, and she fretted from his restlessness. To think of him maimed or killed?

Her heart was heavy. He'd leave soon. If only things could stay the way they were. A sixth sense awakened and ice spread in her stomach, veering her mood. She stood and paced. "I don't want you to go back."

"I have to go back," he said carelessly.

Her hands clenched. The orphanage she had built in New York brimmed with sad, lonesome children, orphans of war. There was a wide gulf between them. "It's complicated, isn't it?"

"Nothing is uncomplicated and for all practical reasons, I'm torn by my duty to my country. The nature of war is that people are killed. The South will continue to fight. Our principles are involved. I am an officer and a soldier. I do what I am commanded to do, just as I command my soldiers to do. As a General, I don't have the luxury of walking away."

But Catherine wouldn't leave it alone. "What of the atrocities? And what about you general?" She hated to think of it.

"Yes, I am a barn burner, destroyer of homes, pilferer of goods," he said. "I don't like such work. But it is not a civilized war." He ripped out the words. "Your Union Army is more like an armed mob. The south will be slow to forgive or forget the damned Yankees who perpetuated the war."

"But it was the South who were the aggressors. Who fired on Fort Sumter? Who was first, may I remind you?"

"Your dear Lincoln who exceeded his power—went over the rights of the constitution, suspending habeas corpus, declaring war without congressional approval. I am a man caught in a trap of time and of duty. You think I enjoy watching my men cut down by Yankee bullets, maimed for life or dead, never to return to their families? You think I love the sight of surgeons plying their vocation, cutting arms and legs with their bone saws...or doctors and their assistants stripped to the waist covered in soldier's blood? I have to persevere. The Cause must be maintained."

"The lost cause," she huffed.

He paid no heed to her bait and stared with a hard, cold-eyed smile. "Most inspiring are the buzzards over us, waiting to pick our bones. At least they like the worms, are indiscriminate in their taste, for they eat both Rebs and Yanks alike."

"Don't you ever doubt?"

His expression darkened with an unreadable emotion. "Only fools never doubt. Sometimes events click in my mind, thoughts about my life...which always lead me to thinking about my death. It's like running my fingers through stinging nettles."

He reached into the basket for a jug of cold spring water. "If anyone could make me forget the anger, the revenge or the hatred, it would be..." He froze. A newspaper lined the bottom. "You said Pleasant Valley didn't have a paper."

Catherine jumped at the bitter scorn in his voice. To come up with a hard and fast reason on why she hid the news from him—he would never understand. "It's not what you think."

His hands trembled as he read the headlines. "May 11, 1864, ten days after my capture. Stuart's dead! Confederate Cavalry General,

James Ewell Brown Stuart killed at Yellow Tavern, Virginia, in the battle for Richmond." Rourke savagely scanned the paper for other news. "The Battle of the Wilderness where I was wounded. Old news. Of course, Union papers claimed it as a victory. Who really knows? Battle of Spotsylvania, May eighth and it's still going on. The Union is moving closer to Richmond. If they seize the capital?" His lips flattened in a snarl.

John raked his fingers through his hair. "Stuart dead? We were good friends. There had been some controversy during Gettysburg when Stuart had ridden off on an independent operation while Lee invaded the North. He had deprived General Lee of the 'eyes' of his army, a singularly grievous mistake that cost the Confederacy. But Stuart had served the South success after success, with his daring, riding circles around the Union Army."

Catherine cringed, "Before my uncle came upon us, I contacted your brother, Lucas in the War Department in Washington to help you."

"And you're telling me this now. It's a wonder the whole Union Army hasn't swooped down on me."

He was burning for a fight. "I'm leaving now." His face was a mask of granite, upset by the turn of events, and—by her deception.

"Give up the war, Rourke. Stay with me."

"How sweet the siren's song." His voice came honey smooth, yet tinged with his contempt.

She turned toward him, plunked her hands on her hips. "Follow your stupid leaders to slaughter. Lead your men to their death. There cannot be too much left to fight. The Union controls the Mississippi, the Union blockade has a stranglehold on the

Confederacy, the North has the munitions and the numbers, Lee has failed at Vicksburg, the war in the west is lost, Sharpsburg, Shiloh, Fredericksburg, and Gettysburg. When will it end? When will you stop? The South has been defeated."

"To win is to outthink and outfight the other. The Confederate soldier is a different breed—obstinate, brave, stubborn. As the South continues, we will move with steady perseverance. I am an officer. I will stay with her."

"Fools and duty." She dropped on the blanket and refused to look at him.

Without warning, Rourke grabbed her into his arms and pinned her beneath him, the newspapers scattering in the wind. He traced the line of her cheekbone and jaw, as if blazing everything about her into his memory. "Catherine, live with your uncle until I deem it safe enough for you to travel. Get to Washington and I'll arrange passes for your journey through Virginia to my home."

She made a cry of protest. She should tell him who she really was. Now. She bit her lip, living in a delusion, deceiving him, her cowardice, a failure to act in the midst of fear. Fear of his hatred.

"No disagreement, Catherine. There is little time left, and that time has to be cherished."

So little time. Why muck it up with the truth?

Leaving her mouth burning with fire, she was shaken at her own fervent reaction and slipped her arms around his neck. John yanked up her skirts and she opened her thighs, meeting his deep thrusts, trying to make him forget, to bend him to her will, hoping upon hope he would remain. Her heart tore apart, flooded with aching tenderness, holding fast, the time for things meant to be, the last instance where after everything else, this would remain as what really mattered.

Sated, they lay entwined, Catherine secure in his arms, knowing the strange peace was about to be shattered. Under extraordinary circumstances they had been brought together and wed, only to be torn apart by those same torrid currents. She committed to memory every line and plane of his profile. Marriage was to be long and enduring, yet what lay unspoken between them expressed volumes. She had no misgivings of their joining, only sad regrets it was to end. A gust of wind blew, as if cautioning her, and Catherine shivered, choosing to ignore its warning.

Chapter 9

John made preparations to leave, stashing staples of food, blankets, and extra clothing into a bag, saying little and waiting for darkness to fall. Catherine gazed out her window. Everything was gray. The sun had hidden in the thick gray clouds, the rocks and crags of the mountains, a sharper contrast of gray and even the horizon was lost in a choking gray mist. It was about to storm. It was a safe wager the rain would be gray.

There was a knock at the door, and Catherine turned to answer. Samuel placed a letter in her hand and disappeared. Where had he gone in such a hurry?

No postscript. Who could have sent it? Under John's watchful eyes she opened the note and began to read. Ice froze in her veins. *Francis Mallory.* He held Uncle Charlie hostage. Jimmy O'Hara's warnings crushed her. *"He's not a man to be dickered with. I've seen him kill men with his bare hands. He killed his father and brother to get what he wanted."*

"What is it?" John demanded.

Catherine closed her eyes. Images flashed, Mallory in the ring, his face anything but human. How to save Uncle Charlie? He was so old, so very dear to her. *What was she to do?*

"What the hell is it?"

"My plans." She stuffed the letter into her pocket and moved toward the door. All her plans had gone awry. She was married now and Agatha could not force her to marry Mallory. Hopes of hiring bodyguards and fighting Mallory, slipped away. What a careless illusion to think she was safe from Mallory's tentacles. Of course, his hired goons tracked her down. To free her uncle, she had to give herself up.

John swung her around. "What's wrong, Catherine?"

"Forgive me." This was not his fight. If only she could tell him, but her life, a complicated mess had reared its ugly head. She must keep John out of harm's way. Mallory would kill him. She had to keep him safe.

"I have to go to town to see about Uncle Charlie. He is not feeling well and I must care for him. So this is where I say good-bye and wish you a safe journey." Her legs like wooden pegs, she moved, and kissed him like she had never before. Breaking away from him, she dragged her feet out the door and up the road.

She blinked. Mallory stood beside a coach. To be sure, he'd not risk losing his prize. Neat as a pin, he was flawless as always, dandified in his formal black suit.

"Where's my uncle?"

"You be a good lass, now, and we'll determine his whereabouts." He smoothed his well-oiled military style mustache with the tip of his finger. "You have left me on a merry chase. Me being so noble and proposing, might make me think you snubbed me. I don't like being snubbed." His ferret-like eyes moved up and down her body. "Keeping in the company of a certain Reb?"

So he knew.

"Your uncle with the help of a few of my good men was persuaded to confess—" Mallory sneered. "—many things."

"If you've done anything to harm him, I swear—"

"You're not in a position to swear anything, my dear. I've learned you've been busy, taking care of General Rourke, Army of Northern Virginia. Sounds like treason to me."

"Don't talk to me about anything nefarious with your criminal history." Thank God, Father Callahan had not divulged they were married. She prayed John would think Mallory was a visitor she had diverted and—to hope John had escaped out the back.

A shadow moved through the bushes. Samuel. She warned him with her eyes. When he ducked farther into the brush, she let out a breath.

"What's he like?" Mallory's black eyes glittered. He grabbed her arm, seeming entertained when she flinched. "Never mind. We'll know shortly."

Catherine screamed to warn John. Mallory clamped his hand over her mouth and crushed her to him.

"Catherine," Mallory hissed into her ear. "Behave and call your Rebel friend out here. Be quick about it, before I lose my patience."

Catherine wouldn't budge.

"Do it now, or I'll have him hanged as a spy, and your uncle will experience an untimely death. However, if you choose to cooperate, and I believe we both know what that means—" Mallory let his words hang. "…I'll let your Reb friend go."

"How can I be certain?"

"You have my word."

A chill crept up her spine.

Mallory motioned his men to move up onto both sides of the porch.

"He's dangerous. Too dangerous," Mallory's men protested.

The larger of Mallory's goons wiped his nose on his coat sleeves. "He's the devil himself. Rides ahead of his troops, slashing Yanks, men drowning in a sea of blood."

"Bullets fly off him," added another.

"Nonsense. I pay you bloody fools good coin. Get him before I pull the trigger on you myself," ordered Mallory.

"Remember," Mallory warned Catherine. "Your uncle is comfortable for the time being. Make sure you act the part when the general comes out, so he stays that way."

Hating herself, but caught in a horrible nightmare with no answer to her problem, Catherine called John. She was Judas.

John heard Catherine call to him. Once out the door, he saw a dandy holding her, and the distressed look on her face. He bolted toward her. He didn't make it to the end of the porch.

Men fell on him. In answer, John roared out an awful challenge. He punched one in the nose, making a popping sound, dousing him in a shower of blood. With lightening quick ease, John broke free and swung his elbow into a man's windpipe. The thug emitted a shuddering breath and somersaulted down the stairs. The rest backed off. Not surprising. These were not seasoned fighters. Who were these thugs? His eyes fixed on every one of his prey. Two down, six to go. He'd been looking for a fight.

With an answering rebel yell as bloodcurdling as that of a beast, he rushed to meet their numbers. Just as their bodies crashed together, John grasped one of the huge wrists and broke it in two. He stopped and hit the next thug with a colossal right that came all the way up from his planted feet, and felt his fist drive right through and beyond. His falling body weight whipped his head out from under his moving hand, allowing the momentum to carry him onward, shoulder first into the guy behind him. He kicked a thug between the legs, and the man's head jerked downward at the same time John's elbow sailed upwards, doubling the power of the blow. He aimed another savage blow at the head of another man, breaking his jaw with a high cracking sound. Too shrewd to allow anyone to get behind him, John jerked his elbow, breaking a man's ribs, the driving force crashing his assailant through a window. Springing to one side and then to another, John outpaced them, owing his supremacy to his hardened experience as a soldier.

A well-aimed fist for John's head came from a meaty assailant and if it had landed, might easily have crushed the side of his skull. But John was too swift and, dropping beneath the strike, delivered a mighty blow into the pit of the giant's stomach.

"Boys!" Mallory ordered, and out of nowhere, more fell on John.

Before he could wrench free again, ten men lunged, seized him in their arms. Pure opposing numbers his undoing. Grappling him to the floor, they kicked and punched and manacled him. When he was physically subdued, they stood him up with his legs and arms spread wide, none of them brave enough to be near him alone.

Several more men held guns on him, keeping their distance after witnessing what he had vented on their comrades.

Catherine ran to Rourke. Mallory snapped her back so hard she thought her teeth would break. "Remember your part, my dear. We don't want things to get too messy."

"General Rourke, since we haven't been introduced, I'll do the honors. I'm Francis Mallory, Director for United States Intelligence," he lied, giving himself a title. "Of course, you've already had the honor of meeting Miss Catherine Fitzgerald, our cleverest spy."

As the words sunk in, John stood stock still, shock crossing his face. Then, consumed with rage, he charged like a mad bull, fighting against his chains…wild, untamed, savage.

"You deceitful bitch!" He shouted from the porch. The goons closed in on him and Catherine cringed, one of them giving him a short, hard jab in the side, and as he doubled over, the other brought his fist down on the back of his neck. John crumpled to the floor, his breath coming out in short, painful gasps. The goons gloated over him, ready to use their wares again.

"Stop it," Catherine screamed.

Broken-hearted, there was nothing she could do but stand there and listen to John's verbal abuse echo through her head. Mallory's skill for the dramatic had done the trick—his ruse irreparably damned her in John's eyes. Of course, he toyed with them, sadistic, like when he was in the ring and crippled men for his sick pleasure.

She again took a step toward John. Mallory yanked her back. "Remember your uncle, my sweet." Her skin crawled. How could she have ever thought this man charming at one time?

But it was when she looked at John that she wanted to flee. When he lifted his head and glared at her, his eyes, that moments before held such warmth, were cold shards of ice. How he hated her. And she thought for one awful second that if, turned loose, his long sinewy fingers would wrap around her throat.

"General Rourke," Mallory called from a safe distance. "You're a fine catch. As a true Son of the South and guest of the United States, we wish to thank you for all you have divulged."

"She's our best, General Rourke," Mallory taunted. "But don't be too down in the mouth. Miss Fitzgerald's craft has been long practiced, and may I add, she is our most treacherous strategist in intelligence gathering. Many have confided in and fallen prey to her charms."

"This isn't finished, Catherine." John growled between clenched teeth. "Even if I have to go to the ends of the earth, I'll hunt you down."

Mallory snorted. "I think not, General Rourke. However, we are going to release you. In time, of course, after our northern newspapers full of your secrets have reported the vulnerabilities of General Lee's army. Interesting, isn't it? The end game has always been won with seduction and spying. They go hand in hand. Am I not correct to assume so, General?"

"Let me go, and I'll show you an end game, Mallory."

"Impertinent fellow." Mallory smirked. He placed his fingers over Catherine's shoulders, pushing her in front of John. "Lovely is she not?"

John's eyes blazed through her. Nausea rolled in the pit of her stomach. How Mallory relished his new role. How twisted and warped he was. She wanted to kill him.

Mallory continued his speech. "The North's most prized possession and weapon is our beautiful seductress, Catherine. Like I said before, General Rourke, you are not the first to be enticed by our finest skilled intelligence operative."

She stared straight ahead. A veritable liar, Mallory had painted her as a very clever, complicit whore, succeeding in sowing distrust and hatred. Oh, why hadn't she told John about Mallory? Because she was too afraid he'd hold her in contempt for her family's fortune was steeped on the South's blood.

She could not look at her husband. He had loved her and for that love he was betrayed. Never would he forgive her. Her head drooped. Time had slipped through her fingers. Not telling him her secret was like a cancer to the soul, eating away what was good and reaping destruction.

Francis pinched her. "Look alive, girl, act the part." *Would Mallory release John? Uncle Charlie?*

"I'll leave no stone unturned to find and repay you, Catherine, for your deceit." John seethed his words.

"Enough," shouted Mallory and the butt end of a rifle cracked against John's skull.

"Mallory wants him done, Joseph. You ready with the hole?"

John came to attention. Every part of his body ached. He swung his head to the side and peered out an opening between the slats in

Catherine's barn. Five to six strange looking guards, dressed more like thugs than Union soldiers. The North must be reaping from the bottom of the barrel. He sank against the wall. Slivered light filtered through the gaps in the siding. He'd give them a fight to remember before they laid him to eternal rest. In fact, he'd take a few of them with him.

Suddenly a barrage of gunshots cracked and scattered over the outside of his dwelling, spraying up dust and splinters over him. He ducked, holding his manacled hands over his head. Who the hell was out there? Too heady to believe he was being rescued by Rebel troops. In agonized moans and cries of surprise, the guards hit the ground. He peered out the slit again. In a matter of seconds, the guards were immobilized. The door burst open. Light poured in, blinding him, and silhouetting the lines of a Union uniform.

"Well brother, what kind of mess have you gotten yourself into now? The Scourge of the South has to have me bail him out of trouble."

Chapter 10

"Lucas!" He could not have been more surprised if St. Peter had walked through the door. "How——"

"Tell you the how's later. I don't know how many others may return to help their friends."

Once outside, John surveyed the six bodies on the ground. "Remarkable for someone who polishes his rear in Washington. Almost as well as myself."

Lucas grinned. "Had lots of practice on my older brother."

"Indeed."

"They won't be walking for a long time. I shot them in the legs. They'll have an awful headache when they wake." Lucas smoothed the butt end of his gun, retrieved keys from a fallen guard and unlocked John's chains.

Samuel brought around two horses. "This young man apprised me of your situation," Lucas said.

John held his hand out. Odd the war he was fighting. He was freed by an escaped slave. "I owe you a great debt, Samuel." John rubbed his wrists. "Very fine mounts."

"Fast," Lucas said.

Lucas like their brother, Ryan, a colonel in the Confederate Calvary, had a good eye for horseflesh. Lucas tossed a bag of gold dollar pieces to the boy. "Thanks, Samuel."

Spurring their horses into a swift gallop, both brothers headed into the mountains. From Pleasant Valley, they rode hard in a westerly direction in case anybody was following them, careful to lose their trail. Then doubling back east, they rode to a railway station in Elmira. Uneasy in a new suit of clothes his brother had procured, John looked like any other civilian traveling with a Union soldier.

"Limp, so it looks like you've been wounded and are out of action. Otherwise people will speculate why a big ugly brute like you is not in the war. What's more, don't talk. Your accent is heavier than mine and sure to draw attention. Your face is another problem, highly recognizable, so keep your hat pulled low. I'm taking a great risk to be hanged for treason, and you, hanged for a spy out of uniform."

John gritted his teeth. The witch had burned his uniform.

Lucas paid for their tickets and they boarded a train. They passed the North's infamous *Hellmira* prisoner of war camp, the worst of the Northern camps with a survival rate worse than the South's Andersonville, and John's original destination. Rail thin men stared blankly out a fence, starved and left to lie in thin canvas tents with no blankets, little clothes, and no shoes, exposed to the severest of northern winters. High above, latrines drained into the camp's water supply, an incubator for smallpox and dysentery to descend.

The ride was uneventful except for two young ladies sitting across from them. Enamored with the brothers, they took all kinds of elaborate pains to capture them in conversation. John had enough of women to last a hundred lifetimes. He left the conversation up to his brother in the *adorable* Yank uniform. Feigning illness, he pulled his hat down over his eyes and tried to sleep. He dreamed wonderful dreams of revenge—once he got his hands on Catherine Fitzgerald.

On the Baltimore and Ohio railroad they made steady progress south. Baltimore. Frederick. Harper's Ferry. In many of these places, he had fought during the course of the war. All were Union controlled now. He shifted in his seat when more men in Union uniforms crowded the train, replacing the two women across from them. Lucas wove a tale, suggesting his brother of having peculiar and strange symptoms, similar to consumption, but of course—not consumption. He even went so far as to keep them in the strictest of confidence by leaning over and whispering loud enough for the benefit of all the passengers that his brother had a monstrous rash. However, he couldn't tell where for the delicacy of ladies present. For this, Lucas received a sharp elbow in the side from him. Lucas had overplayed his part.

"Is it itching you again, brother?" Lucas turned to him with all the sympathy he could muster. For his concern, Lucas obtained a cold warning glare. Lucas turned again to his horrified audience. "Terrible affliction. Sometimes the itching turns to horrible fits. Been to all kinds of doctors. Why one time—"

The two soldiers across from them moved away. John kept coughing to add to the horrors of the tale.

They disembarked in Martinsburg, Maryland, bought fresh mounts and headed south. Out on a lone country road, they were able to speak.

"How did you find me?" John asked.

"I received a telegram from Catherine Callahan, cryptic in wording, but I gleaned the intention was for me to come and get my older brother. Since you were missing, I was curious and made the trip. Once in Pleasant Valley, I was pointed out of town to the schoolmarm's home, and then headed off by Samuel who apprised me of your situation."

Catherine Fitzgerald. Betrayal. Her name floated sourly over his tongue.

So soon...my plan... Cryptic at the time, her last words went round and round inside his head as he tried to piece events together. She'd been interrupted, upset with her superiors moving in on the complicated operation too soon, wanted to ferret more information from him. What a fool he'd been.

Nothing, I have to go. The letter was the signal, lured him outside, knowing he'd come to her. Like Mallory said, the cleverest of Northern agents. He closed his eyes, her hair, her lips, her breasts, everything about her spelled seduction. Had given herself to him, figuring a general was worth the prize.

"Get it out, John," Lucas ordered. "It'll eat you alive if you don't. We may be on opposite sides, but I know that it can't all be me."

They had said little on how they parted before the war, and it was the first mention of those strong feelings that had so fiercely divided them.

"We're brothers, after all. It's blood that counts." Lucas goaded. "Maybe we should get off our horses and have us a good boxing match to loosen things up. Like the old days. Remember Billy on the farm next to ours. He disappeared and no one knows where."

"It's not you, little brother. I've come to terms with your views a long time ago. I don't agree with your position, but I respect it." Billy was a master at boxing, had grown into a legend, and the Rourke boys had cut their teeth under his hard lessons. Those golden days were long past. Billy was a runaway slave.

I will not let you go. Catherine had told him before they made love one last time in the glen. She had meant every word. Standing next to Mallory, she never flinched, stared straight ahead, impassive and indifferent—a heartless triumph. He'd seen a long line of battles, maiming, killing, and death, yet, on her porch wrapped in shackles and beaten, he had stood on the coldest place on earth.

"You're a changed man, John." Lucas tried to throw wide the doors.

The war had changed all of them. They passed under the welcomed shade of trees that canopied over the road. "Thank you."

"I know you'd do the same for me. How were Mother and Father when you last saw them?"

Lucas needed to catch up. He had not been home since the war started and he missed everyone. "I was home a few days during Christmas. They are doing well. Fairhaven could be in better care, but the war has taken its toll on everyone's economy."

Lucas turned serious eyes on him. "What happened to you up North? And don't clam up on me. I have big shoulders. Maybe not as big or as revolting as yours, but I'm a good listener."

John stared forward over his horse's ears. When they were younger, they shared all sorts of things, but as they became older, he kept his own counsel.

From the beginning of time, women had been the downfall of men, ever since Adam and Eve. Wasn't he one more notch in the annals of history? Duped again by a woman, except this time, it was worse. His men and the Confederacy were at stake. How he itched to get his hands on her.

Hadn't he always measured the pros and cons, drilling his instincts, creating an image of his adversary's reasoning, logic and motives? As a general, his recurring triumphs in circumventing the enemy had been his judgment of the nature of his enemy, yet to have been blindsided?

How well she blended in, fearless, a soldier working on an invisible front, an altogether brilliant and contrived master stroke. John racked his brain with what he had divulged. He had given her strategic information, including personality profiles of the South's greatest leaders. But how broad ranging was its importance? Troops were always in motion unless entrenched. They were also classified. Had he disclosed any plans, any important strategies, weaknesses, strengths, troop numbers, locations, future attacks? None that the North would not already know, so the information he had given was insignificant, redundant, and too outdated to be of much use. With her plot aborted ahead of time, Catherine's ingenious flair for intrigue was wasted, her ruse, ineffective, making what little information she gleaned not worth a tinker's damn.

"I'll make her pay with every ounce of her blood."

Lucas snapped his head around. "I'm all ears, big brother."

John provided an abbreviated version of the story, leaving out certain details that Lucas of quick intelligence probably filled in for himself.

"So Miss Callahan and Miss Fitzgerald are the same." Lucas mused aloud.

John did not comment.

"I have an affiliation with the war department and have listened to some tall stories on spies, but to tell you the truth, I've never heard of Catherine Fitzgerald or Francis Mallory ever being associated with the office. Your interlude was far more sophisticated than anything I've heard of—a marriage, a priest. Why would they go to such an extent without gleaning information?"

With his hand, John flicked the flies gathering about his horse's head. He was careful where his brother was concerned, had heard rumors Lucas's association with the Union Office of Civilian Spying, ferreting vital military information through the intrigues of a slave network as well as a myriad of men and women who contributed to civilian spying. If anyone would know of Catherine's scam it would have been Lucas. "How should I know? I don't want to hear her conniving name again."

Lucas wouldn't give it up. "Doesn't make sense, why would she wire me?"

"How the hell should I know? Maybe she hates all men."

"How exactly does this Mallory fellow fit in?"

John smacked away a low overhanging branch. "Obviously she reports to him. Next time I meet that Mallory fellow, I'll be obliged to cut his throat."

"You are sanctimony and empathy in person." Lucas mocked him. "Did you ever think that there might be more to the story?"

John dismissed the notion in a flash.

They pulled up to a modest farm with a collection of red sheds and barns. There was a huge white clapboard house with a large sunburst window over the door which seemed incongruous with the desired architecture that demanded simplicity and purpose.

"Most remarkable," John drawled, "the immaculate condition of the whole property."

"These are good friends of mine, John. I've made arrangements to stay here for the night."

John hesitated, scanning the property. "Nobody's here."

"They're Shakers. It's prayer time and their probably at their meetinghouse with the main part of the community over the next hill. Good peaceful people. If everyone shared their philosophy, we wouldn't be compelled to be in this terrible war in the first place."

After bedding the horses down in the barn, John followed his brother to a small fresh white-washed barn to the rear of the house where they would sleep. Holding the door open, Lucas made a broad exaggerated sweeping of his arm, motioning for his brother to enter. "Age before beauty," he grinned.

John smiled at Lucas. "It's good being with you, brother. You're the one person in this crazy world I can trust."

He walked in the barn. The door slammed shut. He pivoted. *Clunk.* An outside bar fell into place. "Lucas, what kind of idiocy are you up to now? I'm tired. I've slept little over the past fifty-two hours, and I'm in no mood for stupidity."

"I am sorry, big brother, but it has to be this way."

"You son of a bitch." John roared, slamming his fist into the door.

"As a Yank soldier, my dedication is to the Union. I cannot allow you to keep leading battles that'll kill more Yanks and prolong the war. You're a great general, in fact, too good. It's my duty to see this war stops. Most important, you're my brother, and it is my duty to protect you. I don't want to see you wind up in a Northern prisoner of war camp, crippled, or worse yet, dead. I know you find this hard to understand but it's for the best."

John kicked the chamber pot letting it fly across the room. *Clang*. The metal pot bounced off the opposite wall and whirled in the corner. Duped again? Betrayed by his brother? The world was a population of liars.

"How am I supposed to eat?" He could rush the Shakers when the door opened.

"I can read your mind brother. There's a small door at the bottom to slide your meal tray in and out. Unfortunately, it's not big enough for you to escape. I have left a sizable sum to pay the kind Shakers for your care and meals. Who knows, maybe you'll be converted."

"I'll kill you with my own bare hands."

"Not very peaceable for a future Shaker."

"Open the door and I'll teach you about peace." Rourke smashed his fist into the wall.

"I'm glad you're locked on the other side. On too many occasions I've felt the sting of your fist, and in your present mood, I'm sure there'd be plenty fare to sample. Be advised you cannot punch your way out of there. Used as an ice barn, the walls are twelve inches thick. There is no way out. Hope for a quick end to the war, brother. Then you can go home. I'll leave your horse. The Shakers will care for it. As soon as I get back to Washington, I'll send some reading materials your way to help pass the time. Try and be comfortable. I'll see you after the war."

"I'll see you in hell!" John shouted after him. He heard Lucas chuckling and the hooves of his horse cantering away.

After a whole hour of looking for a way to escape, John gave up and took stock of his surroundings. So this would be his prison. The inner walls were of rough lumber a foot thick like Lucas had indicated. Small arrows of light escaped into the gloom, making it seem more like a church. His nose twitched with a light smell of mold mixed with a stronger odor of whitewash.

There was little in comforts. A cot was provided with several warm blankets, a pillow, and bordering it was a candle stand on an end table. The brass chamber pot remained in the corner upside down where he had kicked it. John picked up a Bible on the end table, left by the fastidious Shakers. They were already trying to convert him. He placed it back down on the table. He'd be the last person they could save.

John threw himself down on the cot, swearing his brother to eternal damnation a hundred times over. Little did the repetition do to lessen his morbidity. Folding his hands behind his head, and dreaming up certain revenges on Catherine Fitzgerald did give him pleasurable pause. Something Medieval came to mind. Or perhaps, a style adopted from the Inquisition. Those people knew how to inflict pain.

Thumbscrews?

Too simple.

What then?

Scourge?

Too effortless and uncomplicated.

What else?

The rack. Now there was a workable notion, having her stretched out on a rack. Many more methods of reprisal came to mind but he dismissed them all as they were too good for someone like Catherine Fitzgerald. Not cruel enough.

He needed something more elaborate and clever. Something more punishing, lasting.

While entertaining his morbid thoughts and staring at the ceiling, a slow pleasurable smile started to spread until it broadened into a wide grin. John laughed out loud for it was something his noble and thorough brother had not thought of or seen. A small batten door, high above in the gable roof and almost invisible to the naked eye, beckoned him. As a betting man he'd guarantee the Shakers knew naught of its existence.

A problem remained. How to reach the door without a ladder? Against the wall, he leaned the cot on its vertical end, put the end table on top followed by the chamber pot. He could almost do it. He'd have to jump high. Might fall and break his neck. Add the Bible? No. He'd take the risk.

To that end, he climbed, balancing on the chamber pot. The structure wobbled beneath his weight. Adrenaline spiked. A rung covered with spider webs in the beam was next to the batten door—a four foot vertical leap to reach. With his heavy weight, one jump, everything beneath him would crash to the floor. *One chance.*

With every well-honed muscle, tendon, and tissue in perfect unison, John bent low then thrust high, stretching, reaching. His hand gripped the rung. Back and forth he swung. *Crash.* The chamber pot and end table smacked against the floor. His arm muscles strained, and his free hand worked the bolt. The pin snapped open and the batten door swung down. John choked on a cloud of dust.

Swinging his body again, he used every ounce of his strength to grasp the roof and heave himself up into brilliant sunshine. Fresh sweet air burst in his lungs. Sliding down a shingled-sloped roof, he caught the edge, dangled, then dropped to the ground. He dusted off his clothes, congratulating himself on the marvelous rapidity of his escape.

None of the Shakers had returned. John passed beehives, honey permeating the air, and took the shortest route to the house. Grabbing two loaves of fresh baked bread, a smoked ham, an apple pie, and a jar of honey, he wrapped his booty in a table cloth, feeling no remorse stealing their dinner. After all, his brother had already paid for an extended stay. Too bad the Shakers wouldn't have another recruit. He penned two letters, one to the Shaker family, begging their forgiveness for borrowing their meal. The other letter, he implored, the Shaker's Christian charity to send to his brother, Lucas.

> Dear Lucas,
>
> I understand and forgive you for what you did.
> Soon I'll be dining in Washington—with my
> troops.
>
> > Sincerely,
> > General John D. Rourke
> > Army of Northern Virginia

Chapter 11

New York City

With a fluttery hand, Catherine pulled back the drape of the Fitzgerald coach. Her spine straight, she sat on the luxurious cushions, her gaze planted out the beveled windows. New York was more robust than she remembered, despite the fact that it had only been weeks since she had departed. The changes were not for the better, the streets, the passersby, the shop windows, remote in the heart of war. Horse manure piled up on the edges of the street, a man dozed on a barrel, and a wagon backed-up ninety degrees to a sidewalk. The city had changed. Did no one realize the horrors of war that were being fought? Were they isolated and indifferent that it all was so casual? Were thousands of men left crippled and dying while no one cared for anything but the profit in their own pockets?

Catherine bowed her forehead on the cool glass, disheartened by the turn of events. That wretched scene two days before where John believed she had betrayed him. Pleasant Valley, a lifetime ago, the hatred scorched in John's soul, his bitter smile and final vow, promising he would hunt the ends of the earth to seek his revenge. How she had longed to go to him. To tell him none of it was true.

Mallory had set his trap and she had stood powerless while Rourke had been beaten and dragged away.

From Pleasant Valley, Mallory hauled her back to the city, Agatha meeting them at the train station. Agatha had pressed a telegram into his hand. Mallory swore at his guards and crammed the message in his pocket. Across from her, she sensed his ferret-like eyes studying her and wondered what the message contained that caused him to crack his knuckles. She flinched when he tapped the bottom of her chin with the head of his silver-topped cane.

"I'm bored with your pouting." He tipped her face around. "It is time to have a talk. Your stepmother, Agatha is in full consent——"

"Full consent about what, Francis?" Her fingernails curled into her palms, making half-moons. She did not need to ask.

"You have left us on a merry chase. Your stepmother has been concerned about your wild ways and feels it is necessary for you to settle down," said Francis.

Agatha gave a dismissive nod, her mounds of flesh, quivering with superiority. Her father had been depressed when he married Agatha who had put on a show of rainbows and sunshine. The week after the vows, she turned into a demanding shrew. "Francis has condescended to offer for your hand, and I am condoning the marriage in light of your sinful behaviors. To think of the repercussions if your little episode were disclosed…you'd be ruined. It was bad enough when you cavorted with those ragamuffins at the orphanage, and then when you brought that miscreant, Jimmy O'Hara home. Since you are not capable of protecting your reputation, I am taking *your* responsibility into my hands by accepting Mr. Mallory's generous offer."

"Agatha, do not delude yourself that I believe for one second you would do anything for the benefit of my welfare unless you profited from it."

Oh. How she'd like to throw the fact that she was married to John in Agatha's face. No. She could not risk John's or her uncle's life.

"Well I never——" Agatha sputtered into an apoplectic fit. "To think of that horrid place you spent…a holiday or whatever you want to call it…how could you live with such vermin! To think of the shame brought on the Fitzgerald name."

"I have done nothing to shame the Fitzgerald name. Agatha, you have sold out the Fitzgerald's." Catherine glared at both of them. "You don't think I know about your agreement."

Francis licked his lips. "I never said you weren't bright, lass. A fiery temper to match. I anticipate our wedding night." He dared to run his cane down her arm.

She shoved the cane away. "I'll never do what you say. I will fight, runaway, and I will not marry a low class vile swindler."

Suddenly Mallory was atop her, grabbing her around the neck. Caught off guard by the magnitude of his rage, his hands pressed deep in a deadly chokehold. No air came down her windpipe. His face mottled red. His black eyes bulged, and he tightened his grip. Black spots appeared.

Agatha gasped. Catherine clawed at Mallory's hands. The light in the carriage dimmed. Her world tilted.

"I will never hear those words from your lips again. You will do everything I command now and in the future. My patience is gone."

Agatha grabbed at Mallory's hands. "You kill her, our objectives will be for nothing."

Mallory threw Catherine against the seat. Her head snapped back. She sucked in gulps of air. Tears stung her eyes. She placed her hands on her throat, massaging the terrible pain. Fool. She had overplayed her cards. If Agatha had not counteracted his frenzy…it would have been her last breath.

"Get this straight, lass, there will be no more avoiding what is already clear. If you want to see your uncle alive, you will do everything I say." His black eyes glittered as he traced the top of her breasts with his silver-headed cane.

Catherine hated him. Mallory had not mentioned John. The telegram…had John escaped? She clung to that hope.

Mallory smoothed a finger across his mustache. "There is the subject of Fitzgerald Rifle Works. Our engagement will be announced, and you will relinquish control of the company to me. Everyone will expect the man in your life to bear the responsibility."

Better to keep her mouth shut until she could escape.

"I believe it is high time you've had a strong hand in your affairs, Catherine." Agatha purred. "It will be a lovely wedding. You will be a handsome couple."

Catherine was too dazed to notice her home on Fifth Avenue, a Venetian Gothic, an architectural triumph, her parents had lovingly created, placing the Fitzgerald stamp on it for generations to come, and now muddied by Mallory's insertion. The carriage stopped under the porte-cochere. Mallory handed her down, charm back in place. In stunned silence, she walked into the foyer.

The butler's eyes grew wide. "If there is anything I can do——"

Her hair had been torn from its pins, and she pulled it around to hide the dark bruises on her neck. "I wish to retire, Donnelly," she said, clenching her hands to keep them from shaking. "Would you be so kind as to send Brigid to me?"

"Catherine," Mallory barked. With slow grace, she turned on one of the double staircases, her head held high. No. Mallory would not see her terror.

He took her hand, kissed it, his tongue slithering over her wrist. She snatched it away.

"Do not fear for your safety," he said, obviously for the benefit of the curious servants who had gathered to welcome their mistress. "I have posted armed guards around your home for protection. You may sleep well." He smiled his threat.

A prisoner. No escape. Mallory would make sure of it this time.

Brigid O'Brian rushed into her room and locked the door.

"Good Lord, Miss. What has happened? There is a guard outside and Donnelly said—"

Catherine had been fingering the silver brushes on her vanity, but when her lady's maid and dear friend, Brigid entered, she flew into her arms and wept.

"Why those—" Brigid uttered every Irish curse known upon Mallory's and Agatha's person.

When the plump maid saw the dark bruises upon Catherine's neck, she cursed Mallory and Agatha further into perdition. "They'll get their due when the devil gets a hold of them." Brigid took over Catherine's care, ordered a bath to be brought up, along with some creams that would help fade the bruises.

"Cook has sent up warm buttered croissants and soup, her special. You must eat."

Catherine was comforted by her loyal staff. "Jimmy O' Hara. I must get in contact with him. He is the only one to help me escape, but my every movement will be detailed and reported to Mallory by his men."

I shall have to pay a visit to the orphanage to see how young Jimmy O'Hara is faring."

"I am desperate. I cannot marry Mallory, I am already married.

"Married?" Brigid slapped her hands on her cheeks.

Catherine gave a brief synopsis of her time in Pleasant Valley. "Mallory will kill my uncle and John."

The very next evening Catherine stood by her window and smiled. Further down the block, a fight ensued. The guard beneath her window was drawn away. A shadowy figure crossed the street and scrambled up a drain spout and crawled headlong into her bedroom.

Catherine hugged Jimmy and explained her difficulties. "I want you to take my mother's jewels and sell them for the highest price. You have connections?"

Jimmy snorted. "You are speaking to Jimmy O'Hara."

Along with other gems, she laid sparkling green stones set in diamonds in his hand. Her heart twisted. "The jewels are worth a fortune, and all I have to barter with. The emeralds were a gift from my father to my mother at the time of my birth. But my uncle and General Rourke's lives are at stake."

"I'll do everything I can. We'll ruin Mallory for his evil ways, you'll see." He stuffed the jewels in his pocket, scrambled out the window, slid down the drain spout and vanished into the night.

The following week her life was between the hammer and the anvil. Announcements touting the betrothal of Francis Mallory and Catherine Fitzgerald were made in all the major newspapers. The *New York Tribune*, acclaimed Mallory, *a fine dashing figure* and Catherine *as one whose beauty and refinement was without equal.*

The year's key event came with a host of invitations to balls, receptions, and parties held in their honor, and all of which Francis Mallory insisted on attending. Catherine was spun into an exhausting whirl of galas. No one wanted to be left out on the greatest occasion of social prominence. After all, the Fitzgerald's name and fortune were likened to royalty, the distinction beyond compare.

To the public eye, it appeared that Francis Mallory gallantly unburdened the winsome beauty of her business. To Catherine, it was the bargain to free John and Father Callahan.

Day after tedious day dragged by and Mallory never missed an opportunity to remind her that their fate rested in her hands. She could not sleep or eat. Jimmy and his crew combed the city for Father Callahan and John. He would find a trail and then it frustratingly would turn cold. Never giving up, Jimmy sent a boy to Pleasant Valley. His nightly visits kept her hopes alive.

"It wouldn't be proper." Mallory astounded her by insisting on a long engagement, granting a reprieve from the actual wedding. Catherine suspected another reason. He wanted to milk the engagement and its publicity as long as possible, enabling him entry into the blue-blooded society he craved. Everyone knew of the thug part of his background, somewhat whitewashed when he had swindled the Mallory fortune. Others chose to forget his pedigree or were too frightened to mention his nebulous past. With Catherine upon his arm, he would cement his ticket into a world that would have rejected him in any other way.

The servant poured Catherine's tea in the breakfast room. Every morning, Mallory prevailed over her home, insisting that she have all meals with him. Her hands curled into her napkin. If her brother were here none of this would be occurring. He finished his eggs, picked up a pile of mail, one by one, sliced through each envelope and read.

He paused overlong on one correspondence, rolled his waxed mustache in concentration. "Washington. A change in scenery will be wonderful. We'll mix business with pleasure."

She could not have been more surprised if he had declared an expedition to China.

What game was he up to?

Finally, Agatha, Catherine, Brigid and a few selected servants with Mallory leading the way, boarded a train to Washington. A few hours into the journey, an odd figure moved down the aisle. To think she barely recognized him, *Jimmy O'Hara*. He had adopted several disguises of late. With a conspiratorial wink he gave her, he fell into Francis Mallory, offering numerous apologies. Catherine excused herself, and under her guards' watchful eyes, made her way to the ladies lounge. She closed the door, and breathed, releasing tense muscles, and then someone tapped her on the shoulder.

Catherine whirled. "Jimmy, you gave me such a start." She scanned the lounge.

"No one's here. Has Mallory been bothering you?"

She adored him for his concern. "Nothing I can't handle." Mallory was unpredictable. How long could she hold him off? "Any news?"

Jimmy had a wide open grin.

She hugged him. "You dear boy. You found them."

"Yes and no."

"What do you mean?"

"My friend returned from Pleasant Valley. They talked to a kid named Samuel. He told them someone had helped General Rourke escape the day you returned to New York. Did a lot of damage to Mallory's goons, but he couldn't say who."

Catherine's fingers flew to her throat, recalling how Francis had tried to strangle her in the carriage. "No wonder he was so angry when we had stepped off the train that day and Agatha had handed him a telegram. It was about John's escape. But who? There is no one I can think of in that little town who would have helped him."

Catherine returned to her seat, Francis raging about his wallet missing. *Jimmy.* It was the first time Catherine had smiled in a long time.

Chapter 12

After four days of hard riding down the Shenandoah Valley, John joined up with General Lee, his old commander astonished from General Rourke's reappearance from the dead. John gave a brief summation of his capture, and escape, albeit minus certain details. Lee rejoiced at having one of his favorite fighting generals' return. Like the prodigal son, John was immediately reassigned by Lee to his old division.

A very tired and weary General Lee brought John up to date on Grant's hard push south. They had withdrawn from the deep gloom of the Wilderness where John had fallen, had left behind the enormous struggles at Spotsylvania, then North and South Anna, including names such as the Bloody Angle. Lee had received reports that Joe Johnston's men were being pushed by Sherman through Georgia and, of course, the sad news of General Jeb Stuart's tragic death. Casualty lists were staggering as Grant persisted with his campaign. Twenty-four thousand Confederate soldiers were killed, wounded, or captured. John cursed time and again for dallying north when the Confederacy so desperately needed him.

That evening he met with General Lee and some of the officers at headquarters in Shady Grove Church. Discussion centered on reports of Union movements. Scouts told of various activities on the Confederate left and even more on its right. General Lee listened as several officers made light of Grant's leadership to the point of scoffing.

"Gentlemen..." the gray-haired army chief addressed his commanders. "I think that General Grant has managed his affairs well up to the present time."

But General Hill was in a more argumentative mood. "General Lee, let them continue to attack our breastworks, we can stand that very well."

"I'm still thinking in terms of offense, not defense. This army cannot stand a siege," Lee said, rising to continue his rounds. "I'm thinking now of Richmond or further ahead to Petersburg. It is imperative we hold the line at Cold Harbor. Our misfortune is that our opponent, General Grant, knows the importance of Cold Harbor as well."

Listening to all the reports and making a quick survey of the maps, General Rourke also realized the importance of Cold Harbor. It was twelve miles direct route to Richmond. Like Lee, John understood never to underestimate the tenacious hammering blows of Grant.

"Have Wilcox's and Breckinridge's commands solidified Turkey Hill?" Lee asked. It was a sore point, for earlier in the day he had ordered Hoke and Anderson to stretch their lines southward and secure the area. It had not been done and Yankee pickets had seized control.

"Yes Sir. There was a sharp fight, but we cleared the hill. Our artillery now ranges the Chickahominy bottoms on the right."

"Good," Lee said. "Now my forces will be secure from being flanked."

"My corps have come up against the main body of Union troops," said General Jubal Early.

"This further confirms in my mind that our next engagement will be at Cold Harbor. That will be all gentlemen," Lee said.

General Rourke made haste to his division, greeted by the cheers of his men as they crowded around his horse. However there was little time for welcoming as he learned that the enemy was concentrating in the woods in front. He ordered his men to solidify their entrenchments, which they met with great zeal as their commander had returned to lead them to victory.

John walked into his old tent to pore over the maps. He was singularly exact in matters of this kind...in surveying his maps and knowing his battle strengths. The maps showed wooded lands and swampy terrain. He scanned several picket and scouting reports. Within two minutes of careful observation, he decided what best strategy to undertake with his men. When he was finished he exited his tent and gazed at the oak tree across from him. It had the same peculiar bent as the oak in Catherine's yard.

An orderly hit a tent stake with his foot, dishing out an avalanche of rainwater off the canvas roof, distracting him. At that same moment his adjutant, Ian MacDougal, appeared, extended one burly arm and offered his equally burly hand.

"Glad to have you back, Sir"

Shaking the man's hand, John smiled. The man's strength hadn't waned. A fierce fighter, MacDougal was like an ancient Scottish warrior down from the Highlands. A large barrel of a man, leaner at present, with keen blue eyes that missed nothing and canopied with thick, bushy eyebrows that drew together in a line when he frowned. His hair was a shock of wild red, matching his fiery personality.

A lively man at one time, his forty-five years had been muted by the war, but mostly from the loss of his wife with whom he'd lived an idyllic life on a farm in northern Virginia. She had scoffed at Ian's need to fight with the rebels, seeing no sense in the war. She had remained behind, taking care of their small farm. When a battle was fought over her threshold, she filled her home with injured Yanks and nursed them back to health. One day, a stray cannonball hit her home, killing her instantly. None of the Union soldiers were hurt. Ian MacDougal took the news hard. John had never seen a man cry like MacDougal did that day, nor had he seen him cry again.

"Yes," John returned stiffly, taking the old warrior by complete surprise. It wasn't the normal greeting he would give his adjutant. Their relationship was beyond that of a commanding officer to his staff. Since the first summer of the war, their rapport had evolved from mentor into friend. "Let's walk," suggested John.

Together they walked up on a hill, but the trees kept them from seeing much ahead except for the encampment of his men below. The cook fires were lit for the night and the sights and sounds of men preparing their meager evening meal filled the countryside. John's bones ached from his travels. He longed for his bed...longed to put his mind at rest. But rest was not in the cards. First, he needed time to absorb and to contemplate all the details from his adjutant.

"Do you ever doubt?" Ian's drawl mixed with a slight burr, intoned the air.

John gathered he meant the Cause. It seemed like eons ago Catherine asked him the same question. His thoughts echoed. *Only fools never doubt.*

He paused. "The Confederacy may be bowed but not broken. There are still enough resources available to maintain the Southern armies, and our armies will stand up and fight. Victory will no longer be measured by the land held, but by the continuation of the will to fight again and again and again."

MacDougal ducked his chin, and John passed his eyes over the landscape in front of them. The sun was setting through the trees in swells of rose and indigo, foretelling another hot day tomorrow.

"Man is a strange sort, unique to the earth, yet we have to learn over and over again what it is to be human. It seems like it has to be learned with every generation." Ian let the words drift.

John clamped down on his cigar. The pungent scent of rolled whole-leaf tobacco smoke spiraled through the warm night air. Earthy, pleasant, Virginia tobacco. "There's good and bad. I've only seen the worst of it," he said through his teeth, unable to keep his bitterness at bay.

He couldn't stop thinking of Catherine. Was she on her next mission? Trading her body for information? His mind wandered until it touched on a scene of Catherine in bed with that slimy Mallory fellow.

The vision made his stomach roil and he cast it out of his mind, yet his thoughts roamed to when Catherine lay atop him in the glen, their legs entwined, her emerald eyes, the soft silky peaks of her breasts tracing their warmth across his chest. He could almost feel the silken golden mass of her hair, sifting it through his fingers. Her warmth, her parted lips, stirred his passions to a soaring height like a hawk high over the land and sea, burned his insides, hotter and hotter.

Until he remembered her treachery. Without preamble, he transformed the burning thoughts into revenge.

"General Rourke, the men love and admire you. But you've changed, subtle but different. I'd bet my eyeteeth it was something those Yanks did up North. Simmering beneath the surface there's a rage. It's one thing to hate, but to hold it inside—is unhealthy."

As the sun's trail progressed downward from the sky, the sad-sweet tones of "Home Sweet Home" filled the air. There were many voices, baritones, tenor and bass with power among them, and for an hour the camp resounded with their melancholy music. There was a sentiment in the tones of these voices that fitted well with the sentiments of their surroundings.

If anyone would note his change, Ian would. John did not comment. "Tomorrow we will fight at Cold Harbor. We must hold our positions. I'm as sensitive to flanks as a virgin." He smiled like Satan in a bad mood.

"How strange. Cold Harbor means shelter without fire," Ian said just as reflective. "The men are feeling very lonely and very bored. I can assure you they are ready for battle."

"Get some sleep, Ian. You'll need it before morning comes."

John woke early to a dark and damp morning, chilled and soured by swamp odors wafting in from the nearby Chickahominy River. He grabbed some stale Johnnycake and chewed on that while listening to distant shots as Union soldiers engaged his picket lines. His men, battle ready, didn't even need to hear his orders to rise in their trenches. More than half had already spent the night there anyway. He heard a soldier tell his friend that today was his birthday and he wondered what he would get.

Low mists and fog still clung to the stunted pine thickets as John watched thousands of blue-coated soldiers stumble into companies that had fused to create regiments...which advanced to shape brigades that made up divisions. Like a giant blue viper uncoiling itself, ready to attack.

General Rourke felt a power in the very air, something palpable affected by the raw sight of so many men, shifting to a single purpose.

Then the battle began.

Dense clouds of acrid, burnt gunpowder rolled upward over artillery and infantry emplacements. The crack of gunfire and cannons burst into the air. A Union shell screamed through the length of his Confederate line, coming close, and its wind seeming to slam every man in the regiment. An agonizing cry emitted from a soldier as the shell tore his arm off.

"Now!" General Rourke ordered. The Confederate response was quick in answer. Ranks of Union soldiers exposed across the ridge were reduced to the terrific gunfire of Confederate musketry. The Yank soldiers pressed to a hundred yards of his frontline before they stopped cold. An awful trail of dead and wounded lay abandoned in their wake.

"Give them double charges of canister. Fire, men, fire!" John roared above the din. The order was obeyed with promptness, but still an ocean of blue came again and again in appalling numbers creating frightful gaps in his line. General Rourke's men labored under murderous fire, and it looked as if a thousand deaths awaited them. The rebel soldier whose birthday it was went down with a ball in his thigh.

So near was the regiment to the Confederates' second line that many Yanks were captured before John's intent to fall back. They waited for the onslaught of the next Union column that hit like a battering ram. John jumped astride his horse, hustling more Confederates into flanking trenches.

"Wait 'til close enough to fire."

The Rebels behind the entrenchments rested their guns upon the works, firing volley after volley. The blue line fell, carried away like wheat from the chaff.

John worried about their lack of ammunition with the ceaseless drumming and plowing of shot, making the field look like a boiling cauldron.

He waved his sword high over his head. "Charge!"

With a bloodcurdling Rebel yell, his men broke into the sea of blue, striking, hacking, firing. On they rushed with General Rourke spurring his horse, leaping high over the works and into the terrible melee of death. His horse reared and many balls that would have struck him missed their intended target as John fought on, bringing his horse under control. In retreat, the Union line melted into the distant forest, leaving a swath of blue carnage.

Later, in Richmond, General John D. Rourke was hailed as a hero returned. A combat artist, who captured his image in the great struggle of Cold Harbor, rushed his artwork to be copied onto boxwood blocks by staff engravers of the Richmond Examiner for several thousand printing runs.

John did not feel like a hero, nor did he feel the bloody standoff was the portended victory the newspapers allowed.

Chapter 13

The Fitzgerald home in Georgetown was a modest, red brick mansion that boasted a huge foyer, drawing rooms, a library, dining room and sitting room, yet was nowhere near the luxurious comportment of her family's New York home and one her father had built when he visited Washington to secure government contracts.

It was a hot steaming night toward the end of June when Mallory, Catherine, and Agatha arrived home, staying late from yet another ball.

Mallory chided her as they mounted the steps. "You're very quiet this evening."

He meant she wasn't acting the part he wanted her to play. "I have had a headache forming all evening."

The butler opened the door. "You've been having quite a few of those lately," Agatha snapped, her rolls of flesh sweating around her neck from the humidity

"It was a lovely ball, don't you think, my dear?" Mallory prodded.

Catherine jumped when he clamped his hand on the back of her neck and began to knead there. She stiffened with the familiarity, didn't dare move, the bruises on her throat had barely faded. "Yes, lovely," Catherine echoed what Mallory wanted to hear. A cat and mouse game to keep him at bay and to stall for time. Her movements had been non-existent. Mallory's army of thugs followed her everywhere. Her chest tightened. If only she hadn't endangered Father Callahan in her affairs. When the butler took their coats, she stepped away from Mallory.

Her likeness had appeared in Harpers Weekly, announcing her engagement to Francis Mallory. Of course, a young socialite from New York was sensational news in Washington, especially since it was wartime and her company furnished rifles for the war effort.

Her life had taken on a surreal nature, receptions and glittering galas were given in Washington to receive the striking couple. The circle which claimed Catherine as their own now included Francis Mallory, proclaiming them as the toast of Washington society. Francis shined and beamed every minute. A bitter taste rolled over her tongue.

He determined what she should wear, who to speak to, what to say, and who to dance with. If she spent too long conversing with someone of whom he did not approve, he would be at her side, clamping his huge hand on her elbow, guiding her away. The past week wore on her nerves, anything to get through the daily tedium of social engagements and his incessant ultimatums.

"Lovely idea, don't you think," Mallory said, "traveling to Washington, killing two birds with one stone. I can sell more rifles to the war department and enjoy some balls and parties with my exquisite fiancée."

He pinched her to get her attention. "What an enchanting little symbol you are, overwhelming the public. Washington women are quite dull and plain-faced in comparison. I noted, Secretary of War, Edwin Stanton, paying particular attention to you. That's good for business. Our venture to the Capitol will be a profitable one. Your presence will sell more rifle contracts than I'd ever dreamed."

Mallory perused the high plastered ceiling decorated with medallions of shells and *fleur-d-lis,* and summoned his blessings. "We were quite the honored guests. It was Catherine they seemed to pay the most homage to. Don't you agree, Agatha?"

Agatha begrudged Catherine even the merest of compliments. But when Mallory spoke, she fell all over herself to answer. "It was quite an occasion." Agatha pursed her lips, causing the fine purple lines webbing up her cheeks to darken.

Shoulder to shoulder, Catherine and Mallory mounted the stairs in what had become a ritual. With her back straight, she stared straight ahead, never looking at Mallory, afraid that if she did it would be all the encouragement he'd need to enter her chambers.

Outside her room, Mallory tugged her hair loose and coiled it in his hands. She froze. "Soon I'll sample your charms and the experience will be delightful. I would not want a soiled dove…you are sure that the Confederate General took no liberties?" When he saw her quick intake of breath, he laughed. "Remember your uncle is comfortable as of present."

"And what about General Rourke? Have you released him as promised?" She knew John had escaped, yet dared to taunt Mallory.

Mallory slammed his knuckles into the wall, withdrew his hand from the hole he made through the plaster, wiping the dust to the floor. "Do not ask that question again."

She flinched when he brushed his powdered knuckles across her cheek, his lips twitched back from his teeth. "You are so lovely, but I am not convinced your relationship with the rebel was as innocent as you profess. Are you sure you are telling all there is to tell?"

Never would she rise to Mallory's bait. After a moment of strained silence, she pulled her hair from his grasp, moved into her room and closed the door. The clink of a key rasped in the latch. Mallory locked her in. Her hands shook, pressing them to her temples. Dear God, she needed more time. Where was Jimmy O'Hara?

The city grappled with darkness and heavy mist. Low hanging clouds dribbled fine droplets of moisture casting every surface in an obsidian-like sheen, while below, the swollen Potomac purled and foamed around rocks and islands. Catherine jumped when a dark figure scratched at her window. Jimmy O Hara. She pulled him in, and then lit a lamp. Jimmy produced a newspaper and she ripped it from his hands. Francis had prohibited any periodicals for her to read. He wanted to keep secret the fact that General Rourke had escaped.

Thirsting for outside knowledge, she snapped open the paper. *The Richmond Examiner* dated June sixth, a couple weeks old. "How did you get this from across the lines?"

"I have my sources." Jimmy smiled cheekily.

On the front page, a dedicated combat artist had sketched John through daring enterprise during a dramatic instant in the Battle of Cold Harbor. In the center of the chaos was General John D. Rourke, portrayed as she had imagined him in battle, armed to the teeth, gauntleted, jackbooted, wielding a sword in one hand and a pistol in the other, astride a rearing black stallion. According to the report, he was insurmountable in glory, a valiant hero.

He was a fool. Bullets blazed around him. Swords thrust. He would get himself killed.

Not that she cared.

But she did care.

If only she had told him the truth about her circumstances. He deserved no part of her personal war. With a sigh, she was glad he escaped. She could not stop from thinking about their time together, never to forget a single detail of his face, the warmth of his touch, and his mouth upon hers. Memories would haunt until her dying days.

She loved him. Her heart lurched, unable to deny the evidence. What a fool she had been not to tell him. Yet to John, the greatest sin was betrayal. With certainty, he believed she had betrayed him. She glanced again at the picture and froze. Fixed in his eyes breathed determination and his ruthless resolve to fight northward.

She dropped the newspaper. She wondered if he was coming to get her. To exact revenge for her betrayal. She prayed Grant would not fall short where Lincoln's other generals had failed. John would hunt her down as promised.

"He's quite a general."

Even Jimmy, a staunch Northerner was impressed with John's record.

"The only place you'll be safe from Mallory is south." Jimmy reminded her.

Catherine laughed at the ludicrousness of Jimmy's suggestion. To trade one madman for another? She dropped to her bed. Didn't the Union Army separate her from the more dangerous of the two? Was that enough? "And what of Father Callahan?"

"I am positive Mallory has him in Washington."

"Are you sure you can find him, Jimmy?"

"Can the pope pray?"

Catherine smiled and ruffled his hair. Tilting her head to the side, she said, "Are you sure you're only thirteen years old?"

"Morning, Miss Catherine. Brigid bustled into her room with a tray. His Excellency has ordered you up and about for an outing."

"An outing? Mallory's never insisted I do anything this early. Where am I going? What am I supposed to wear?"

"Put on this brown dress."

Catherine wrinkled her nose "It's horrid."

"That's the idea," Brigid said.

Her maid shook out the dress and lowered it over her mistress's head. "We need to tone down Mr. Mallory's interest in you. Not that it would do any good. You'd look fetching dressed in farmer's britches. However this dress will have the least effect, I am thinkin'."

"I wish I had the opportunity to talk to Secretary of War last evening about Shawn, but Francis dogs my every step."

Brigid took a brush in hand and began brushing Catherine's hair in long strokes. "You'll find someone who will listen. I have confidence. The servants cannot stand Mallory or his thugs. If your brother was back, Francis would be behind bars."

"Where is he taking me?"

Brigid shrugged. "All's I know is that his Lordship is awaitin' in the foyer. I have half a mind to shy his lean carcass over to Richmond and let the Rebels take care of him."

"Never mind about that this morning, Brigid. It's too fine a day." Catherine threw down the *Richmond Examiner* on the vanity.

Brigid's brown eyes grew as large as dinner plates. She took hold of the paper. "Is this really General Rourke? Your husband? A fine specimen of a man, yes he is."

"He won't be so fine if he gets a hold of me, since. Francis convinced him I was a spy."

"I don't believe that for one minute. All he has to do is look into those emerald eyes of yours and everything will be happy times again."

"Never—delude yourself with romantic notions where General Rourke is concerned."

"Would certainly make my heart swoon. And to think you were married in a week. How dashing he must be to have swept you off your feet. How passionate."

"You don't know John very well. He's set on revenge. In his present state of mind, he'll draw and quarter me and take pleasure in doing so. The farther I'm away from the southern border, the safer I'll be."

"But your General Rourke is a handsome devil." Brigid quit brushing and looked dreamily into the mirror. "My dear departed mother always said, sometimes something comes over a woman, and it's like she's connected to everything in her life that's precious to her. Almost like she can reach out and lay her hand on her man and draw him to her, even though he's not really there. And with him comes all the memories, and they wrap around her like a quilt, the warmest, most comfortable quilt in the world, and she knows it all, and feels it all, and the thing she knows the most is that it's all right. No matter what happens, it's all right because she loved her man and that won't ever go away, no matter what. A perfect love. That's the feeling that comes over a woman sometimes, and I hope I get that feeling for a man someday."

Catherine clasped the warm hand of her maid whom she had come to call a true friend. "I have no doubt you will, Brigid."

Plump and crowned with thick lustrous brown hair and dancing brown eyes, Brigid was a spirited girl, given for the most part to practical matters. The oldest of five siblings, she had already outlived two of them as well as both her parents. The curse of the potato famine had been the impetus to bring them across the Atlantic to a new world full of promise and hope.

"I'm twenty-three years old and have found no one who meets my fancy. All my sisters and cousins were married no later than nineteen years and most of them with wee babes suckling at their breasts before they were a hair over twenty. I would die and go to my maker happy to find a nice Irishman. But never a Scotsman." Brigid shuddered.

Catherine mouth fell open. "What do you have against the Scots?"

"My dear departed mother told me they're absolute woodenheads. They come down from their hills sighing for the warpath, yearning to drink their enemy's blood. They don't need a reason to fight. They fight about fighting. They rage and rave about war, considering it an inspiration of genius. They gather together, plotting and planning, dizzy with astonishment, admiration and delight of themselves while the rest of the world looks upon these fools for their idiotic blunders. Give me an Irishman any day, but spare me the Scots!" Brigid finished with dramatic flourish as she plucked the brush from thin air and began brushing again.

Catherine was dizzy from Brigid's dramatic pronouncement. "Never in a million years would I have guessed your disdain for the Scots. What about our driver—he's a Scot?"

"He's half-Scot. His mother betrayed the fine Irish race by marrying the most godless creature under the sun—a Scot. How can I hold the sins of his mother against him?"

"Benevolent of you."

Brigid slapped the brush on the vanity. "Just in case, I cross myself when he passes."

Catherine burst out laughing.

"There you are all smiles again. That's the way I like to see my girl."

"If only Jimmy could find Father Callahan. Then I'd disappear again." Catherine sighed.

"Now don't you worry about young Jimmy O'Hara. If he says he'll find your uncle, he will. We'll beat that spider-legged devil Mallory. Yes we will."

"An entertainment for you my sweet." Mallory declared more to his men than to her then stripped off his coat and shirt. "A different enterprise which I think you'll find rather charming." Her eyes adjusted to the dim interior. A raised platform like a stage was in the center of the musty barn.

Mallory's men threw wide the barn doors and herded two Confederate soldiers with heavy, clinking chains. Catherine gasped. Starved, filthy and with deep-set eyes, the soldiers haunted her. Mallory waved his hand and two of his men closed in on her, escorting her to the crates.

Mallory snapped his fingers and ropes went up around the stage. He was to fight these men? In a twisted, sick sordid sense, she knew Mallory was showing her he could beat General Rourke by beating these defenseless men.

Mallory ducked under the ropes. "Gentlemen, the north will be victorious over the south."

"Get 'em in here boys. Damn pathetic," said Mallory, sniffing the air. "Is this the best you could get out of Capitol Prison? I paid a good penny for this lot."

"Will you dry up and blow away?" Mallory taunted a gray-haired, gaunt prisoner. His men laughed, and then he pulled on an invisible string. "*Ding!* There's the bell laddie. Where's the fight in you Southern bastards? You mean to tell me there's nothing left?"

Mallory shuffled in the ring. He pushed a fist up against the Southerner's chin. "Just testing. That will teach you to cover up for when I really tag you. Do you think you can remember that?"

Catherine's hands fisted. The rebel stared back. He simply didn't care.

Angered by the soldier's lack of participation, Mallory slammed him flat with one hard punch. Blood trickled from the soldier's broken jaw. Catherine shot-up from her crate and moved to the soldier. Mallory waved his hand. Two of his men shepherded her back. Mallory's goons carried the soldier away.

"Last week at least they put up a little fight. You there, boy. You look like you have a little fight left in you. Your friend couldn't suck eggs."

A tall lanky boy of about nineteen years who stared out with pale tired eyes stood mute.

"Happy days, laddie."

Mallory's goons jeered.

The boy came out of his corner as if he really meant to make a fight of it. His stiff jabs made Mallory clumsy and flatfooted. Mallory threw a wild right, almost knocked himself down when the boy ducked.

Ten seconds passed before the Rebel feinted to the body, sucking Mallory into dropping his hands, and the boy crossed him with a straight right to the jaw. The blow caught Mallory by surprise.

"Never do that, Rebel boy." Mallory warned, his face white, his thin lips drawn to a thin line.

The Rebel boy waited in the corner, poised, ready, and Catherine wanted to stand up and shout for joy that someone stood up to Mallory.

Mallory came at the boy then, ready to connect with his ponderous right. But the Rebel boy danced around, scoring with sharp punches, defying the slow-moving Mallory.

The boy kept trying, like chopping down a huge oak. He knocked Mallory off balance with a smart left jab to the mouth that sent Mallory stumbling into the ropes. Blood began to trickle out of one corner of his mouth and down his eyes. At any moment Catherine expected to see Mallory caving in, but not before she saw his nod. Several of his men jumped the ropes, holding the Rebel boy down. They chained his feet together allowing no room for movement.

The boy fought back.

Mallory's eyes glared red. His left hand shot into the boy's shoulder. The wallop unbalanced the boy, sending him crashing to the floor. The men cheered Mallory as he climbed on top and pushed his fist repeatedly into the boy's face. The boy struggled to shield his face. With punishing blows, Mallory pawed the boy's face until his mouth became a bloody mess. Mallory's fists were sticky with it too, and each time he brushed the boy's face they left an ugly red blotch. Mallory kept boring in.

"Stop it." Catherine screamed, but Mallory kept on. She sprang under the ropes and laid her body between the boy and Mallory, shielding him.

Mallory quit, but Catherine remained, cradling the boy in her arms. "You animal," she seethed. "You're nothing but a coward,

Francis Mallory. Someday you'll meet with someone on equal ground. I hope I'll be there to witness it."

Mallory wiped his hands on the boy's shirt.

"Perhaps your uncle would like to go a round or two?"

"You wouldn't dare——"

"Suit yourself." Mallory signified with a shrug.

Before they left, Catherine begged what looked to her as one of the more compassionate guards to get the injured Rebels medical attention.

Mallory overheard her. "Of course my dear, anything you desire."

She knew they would get nothing.

Chapter 14

*M*allory clasped her elbow. "Make sure you pay particular attention to Stanton, Seward and Giddeon Welles," he whispered into her ear then greeted important guests. A twirl of colors in silks and satins bedecked the ladies as they danced around the ballroom with their partners, handsomely dressed in sharp navy blue uniforms trimmed with bright brass buttons.

"How could you beat those defenseless men?" She was still reeling from his depraved sparring earlier in the week and had no doubt he continued his activities. Washington's political elite stood off to the sides while their wives sat on blue-silk embroidered sofas, their shrill laughter in discord to her dismal mood.

"Perhaps your sympathies lay more toward the south?"

"Go back to the hole you crawled from," she dared and broke away from him when Edward Stanton bowed before her.

"Miss Fitzgerald, it's good to see you again. I hope you are enjoying your extended stay in Washington. How well I remember your travels to our fair city with your father."

Catherine extended her hand and smiling, said, "It is good to see you, Mr. Secretary." How easy to report Mallory to any one of them. No. His threat against Father Callahan was real.

After a few minutes of conversation, she was twirling around the dance floor, besieged by a swarm of requests, responding with a flirtatious gaiety that disguised her turmoil. Only once, she begged to catch her breath. With a bold wink, a servant pressed a cup of wine punch into her hand. Catherine widened her eyes. *Jimmy O'Hara.* He made beeline across the room and dropped his tray on Mallory.

"What do you find so amusing?" A colonel with an enormous girth from the War Office puffed out. He had a beefy face, and when he smiled, his upper lips curled back like the muzzle on a horse.

"Oh—nothing." Catherine said. Jimmy O'Hara pocketed Mallory's wallet while wiping wine stains from his pants.

"Thank you, Colonel McCullough, I'd love to dance," she said, reading the look in his eyes and permitted him to lead her to the center of the dance floor.

Sweating, the Colonel yearned for conversation. "Soon we'll have those Southern turncoats crushed under our heel."

"Really. Have you just returned from Cold Harbor?" He was a political appointee who had never seen action.

"Why no, I'm nursing an injury."

"At what field of battle, Colonel?" she asked demurely.

"I fell off my horse at the advent of the war. The doctors have warned my diligent care." He grew red in the face. "But we'll get those Rebels and slam down their leaders. Hang every one of their generals for treason. Justice will reign in the end."

"You fell off a horse?" Feigning a look of total feminine confusion, she refused to let it go. What would the pompous Colonel

McCullough think if he knew she was the wife of one of the South's infamous generals? The buffoon stepped on her toe.

"I feel like I have two left feet." He blushed.

Her laughter vibrated through the air. "Nonsense. You're doing splendidly." Her foot ached. She longed to fly away, but Mallory kept a watchful eye, as did his men positioned around the room.

An officer in a smart blue uniform tapped her current partner and rudely broke into the dance. Catherine was about to protest when two steel-blue eyes bored holes into her. She lost a step then, before his arms circled her waist in a strong grip and swung her into the rhythm of the dance.

"Miss Fitzgerald, I presume?"

Catherine gasped. He looked so much like John, so similar in appearance, the eyes, the dark hair, the angled curve of the jaw, why they could be—

"Brothers," he confirmed her suspicion.

"Lucas?"

He lifted an eyebrow in that same infuriatingly arrogant manner. "You have a lot of explaining to do, *Mrs. Rourke.*"

Her mouth fell open. "How did you know?"

"I am curious about the woman who entrapped my brother. John confided everything. It was a matter of putting the pieces together—"

"You have seen him? Is he well?" Her voice rose in pitch. "You were the one who helped him escape. Thank God—"

"You're happy he escaped?"

"Of course, except the fool is fighting again and is going to get himself killed. Couldn't you have done something to keep him out of the war? That's why I telegraphed you in the first place." Catherine glanced over her shoulder. Mallory stopped conversing and came straight for her before he was waylaid by an officer.

She trembled in Lucas's arms. When the music stopped and before the next refrain began, she begged, "Please keep dancing with me. See those men around the room." She inclined her head toward some large well-dressed thugs. "Those are Francis Mallory's men. My mistake was never telling John who I was. I thought he'd hate me for my association with Fitzgerald Rifle Works since our repeater rifles are used to kill rebels. My brother had disappeared during the war and with no one to protect me, and—I had to run away—"

She summarized her whole state of affairs from finding John and nursing him back to health, to her Uncle Charlie's insistence they be wed. She then relayed Mallory's finding her, his warped lies to John implicating her as a spy, Father Callahan's kidnapping, John's beating, and Mallory's extortion. "I have never told Mallory that John and I were married. He would have killed him. My only hope had been to rely on his promise to release John, if I went along with handing over the Rifle Works and marrying him."

"He didn't. They were ready to hang my brother until I broke up their party," Lucas said.

A cry of relief broke from her lips. "Thank God. Involving John and Father Callahan in my personal war has left me with nothing but worry and guilt. Mallory's a dangerous man and has killed many people. I'm his prisoner, but until my sources come up with Father Callahan's whereabouts, I must bide my time, and cause Mallory not to have any suspicions."

Lucas eyeballed the guards holding up the walls. "The pieces of the puzzle fit well. My instincts tell me you are disclosing the truth and I always act on my instincts. I have a special position in the military with advantageous resources. After I left my brother, I did research, stymied by your background. A benefactress of an orphanage, raving reports on your work with Dr. Parks at Mac Dougall Hospital—did not fit the profile of a relationship with an underworld criminal with a reputation a mile long such as Mallory. Nor did you fit the description of a spy. I requested an invitation to this event to observe."

Her mouth fell open. She had been observed? Of course, he'd have his suspicions.

"Everyone knows Mallory is a thug. How does he weave into society?"

Catherine exhaled. "Part what he has grabbed from the Mallory fortune, part from me, but I think there is an under-scored celebrity to him with his powerful connections to the Tammany political machine. Boss Tweed's ring is strong and solid, strategically deployed to govern key power points of New York City. They control the courts, the legislature, the treasury, and the ballot box. Their frauds are grandeur of scale and possess an elegance of structure via money-laundering, profit sharing and organization."

Mallory barreled through the crowd. She dug her fingers into Lucas's coat sleeves.

Lucas angled his head when Mallory was intercepted. "Don't worry. My men have been ordered to keep Mallory busy." Then Lucas narrowed his eyes on her. "You have a care for my brother?"

She looked into his eyes with all the sincerity in the world. "I love him."

"You have a serious problem, Mrs. Rourke. My brother will not permit you to collect husbands."

Her shoulders slumped...so little time. "Could you help me? My brother Lieutenant Colonel Shawn Fitzgerald is missing— I believe Mallory has had something to do with his disappearance. Please see what you can do to discover what happened to him. And my uncle, Father Callahan...he is hidden somewhere in Washington. Can you find him? Get with Jimmy O'Hara. Perhaps the two of you working together?"

Lucas smiled. "Of course. I will champion your cause. You have nothing to worry about. As my brother's wife, I will do everything in my power."

Tears of relief stung her eyes. "But how?"

"I have my devices." He was succinct and would give no more.

"There's one more thing," she said, clinging to him. Oh, he was part of John, a life rope thrown to her. She didn't want to let him go. "Mallory has been taking Confederate prisoners out of Capitol Prison for his personal bouts, except it is one sided and he beats these poor men brutally. I beg you to get the men who have been hurt by Mallory the medical attention they need. I'll repay you as soon as I am able." She felt his muscles tighten beneath his coat and a vein throbbed dangerously on the side of his jaw.

"Taken care of. Jimmy O'Hara—how do I get in contact with him?"

"Jimmy O'Hara will find you. And what of John? He believes I have deceived him."

Lucas nodded. "In John's present mood there will be no mercy. I'll write him a letter and explain everything."

"You can send him a message?" A warm glow of hope flowed through her as Lucas whirled her around.

"It will take some time. It's been done throughout the war. You are an angel, Mrs. Rourke, caring for everyone around you to the point of endangering yourself. Your courage is admirable. My brother is a lucky man."

Mallory broke in. "Catherine."

He jerked her arm and when Lucas stepped in to intervene, she shook her head. She exhaled when Lucas backed off. "Thank you, Colonel Johnson," she said, using a false name while Mallory pulled her away. "You dance divinely."

"A pleasure, Miss Fitzgerald. I look forward to having the honor of someday introducing you to my family members. They will be most happy to meet you. Until we meet again." He inclined his head with the briefest of smiles.

Chapter 15

$\mathscr{S}$ince the temporary success of Cold Harbor the past few weeks had been hard on General Rourke and his Confederate soldiers. General Ulysses S. Grant, Army of the United States, had cleverly concealed the movements of his massive army south across the James River to begin a siege on Petersburg. Except for the failed two-corps lunge by Grant, the lines of Lee that protected the vital railroad center, supplying the capitol of Richmond, held fast. The eastern offensive by the iron-hammered General Grant had wound up in a stalemate and a digging contest between both sides resulted.

The future hinged on the turn of Grant's strategy for there could be no denying that heroic Confederate defensive efforts demanded stout offensive measures against the Yanks. General Robert E. Lee clung to his lines by sheer will and wile against the massive numerical and material superiority of the North.

While Lee held off valiantly, the Kearsage and Alabama warships engaged off Cherbourg, firing at each other across the narrow circles they navigated in the choppy waters of the English Channel. In continuing the anaconda approach, General William Tecumseh Sherman, U.S. Army, maneuvered in Georgia, hounding

Confederate General Joe Johnston's army. General Jubal Early had been sent by Lee to check Yankee General David Hunter who had been terrorizing the civilian population by burning homes and fields along the Shenandoah. General Early removed Hunter from all tactical calculations, checkmating him at Lynchburg and chasing him over the Alleghenies. Lee now ordered Early to head north crossing the Potomac River on a daring raid to Washington.

"Strike as you can," Lee ordered General Early.

Rourke and his men had left Cold Harbor, marching south to fortify the vulnerable entrenchments protecting Petersburg. Lee then sent John under General Early to bolster the Shenandoah, defending the crucial breadbasket of the Confederacy. John's original optimism plummeted when he was left behind to guard the Valley and not allowed to proceed on with Early.

Yet he understood General Lee's calculated maneuvering on two accounts. First, it was hoped General Early's menacing attack on Washington would force Grant to send troops from Petersburg, thereby reducing the threat at the South's vulnerable underbelly. Second, it would spur Grant into staging a reckless attack, Cold Harbor style, which would functionally bleed him down for being disposed of by a counterattack that would follow his repulse.

General John Daniel Rourke had made camp outside Lynchburg with steady patrols up and down the Shenandoah Valley, keeping a keen eye out for Sheridan's Calvary. There would be no more abuse of citizens in the Valley under his guard. If he was to curb Grant's bulldog grip to chew and choke, then by God he'd do it.

John sat outside his tent, legs stretched out in front of him and crossed at the ankles, and with a cigar clamped in his mouth.

Enjoying a momentary respite with his men, he listened to the light banter.

"Boy, I sure do miss the chance to take a few potshots at Lincoln like Old Jube is going to get to do," one of the younger officers said.

"Mind you, I'm chomping at the bit to see some of that action myself," confided Lieutenant Johnson.

John rolled his cigar around in his mouth. He too, envied Old Jube but was content right where they were. Unlike their brothers at Petersburg, food was in great supply. In addition, many of the women of Lynchburg were happy with their boys' recent victory and rewarded them with a steady supply of home baked items to fill their diet. His men were scrawny, ragged and needed time to recoup. Their boots, if they had any to wear, were falling to pieces, their gray uniforms were patched and over patched, and their worldly possessions reduced to what each man could afford to carry on a long march.

A mail carrier rode in and many of the men grew quiet, having a private moment, reading letters from loved ones' back home. Absorbed in several dispatches, John rose to take them into his tent, but paused when the mail carrier interrupted again with several periodicals traded from northern pickets. John picked up a handful to glean critical information. The best spies were Northern newspaper reporters notorious in detailing Yank strategies and locations. Of late, Grant had put a stop to the practice.

A shrill whistle emitted from the teeth of one of his men. "She sure is pretty for a Yank."

"Who is she?" A corporal asked.

"Why would you want to know? She's getting married anyway."

"I'd have a chance——"

"Like giving Lincoln a lecture on politics and him listening."

The soldier's friends laughed at him.

With a nose like a beak on a pelican, the indignant corporal persisted. "I'd bet she'd be the first to dance with me, finding me the fairest of you all."

"If there'd be a hanging for beauty, rest assured, you'd be last in line."

John allowed a slow rumble of laughter at the imparted truth.

"She'd be hard put to resist my charms." Lieutenant Johnson boasted.

John's lieutenant had a face wrinkled like a dried apple in the hot sun. Many called him Grandpa.

"And those charms are——"

"I'm witty, clever, intelligent...the list goes on, but I don't need to bore you boys with familiar knowledge. Nor do I wish to pain you with standards you could not live up to."

"I don't recall any of those specific charms," scoffed another officer.

Lieutenant Johnson stroked his beard at the rebuff. "Is it me? Am I getting wiser or is it the young who are becoming more stupid?"

"It's just that those charms you mention are naked to the visible eye."

"Then wallow in your ignorance." Johnson protested and John grinned around his cigar.

"It says here she's rich, too, an heiress to Fitzgerald Rifle Works in New York City. Why I've stolen a couple of their guns off

Yanks. Repeater rifles. Good guns. They're shiny and sleek—like I'd imagine dancing with this gal."

"Ain't she a beauty, General?' drawled a West Virginian, pointing to a likeness of a woman in *Harper's Weekly*.

Fitzgerald. John imagined there were a lot of people with the name. He chafed at the reminder of his wife...the liar...the spy. He finished the last of his dispatches and handed them to his adjutant to put in his tent. He stretched then lounged again in his chair.

"Here's an article on the same woman in the *New York Tribune*. Bet her family made a lot of money on this war. It says here Catherine Callahan Fitzgerald is to be wed to Francis James Mallory both of New York and is to be the toast of—"

"What!" John exploded from his camp chair and grabbed the papers. With his cigar clamped between his teeth, he said nothing, confirming what the soldier had read aloud. All the eyes of his men were upon him.

"You bite that cigar any harder," Ian MacDougal commented, "You'll bite it in two."

Ignoring him, John glanced at her photograph in *Harper's Weekly*, and then the article in the *New York Tribune*, dated in late June. He couldn't believe his eyes. His lying, cheating wife was marrying that Yankee scumbag? Just as diabolical, she owned Fitzgerald Rifle Works. How many of his soldiers had died from those rifles?

Many of her evasions made sense now. She had gone by the last name of Callahan. Yet, Father Callahan solemnized the ceremony using her surname Fitzgerald. Like a steaming locomotive, memories slammed into him, her fine manners and delicate ways, the way she spoke, cultured, intelligent, the way she carried herself. She couldn't cook, crossed her fork and knife on her plate. Of course. She had an army of servants to wait attendance for her every waking need. Born with a silver spoon in her mouth, she no doubt took up spying from sheer boredom. He stared at the papers, burning with inner fury.

"What is it, General?' Has Lincoln surrendered?" The men laughed, but the deadly countenance of their commander was not a laughing matter. In seconds, the men dispersed...except MacDougal.

Rourke chuckled nastily, an affront to the silence. According to *Harper's* she was in Washington on an extended stay. So close. Enjoying balls and teas and—other entertainments? Indeed, he could imagine what other entertainments. How he itched to get his hands on her.

Concealing a growing impotent rage, he wished he were in Old Jube's boots right now. There would be no doubt John would capture Washington just to get to her.

MacDougal scratched a Lucifer match alight and crouched over its flame. "You look like you got struck by lightning." His adjutant made a way to open up a conversation. "Your innards are filled with rot-gut whiskey. Wisdom tells me it's time to open the book or have you ceased to imbibe wisdom?"

John was in no mood for banter. Another dispatch rider thundered in, sending up a spray of dust. He dismounted and saluted.

"General Rourke?"

"The same."

"I've come from General Lee." The courier announced.

"I gathered." John drawled and opened the sealed packet. A part of him hoped he didn't have to move his troops again. They needed rest. Yet another part of him wanted to fight, to slam his fist in somebody's face.

"It looks like I have to pay my respects to General Lee. Ian, I'll have you accompany me. Lieutenant Johnson," John called over to the surgeon's tent where Johnson had wandered. "You're next in command. I'm sure you'll fill the shoes adequately until I return."

General Rourke came upon General Lee at his headquarters inside the entrenchments at Petersburg. He looked more tired than usual, menaced by an intestinal disorder but, as always, remained impeccably dressed. Lee did not waste time with pleasantries but moved on to business.

"I need someone I can trust to ride through to General Early with a message. I sent my son, Robert, but have not heard back from him." Lee paused but never revealed his worry. "This is a matter of grave importance for the Confederacy and cannot wait his return. A combined operation by naval elements and undercover agents is planned for the liberation of seventeen thousand Confederate prisoners at Point Lookout, down Chesapeake Bay at the mouth of the Potomac. After General Early closes in on Washington, I need him to be at or near Point Lookout on the night of July twelfth in time to assist setting free what would amount to a full new corps for the Army of Northern Virginia."

"Yes, Sir," said John, concurring the importance of resurrecting more fighting men to sustain their rapidly depleting army.

"If things work out right, if God wills, General Early will be successful in uncaging veterans' south, armed with weapons taken from the vastly supplied stores of arsenals, ordnance shops, and armories in the Federal Capitol."

Lee poured over the maps. "We need two days. That is to say, if there is no delay en route. A battle or sizeable skirmish, anything that would oblige a major portion of Jubal's army to deploy or engage will eat up valuable time."

"Understood," John said. "I'll ride out only with my adjutant." He paused before he left. "When I meet Robert, I'll send him this way."

"Of course." Lee hesitated, but then dismissed Rourke. As John climbed into his saddle, the general came outside. "God go with you."

John saluted. He felt like he was leaving his father behind. He was also elated. He was heading north. He'd arrive when Early made his strike into Washington. Maybe he'd have lunch with his brother after all. That is—after he finished business with Catherine Fitzgerald Rourke.

Chapter 16

*M*allory had cut their attendance at a dinner party short and returned home. The heavy booming of artillery and rifle fire had unnerved him. Washington panicked with rumors of Armageddon. Rebel columns had knocked what little Union resistance there was out of their way and drew closer by the hour. Hysterical citizens wailed.

Descending on their city doorstep, an army of a hundred thousand Confederate firebrands, screamed vengeance for the destruction of their homeland. Influential leaders harassed President Lincoln to bring Grant's army back north, despondent that he had left them to suffer their fate. Galvanized into action, every available militiaman, War Department clerk, and dismounted cavalry mustered in the outworks. Northward, communications had been cut-off by rail, wire, telegrams and newspapers by the insurgents. Hundreds of refugees swarmed the city with tales of murder and mayhem, adding to the impending doom.

Mallory's voice held a rasp of acidity. "The situation is very grave. Rumor has it, Mr. Lincoln has boarded a naval ship and abandoned the city. Only a few fools are left to guard Washington. How stupid to keep the Union Army fortified around Richmond. Why

Lee's whole army is left to torch Washington. Lincoln is a fool. Grant is a fool."

"Perhaps you should consider volunteering," Catherine said.

"And leave my darling fiancée unprotected. I would not think of it."

"Of course," Catherine acceded. "Perhaps General Rourke and his army will call on us tomorrow morning. We could invite them for breakfast," she said matter of fact, rewarded with a momentary flash of horror across Mallory's face.

"I recall he'd be more interested in having his revenge on you." Mallory let it hang.

One of his men entered the parlor. Catherine used the opportunity to flee to her room. A smile came to her lips with a letter from Lucas that had magically appeared in her reticule. Lucas had put a halt to the Rebel soldiers taken from Capitol Prison for Mallory's abuse, making sure they had the medical attention they needed and swift retribution for the guards who had profited from the scheme. Through his frustration and admiration, Lucas had detailed his introduction to the thirteen-year old hooligan, Jimmy O'Hara. Lucas's wallet had been stolen. To his chagrin, the wallet lay on his desk an hour later in a heavily guarded office. Jimmy O'Hara, just barely out of his nappies, had provided Lucas with a different ambit—a view of the Irish underworld with its underpinnings centered in New York City and spreading its tentacles throughout the growing nation. Mallory had been crafty, moving Catherine's uncle about Washington. Where Lucas had failed at the turn of a coin, Jimmy O'Hara had succeeded through his network. Lucas hoped to visit a nondescript hotel on the west side this very night. Once he had her uncle, then he would help her escape Mallory.

Catherine would hire an army of Pinkerton agents and body-guards. She would use her connections in Washington to find out what had happened to Shawn and then block Mallory. No more would she be under his thumb. Jimmy had informed her that the new Fitzgerald foundry in New Jersey was near completion, so the Rifle Works wouldn't need to depend on Mallory Foundries. Since she was married, lawyers in Washington and New York would be secured to arrest control of her family's wealth. Then she'd toss Agatha out. So much depended on this night.

For Catherine, getting away from Mallory's oppressive presence did not make her any more secure. The rumors abuzz in Washington had raised the hairs on the back of her neck. John was miles away, defending Richmond. Wasn't he? She rounded the balustrade. Tremors spiraled up her spine. To fall into his hands? She clutched her throat.

A strong wind blew against a huge darkened stain-glass window and it rattled in the sashes. A terrible foreboding touched every fiber of her being. Ridiculous. Giving herself a little shake, she entered her room and pressed her forehead against the closed door. Mallory was downstairs. Good. *Safe. Lucas would find her uncle. He'd help her escape...*

No sound in her room. Odd? Not even the wind—an unnatural quiet. Catherine shivered.

The room was obsidian black, the only light that of the moon through the branches of the oak outside casting gloomy shadows across the wall. A tranquil room. Nothing to fear. She struck a match and lit her lamp. Light exploded to the far reaches of the room.

A man's dark form loomed large...a form she recognized instantly. "J-John." She blinked. No. It can't be...

Had she summoned up an image of him? Sitting on a gold brocade chair, his legs stretched out in front of him, he tipped his hat back. "Yours truly, my love."

A cigar poked from between his teeth and a Colt revolver lay across his lap. His right hand rested on the handle of his pistol, the easy grace of long habit. He grinned around his cigar, a slow...dangerous smile. "I happened to be in the neighborhood and decided to pay a visit."

She drank in the sight of his face—a face that aroused deep and profound memories. There was no helpless or injured man about him now. With his Rebel uniform open at the throat and exposing his sun-burnished skin, and his tight-fitting gray pants, he looked a mix of raw predatory instinct, and undeniable power. The expressive sweep of his dark brows and the sensuous bow of his lips—lips she remembered only too well—even now, she could remember their smoothness, taste and feel.

She put her hand up. "I've done nothing wrong."

"Your pardon, but at the present moment I am devoid of all strenuous emotions, so any of your remarks are of no consequence."

So menacing, so threatening, far more than she could have imagined. She was damned. Her shoulders dropped. "Let me explain."

"You are mistaken my dear wife if you think I would listen." He threw the New York Tribune at her feet, her engagement announcement to Mallory. "Bigamy even in the *amoral* Union States is illegal."

"I did everything in my power to protect you and Uncle Charlie—"

He cut her off. "No more lies. You are a harlot, plying your wares for excitement. Spying must be glamorous business to attract a wealthy woman. You are good. Damn good."

Catherine drew in a sharp breath as if he had slapped her. She had been surprised and even happy to see him again, but his slur upon her character was too much. "How dare you."

A muscle ticked in his jaw. "That was just an interchange of compliments. What intrigue are you involved in now? I should expect you are using that lush body of yours for further procurement of information."

"Mallory promised if I did everything he wanted, he'd release you. He has my uncle, and I'm going crazy with worry that he will kill him."

"Delightful story. I'm charmed."

"Charm is beyond your reach. Of course, you would never believe the truth." Memories swirled, her stomach clenched, his promise of revenge. "Nor will you be satisfied until you've had your revenge."

"Madam, I have traveled far, plagued by the memory of the generous way you received and entertained me during my...convalescence. There were many fascinating moments. How endowed you were with...certain assets...that would cause a man to forget... to forget his men, his country. Too bad you didn't receive one bit of information that wasn't already available. No doubt, you paid the price, your patriotism, admirable. One satisfaction I own is that I was the first. How many have you seduced since?" He laughed when she flinched.

Let him think what he wanted. Oh, to put him in his place. "The consequence of such disadvantaged fame fashions you a symbol of the destructions of the Confederacy that the North desires to eradicate. I could scream and bring the house down."

With lightning speed, John was upon her. "I think not." He put a hand over her mouth, his other hand clamped on the small of her back, holding her against him. At full strength, he was lean and powerful as a wolf. She pushed against his chest. He gave her a rough shake that threatened to snap her head off. Her pins fell to the floor and her hair tumbled down her back. Catherine stilled.

"That's better. You are not so proud when you fear."

She lifted her chin, summoning what little courage she could assemble. "Do you think I'm afraid of you?"

Silence loomed between them. His rapier glance passed over her. *Lucifer in butternut.*

"Yes, my loving wife," he smiled, his even white teeth showing. "You should have cause. The hand of your betrayal preys on my mind. I have fought the devil's own and risked all to have retribution.

She tossed her head. "Be informed that nothing will come to pass, for I am going nowhere with you."

"But you will——"

Never had she seemed more beautiful, more desirable. Her emerald eyes shone with unshed tears, dark and luminous—and pleading.

Her bosom barely covered by the satin she wore heaved against the taut rich red fabric. He remembered the soft silkiness of her breasts and he ran his callused fingers across them.

"I cannot go with you even if I wanted too. I have too much at stake. I beg you, John, if you have any shred of decency or chivalry left in you, take your leave."

"None of these attributes belong to me," he murmured. Would she weep? In her pride, she steeled herself away from him, determined not to break down, at least in his presence. His mission for Lee in delivering the personal message to General Early had been fulfilled, but freeing the seventeen thousand Confederate prisoners from Point Lookout had been unrealistic. With Early's attack on Washington, John with his adjutant had used the distraction to slip into the city under cover of darkness. Wasn't his *dear* wife surprised with his visit?

"What do you propose doing with me?" Her tone was light, in spite of her trembling.

"Take you south. We have methods for spies in the Confederacy. I have entertained several."

"You forget yourself, General Rourke. Need I remind you of basic geography? You are in the heart of Yankee territory. The Capitol no less. I refuse——"

"You will be sorry to test my patience further," he drawled, pressing her flat against the wall with his body. "Ever since our rude parting, I could not put behind even the minutest detail and I vowed that neither starvation, disease, death, nor pestilence would keep me from you."

"And when Mallory comes? No? Is it fear?"

Did she dare to test him? "I do not fear, not in the least, I shall be delighted to welcome your paramour and allow him to digest eight inches of my steel."

"Your skill at destroying is indeed legendary," she said, imitating his sarcastic tone.

"I thank you for your flattery. It will be neatly done. I admire your courage. Most women in your place would be pleading for mercy. But you are not just any woman, are you, Catherine? A highly trained professional, proficient in your art, practiced." He moved from her then, grabbed a black cape and threw it at her. "As much as I'd like to stay and have you practice your art on me, I feel compelled to put as much distance between me and your friend—Abe Lincoln and his cohorts."

A brown-haired young woman entered the room and closed the door behind her. "And where do we think we be leaving on a dreadful night such as this?" The woman appraised him, and at that moment, a genuine look of surprise lit her face. "General Rourke!" She bobbed a curtsy. "I'm pleased to make your acquaintance."

"The pleasure is mine ma'am." He tipped his hat with just the right amount of insolence. "But since I have another engagement, I have little time for paying my respects. Who is she?" He jerked his head toward the woman.

"Brigid—my maid."

Brigid spoke up. "It's a terrible night for travelling. Would you be willing to come back when the weather is more suitable?"

John clamped harder on his cigar, the ludicrousness of her statement almost laughable. "I apologize for the present state of the weather. But it's out of my control."

"I'm not going." Catherine threw her cape at him.

"He is a handsome devil, just like you said, Miss Catherine."

Catherine sputtered. "I never——"

"A bonny man, much handsomer in person than the newspaper allowed, and Irish too. My dear departed mother——"

"Brigid!"

"Catherine." Rourke threw the cape back at her. "Is my directive too difficult for you?" he said, his voice sharp with annoyance. "Or shall I try to frame an easier one?"

"What an impatient nature your husband has," Brigid said.

Catherine began to pace back and forth, undaunted by his tone. "Pigheaded, stubborn, conceited, arrogant——"

She spat out her words with such outrageous facility that John could nearly see the humor in it. "You're right," he admitted, gritting his cigar at the woman whose outrageous insults peppered him like a gatling gun.

"And just how are we to depart? Just fly out the window... parade right in front of Mallory's men guarding the house?"

"Mallory's men will have a sufficient enough headache to last a lifetime. He patted the butt end of his pistol." John grabbed her, and she sunk her teeth into his hand.

He took hold of her then, wrapped the cape around her head and body, and threw her over his shoulder. "Do not test my patience again," he bit out. "It will be your last."

"I'm suffocating." She shook her head, kicked her feet. Rourke smacked her bottom and she stilled from the insult.

That's better," he mocked. "Better you learn to fear me. Listen what I have to say, *Mrs. Rourke.*" He ignored her renewed terrified struggles. "Without a doubt, I am going to lower you out the window. If you give me anymore trouble——"

"The window? You are mad. It's three stories high. If you drop me, I'll break my neck." She gulped air.

"Then I recommend you be silent." He cinched a rope around her then lifted her out the window, lowering her, the rope burning his palms.

"Excuse me, General Rourke. You're forgetting a detail." Brigid said her fists dug into her hips.

John continued lowering Catherine out the window. He had assumed the maid would give him no trouble, but questioned now his earlier intuition. His Colt lay three feet away. "What is that?" he asked.

A moan arose from Catherine's throat dangled between sky and earth. John kept releasing the rope, trying to think of something else to say to stall for time. Since there was no way to silence the maid without letting go, he prompted her into casual conversation. "You were saying——"

"I would like to make a deal with you."

"What makes you think I make deals?"

"The fact, I could scream loud enough to wake the dead all the way to Tipperary. Of course, Mallory would be here in a heartbeat and he'd put a bullet through your head."

"You'll have to do better than that."

"I am very loyal to my mistress. Most importantly, I'm scared to death of being left behind. Once Mallory learns Catherine is gone, there's no telling what he'd do to me."

John remembered Mallory's warm reception in Pleasant Valley and held no doubt on what foulness Mallory would wreak upon the woman. It was none of his affair.

Her voice broke. "Besides I could help you."

Rourke hated to hear a woman beg.

"I don't need a lady's maid." He shot her a curious sidelong glance. "Can you cook?"

Brigid looked him square in the eye. "Does the sun rise in the east?"

Since John's personal cook had been shot at Cold Harbor, mealtime had taken a downturn. He recalculated the benefits of taking the maid with him against the difficulties she'd create by slowing him down. He hesitated then jerked his head in a reluctant nod, cursing his stupidity for taking on the additional responsibility.

"You realize the journey will be dangerous. There are no guarantees."

Brigid held her head so high she could paint the ceiling with her chin. "I could survive an invasion of Cromwell."

John snorted. With certainty, the tough Irish maid could more than outlast the seventeenth century's ruthless nunnery burner.

"I have one small request."

Did he hear her right? "What is it you require?" He ground his teeth. Was he bargaining with a lady's maid? What next the family dog?

"I need to pack a few things."

John looked at her hard. Brigid could alert Mallory. He decided to trust her. "Make sure you pack light. You have one minute, not one second more." He glanced over his shoulder, out the window. Catherine was almost to the ground.

Brigid was back in one minute, handing her bag to Rourke.

"This bag must weigh sixty pounds! What did you pack?"

"Some medicines, one whole cooked turkey and a ham."

"You're a woman after my own heart."

For that he received a big smile from the Irish maid.

Huge arms grappled Catherine and snatched her out of the air. Her feet upon solid ground, her breasts were scraped. Someone untied her, spinning her around and snatching off the cape. Catherine pushed her hair back from her face. A tall brawny man loomed over her with thick bushy eyebrows pulled together into a singular frowning line.

"Who are you?" Catherine whispered to him, but he said nothing. Seeing which way the wind blew, she turned her back to him. Mallory's men lay unconscious, tied and gagged next to the house. Other than the guards that remained in the house, John was thorough.

"Such a nice night for a stroll," she said between bright flashes of lightning and rumbles of thunder. Or was it cannon fire?

A bag flew out the window and the Reb caught it.

Catherine's jaw dropped. Was that Brigid dangling out the window? John had no morals. He kidnapped her maid too.

A scant few minutes later, all three were on the ground. John made cursory introductions to his dour adjutant, Ian MacDougal.

"Good Lord! He's a Scot. Lord have mercy on us all," cried Brigid as she stared at the expressionless face of the towering adjutant, and then crossed herself.

"What's wrong?" John pushed Catherine up on his horse while Ian did the same with Brigid.

"He's a Scot," confirmed Catherine.

"What's so bad about being a Scot?" John growled. "I thought she'd object to him being a Rebel."

"It's worse than Cromwell," said Catherine.

"Lucky for her." John put spurs to his horse's flanks and she grabbed the horn to hold on.

"And why is that?" Catherine ventured to ask.

"Because you're riding with the devil."

Chapter 17

Riding south then east, John spoke to his adjutant. "Our escape route from Washington has been cut-off by the arrival of Grant's corps shipped up from Petersburg. General Early has succeeded with that part of his mission and may well relieve Old Abe of his arsenals. Lee will be pleased. But every minute that eclipses is valuable riding time lost. Washington is on full alert."

There was a shout. Union soldiers yelled for them to halt. They wheeled around their horses and galloped in the opposite direction, gunshots whistled past. John bent over her to shield her from the bullets.

"Do you have a plan to get us out of Washington without being maimed or killed?" she hissed.

He did not answer.

"Well then, I guess the simple fact remains you don't have a plan. What are you to do?"

"I think——" he spoke to his giant of an adjutant.

"Think! You should not try to think. One cannot think without proper machinery. Richmond is one hundred miles through Union lines. Why not sashay down to the rail depot and purchase train tickets or, ask Lincoln for his carriage?"

John cursed. "I have a better idea——"

"So you do have a plan. I am awestruck."

"I always have a plan, it's my peculiarity," he drawled, his temper cool in the face of crisis.

"But is it a good one?"

"Excellent. All the priests and popes could not devise a better one." The contempt in his voice forbade any further argument.

No doubt, his life training left so little space between decisions and action when an emergency confronted him that there was not even room for a shadow of uncertainty between them. He could not ride out of Washington, the way he had intended. Ten, maybe fifteen Yanks dogged them. John cut through alleys.

To Catherine, everything was a blur as they raced across the city. Hoof beats clattered on cobbled streets then gave way to the softer pounding of dirt-lined streets. She clung to the horse's mane for dear life. She wrinkled her nose with the scent of sewage and garbage that spiraled through the air. They headed down a seedier side of Washington with rows of saloons, and brothels. Mallory had joked about the seamier side of Washington, nicknamed, *Going down the line,* where Union soldiers supported the over four hundred and fifty bordellos that had blossomed during the war for 'horizontal refreshment'.

When John pulled up in front of an ostentatious storefront, her mouth dropped open. Overhead, a large marquee trumpeted, *Bouncing Betty's.* He hauled her off his horse. For the first time she was speechless.

As their eyes met, she found her tongue. "I will not suffer the indignity of entering——"

John pushed her up the steps. "You should feel quite at home, don't you think?" She struggled against his strong arms, helpless he dragged her into the dimly lit interior of Bouncing Betty's establishment. Hair lifted on the nape of her neck. What did he intend?

She blinked. *Red.* Everything was cloaked in gaudy burgundy red. Red velvet wallpaper lined the walls. Red drapes hung over doorways and windows, red-globed lights, red stair railings and wainscoting, matching red spittoons and lush red oriental carpeting. Reclining on several red velvet couches were a number of scantily clad ladies all dressed in…red.

"Johnny," hailed a husky voice from across the room.

"You have friends here?" Catherine shot him a look of disdain.

A woman moved toward them with red painted lips and cheeks, and corseted like a well-trussed turkey on New Year's Eve. What was most remarkable was her flaming red hair and low décolletage, impossibly housing gigantic pendulous breasts that swung to and fro with the sway of her hips. This…must be the famed Bouncing Betty.

"What brings you in tonight, Johnny?" Bouncing Betty asked. "Our boys wrestling with the Yank Army? I reckon Old Lee be running Abe Lincoln out of the White House on one of his own fence rails."

"For sure all the pale lawyers and plump politicians are long gone. No doubt only the good souls are left behind." He smiled at Betty, his laugh, sardonic and scornful.

Betty threw back her head and gave a loud hoot. "You got that right."

"My adjutant and I performed a detail for Lee. We wish we could have more time to visit, but the Union Army is close on my heels and I need a place to hide out. I'm sorry to put my troubles at your doorstep but I have no other recourse."

"I can help you." Betty smiled up at him, her rouged cheeks cutting wrinkles across her face. Inclining her head toward Catherine, she drawled, "But who's gonna take care of her?"

"We're together," he emphasized. "I am also travelling with two friends. They are stabling our horses. We have no time to spare. Half a Yankee regiment is hot on our trail."

"You've come to the right place. Girls!" She clapped her hands and mobilized several women up and off their red sofas. "We're having several Yank soldiers as guests in a moment. You know the drill. Treat them real nice, keep them more than occupied, and you'll get an extra tip from me in the morning."

She cuffed an elderly man awake. "Gus, get Johnny's friends in the stables and bring them upstairs. Fast." She commandeered John's arm and moved up the stairway. "This way—"

Catherine's hands clenched. To think they were on a first name basis. What was his connection to the efficient and obvious Southern sympathizer?

Bouncing Betty hung on John, and when she leaned over to whisper something into his ear, Catherine swore her breasts were going to fall out of her corset and right into his face. When John smiled at Betty's well-aimed charms, Catherine's blood boiled.

"Why is your little friend glaring at you, Johnny?" Betty glanced over her shoulder and with condescension looked Catherine up and down. "Worried?"

"As a matter of fact, I am concerned." Catherine stared back. "If you get any closer to him, he'll suffocate."

John chuckled. "There are worse ways for a man to die."

"Your little friend sounds jealous," Betty purred.

"Nonsense." Catherine forced the scowl from her face. Never in her life had she felt jealousy toward another woman over a man, even if the man was her husband. No way would she fall prey to that urge now.

She addressed her comments to her husband. "You are mistaken. The loose women you dally with are of no consequence to me. So wallow in your frivolity with your insignificant acquaintance, it's no concern of mine."

"Know the general long?" Betty asked and steered them into a room with exotic appointments and pulled the drapes.

Catherine took stock of the crystal candelabras and other rich accoutrements. Flowered murals with peacocks adorned the walls. Bouquets of peacock feathers fanned out in mammoth cloisonné vases. The room's prominent feature was a huge bed, covered with a turquoise colored satin coverlet, and piled with pillows of turquoise satin and trimmed with turquoise tassels.

When Catherine made no reply, Betty made it a point to continue her conversation. "Johnny and I go way back, don't we Johnny?" Betty flounced her broad hips up to Rourke, and stopped dead in front of him. "You better take your clothes off, General... if you get my drift."

Like a dry twig under foot, Catherine's temper snapped. "You get away——"

Betty looked down her nose. "Quiet, honey or you'll wake the dead." She laughed and moved away. "It's almost like you two were married." From her wardrobe, Betty grabbed a Union Colonel's jacket and hat and draped it on the bedpost.

"We are," John said.

"Thought so. Never saw a woman so possessive about a man," Betty sighed. "Too bad it wasn't us John. I always had a particular fondness for you."

"I never——" Catherine sputtered, but Betty interrupted her.

"You get undressed too, honey and get in bed."

"I will not. This is the end of this ridiculous charade. I'm leaving."

Rourke grabbed her arm and spun her around. "You'll not compromise, Betty. She's a good friend. I'll not see her hang for the likes of you. Get undressed, or I'll tear your clothes off."

Betty laughed and patted her red hair. "You have yourself a real wildcat with claws, General, should be an interesting evening." She winked at him then ambled away, closing the door and leaving Catherine feeling tawdry.

John smiled then, a menacing smile. "Let's stop the pretense. We are both aware of your profession. This is not an establishment you would normally work out of, but what's the difference? Except what you do, I hold in contempt. Betty at least has my admiration. She is honest and has a heart. You however, are a spy, the worst kind. Don't look daggers at me. I am no stupid fresh-faced raw recruit."

Her lashes fell. To have come so close to a happy reunion. There were some roads that could never be revisited, no matter what lay at their ends.

She heard horses pulled up out front. Rourke lifted the drapes, then snapped them down. "Yanks, I'll insist on your full cooperation or else."

"I will not. You brought this down on yourself. You chose to leave the south on a fool's errand."

John reached her in two easy strides, spun her around then undid the row of tiny buttons down the back of her dress and yanked the garment off. He pulled a knife from his boot and before she could shriek, cut the laces off her corset and tossed the clothing across the room in a heap. "I will not put up with any more of your defiance nor will I be taken prisoner."

She stood before him naked, yet proud, despite his attempts to humiliate her, and she didn't like the hungry look in his eyes— the look of a man who had marched through hell and back to get what he wanted. He stripped off his jacket and shirt and stuffed them in a chest. He picked her up and deposited her on the bed, and then straddling her, he pulled the coverlet up to conceal them.

"Now is your time to act the part you were born for, my sweet. One slip, and I'll—" The booming of heavy boots hammered up the stairway and thundered toward their room.

Catherine was about to scream for help but John silenced her with a kiss. The door busted in. A number of Union soldiers stood in the hallway witness to an act they could only imagine. Catherine yelped, her shame eternal, but John held a pistol at her side, warning her.

"Gentlemen?" John asked in his best imitation of a Washington accent. "Is there a problem?"

"Ah-uh-no, Sir." The sergeant stuttered, glancing at the Colonel's jacket hanging on the bedpost. "We were looking for an escaped Rebel."

"As you can see——" John laced his tone with irritation. "I'm busy. If you don't mind…"

"No Colonel," The sergeant chafed, growing red-faced. "We were directed to this establishment. There's a dangerous Rebel loose in the Capitol. If you see anyone or anything suspicious——"

"I'll be the first to tell you," John snapped. "It's a short night boys. I've paid a good sum for tonight. But Miss Candy, I'm sure, will be obliged to sweeten your appetites tomorrow night if you are so inclined. Won't you, Miss Candy?"

He jabbed the muzzle of his revolver in her side.

With a whimper, she doubled her efforts to be free of him. The soldiers laughed, enjoying an officer having fun with a woman.

"Yes Sir." The sergeant smiled with the eagerness of a puppy, tail up, nose wet and impatient to play. "No one suspicious here. We'll continue our investigation downstairs and interview the ladies. My apologies, Colonel." He tipped his hat, stepping through the wreckage and left.

"How dare you put a pistol on me," she hissed.

John laughed and wagged his index finger that he had used for a pistol. A cruel set came to his lips and a naked hunger in his eyes burned into her. While he voiced no words, she heard his thoughts as if he roared them. His fingers threaded into her hair, and then his knuckles brushed warmly over her cheek, her bare shoulder. "We have some catching up to do *wife*." He lay with his full weight upon her. His hand slid down her taut stomach to the swell of her hip and

206

then back up again to outline the circle of her full breast. He kissed her, forcing her to endure his punishing kiss.

It had been so long...she curled into the curve of his body, and a hard rise protruded from his wool pants, rough against her skin. The mere touch of his hand sent hot, wild shivers running through her, and she moaned aloud, aware of the heavy pounding of his heart, and her own throbbing a frantic new rhythm.

"No." Catherine squirmed beneath him. "You were freed, back to your beloved homeland to preserve your insidious war. You have magnified me a hundred times over to be a villain. Have you no regard for the truth?"

"Your paramour, Mallory, had his thugs bound and beat me, then ordered to finish me off. The hangman was cheated, the Union Army thwarted, and for the time being, the Grim Reaper frustrated. You have made life a challenge, and I have met it, and now, we have come full circle. Don't for one second, deny your deceit."

"You are a fool!" Catherine hissed, and then gasped in alarmed surprise as his arm coiled around her like a striking snake, hauling her up against his chest.

"Don't ever," he said, enunciating in an awful voice, "use that tone on me again. For weeks I have served up the tantalizing prospect of having you beneath me. Can you begin to understand what can make a man fight and win, to keep his mind off blistered feet and burning muscles and torrid sun? Dreaming of champagne, of wide beds and soft white sheets, of a woman who betrayed me and who I will use at will to be at my beck and call for my every need when it arises. But now is not the time."

He jerked her to her feet. "Get dressed!" he rasped.

They met MacDougal and Brigid in the hallway. Catherine expected to find an outraged Brigid. She looked twice. Her maid stood starry-eyed, hauled up underneath the tall Scotsman's arm in an embrace.

Catherine pulled her reluctant maid aside. "Brigid, you've been kidnapped, forced against your will into a brothel and—" Catherine hesitated looking up at the formidable Rebel who she dared not offend, "—if I recall, you've had less than an inclination for a particular nationality."

"He's so romantic."

"Romantic." Catherine blurted. "He didn't take any liberties, did he?"

"Ian's a perfect gentleman. If only my dear departed mother told me the Scots could kiss so well," Brigid sighed.

"Ian?" Catherine repeated. "You're on a first name basis?"

Ian pulled Brigid back to his side, and John prodded Catherine ahead. Turning her head, Catherine witnessed the unadulterated dreamy looks her maid and Ian cast each other. Unbelievable.

Betty led them down a back stairway to the outside. "The Yanks are still here. My girls will keep them busy. Ride due west. My sources say it's your only avenue of escape." She kissed John good-bye. "Until I see you again."

To Catherine, she said, "You are a lucky woman."

Chapter 18

*I*f the moon did come out, it would be shrouded by clouds. The smell of moss and rotting leaves floated up from the earth. There was no breeze, just a hot humid night awaiting the release of an impending storm. The air was electric. Catherine looked behind her at John. In the minimum light, his face appeared marble with no show of fear.

He stopped to double-check his compass and waited for Ian to bring his horse abreast. "With numerous miles and three hours before dawn, I want to put distance between us and Washington. Crossing lines will be tricky. Our surroundings have changed from a point on a map to a battlefield. My above average hope is to stay away from the tight formations of Union companies and not run into a stray company. Staying on the fringes and hoping to fall into General Jubal Early's columns is the best we can pray for."

"Let's hope panic shooting pickets don't wedge bullets in our sides," Ian warned and Brigid wailed. "Don't worry, darling, I'll protect you with my life." The big Scot comforted her.

Darling? Catherine worried about her maid. But the fearsome adjutant looked like a man who could take care of himself. John wouldn't have picked a henwit for such a risky mission. No, he would pick someone like himself, dangerous and deadly.

John spurred his horse. He was a matchless rider, running at a full gallop across the fields to the south, gliding over fences in effortless motion, every bone, muscle and tendon of horse and rider working in spectacular, perfect symmetry. Did he see in the dark?

Sounds from nearby units filtered through the forest and a surge of quick time marching streamed to the west. In the road parallel to them, cassions of horses, pulling cannons galloped by and disappeared ahead of them.

The pace was quicker. With his gloved hand John stroked her hair as if assuring him that she was there. He drew her hood over her head shielding her from the briars that might snap across her face. The gestures were telling. *He did care.*

They raced through the thicket and woodlands, the horse jumping over fallen logs. *Were they alone in the woods?* Her head jerked up, the steady drumbeat of hooves galloping through the soft earth, slashing through brush, and crumpling thickets. John too, heard, and she started to ask, but he waved his hand, silencing her. A shot cracked off to the right and John's head snapped toward it.

Were they discovered?

A deer dodged through the bush ahead of them. John and Ian froze. Yankee pickets moved east of them. The hairs stood up on her arms.

"If you dare make a sound——" he whispered in her ear, his contempt, a deep warning.

Catherine could reach out and touch them through the bushes, even count the hairs in a man's whiskers. They were that close.

On foot it would be a shoot-out, then hand to hand fighting. To be pierced by a bayonet?

As quickly as the Yankee pickets sidled past them, they were gone. Waiting for them to pass over the ridge, John moved again, melting into the darkness. He switched direction bearing harder into the brush, bending saplings and sidestepping trees, punishing his horse. The animal's flanks lathered from the double load. At the edge of a clearing, they paused for Ian to catch up. Brigid draped lifeless in his arms.

"What did you do to my maid?"

The adjutant shrugged. "She fainted at the first sound of a bullet."

"Impossible. Brigid would stand firm in front of a charging bull."

"Quiet." John breathed, listening, and then peeling his Union top coat off, he stripped to his butternut and doffed his Rebel hat. Ian did the same. No doubt, getting caught wearing Union garb guaranteed a hanging or invited a bullet from Rebel pickets. Both horses were prodded over an open field. Bullets exploded around them. Union infantry from the road had discovered them. John spurred his horse, urging his mount to get out of range of rifle fire.

"This way." he shouted, heading deep into the cover of the woods ahead of them.

Catherine held her breath. No way could they keep up this pace through the woods. The horse followed an erratic path and at once sloshed through a creek bed, water soaking her skirts. All the fear eating her pushed outward. She was on fire. Every sound exploded in her ears. Every sight burned into her mind as if it were her last.

The horse carried itself low to the ground, out of sight. Like an invisible phantom of the night, its strong wide hooves secured confident footfalls, dodging branches, leaping ravines, and fallen logs. More shots. Too fast. Gunpowder spiraled in the air. Her teeth clamped down on her knuckles to block her scream. John and Ian fired off a few shots and picked a new direction.

"Hell, General, we're flanked on both sides. These woods are crawling with Yanks. What do we do?" John scanned the night. "General Early must be in retreat. Plow straight ahead."

Her hands shook. "You'll get us all killed."

John checked his compass again.

Mary Mother of God! With all this zigzagging, he has us lost! Another bullet whizzed right by her ear before slamming into the trunk of a tree beside them. *The fool!*

Another round came, and another en masse, emanating from the mysterious darkness. They flew until a single roll of crackle gave way to a solid roll of shot. John crushed her belly-low over the horse, to make as small a target as possible. Bullets whizzed by, miraculously missing. At any moment their mount would be shot from beneath them breaking both their necks. It just wasn't pickets anymore. Branches flew off the trees as spent bullets kicked-up the leaves.

She was in the arms of a madman! God save her! As quickly as the volley started, it ceased, as if the Yankee leaders decided it was a waste of ammunition on such small quarry. Their respite was momentary. Yank Calvary shouted from far atop an opposing hill on sighting them. John kneed the horse across a small clearing, heading east, and then when obscured from view, veered west, plunging into another endless forest. They came upon several mounted Rebels.

"You're late, General."

"Better late than never," he said and dismounted, dragging Catherine off the saddle. Her legs buckled. Hours in the saddle had numbed her legs. She fell into John. He held her up. If the men were surprised they said nothing, seeing nothing unusual of their general with a woman.

"There's Union Calvary in hot pursuit." John drawled, matter of fact, as if they were taking a Sunday stroll around the block. "I believe we confused them for the time being, and without a doubt, take great pleasure if we lost them, but be sure they haven't forgotten us."

To Catherine's great agitation, the men showed no alarm, treating the occasion as mundane as the rain that was beginning to fall on their heads. All the fears culminating over the last few hours exploded.

"Are you insane?" she spat.

"Keep silent," he ordered, "Or you'll get us all killed by Yankee bullets."

No way was he going to tolerate her insubordination in front of his men and no way was she going to keep silent. His command unleashed all the fury she had stored up. "It will be a Yankee bullet and from my gun, General. You have kidnapped me against my will, dangled me out a three-story window, thrust me into an unspeakable establishment and have ridden me through the bowels of hell. Do you realize all night I have prayed to the higher angels to let me live, so I could murder you myself?"

"I'm warning you—"

"I'm through with your warnings and bullying. When I get done, you'll be nothing but a social curiosity for the hawkers of Barnum and Bailey."

"Catherine."

She jabbed a finger in his chest. "You, Sir are a lunatic, thoroughly wise, in your ability to direct a universe of madness."

The mounted Rebs snickered. It was the first time, the Rebels showed even hint of any emotion and she turned on them. "How dare you think it's funny. Why I'll take a horsewhip—"

Before she knew it, she had his gloved hand clamped on her mouth.

"General Rourke, you're sure going to have fun with that Yankee spitfire."

"Before you boys get any wrong ideas, this Yankee spitfire happens to be my wife and deserves all the respect that position accords her," John snapped.

"Yes, Sir! No offense, Sir." They saluted and sat bolt upright in their saddles. "Our apologies, ma'am. We had no idea." Not in the least did they desire the full wrath of General Rourke on their hands.

A cavalryman rode forward, a new arrival, an officer, and one who John seemed to recognize.

"Colonel, didn't know you were in the neighborhood." John addressed him while the other swept his feathered plumed slouch hat into a broad graceful arc before returning it to his head.

"Did I hear something about a wife?" The Colonel edged his mount closer.

Catherine bit John's hand then kicked him hard in his shin, gaining her freedom and a curse from the general.

She ran to the Colonel, clinging to his leg for dear life and pointed to John. "Please, Colonel. If you have any honor, please get me away from this lunatic."

The Colonel stroked his chin thoughtfully. "I have to agree with you. He impresses me as a lunatic at times. In fact, he thrives on it. It's his sworn commandment: Thou shalt at all times be a lunatic."

Catherine had the distinct feeling, the Colonel was just warming up and ignored the dark looks John cast her way.

"Why I've heard he's a veritable legend in lunacy, the absolute envy of every crazy man on earth. But it's his fine practice at lunacy that gives him his name." He leaned low, confiding in her. "Absolutely scorns any kind of deliberate sanity. Howls at a full moon, bites the dog before it bites him, and becomes thunderstruck with the notion of running naked on a storm-drenched night. Another peculiarity is—"

"Colonel." John cut him off.

The Colonel could not be dissuaded from his reflections. "Now he is kidnapping women. That certainly is a thoughtful revelation." The Colonel paused, more for dramatic effect. "What is most awe-inspiring about the general is his absolute humility on the subject. But it should come as no surprise."

"So you agree to help me." She was so happy she could wrap her arms around him.

"In all my years of knowing General Rourke, I have never known anyone who has challenged him so, *Mrs. Rourke*." He choked. "To help you would be difficult."

"But why?" She would not give up. She could charm the colonel.

"You are one of the most beautiful women I have ever seen, and I'm hard put not to be enchanted by you…"

Catherine turned her nose up at John's murderous expression. The colonel was melting and he was making John jealous. Of course, he'd help her.

"I've been to war too long." The colonel gave his head a shake. "I cannot help you, because, I have the deepest admiration and affection for General Rourke's…lunacy. You see, he is my brother."

Catherine glanced from John to the colonel. Same build, same tone of voice, and she surmised, the same colored hair and eyes. With a small cry, she let go of his leg.

He saluted her and chuckled from her horrified discovery. "Colonel Ryan Rourke, Confederate States of America at your service. It's an honor making your acquaintance…*Mrs. Rourke.*"

"Madness must run in the family," she said and stood back from him, crossing her arms in front of her chest, glaring at both of them. He had been joking, and she had made a complete fool of herself. "The Rourke family must populate the whole planet. It's my penance to meet every one of them."

"Not every one of us. Outside of us four boys, you'll love my father and dear sweet mother. They are the exception," Ryan offered.

"They have my pity." Catherine said, the spirited tone of his voice incensing her more.

"My belated congratulations, General Rourke." Ryan regarded his brother with amusement. "You've courted trouble all your life, now I see you're married to it. I wish you a full and happy life together. That's if you don't kill each other first."

John sighed. "It's a long story——"

"And a tale I'll be most interested in hearing, but for now my scouts have indicated a whole Yank Cavalry breathing down our necks. Teddy here——" He jerked his head to a soldier. "——can see easily to your needs. Since your horses are tired, leave them here to graze. I'll make sure they're returned to your camp. We'll offer the Yanks a merry chase away from you."

John saluted all the mounted men. "It's good to see you, Ryan. And thanks."

"No trouble at all." He chuckled and tipped his hat to Catherine. "A pleasure, *Mrs. Rourke.* Until we meet again."

Ryan wheeled his horse around and with a gauntleted hand raised up, shouted, "Head out boys." They disappeared out of the woods and into the meadow where Catherine listened to the most ungodly, hellish screaming she had ever heard that rattled the nerves up her spine. "What in the world was that?"

"That, my dear wife, is the Rebel yell."

"Lead the way, Teddy." John ordered.

Glancing back, she glimpsed the big Goliath cradling her maid as if holding a fine china doll. It was an odd picture…a giant who could scare the hounds of Hell, and then, so solicitous over Brigid.

"We'll have to move with speed, Sir," Teddy warned. "Yankee infantry are moving in and out. I couldn't really tell if the pickets are forward or farther back."

"Lead on, Teddy." She commanded, daring to outstrip her husband, and earning a shove forward. They travelled on an old trapper's trail running counterpart to a small stream.

After roaming a distance of two miles in the rain and not coming into company with any Union soldiers, the adjutant spoke. "We were a mule's kick from them Yanks, General. You know Bobby Lee wouldn't be pleased to lose you."

Catherine fell. Her skirts were soaked and tangled around her legs. John pulled her along. Bullets popped in the distance, lending credence that the lines were behind them. Teddy led them to the safety of Rebel pickets. Given fresh mounts they continued on their journey down the Shenandoah and soon the cold rain stopped. She sniffed then wiped at her nose. The first few stripes of dawn scattered a prismatic display of coral then daffodil yellow rays over the breast of the mountains, chasing away the dark sapphire blue of the night.

Ian's horse had taken a stone in its shoe, so he begged leave at a neighboring farmhouse for repairs, promising to meet Rourke back at camp. It was the last Catherine saw of Brigid, clamped to Ian's chest.

John's silence jarred her. The iron door had swung shut, heaving its hush. Catherine had a boiler full of turmoil inside her. She would have the last word. "Allow me to congratulate you."

John tapped his heels into his horse. The gesture banished conversation.

"So your ears do work, General. That's good news. I suppose a leader of your rank should possess all his faculties before age, stupidity, and outright stubbornness erase them."

Catherine whipped the dampness from her skirts. "Astounding isn't it, how the male mind works. It can move, it can shoot, it can kill and destroy, but it can't seem to speak—"

John said nothing, and Catherine hastened her horse to a faster canter, coming up beside him. "There's an easy explanation for that, isn't there, John. Your conversation is like looking at the wrong end of the kaleidoscope where everything's a jumble. You try to form a simple sentence and like it, you consciously store it away in your mental chamber, and brick by brick you are mystified. And likely enough with the structure up and running, you feel complimented. Now see how easy it is to be a general." She snapped her reins on the horse and trotted in front of him.

Chapter 19

They passed the sentries, riding as the day receded and into a deep valley. She smelled the smoke of campfires first, before she saw the rutilant light. Hundreds of white tents were pitched in long rows. Soldiers conversed, sitting around campfires. A Rebel camp.

"We're home," John said.

After numerous hours in the saddle at a murderous pace and with no rest, her muscles screamed with the pain of dismounting. She would have collapsed except that Rourke caught her, holding her until the circulation reached into her legs, and then moved away.

"Thank you." She swallowed a lump that lingered in her throat. What little fight Catherine had left took flight. Living in a nightmare of gigantic proportions and trying to escape was useless. From Mallory to John…had she traded one madman for another? What new misery awaited her?

A man with a beaked nose and, close set eyes stepped forward with a slow smile. "We were worried about you, General. Any word on General Early?" He took off his dusty hat and smacked his knee with it.

"Mission accomplished, Corporal Austin." John said and then turned his attention to an elderly Rebel, his face wrinkled from the sun. "Any problems in my absence, Lieutenant Johnson?"

"None Sir. Kept a keen eye out. So far, all's been quiet in the Valley.

"Glad to hear it. The boys need a rest. I'm proceeding onto General Lee to report."

"Lee?" Catherine cried, weary of any imminent argument. "I can't ride any farther, and I can't stay here with these——" Several ragtag soldiers peered from their campfires.

"Rebels." John lifted a brow, his tone full of contempt. "These are my men. The Army of Northern Virginia's finest."

"But——" She trembled not able to find words. *He was leaving her?*

John reached her in two easy strides and yanked her away from earshot of his men. "There's a war going on in case you've forgotten. Do not think of trying to escape. With certainty you will risk the treatment of a camp follower plying her avocation. It's your choice."

He dropped her arm as though to touch her disgusted him. Mounting a fresh horse, he waved his hand to his men. "This is *Mrs. Rourke*," he drawled. Barely sparing her a disinterested glance, he spurred his horse and rode off.

Catherine stood motionless, the campfires creating eerie apparitions of the soldier's faces. They stared with such intensity. Would they teeter head over heels?

Alone, isolated and very frightened, she raised a shaky hand, to smooth her tangled hair. What a mess she must seem, smelling like horse and sweat. Looking up at the starlit night, thinking about her unknown fate at the hands of these men, tears formed in her eyes. Exhausted, overwhelmed, and miserable, she despaired having to endure yet another trial. Like a public oddity and feeling a thousand eyes on her, she glanced at the Rebels with their long black beards, gaunt faces and dark eyes.

A lamb in front of a pack of wolves? Rubbing her hands up and down her arms, her teeth chattered. She waited for someone to do or say anything. Her throat squeezed so tight, she coughed.

En mass, the Rebels jumped from the campfire and surrounded her. She jerked back. All she had meant to do was clear her throat. *Were they going to kill her for a simple cough?*

A soldier draped his ragged coat over her shoulders. "So you won't catch a chill."

Another thrust a cup of coffee into her hands. "To warm your innards."

And yet another escorted to a stool and seated her by the fire. "To keep you warm, Mrs. Rourke."

The mob was so genteel and labored so hard to give her every pleasure they had to offer, that she smothered a laugh from her initial fright. Never had she been wrapped in such demonstrative affection or warm-heartedness. Zillions of questions were thrown out, their curiosity getting the better of their gentlemanly manners.

"You really the general's wife?"

"When you get married?"

"How come we didn't get invited to the wedding?"

She didn't tell them it was a forced ceremony, an irate priest condemning her and the general for an adult sin. No, she dared not tread that subject.

"It was of a sudden," she squeaked.

"Love at first sight," nodded a soldier with a burnished Alabama voice. "I knew the general would be that way boys. Quick and fast like lightning he always is."

"Ain't she the prettiest picture my eyes have ever beheld?"

One man rose to touch her hair as if it weren't real. "Pardon me miss. I've never seen hair so golden. I thought I died and went to heaven."

"Please tell us about yourself."

Where did she begin and how much did she tell? Of course, a modified honest approach was the best. She bit her lip, glancing at the sea of faces with more men arriving from other campfires. "I'm from New York. New York City to be exact." She hesitated gauging how that would sit. She could cut the silence with a knife.

"A Yank?"

"Will you hold it against me?" Her voice drifted in a hushed, pathetic whisper.

"Nope, not if the general don't," the men chorused. "You're all right by us."

She stretched her fingers by the fire to warm them. The general's wife was big news.

"Are all the women up north as pretty as you?" asked a young soldier who still looked hardly more than a boy. His hair all curls, like a French prince, he swept off his hat and held it to his chest, the feather plume frilling in the air.

"There are many pretty women in the north." She admitted, amused that these fearsome Rebel warriors had such an interest in Yankee women. "There are also women who are good teachers, artists, mothers, nurses and more. I am sure the South has many such ladies."

A soldier with heavy lidded eyes and a lock of hair combed unevenly over his head spoke next. "We apologize for our rough condition."

"It all goes with rank ma'am," said a black haired soldier with the most guileless face she had ever seen. "A general has one hole through his pants, a captain two and a private has many holes in his britches."

A warm glow flowed through her. Their hems were frayed, butternut uniforms tattered with shiny bottoms, very unlike their Union counterparts with new woven navy uniforms. Yet they held elegance, grace, and kind-heartedness, and she could not help but feel an immediate peace and admiration in their company. "I find all of you quite dashing and wonderful. Most of all, I feel honored to meet every one of you."

Some stroked their beards others nodded their heads pleased with her words of acceptance. Tree limbs snapped and drew her attention.

"What are you doing, Danny Boy?" One of the soldiers yelled to a boy near the trees.

"I'm bending saplings, weaving them together to use as a defensive barrier. I want to see how it works. I read that's what the Gauls did to ward off the Roman Cavalry."

"I don't think we have to worry about any Roman Cavalry."

This brought a round of guffaws. The boy blushed apple-red.

A Rebel with a rather jaundiced, ill-favored face by the Lord's creation, stepped into the center of the ring, his thumbs hooked under his suspenders. Catherine's head creaked backward at the Paul Bunyan-sized man. "I want to announce that a letter from home has confirmed Miss Nancy Ann has agreed to marry me."

"You mean you're engaged to be married?" Danny Boy asked. He was no more incredulous than the other men were.

The enormous Rebel picked Danny Boy up, held him eye to eye. "You find that circumstance extraordinary, perhaps?"

"I-I find—it cause to give you congratulations."

"Good." The giant dropped him in the dust and walked off.

Lieutenant Johnson laughed. "Danny Boy, your tact surpasses your truthfulness."

Another young Rebel, nicknamed Gus, with a peach-fuzz face and soft lingering drawl of a Mississippian, volunteered an anecdote. He clapped his hand on the back of the soldier sitting beside him. "Eustace here, his heroic deeds are mind-boggling. Saved a cat from a whole Yank company firing down on him because he didn't want the cat to get hurt. Isn't that amazing—"

Eustace bolted from the ground and grabbed the younger man's jacket. "Listen boy, I've shot men in the belly and had their lunch on my shoes. So don't think I'd blink before I'd put any of you six feet under." He dropped the boy and ran for the woods, leaving all the men guffawing.

"Saved by the quick-step. Don't use the poison ivy leaves!" yelled Gus, sending another round of laughter through the ranks.

Lieutenant Johnson bowed and shared a confidence. "Eustace is surly. His missus died with his stillborn son and poor Eustace hasn't been the same since. The boys try to get him out of his stupor."

Catherine stared, tongue-tied from the tragic circumstances surrounding Eustace's life, and the odd but gentle concern shared by his companions.

"Mrs. Rourke you sure are a lucky woman to be married to one of the finest generals of the Confederate Army. I have to say, no general can attest to be a general unless he has won his spurs. General Rourke possesses the requisite spirit and boldness to seize the various chances for victory that are offered him. He is a brilliant commander, your husband."

"And brave too," said a soldier with ruddy brown skin, dark-brown eyes and the bearing of a loyal mastiff. "I was injured real bad. He carried me three miles, one night, through artillery and musket fire. Saved my life. Yes, he did."

"He's like an oak tree, stubborn and strong, can't tear him up by the roots. I guarantee any hurricane that goes by will not bend him one bit. Trust him with my life, I do…as do all the men here," Lieutenant Johnson said.

There were several soft murmurings in agreement. Their deep respect and fervent loyalty astounded her. In full measure, General Rourke was loved and venerated by his men.

"Mrs. Rourke?" A tall rawboned man with his brogans tied and slung over his shoulders bowed his head. "Do you by any chance write?"

Catherine blinked. "Why yes."

"Do you think you'd be willin' to write a letter to my wife? My son died at Cold Harbor and she…still doesn't know."

"Of course. I would be happy to help you with your correspondence." Catherine was appalled they had no one to write news to their loved ones.

The lanky man thrust a pencil and paper into her hands. "You know there were ninety of us from our town in Alabama. I'm the only survivor. One woman lost her husband and six sons. So I'm not too bad off. Others have suffered more."

Catherine could hardly write. She wanted to scream at the world for its madness. She wanted to break down and cry. Instead she asked him his name and the name of his wife and composed the most beautiful letter she had ever written. It was a wonderful testimonial to the heroic deeds of their son. His wife would have comfort that her only child had not died in vain. The father, Charley, asked her to read it aloud before he sealed it in an envelope. There was not a dry eye in the whole camp.

More men asked her to write letters, but Lieutenant Johnson intervened, and Catherine was thankful. "Mrs. Rourke needs rest after her long journey. I'm sure she'll be happy to do your correspondence tomorrow." He then escorted her to the general's tent. "Thank you, Ma'am. The general has married himself a fine woman."

Catherine woke to a deep modulated drawl of a man's voice.

"Mrs. Rourke? Are you all right?"

Through half-opened eyes, she peered up at sun-washed canvas, dappled with the shadows of fluttering leaves. She struggled to get a bearing on her surroundings.

She was in a Rebel camp.

She was in her husband's tent.

"Mrs. Rourke? It's Lieutenant Johnson. It's midday. I thought you'd like a bath and something to eat."

Her eyes burned. Her body was engulfed in tides of weariness and tenderness. Sitting up, her blood rose. A vivid recollection of the past few day's events came to fore and she grimaced. She had fallen asleep in her muddy cape. "I never sleep this late."

"A bath? Food?" Catherine flew to the door and threw open the flap, the bright light of day blinded her. Lieutenant Johnson had procured several buckets of steaming water and a copper tub. "You are the dearest, sweetest man in the world. Please bring it in right away."

Lieutenant Johnson did as she requested, lifting in the tub and emptying the buckets of water. Joy bubbled in her laugh at the contemplation of a hot bath. It was impossible not to return Lieutenant Johnson's broad smile as he deposited a plate of biscuits and a cup of coffee on the table.

"Do you have any idea when the general will return?"

"No ma'am."

"I see." She scraped the mud off her collar. Of course, John departed with no word of his comings and goings. "Has his adjutant, Ian McDougal, arrived with a woman by the name of Brigid?"

"Yes ma'am. She's restin' in the adjutant's bed."

"The adjutant's bed?"

Lieutenant Johnson threw up his palms. "No ma'am. I mean, yes ma'am. She's waiting for you to come and visit." He laid out a cake of soap and a towel, high-tailing it out of the tent before she could ask any more questions.

She shook her head, mystified with that revelation then stripped out of her clothes and stepped into the copper tub, sighing. She washed away the dirt, grime, and filth, allowing the warmth of the water to ease the soreness of her muscles. Sounds and conversations drifted from the camp around her. As a well-bred young lady, she had been kept from more common conversation, especially discussion that carried a forbidden nature. Like a recalcitrant schoolgirl, she eavesdropped.

"Come on, show us your sweetheart's picture, Billy," someone coaxed.

She heard the clink of tin cups. The reluctant Billy must have handed the picture over for the assessment of the men.

"Why she's so homely, her face would stop a plow pulled by ten mules."

"She is not," a younger, high angered treble voice warned the man who dared to make fun of his sweetheart. "I challenge you to a duel."

"Forget the duel, Billy, and don't get all wet in your drawers. We have enough dueling to do with the Yanks. Besides, I might introduce you to a real woman in Richmond. Her name's Hopping Hetty. That's if you can find your pecker."

This was answered by a round of guffaws as Billy, now quiet, apparently contemplated the prospect of meeting Hopping Hetty. Catherine dropped the sponge. Was John as familiar with Hopping Hetty as he was with Bouncing Betty?

"You have Satan's own tongue," harped a soldier with a loud stentorian voice. "May the Lord destroy all poisonous lips, and the tongue that speaketh evil things."

"Save yourself, you old reprobate. You'll preach salvation to anyone who'll listen or to anyone who won't. And if you think I'll go into that little hot box of a church back home to listen to

Reverend Potts screech, you can forget it. God's not going to be stayin' inside on such a nice sunny day. No siree. You'll be finding God down by the river, and I'll be keeping him company, hooking catfish."

Catherine sank below the waterline, the water sloshing out of the tub. She smiled from the Rebel's logic. How often had she felt God pouring down his rays of sun upon her gardens?

"Tell me more about Hopping Hetty."

Billy wasn't going to let it go.

"You got more questions than a bride on her wedding night," answered the voice who had offered Hetty's services. By the way he ground down hard on his R's, Catherine guessed he was from Maryland.

"The words of the Lord are pure words—as silver tried by the fire, purging evil from the earth. Woe to those caught by the wickedness and snares of the devil," said the Bible thumper.

"You should join a monastery."

"It's the sin. I couldn't live with it," confessed the Bible thumper.

"And I couldn't live without it."

Catherine brought her hand up to stifle her giggles, amused by their gentle camaraderie and subtle wit.

"Harold, let it up." A soldier called after him. "He never got religion until he got shot in the Bible. He had it posted inside his shirt, when *bang*, a shot knocked him to the ground. He thought for sure he was dead. Showed me where the bullet stopped on the twenty-third psalm." The men mumbled their understanding.

The conversation drifted from the ludicrous to the even more absurd. To keep up with the range of topics grew impossible. If her mother were alive, she'd be mortified. Yet Catherine thought all their accents and language so beautiful. Their rhythms, their cadences, and their charming communications came through, endearing them all to her.

Between rinsing her hair and worrying about her clothing, Catherine took stock of her cape, dress and remaining undergarments tossed over the chair. Her dress, torn from brambles was beyond repair and the heat from the relentless Virginian sun would make it impossible to continue wearing her mud-caked cape. *What was she to do?*

Her gaze roamed the interior of John's tent. A desk with an inkbottle and pen, next to that, a crate of rolled parchments, crates of books, a lantern, a canteen and a mirror hanging from a center pole. Guns with cartridge boxes were placed alongside a washstand that contained a shaving brush, razor and strop. Everything arranged neat and in impeccable order with all soldierly accompaniments, masculine and reflective of the general.

A couple of trunks lay at the end of the bed. Catherine leaped from the tub, wrapping a towel around her. Like a woman possessed, she threw open the trunk, rifling through the contents. To her delight, she found a brush and—women's clothing? *John kept a woman?*

She slammed the lid. Of course, someone with his rank and looks would attract women, all kinds of women. No doubt the South was littered with his paramours, from Bouncing Betty to Hopping Hetty.

She read the engraving on a small brass plate on the trunk and frowned, Union issue. *Property of Colonel William E. Briggs, Western*

New York Artillery. The same brass plate was nailed to the footboard of John's. Her husband was a thief! She plunked her hands on her hips. *What was worse, a libertine or a thief!*

Catherine knew of Colonel Briggs and the fact that he traveled with his gracious wife. Throwing open the trunk, she sorted through a variety of ladies clothing items. Not as elegant as her own wardrobe, yet she approved of Mrs. Brigg's taste. She held up a blue cotton day dress, sizing it, her mouth curving into an unconscious smile, pleased Colonel Brigg's wife was the same size. The unfortunate loss for the Colonel's wife became a windfall for Catherine.

After brushing out her hair and drying it, Catherine donned the pale blue gown. It was a little tight in the bosom. She would have to make do. Had her uncle been freed from Mallory's thugs? How she worried about him. If only John had not kidnapped her. What was she to do? *Escape.* The mantra roamed through her head. Could she gain the trust of John's men and escape?

Lieutenant Johnson appeared outside her tent again. "I thought you'd like to go for a walk, Mrs. Rourke. I would provide escort."

Checking her image in the mirror, Catherine beamed and an expression of satisfaction shown in her eyes. Straightening herself with dignity, Catherine threw open the tent flaps and stepped outside. "I would be honored, Lieutenant Johnson," Catherine began and then noticed the look of utter astonishment upon his face.

Is there a problem, Lieutenant?" she asked feigning surprised innocence, yet enjoying her new objectivity.

"Yes ma'am. I mean no ma'am. I apologize, ma'am." The lieutenant fought for words. "It's just that——" He rubbed his jaw with his thumb and forefinger, looking worriedly about the camp and muttered something she barely caught.

"*General Rourke did not enlist eunuchs.*"

Chapter 20

*J*ohn saluted Major Hodge. "Request permission to see General Lee."

Covered with dust and exhausted from his hard ride, John stood at attention. General Lee moved through his camp like Moses through the Israelites, everyone parting, and then stopped in front of his headquarters where General Benson, General Longstreet, and several other officers gathered. Lee paused as his aide de camp apprised him of General Rourke's arrival.

General Lee pivoted, his clear blue eyes, glacial now, focused on John and bowed his head with the barest of acknowledgement.

Taken aback as to what merited his commander's ire, John stepped forward, saluted, and made customary salutations to the other officers.

Always formal and without expression, General Lee broached the discussion first. "General Rourke, there are rumors, strong rumors surrounding your exploits in Washington—kidnapping the heir to the Fitzgerald Rifle Works? To lose a general on such a foolish escapade?" Lee's cool blue eyes bored into him. General Lee never shouted. His words spoken with terseness defined his greater anger.

"It is a very long story. I can explain, Sir."

Lee raised his eyes. "You have a lot of explaining to do, General Rourke, but you will remain silent until I'm finished. Kidnapping a woman, and one I might add betrothed to another man is unchivalrous, if not uncharacteristic. That is not what the Army of Northern Virginia is about. I gave express orders for General Early to invade Washington. I don't recall ordering you to do the same."

Normally grim and grave, General Longstreet lounged back in his chair behind General Lee and, smiling, Longstreet said, "What are we to do with him?"

No doubt, the general itched to heap coals on the fire.

General Lee turned his gaze on Longstreet who lost his smile and cast his countenance into a proper serious frown.

Leaning against a tent pole and leisurely smoothing his mustache, General Benson spoke. "This is a most serious situation, with most serious consequences. I am sure kidnapping a betrothed woman is a grievous offense," he said, fanning the flames, to make John sweat.

John glared at him. Benson and he had been close friends at West Point and had grown up in the same county. Both had gotten into competitive skirmishes during their boyhood days as well as during their military schooling. John could beat Benson with one hand tied behind his back.

"Foolish. Very foolish." Lee shook his head. "What kind of leadership example is this for your men?"

General Longstreet leaned his stool back on two legs, reviewing the matter. "I don't think this has happened since the uncivilized, barbaric Romans fell upon the Sabine women," he commented with rare humorous glee.

"What is the world coming to?" Benson added, not to be outdone by General Longstreet.

"A most hurtful embarrassment to the Confederacy," conceded Longstreet.

"What other death defying missions can we send General Rourke on? Another ride into Washington to steal Lincoln's dog?" Benson could not contain his mirth. John glowered down on him.

"Enough of this," Lee said. "General, if I didn't have such a shortage of leaders...and good leaders...I'd court-martial you here and now. But I can spare no one. Pray tell me, General Rourke, how you happened upon this activity."

Finally able to speak, John exhaled. "Miss Fitzgerald is my wife."

"Your wife!" All three generals echoed.

Benson gaped. Longstreet dropped his chair on all fours. Lee gazed at him, his astonishment genuine.

He had a lot of explaining to do.

"The Northern papers contend that she was engaged to Francis Mallory," Lee apprised him. "I assume you were married just last night."

"Not quite Sir. A little earlier than that."

"I find it hard to believe you were married while on horseback running between lines."

"Earlier than that, Sir. A couple of months ago."

"This is interesting." Longstreet stroked his beard.

"I left out a small detail, Sir, when I told you about the Yankee woman who rescued me."

"Apparently so. Go on, General Rourke——"

A tense silence loomed between them. John stroked his throat with what he must divulge. "I was…we were…caught in her bedroom. Everything was circumspect, Sir. It was…" Glancing at Benson's hilarious countenance, the muscles of his forearms hardened beneath his sleeves. There was no need to go into further detail. He made a mess of it.

"It was what, General?" Lee frowned, waiting.

"A shotgun wedding to the South's most notorious bachelor!" Benson hooted.

"Is this true?" Lee exhibited greater concern.

Under Lee's scrutiny, John sweated tenfold. He sounded like some greenhorn sapling.

"Yes, Sir. Her uncle, a priest, was present——" he cleared his throat, "——and the wedding took place immediately."

"Did the priest use a Fitzgerald repeater rifle to consecrate the vows?" Longstreet chortled, which drew stares from across the camp.

"She must have fallen head over heels for you because she picked up another fiancé right away." Benson slapped his knee, but stopped short when Lee's smoldering gaze fell on him.

A vein pulsed in John's neck. He kept a lid on his temper, mindful to push through his paper-thin veneer of respectability. "There is more to the story, General Lee, but I don't think I need to bore you with all the facts," John said, desiring to wring the facts out of Catherine's neck.

"It's been interesting," said Lee.

"If not entertaining," agreed Longstreet.

"Do continue," begged General Benson, humor still plastered on his face. "It is not often we have such compelling or engaging tales to share."

"My wife is most probably quite frightened by the ordeal. I beg to leave and get back to her and my men, Sir," John said.

"You may, General Rourke." General Lee tipped his head.

But Benson gloried like a kid with an early Christmas present, refusing to give it up. "Here's a man with all the female hearts in the South aflutter...made a vow to stay away from the state of matrimony, likening it to a mountain lion. What was it you said, General? You stay away unless you want to get scratched."

"I assume——" Lee interrupted, "——if I question Mrs. Rourke, I will find her most agreeable to this arrangement?"

"Yes," John said, though he had no idea what type of temper she would be in upon his return.

"Very well. Dismissed."

"Thank you, Sir." John saluted and mounted his horse.

"One last thing." Lee looked up to him. "I assume she can be trusted."

"Absolutely Sir." He spurred his horse forward, worried what he'd discover in his absence, and then wheeled his horse around, returning to the communication tent next to headquarters. He had forgotten his dispatches.

"Now look at that," John overheard Benson comment. "See how General Rourke spurred his horse to get out of here."

"What is your point?" Lee drawled, his vexation with General Benson evident.

"For the first time, I saw a stripe of fear run down General Rourke's face as if he'd get back to his camp and find his wife collecting another fiancé." Benson guffawed.

Longstreet chuckled.

"General Benson," Lee said. "Your conversation thus far has a curious sound in my ear. To believe that such talk ever comes out of a person's mouth was a time when time was of no value to a person. Your talk wanders all around and arrives at nowhere and thus far, has consisted only of irrelevancy."

Chastised, and seeing John's warning glare, Benson wisely displayed the relevancy of a remorseful countenance.

Lee's tone was as critical as it was to praise. "General Rourke is an outstanding general, one of the best, as is present company included. Gentlemen, we should retire for we know not what tomorrow brings."

Chapter 21

*C*atherine moved to Lieutenant Johnson's side. "I have made it my personal mission to meet every man in my husband's camp."

"That's impossible. There are over four thousand men in this camp."

"My mother always said there is always a good outcome in meeting new people and enlarging our circle of friends even though we might not have matching viewpoints regarding the war. Besides, some of the men may need my help." Catherine frowned when he stopped to make sure all six chambers of his Colt revolver were filled with fresh balls, gunpowder and with percussion caps in place. "Why are you checking your pistols?"

The lieutenant wrinkled his beak-like nose. "General Rourke's men are not blind. Laying eyes on you, Mrs. Rourke, will be like seeing clouds in the desert and expecting immediate rain. I'm not taking any chances."

Nonsense. She had plenty of experience with men in New York. Exuding calm and focus, she outpaced the lieutenant to a group of men sitting around the outside of a tent. Before she could introduce herself, she met a tsunami of lecherous grins and jaw-dropping predatory hunger. How naïve she was to expect these men, hard-driven men…, and made more so by the war, to behave like the men of her drawing room acquaintance.

One soldier was bold to speak, making known his depraved thoughts. "She is pretty. I'm thinking of a deer running his tongue up a saltlick."

The men laughed and had mistaken her for a camp follower. Heat rose from her toes to the roots of her hair. Lieutenant Johnson edged beside her, and she straightened, fortified by his presence and the two Colt revolvers on his hips.

Lieutenant Johnson sustained strong eye contact with the men that ceased any forthcoming ribald comments. "Allow me to make introductions…this is General Rourke's wife." He let that part of his sermon snake around them.

Smiles froze. Eyes rounded as big as silver dollars. Some choked on their food. "The general's wife? We-we apologize, Mrs. Rourke. We had no idea. This won't get back to the general?"

She suppressed a smile. With certainty, the status of the general's wife brought instant acclaim and immediate respect. "I came to ask if there is anything I can help you men with."

A haggard man with shoulders as wide as a bull buffalo's stood. "My wife is very pregnant with our first child."

Catherine inhaled. He should be home tending to his wife, not at war. "It is natural to have worries, especially with your first child. Does she have someone in your absence to care for her?"

"Her mother lives on our farm." He answered with woe.

"Then you should have faith that your wife is in good hands. Why don't you and I sit down and pen a letter to your wife that will give her comfort for the blessed event." Catherine sat on a stool the men provided and composed a letter of love and regard to his pregnant wife. The letter was not so much for the wife, but as an opportunity to counsel the expectant father that he too, would journey through a myriad of intense emotions for one of the most miraculous of life's experiences. As the sun poured out from behind a cloud and bathed the day in its golden rays, the men nodded their heads and gave their reassurances, clapping the soldier's broad shoulders until he was smiling and relaxed.

"Can you write a letter to my sweetheart? To my wife? To my children? To my mother?"

She treated each and every man with concern, listening to their sufferings and sorrows and hardships. With diligence she wrote impassioned correspondence to wives, mothers, and sweethearts back home. She listened to the men who were lonely and needed to pour out their troubles, and with tenderness, she addressed them with affection like a mother would a child.

"That's enough for the time being," said Lieutenant Johnson and she mouthed a *thank you* for her back ached from sitting so long.

The men protested her departure. Many were illiterate and thirsted for communication to their loved ones. "I promise to return, but first I would like to meet the rest of the men."

"This is my toughest and most dangerous duty in escorting the general's wife," said Lieutenant Johnson, holding a straight face, and the men moaned. He took her hand and helped her rise.

"That should be my duty." A soldier massaged his chest.

"There are earthquakes. There are tornadoes, but…it is the green-eyed monster, which doth mock the meat it feeds on," Lieutenant Johnson goaded.

So the lieutenant was a student of Shakespeare. She strolled beside him unable to get out of her mind the deplorable conditions of the men. "I must speak with the general about the lack of proper clothing, shoes and food when he returns. I realize the war has brought unfortunate circumstances, but we must improve the conditions of the men."

He lifted his chin. "The general has married a saint. It would be my pleasure to escort the sweetest tempered woman in the world to tour the hospital and commissary."

She narrowed her eyes. There was more to the request. Was it a test? "I am not faint of heart. I have assisted with surgeries at MacDougall Hospital in New York and have seen the worst."

When Catherine entered the hospital tent her stomach churned from the stench of unwashed bodies and unattended men. "Where is the doctor?" Her voice cracked through the stillness.

"Dr. Hancock." Lieutenant Johnson angled his head to a rotund, soiled man drunk in his cups and snoring in a chair.

She kicked him in the shin. He exploded from the chair, swinging a meaty fist. Catherine ducked. The doctor spun around and toppled over.

Catherine seethed her words. "What are you going to do about the deplorable conditions of this hospital and the patients? These men need to be washed and their bandages changed. Everything in this hospital must be boiled, rinsed, dried, sterilized and fumigated. Now. Including you, doctor."

The doctor got up, weaved, and then leered at her. "Who's going to make me?" He had the audacity to look her up and down, while scratching a louse beneath his shirt.

"I am." Her nostrils flared. "These men will die if these despicable conditions are not changed."

"Then do it yourself." The doctor obliged, mocking her with a sweep of the hand toward his hospital.

"You call yourself a doctor. You are nothing but vermin. Get out of here before I report you to the general."

"Suit yourself, Miss high and mighty, but the general always listens to me." He slapped her on the derriere as he passed.

Lieutenant Johnson drew his revolver on the surgeon. Catherine pulled on his arm. "Let him go. He's not worth the trouble. We'll have to make do on our own. Go get a few men who you know are fastidious in cleanliness. We will need all available hands to bail us out of this God forsaken mess."

"I know you're a Yank, but I like the way you took command and put that worthless doctor in his place. Too many men have died from his incompetence. I'll get men right away." The lieutenant saluted, and to his consternation, dropped his hand.

Catherine bit her lip. She was not an officer of the Confederacy.

Catherine, several soldiers and Lieutenant Johnson spent hours doing backbreaking work, getting the hospital in order. She ordered everything boiled and sterilized, including tools, bandages, and bedding. The patients were bathed and their wounds redressed.

Particularly helpful was Danny Boy, who seemed to guess her every requirement before she even thought about it.

Danny Boy assisted her in removing a ball out of a soldier's leg that the bungling doctor could not seem to do. At first Catherine thought it was lodged in the bone but upon further reflection, considered it just like her husband's wound. With the proper sterilized instrument, she successfully removed it, saving the soldier from infection and losing his leg.

Samuel, the Paul Bunyan-sized man, was wonderful in lifting the patients so they could clean the beds and also take the soldiers out for fresh air. For several hours, she worked, pleased with the overhaul of the hospital and infirmary. She washed her hands and asked Lieutenant Johnson to escort her to the camp kitchens.

Her gaze followed the silent ghosts of cornstalks that peppered the hills. Could she make it to the tree line at the top and melt into the wilderness? Would she be shot by pickets?

With certainty, Brigid would be awake by now. "Where is the adjutant's tent?"

Lieutenant Johnson pointed to a tent beneath the shade of a sycamore, but when her eyes beheld the commissary, she was thunderstruck. If the hospital was in appalling condition, then the camp kitchen was unforgiveable.

"What is it you are cooking in that kettle?" she asked in all manner of sweetness, wrinkling her nose from the horrid smell.

The cook obliged her by opening the pot, his grubby, greasy arms exposed from where his shirtsleeves were rolled up. She leaned over the bubbling brew, the odor like long forgotten, moldy socks.

"It's called Knock 'em Stiff." He thrust his chest out, ladled some of the liquid, took a sip, and exhaled with heavenly euphoria. The cook's long beard was decorated with food items from the past week. He spat near her shoe, not out of insolence, but out of habit.

Catherine grimaced. "Pardon me?"

The cook looked at her as if as she didn't have a brain. "You know, Make 'em Joyful."

She started pacing, stopped, and then pointed at the offending substance. "That stew is not fit for human consumption, dump it out and start over with adequate substance for proper nourishment."

"Pretty lady, you make me dizzy with all that pacing, but you must have taken leave of your senses. I'll not do it. This is the best corn liquor this side of the Mississippi."

"Liquor? You can't be serious. What would the general think? Throw it out." She began pacing again. "Why are you not cooking meals? Why are you pursuing this dim-witted activity?"

"First of all, the general ain't here, so what he don't know, won't hurt him. Stews over there, left over from yesterday." He pointed to a pot in the corner, rancid and fully covered with flies. In fact, everything about the cooking area, like the cook, was filthy, greasy, and a banquet for flies. No wonder the stew was left over. No one in his sane mind would eat it.

"Lieutenant Johnson, have Danny Boy sterilize these bottles and fill them with the alcohol, we can use it for sterilizing instruments and wounds."

"Over my dead body," shouted the cook, using his body to shield his precious brew.

Catherine grabbed a Fitzgerald repeater rifle lying against a stump and eyed him down the barrel. She had enough from the surgeon's lack of respect and would not allow this brute to put her down.

The cook laughed as he sidled up to her, emboldened by his homemade brew. "Now, we know you can't handle a gun, Missy, so give away—"

The rifle exploded, splicing a hole through the center of his hat.

The cook fell back, splayed across a pile of firewood and stared tongue-tied. She pointed the rifle at the center of his skull. Several Rebels looked up from their current tasks, wondering why a rifle shot went off inside the camp. They gaped at the general's wife, wielding a gun at the frightened cook.

Through the roaring din, she breathed her anger, "I can handle this gun because I was born with it in my hands. I could put every piece of it together in the dark. So don't tempt me again because I'll use it on you if I have to. Now get up and start cleaning this kitchen or else."

"To tell you the truth, ma'am," the cook was more respectful, "I don't like cooking for those boys from Alabama and Kentucky."

"What does that have to do with cleanliness?" Catherine shrieked and brushed away a cloud of flies. Her rifle slipped a notch and pointed at his heart.

The cook threw up his hands, as if warding off an evil spirit. "They make fun of my cooking."

"You call that cooking? I call it a tragedy."

"You see, ma'am, I can't cook at all."

Catherine snorted the obvious. "Then why are you cooking?"

"The old cook died at Cold Harbor. I was appointed his replacement. I didn't want no part of the job, but I take it upon my shoulders as a matter of voluntary suffering, ma'am," The cook said, his face a manner of pure contriteness, absolving him from any sin or wrongdoing.

Catherine rolled her eyes with his righteousness.

"I treat it as my repentance to gain me entry into the pearly gates."

"Or to house with the devil. I'll get this camp a real cook. Now start scrubbing those pots and utensils and have it done before I get back."

Lieutenant Johnson started laughing, and so did the others crowding around the cook tent.

"What are you laughing about?" Catherine glared. Did the lieutenant salute her again? In a terrible state of irritation, and before Lieutenant Johnson could ward her off, Catherine marched into the Adjutant's tent.

"Brigid? Ian!" She could feel her face turn fifty shades of red. Her maid in bed with Ian, unclothed and in a very affectionate embrace? "I can't believe my eyes—"

"Out!" ordered Ian.

Catherine needed no such orders.

"Miss Catherine," Brigid called. "There's an explanation. Hurry," Brigid said to Ian. "Get dressed."

Catherine waited outside, her mortification complete as the tall adjutant came out, not particularly happy with being disturbed. In fact, the enormous Scot looked like he'd like to murder her. He jerked his head toward Brigid in the tent. Catherine understood her cue and without preamble, entered the tent.

She took a deep breath. "Brigid, I have known you for a long time, and I'm sure there is a plausible explanation—" Catherine's jaw dropped. A black and blue mark was on Brigid's chin. "Did that brute do that to you? I'll have his hide horsewhipped for beating and taking advantage of a defenseless woman, even if I have to go to the President of the Confederacy."

"Oh that. Don't worry on that little account. Ian has apologized to me countless times. You see, I was making too much noise, and he had to knock me out before going through the lines so we wouldn't get shot."

"He told me you fainted."

"I would have after he told me how horrible things were. He's been nothing but sweetness to make up for it."

"I see." Catherine raised her brow. "And what else has he promised you?"

"He has a large farm in northern Virginia and wants me to come and live with him."

"Live with him? I would hope he would tender a proposal first."

"I almost forgot. We're married."

"Married? How could you forget a thing like that? What's more, he's a Scot." In forty-eight hours, her maid was kidnapped and married?

"Ian's a gentleman," Brigid cooed. "He insisted we be wed right away. He's very principled. Besides what do you have against the Scots?"

"I have nothing against the Scots. It was just you had such a problem——" Catherine rubbed the back of her neck. She couldn't think.

"Anyway, we stopped at a church and Ian commanded the priest to marry us—immediately. At first Ian offered him gold dollars."

Catherine gasped. "He bribed a priest?"

"No. The priest had a northern bias and refused to marry a nice Irish girl to some worthless Rebel trash."

"I imagine Ian took that well. And how did he convince the priest?"

"Why Ian held a gun on him. Isn't it romantic?" Brigid breathed, all starry-eyed.

Catherine was speechless. The whole affair was like putting out a fire after the house burned down. Was the marriage legitimate? "May-may...I offer you my congratulations."

"Oh Catherine," Brigid swooned from the bed. "Ian has nothing but worshipful affection for me. He said my body is like a harp and his fingers are there to pluck the strings." Brigid clapped her hands and looked heavenward, for the Irish are born upon a stage with the Lord as their audience. "He is the dearest, adoring sweetheart that any woman could ever desire, just as your General Rourke is to you."

Catherine rolled her eyes heavenward but, unlike Brigid, her own was a silent plea for fortitude. "Enough, Brigid." She did not want to hear the details of their married life. "I need you to oversee the cook. He needs a little help." Catherine said, careful with the truth. "I know you are an excellent cook and want to find a circumstance where you can display your talents for Ian. Am I not correct?"

With enthusiasm, Brigid nodded.

Catherine left, knowing full well what opinions Brigid would have of the cook. She smiled, feeling sorry for the cook.

Chapter 22

"General Rourke, Lieutenant Johnson told me to bring my complaints to you," the cook said, thrusting his matted chest forward.

From John's visit with General Lee and a week of hard riding, he arrived in camp, his mood intolerably thin, near breaking with exhaustion and the desire to see his wife utmost on his mind. What if she had escaped? What information had she gleaned to pass on? He needed a guard posted, not to protect her—but to protect his men.

"First of all," complained the cook, "Some woman..." he scratched his head where it looked to John as if a bullet had parted the cook's hair. "...a right pretty piece if I might say, with a temper as bad as any badger. She started fussing about a few flies and cleaning things and overall complaining about my cooking. Got all fired up over some refreshment I made and shot me clean through the top of my hat."

To demonstrate, he wiggled a fat finger through the hole. "What am I supposed to do when it rains? Anyways, I never saw a woman work herself into such a painful fury. She started a pacing, and I swear she could fill a room with mist, raise the dead, and make lightning strike. She stomped the ground and snakes fled into the river and drowned. But all that was nothing compared to when she sent Ian's wife—"

"Ian's wife? She's dead." John narrowed his eyes. Had the cook brewed a batch of white lightning while he was gone?"

"Well she don't look too dead, unless out of pure spite she's come back to haunt me. She's worse than that pretty woman. At least the yellow-haired gal is more tolerable. I can look at her and dream a little. That other devil of a woman had me cleanin' and scrapin' 'til my knuckles bled. She beat me about the head, threw a knife at me with such aim she practically turned me into a soprano. Then she boxed my ears and loosed her tongue on me, threatening to send me to where somebody named Cromwell will burn me at a stake and put my head on a pike. Do the Yanks really have someone like Cromwell?" The cook's eyes grew as large as dinner plates.

"There is such a man." John half-listened, observing the object of his desire exiting his tent unaware of his presence. He admired her bravery, and had to admit, his most seasoned men would have had difficulty running through the lines between Washington and his camp, and holding up under such an attack.

She moved to a group of soldiers, each one plying for her attention. One soldier bowed and offered his stool, but not before another rushed to drape a blanket across it so she wouldn't soil her gown. The men laughed at something witty she said, and jumped for any morsel of interest she cast their way.

The cook didn't hear, his attention drawn to picking a nit or two from the back of his head. "Those northern women are powerful mean. I can understand why those Yankee men keep a comin' and a comin' at us. Yes siree, they ain't never gonna stop and to tell you the truth, I can't blame them one bit. They just want to get away from their womenfolk."

John groaned. What else was turned upside down? Lieutenant Johnson arrived with Ian in tow and thrust a plate of stew, and biscuits in his hands. So hungry, he shoveled it in his mouth. He squeezed his eyes shut, savoring the flavors of soft roast beef, potatoes, carrots, parsnips and gravy. He opened his eyes. He swabbed the buttery biscuit through the gravy, took a bite and groaned. "This is excellent."

Ian beamed from ear to ear. "My wife's a very good cook, isn't she, General."

"Your wife?" The cook took two steps back. "You mean that brown-haired woman in my cook tent? Why she's the sweetest thing this side of the Mississippi."

John pivoted. "Your wife?"

"I married Brigid."

John stared. Ian was one of his most predictable men. This development gave John pause—Ian McDougal unpredictable? "May I offer my—belated felicitations? And may I congratulate our additional blessing on our new cook?"

"Absolutely." Ian grinned from ear to ear.

The doctor pushed the cook aside. "Excuse me, General Rourke. I know you are awful busy but a crazy woman came to my surgery and had the audacity to kick me out. Imagine, a Doctor of Medicine."

"I can imagine," Rourke drawled. His gaze roved over the surgeon's head. A soldier thrust a pen and paper into Catherine's hands and another placed a portable writing desk on her lap. He also noticed how beautiful she was when she turned up her face to laugh at what a soldier had commented. He also knew how conniving she could be. To escape, she would endear his men to her.

The surgeon ranted. "In any case, this yellow-haired witch has taken over my hospital and refuses to allow me to perform my proper duties. I insist you do something."

"The surgeon got very personal with the lady, General." Lieutenant Johnson interrupted, earning a scathing glance from the surgeon.

"And General Rourke—" The surgeon sneered. "Lieutenant Johnson supported her, got right into the thick of things. You should know that for when you have him court-martialed."

His lieutenant stood quiet. John was stone-faced. "How personal?"

"I slapped her on the rear," the surgeon bragged. "If I really wanted to have my way with that camp whore, I would have thrown her down on the ground and mounted her."

"Hold my plate, Ian." John's hand clenched. "That yellow-haired whore you just referred to is my wife." Before the surgeon could react, John cracked a hard left to the point of the surgeon's jaw. The doctor's mouth fell open and his knees sagged. John was going to hit him again, except the doc dropped face forward in the dirt, and unconscious at John's feet.

He took his plate from Ian again and with the same easygoing smile, said, "This food is exemplary, Ian. One of the best decisions I've made in this war was having *your intended* accompany us south.

More men came forward, stepping over the unconscious doctor, uncertain about the state of the general's temper. One of the more bald-faced men spoke for the group. "Some crazy brown-haired woman had us picking huckleberries, General. We're fighting men, not berry pickers."

John had just taken a taste of the huckleberry pie. It melted inside his mouth. "It seems to me Ian," Rourke drawled to his adjutant. "What should have been a simple homecoming has turned into an exercise in diplomacy."

This time, Ian stepped forward. "That's my wife you're talking about, and I don't take too kindly about you calling her crazy." Ian looped a right, caught the soldier in the bristles of his cleft and knocked him flat. Ian dusted his knuckles off on the soldier's shirt. "Takes the edge off, doesn't it General?"

"Any more questions?" John asked, scooping another bite of pie into his mouth.

"No-no, Sir," echoed the rest of the men, observing their companions dispatched, and lying prone over one another in an inconvenient pile of horse dung.

"Cook!"

"Yes, General." He half-turned, ready to flee. "I didn't know the yellow-haired woman was your wife. Why she's the nicest lady——"

"This side of the Mississippi," John finished for him. "I want you to learn from Ian's wife how to cook as well as this."

"Yes, Sir. I'll stick to her like a tick on a mule." The cook looked at Ian's formidable countenance and muttered beneath his breath, that Rourke barely caught. "More like she'll be sticking to me like a tick on a mule."

Chuckling, Rourke dismissed the frightened cook. Hearing female laughter, John jerked his head up..., listening to the lyrical seductive laugh of his wife entertained by a covey of his soldiers. He didn't care for his camp to be turned into a ring of parlor flirtations nor did he care for his wife to be the center of those attentions.

"Excuse me gentlemen. I believe I'll see to my wife." John strode to a knot of oaks and stood undetected behind his wife and her acquaintances.

"Really, Mrs. Rourke, what are my chances with you? Please do tell." A sergeant begged, refusing to release her hand until she gave him the answer he wanted to hear. From the meager distance that separated them, a breeze carried the delectable scent of her fragrance, and John inhaled as it twined through his senses. Everything about her was intoxicating. She met the sergeant with a breathtaking smile and John had a bird's eye view of her creamy shoulders and silky breasts, beckoning him from her daring décolletage. John's hand curled around his pistol handle. It was same view his soldiers shared, towering over his wife and ogling her plentiful charms.

She bit her lip to stifle a grin. "Your chances are one in a million, Sergeant Smith."

"So you are saying I have one chance." The sergeant refused to let her hand go.

John had enough. Her clever manipulations of his men, leading them wanting, frothing with anticipation like her personal stable of rutting stallions. He took two paces closer, his shadow swallowing the sergeant. The other soldiers held their breath. "I'd say your chances are zero," John said, his voice, though matter of fact, possessed an ominous quality.

Catherine turned. The sergeant dropped her hand.

"Mrs. Rourke was endeavoring to write a-a letter for me." The sergeant explained.

"I see," said John, and the only sound was the wind climbing through the trees. John caught Catherine by the elbow. "I have returned and wish to have a few private reflections with my wife." He nodded to the remaining men. In silence, they both walked, Catherine with stiff dignity, John with stern discipline into the privacy of his tent.

Catherine jerked away. "Don't you ever treat me like that again. I am not a dog tethered on a leash. Nor will I adhere to your every command. As your wife, you will give me the respect due to me. Do you understand?"

Neither spoke. Both breathing hard, they stared into each other's eyes. Was her heart beating as hard as his?

Why did he bring her here? God he was weary. She stood like a Greek goddess, still and perfect, cold and aloof. A wind beat against the canvas, lifted a tendril of her hair to tease the bristles on his chin.

They had come far. *Too far.*

But he could not risk touching her. To open Pandora's box, Armageddon as a prize? Another breeze crossed the land, cool and sweet. It did nothing to ease the fire ablaze throughout his limbs.

He could see the rise and fall of her breasts with the uneven whisper of her breath—and he could see the pulse beating at her throat, beating there in anger, or was it fear?

He wanted her.

He pulled her roughly, almost violently to him, gathering her into his arms, his mouth covering hers with savage hunger. She cried out from the cruel ravishment of his mouth and pushed away, but he crushed her to him. Her skin was so hot and he craved the feel of her…free from all her clothing. The thought of her naked beneath him, made John's blood rush. Just one more touch.

Though in full knowledge of what he was doing, John's mind cleared enough to understand he was ending his attraction to her, needed to identify he was in absolute control and to destroy the siren that called him to slaughter. But to his shock, the warmth of her pulsing body and her hand, caressing the back of his neck created a red-hot blaze of need.

Not enough. His hands moved to her sleeves, yanking them down her arms, exposing rosy nipples beneath her chemise. He shuddered when he slipped his hands beneath the filmy fabric and palmed the satiny skin of her breasts, their tender buds hardening to the graze of his thumb and forefinger. Her moan inflamed him and he lowered his mouth and suckled her breast. She tasted like wild honey and he pulled with his mouth, surveying the wet sheen on her nipple. His hand seared a path down her abdomen and came to rest on her hip, pressing her intimately to his arousal.

"General Rourke? Excuse me?" A soldier's modulated voice called from outside. The voice seemed light years away, yet was like getting a bucket of ice water thrown over his head. He hovered above her, breathing raggedly, his gaze fierce as he snapped through his passion-ridden brain.

"Make yourself decent." He pushed her behind him, straightened his dusty clothes and wrenched open the tent flaps. She slipped by him. Her hair caught in the brass buttons of his coat. She snatched her hair from his grasp, smothered a sob and fled.

John met the rest of the daylight hours in torment. Part of him wanted to find his wife and apologize, the other part remained embittered with memories of her treachery. Most of his time was spent riding out and checking with pickets, camp disputes, foraging feed for the horses, and taking stock of ammunition and rifle supplies. Shortages. Everywhere there were shortages. How was he supposed to lead an army against the enemy?

In less harassing moments, he read through and wrote dispatches, and then he visited the sick and injured men in the hospital. There he learned of his wife's treatment of his men. The hospital had been given a complete overhaul, clean, efficient, and tidy. To think she had improved the morale of his men. Many sung her praises, calling her an angel of mercy. One soldier informed him about how she saved his leg, and his life.

John moved on to visit with the rest of the men in his camp. Again, they too sung her praises, likening her to a saint.

"General Rourke, Sir. If I may have a minute of your time, please. I'd like to say thanks to you for your wife even though she's a Yank. I never met a woman with so many talents. She can sew and tend wounded and can organize a camp better than any general—present company excluded. And, she has that brown-haired gal cooking food fit for the gods."

One young soldier mentioned how she wrote a hope-filled letter, encouraging his wife who was expecting their first child. More approached him, thanking the general for the gracious generosity of his wife's time. Not only did she handle correspondence to loved ones' back home, but she had become a ready ear, sympathetic to their problems, and feelings of loneliness. Catherine had become a beacon of light for his men.

So she happened to earn their trust? Clever. No doubt she moved about the camp, collecting troop numbers and strengths. John frowned. He had not seen her all day but had guards, keeping an eye on her every movement. Soon they would be engaged. General Grant carried huge numbers of Union troops, placing Petersburg under siege. General Jubal Early's raid on Washington would not go unanswered. The Valley would be a prime target for Hunter or Sheridan's Calvary. It was all a matter of time.

The sun dropped beyond the western ridge of the Shenandoah, and the shadow of night crossed slowly over the land. For a while, the country was much as it had been—the red oaks, dark and towering, frowned on either side of his encampment. The lower limbs and forest floor were stripped of its wood for campfires. The meadow debouched into a close-bitten field, and out of this gnawed land the camp rose up with its hundreds of canvas tents like a swarm of locusts.

But it was the sky that caught his reflection, streaks of amber giving way to indigo, mingling with the darker permanence of amethyst. The pigments were so dazzling and extraordinary, that it gave John pause to witness such creation—and isolation.

John gazed down upon his encampment. The distant sound of a harmonica mingled with the normal sounds of a military camp settling in for the night. The men were talking quietly, laughing about a mutual joke shared around their campfires. His men. Men to whom he had a sworn duty. He would remember these warm little scenes for the rest of his life, whatever destiny prevailed upon him.

Fragments of what he'd done earlier in the day flashed before him. Catherine, warm with passion, her lips, her soft breasts, she had too much power over him. No. He dared not hazard another encounter.

He pushed away from the tree and raked his hair off his damp forehead. Slimy and sweaty and smelling of horses, he walked a mile to the eastside of camp. He waved to the pickets so he wouldn't get shot. They knew he wanted to be alone.

Stripping away his clothes, John walked into the shallows of a creek then dove into a deeper hole. He swam along the gravel bottom for a long time trying to cleanse her from his thoughts, and then when his lungs could bear no more, burst in a shower of spray to the top. With a cake of precious soap, he scrubbed himself clean, swam upstream then drifted down with the current. Calm? Peace? There was none.

What the hell was happening to him? He dove into a deeper pool, searching for the cooler depths, until his lungs ached for sweet oxygen. Treading water, he backhanded the water's surface, observing a wake of driving spray while rummaging for solutions that had no way of emerging. His body was controlling his mind. Celibacy was hell. What man wouldn't be crazy with lust by now? She had every one of them wanting.

He laughed, then cursed his own pathetic weakness as he strode out of the stream. He shook his head, the water spraying from his hair in all directions. Dripping wet, he pulled on his dusty trousers and headed to his tent to get clean clothes.

Chapter 23

ohn approached his headquarters and stopped dead in his tracks. Lounging around a campfire, were several of his soldiers, their heads cranked around, mouths gaping open, all focused in a single direction. He followed the course of their gaze and observed firsthand the object of their aspiring concentration. *Catherine.*

He gritted his teeth. It was one thing to have a lantern lit inside his tent for illumination. It was another situation when the translucence of tent canvas silhouetted her perfect form while she bathed for all to behold. He would have his tent removed to the privacy of the woods in the morning.

John cleared his throat.

"General Rourke, Sir!" They all stood at attention, caught like schoolboys, stealing a pie off the sideboard.

"Sergeant Putt? I want you to do some drills with the men. Ten would be a fine number."

"Ten, Sir?" Sergeant Putt whistled between his teeth.

The men groaned.

"Make that twelve."

"That will take all night," the sergeant protested.

"That's the idea. Now head out."

After his men sallied off, grumbling from the prospect of all night marching, John took deep strides to his tent. He ducked in, tied down the flaps, his eyes riveted to the banquet before him. What had been left to the imagination, concealed by canvas, paled in comparison to what he viewed mere footsteps away.

With her eyes closed, and her head back, Catherine reclined in a copper tub—contraband he'd acquired, courtesy of a Yank camp in Maryland. He had not wanted to take the tub, thinking it too heavy when he preferred to have his army travel light. He thanked providence for the sin of his quartermaster's greed. Such sights stoked a slowly growing fire. Her thick golden hair was caught up on top of her head in a blue satin ribbon. And even in repose, there was both delicacy and refinement. Hungrily he watched a drop of water trail down her neck and over her breast, tear-dropping at that soft enticing peak. With superhuman strength, he resisted the urge to lathe it with his tongue. That same drop crested then tantalizingly traveled down her slender waist where it met the water's edge. The droplet was lost to him, but remaining beneath the waters of the bath was the flare of her gently rounded hips.

Catherine's eyes flew open, and she jumped, water splashing over the tub. Her heart skipped a beat, as she searched for her towel. Damn. Behind Rourke. She sank lower and clasped her arms tightly around her legs to hide her nudity.

"I hope I am not intruding, Mrs. Rourke. I recall viewing every aspect of your delectable form during my convalescence."

A sardonic smile spread across his lips. He dropped into a chair, leaned back, his legs stretched in front of him.

He was half-naked, as if he'd just bathed, his dark hair, wet, clung plastered to his head. His muscles rippled across his abdomen where she had once so lovingly caressed and his damp trousers hugged his narrow waist and hips—and did nothing to hide the menacing bulge in front.

He meant to taunt her. She squeezed the sponge until flattened from dampness. She remembered how he'd kissed her earlier in the day, how he had humiliated her. She had cried for the better part of an hour, vowing to get away from him, and swearing not to let him touch her again. "Why are you not sleeping with your men?"

"Indeed. When I was young, I could have slept on a bed of rocks. I am older and care for the luxury of having my spine resting on a feather mattress." Indifferent to her suggestion, he scented the simple dinner prepared on his desk. "My stomach has been cutting a few capers. May I indulge?"

"Of course, you are the commander. Your sustenance comes first."

"My sustenance has yet to be filled," he said and Catherine did not miss his double entendre.

"Then starve!" she cried, splashing a huge wave of water over the rim and soaking his pants.

He lifted his plate in time. "What a terrible temper you have."

"Spare me, your provocations, General. You might come to the realization that I simply do not care."

"But I think you do care."

He was testing her. She cared not one whit.

But she did care. She felt guilty assuming the Rebels her enemy. They were the same, North and South. As Lincoln had said, they were brothers.

"The men are suffering terrible hardships. They are ill-dressed, some with no shoes, and barely any clothing to speak of. There is a shortage of food. The worms in the flour are as long as your finger. One has to skim the weevils from a substance they call coffee and the hard-tack is so rock-solid, it can stop bullets."

"And—"

A cold knot formed in her stomach for she had dared much during his departure. She remembered what had transpired earlier in the day, and bar none, she feared John's explosive nature and the fact she had overstepped her bounds. "There is an overall lack of medicine and proper medical care. The sanitation—there is no practice. The doctor I find appalling and—" She took a deep breath and looked John straight in the eye. "I took the liberty of firing him."

John finished his meal and put his plate down. He poured himself a glass of whiskey and bit off the end of a cigar and spit it out. "Fine Virginia tobacco." He rolled it between his teeth. With certainty, she could tell his degrees of temper and ponderance with the extent he clamped it between his teeth.

"The South, thanks to the northern blockade and other activities of your Yankee brethren, has been stripped of many needed supplies," he said, considering her. "As to the doctor…he's not really a doctor. I should have let him go a while back, but he was the closest thing I could get to a real doctor. Let's hope—" he took his cigar out of his mouth and pointed it at her, "we'll not be engaging your friends in the near future, for my men will have no medical care until he is replaced."

Her friends? Was he blaming her? She raised her chin and continued as if he hadn't spoken. "The latrines have been dug in upstream and I recommend—"

"You will recommend nothing. This is my camp,"

"And the shortages? You'll allow them to continue, the men to go without all because it is your camp? Your brilliance rivals your hubris, General. To think I am in the presence of Copernicus or Da Vinci himself." She narrowed her eyes. "As long as your men starve—"

"The commissaries in Richmond are not fatted coffers for the taking."

"You could go out and steal. You're not so lofty in your morals that thievery is above you. In fact, pilfering is an art for you." She swept her hand, palm-up to the bed and trunks. "Property of Colonel Briggs?"

John stopped and lit a match to his cigar, until it flamed a glowing red. The smoke spiraled, drifting, and was rather pleasant. He studied her, eyes darkening, a sultry look she well remembered.

"Spoils of war. Graciously donated by your Union Army."

"Then go steal some more."

He grinned, took another swallow, then stared at the amber liquid.

"You are a prisoner of war. You do not give orders and you do not run my camp. I take full responsibility for my men. I haven't decided what to do with you yet. I've been thinking of turning you over to the military high command for sentencing."

"I had hoped for some kind of reconciliation, at the minimum, a friendship, but you are set on Mallory's lies and believing I'm a spy. Ask Brigid. She'll tell you."

"I did but she would back you up regardless, maybe help you escape."

"Ask Lucas, your brother. I met him in Washington. He believed me. He was trying to help find Uncle Charlie."

"I have sent messages. It takes weeks sometimes to get through the lines."

Her breath stalled, the degree to which he had had her investigated. "I suppose you'll do what you feel you have to do regardless of my innocence."

John snorted. "I'll no longer believe anything you tell me. I value my life too much."

Catherine stiffened. "So without ever being in the military, I'm a prisoner of war?"

"You've got that right. Your name will be chiseled in stone among the betrayers: Lucifer, Judas and Fitzgerald."

"As a prisoner of war, it is my duty to escape."

With that suggestion, he pulled his cigar from his mouth. "That is not in the cards. I have posted guards on you around the clock. My men are excellent sharpshooters. They can shoot the eyes out of a pheasant at two hundred yards."

Catherine pasted on a smile of nonchalance. "Are you planning to have your men come after and shoot me?"

"Heavens no, Mrs. Rourke. It's war. I have sent my men into hell and back, through every battle this war has encountered. I am a sympathetic commander. I wouldn't dream of sending them after you."

Paying no heed to his sarcasm, she nearly smirked in calculating challenge. "Then be prepared, General, for I will do my best to subvert you at most any time."

"I would enjoy that enterprise with the greatest recreation." His eyes dipped to the water's edge and he took another swallow of whiskey.

They were alone, except for the thousands of men camped in the distance. An owl hooted and a moth threw itself furiously at the lantern light. The water was cooling, chilblains rioted up her arm, her nipples popped. Catherine ducked lower.

"General Rourke, I am sure there is proper conduct in the treatment of one so lowly as a female prisoner of war. I am sure that even your genteel General Lee would afford me that small status."

John smiled benignly, as if dealing with a temperamental child.

She curled her hands into fists. Oh, to play every trump card. "The Fitzgerald fortune is vast. It could buy my freedom. You could have money for yourself, and add to your little farm back home. You could even have money for your army. Think of the possibilities..."

"Do you think you could buy your way out? You are going nowhere. I know you for who you are—a clever manipulating, deceitful witch.

"My family is one of the North's finest. I have political connections all the way to the White House. Your treatment of me as a common criminal is outrageous, and I won't stand for it any longer. The northern papers will make public my plaudits and order my freedom. President Lincoln will demand my release. The Union Army under General Grant's command will hunt you down."

He launched to his feet. The chair crashed to the floor behind him. He grabbed her by the upper arms and pulled her up, squeezing the flesh bloodless. She was only aware of the pain in her arms, and the tall dark man looming over her. Her husband. A total stranger. She gasped, fought back tears.

"You are speaking of Catherine Fitzgerald or Mrs. John Rourke? Neither exists. You have ceased to be. You are now my prisoner and servant."

"To you, John, love seems like a bad joke and honesty seems foolish. I am the one wronged. And I promise you will rue the day. The truth will come out, but it is too late. For left in my heart is nothing but hatred for you. Your warped sense of revenge is misguided. You have no idea how much you have interrupted everything and will destroy what's left of my family. My uncle will die at Mallory's hands." With a sob, she tried to extricate herself from his brutal grip where he was bruising her arms.

"He's all I have left in the world...he was to be rescued the night you took me and now I'm going crazy with not knowing. Mallory is a thug, coming from the underbelly of an Irish underworld that you could not even begin to comprehend. He has murdered to become part of the new rich, the ones who have stayed behind to reap their fortunes on the war. In New York City, he controls the political bosses and influencers, spending their hideous fortunes on extravagant parties and garish homes, sparing no expense. But he craves the elusive polished spot and proper conventionalities of upper society. I am his ticket to the old money elite. Francis Mallory's bid for the Fitzgerald fortune can be acquired through marriage to me. He promised my stepmother, Agatha, a sizeable fortune for my hand—"

"Enough. You weave a good tale. Your extraordinary intelligence, and exhaustion of every wile is used to cheat the hangman's rope and calculated for your survival."

Not that John ever intended to turn her over to the authorities in Richmond, but he entertained with pleasure the use of her wiles on him. How far would she go?

Why did he feel the need to believe her? Brigid would back her story regardless. Lucas? Why had he not heard from him? Rourke spread his legs apart, seeking to redirect his thoughts. Could he let her go? Return her close enough to the border where she could rejoin the Union Army? His mind warred with reason. To allow her to spy against the Confederacy was out of the question. Too dangerous. With her talents, everything he had fought for over the last four years would lay in shambles. He had to keep her to protect the Cause.

He let her go then. "Get into bed."

"I will not."

He took a threatening step toward her. "Don't even entertain that I would find comfort touching you. Indeed, I can find plenty of solace elsewhere. But since you are my servant, and since I have no morals, I will take you whenever it pleases me."

Ignoring Catherine, he began unbuttoning his pants, until she gave a stifled gasp, and he stared at her in mild surprise.

"What...what are you doing?"

Her voice held a shred of terror. Good. "Undressing. Do you object?"

"You said…" she began, but he cut her short.

"Indeed your modesty is a little late if not contrived. You have seen every aspect of me."

"You will never have me. I will scream so that General Lee will hear me."

He cut her a sharp look that dared her to argue. "Even the Confederacy allows a husband his marital rights, willing or unwilling. I have no intention of taking you this evening, if that's what you're afraid of. I have traveled hard for many days and I'm exhausted. I'm going to sleep. You may join me in the bed if you wish, or, you may sleep in the chair in the corner. It means nothing to me, one way or the other. When I take you, Catherine, it will be when I am rested, and at my full strength, so that I can savor your delectable charms to the fullest. Believe me, you are quite safe tonight."

He threw a towel at her, which she had laid out before her bath. She wrapped it around her, careful to keep concealed, dried off, and then yanked a gown over her head. She stalked to the straight-backed chair in the corner, and sat stiffly upon it, studying the rough plank floor.

"I'll take no chances."

"Suit yourself. That chair is as soft and yielding as the hickory it was made from."

She continued with her stony silence while John, naked now, shrugged, and dimmed the oil lamp. He cursed the sheerness of the gown covering her. It wreaked more havoc on his senses than if she were completely exposed. The bed screeched beneath his weight as he settled between cotton sheets, and threw off the thick quilt that was too warm. For an hour, she shifted in her uncomfortable chair and sighed. No doubt, her back ached and dampness crept down her spine. Everything in the tent grew quiet. The single flash of a firefly brightened a corner.

She eased out of the chair. The floor groaned beneath her feet as she moved toward him. There was a knife on the nightstand. His muscles tensed. Would she stab him? He probed the darkness, his hand moved to the hilt.

Slowly, painstakingly, she lowered herself to the bed. He remained silent, did not move while she pulled the sheet up to her neck and exhaled. Their bodies did not touch. Her scent and heat entwined him.

He tucked the knife under the mattress...just to be safe. "I thought you'd see reason. Now go to sleep."

Her body went rigid, and then she flounced on her side, her back to him. He waited until she was asleep. Her breathing was soothing, and as he lay, feeling her there in the soft, cozy bed, he drifted off to a warm dreamless slumber.

Chapter 24

*S*everal days passed and then another. Catherine barely noticed. Her days had become a precedent of work and sleep. The war had tainted her husband and there was no way out of this mess. No proof of her innocence...no evidence...nothing to exonerate her. Her heart ached, as if torn in two.

From the first day when she awoke to find John gone, she discovered her full-time guard, Danny Boy, with an armload of mending to do. Other jobs were assigned, from helping Brigid in the kitchen to hospital work, to serving John's meals. Each morning, she dressed in one of Mrs. Briggs gowns, and brushed her hair into a neat chignon, only to have it fall in disarray by noontime from lack of pins. Why should she bother to look properly groomed? Instead she let it swirl about her shoulders as she worked, concentrating on completing the day's labor before dusk, so that she could return to the tent and go to sleep.

Accustomed to the rigors of the day, she was no longer as exhausted as she had been at first, lending more time to writing letters for the men. Far away were the glittering ballrooms of New York and so distant the accompaniments of wealth that afforded her every leisure. With irony, she found the grueling routine satisfying, preferring the distraction, relative to spending it with her husband. So far he had not touched her, treating her with icy civility, giving her orders and going about his soldier business without so much as a glance in her direction. Catherine, in turn, did as she was told, whether fetching his meal or darning his socks, biding her time in hopes of escape. A mountain of rock had emerged between them, and as far as she was concerned, that suited her just fine. The less she had to do with her husband, the better.

Danny Boy on the other hand was another matter. He was a tall, strapping boy of eighteen years with an infectious grin, a thick crop of blond curly hair, and mischievous blue eyes. From the Old Country, he held an Irish lilt, was outgoing, exhibiting an uplifting zeal for life—unlike the staid harshness of her husband. He was a hard worker and cautioned her not to overdo. He carried the heavier loads for her, insisting she take time to rest. How could she not be charmed by his fresh appeal?

Catherine had developed a fond attachment to Danny Boy, grateful for his companionship. He made her laugh at the simplest of things and entertained her as if they were experiencing the gaiety of any formal party, indulging her with his comic illustrations and wit. Working side by side with him, a warm and wonderful friendship grew.

One bright and blustery day, Catherine laughed aloud at one of Danny Boy's hilarious stories and caught John staring at her.

"Danny Boy, fetch another pile of mending for Mrs. Rourke. She has too much free time on her hands."

When Danny returned, he spat. "Other commander's wives live quite well in the camps—in contrast to the servitude the general puts upon you. I do not care for it, not one bit, and someday I am aiming to tell the general to his face."

"Do as you are commanded and remain silent." She advised Danny Boy. Why should Danny suffer repercussions by championing her cause?

For her laughter, Catherine was rewarded with a pile of hopeless mending. Prior to her camp experience, her sewing had been confined to an embroidery hoop. The bottomless pants were beyond the miracle of a needle. Did she dare throw them into the nearest campfire? She glared after John, boring holes into his back. Oh, if she were a man, she'd snap his arrogant neck. Yet the same man who showed her such harshness was compassionate to his men.

"Danny Boy, would you be so kind and fetch me the red satin dress in my tent?" she asked sweetly. Ideas spun, and at once, she decided to use her embroidery talents in repairing the men's breeches. The satin dress was the one John had ruined and so, she cut with her scissors perfect hearts and stitched them on the bottoms. Not content with just hearts, she added butterflies, flowers, kittens, and a myriad of other frivolous items. She even held the finished product up for Danny Boy's perusal, earning a broad smile for her creative efforts and admiration of her bold rebellion. He did caution her on the larger pants, belonging to Samuel, speculating what calamity might become of her inventiveness.

When she had finished her task, Danny Boy suggested they take a walk..., the long way...before they began their work at the hospital. Since it was a warm sunny day, and she was still feeling mutinous, Catherine was more than willing to oblige. Soldiers passed the time with a cockfight. Two multi-colored game birds, one named Grant and the other Lee circled one another, baring their vicious talons while the men cheered them on.

Soon they came upon Brigid working in the kitchen in a terrible tempest from the lack of supplies. Brigid complained she didn't care for the way the general was treating Catherine and as soon as she laid eyes on him would bring her complaints again. Then she kicked the cook awake, which he answered in a dreadful howl, and then ordered him to finish scrubbing the pots. The cook fell to order wearing a look of formidable concentration as if scrubbing pots required all the strategy in the world and every whit of his attention.

"They are the dirtiest, rag tag group I have ever seen, but they have a bit of dash that the northern men lack." Brigid winked at Catherine, and then noticing something wrong, she pulled her mistress to the back of the cook shed.

"You seem very happy with your marriage," Catherine said to ward off any questions Brigid might pose.

"I am very happy with Ian." Brigid told her and brightened as any newlywed bride in love with her spouse. Brigid was willing to ride out any storm, any unpredictable future, to endure any hardships.

Catherine was envious of that love, a love so simple, so sincere, and without the complexities that life would throw its way. The war created hurtful divisions. She and John's relationship, a casualty, and any kind of happiness remained precluded by an awful and complex schism.

"The general does love you," Brigid told her, pinning laundry on the line to dry. Nothing escaped Brigid's notice.

"I talked to him at length, told him he was dead wrong about you. He's a brute for now, but I see how his eyes follow you when you are unaware. I see how he comes to attention when the men sing your praises. Oh, it isn't much of a movement, but I see it. I hear him ask Ian from time to time of your whereabouts. Is this the behavior of a man who does not care? Men have different ways of reacting to things than women do. Your general is a great man with many responsibilities on his head. His reactions will be even stronger. Weather it for now. The future will be bright, of this, I am sure."

Catherine sagged against a tree. "Deep down, I know he believes me. I feel it in my bones. But something else is bothering him that keeps him from wanting any attachment, and I believe it stems from the betrayal of his first wife. Somehow, I'm woven into that same fabric. He cannot be vulnerable again."

Brigid snapped damp pants into the air, then took two clothespins from her mouth and anchored the garment on the line. "Men are curious creatures. When he figures it all out, he'll be on his knees, begging your forgiveness."

Catherine rubbed the heel of her palm against her chest. "I suppose I could tell you that I am unhappy, but that is not true. I feel useful and have a sense of home and place here. Sometimes it breaks my heart to write the men's letters of loneliness to their loved ones, knowing not what their future will bring, but at the same time, I find it fulfilling for it is a communication that they would not have. I enjoy taking care of the sick in the hospital, and look upon it as a privilege, but wish there would be no more suffering caused by this horrible war. The divisions have become blurred for me, Brigid. I can no longer tell the difference between Yankees and Rebels. They are all flesh and blood men, coming from mothers and fathers, they have sisters, brothers, wives and sweethearts."

"And when this war is over, they all will be reunited again. We must have this faith." Brigid flashed Catherine a smile then glanced around the cook shed. "Now, I have a wayward cook to keep after. He is the laziest human this side of Ireland."

The cook was sneaking away when Brigid put her foot upon him again. Catherine laughed and picked up a pair of long-john's to pin on the line. Through the divide of two large oaks, Rourke stood surrounded by his men.

"Here's Ben," greeted the men.

"What took you so long?" Her husband scowled. "Anything to report?"

"I walked a hundred miles, Sir, not for the exercise but on account my horse was shot out from under me by some Yanks."

"Couldn't you have stolen a horse?" asked Lieutenant Johnson.

"That's breaking the seventh commandment. However, I did entertain borrowing a horse. But the matron of the house was loathing parting with it and me, seein' how comfortable her musket was in her arms, like nursing a newborn babe, I felt right poorly on separating her from her horse."

"I see," said John, smiling around his cigar.

"There's a lot more to tell. I skedaddled on account I hear General Grant wasn't fooled by General Early's raid and he means to make the Confederate's acquaintance with General Sheridan's Cavalry riding down the Shenandoah real soon. Reinforced to close to ten thousand strong. So I say to myself, better hurry on up, so I can tell the general and be ready to show those Yank boys some real Southern hospitality."

John rested his booted foot on a stump. "If we are met, we will fight back with due haste, giving them a taste of our generosity."

Hidden behind a sheet, she peered over the line. It was well done. His men raised a cheer. His doggedness, calm, tranquility, a Caesar-like steadiness, would encourage his men to fight on. He was their commander, like a champion of some ancient lineage at the head of his legions.

A roughened cavalry unit galloped into the camp, leading twenty well-stocked wagons. The dirt kicked up from the horses' hooves spraying a thick yellow veil of dust around the camp. There must have been sixty soldiers, dark bearded, menacing, yet filled with laughter.

"General Rourke!" The dark haired leader spoke without dismounting. "I have some well needed supplies and ammunition, courtesy of our northern brethren."

"My compliments to you Colonel Mosby. You timing is impeccable," John said.

Brigid pressed forward into the crowd of men and contraband.

"Woman, don't chastise me for stealing," John warned. "I've got what you want."

Brigid lifted her stubborn Irish chin, meeting John's gaze without a blink. "What took you so long?"

John turned to Colonel Mosby, unruffled by Brigid's impertinence, to which he was accustomed. "If I put that frightful female at the border it'd scare away all of the Union Army. But I do have to admit, she's one hell of a cook."

"That's if I can be stocked with good supplies instead of the rubbish you throw my way." Brigid set in, her hands fisted on her hips.

"As you see, Colonel, Brigid and I never disagree."

"Is an elephant disturbed by a cricket? She demanded over her shoulder then ordered soldiers to help her unload foodstuffs from the wagons.

"Quite unusual." Colonel Mosby nodded his head in direction of the insolent woman.

"Be careful what you say," John cautioned. "I would not desire to offend Ian for she is his new bride."

"I hesitate," said Mosby, "whether to offer Ian my congratulations or my condolences."

John threw back his head and roared with laughter, and then the former cook came forward, turning round like a trout circling its bait. "What is it you want?" John barked out.

"You misunderstand me, General, please, speaking serious, first it may seem kind of different to you but you will see it is a tad unusual."

"I'm not in the humor for your jokes. So have a care what you say," John demanded.

"It's just that I'm not particular to having holes in my britches but having butterflies… well that makes me feel as I might swoon over in a faint." The cook turned around and showed two dazzling red satin butterflies, embroidered on his breech bottoms.

Samuel elbowed his way through the crowd and turned his giant backside for all to see. "Hearts! Can you imagine the look on the Yank's faces when they see red hearts?"

Mosby and his men rocked with hilarity.

John was in a different humor. With certainty, he *identified* the defiant intentions of the artist.

"Catherine!"

Squirrels and birds scattered from the safety of their nests to the treetops. She tried to back away without being seen, but he knew exactly where she had been all the time, his eyes burning a hole through the sheet. Squaring her shoulders, Catherine walked around the laundry and forward into the crowd of men with the regal dignity of a queen before her subjects.

"Did you wish to speak with me, General Rourke?" she inquired with captivating sweetness, knowing the full reason for the murderous rage crossing her husband's face.

He pointed to the derrieres of his men and Catherine stifled a giggle for truly her artwork was—incomparable.

"Could you explain the reason for this?"

"Well I didn't have anything to patch them with." Catherine protested, attempting to lull him with her innocence. "With the terrible shortages and all, I was forced to use what resources were at my disposal."

"You will overhaul every pair of pants. I assure you we will have a discussion later."

Catherine was sick of his high handedness and his ordering her about. She opened her mouth about to launch into a few of Brigid's favorite Irish curses that would have scorched his ears, but decided now was not the time.

"I would hope, General," Colonel Mosby hankered for John's attention. "You will not be such a dullard and introduce me to this lovely lady."

John was forced to turn his attention to the Colonel and his men, having forgotten their presence. His jaw clenched. All sixty plus riders had their sole concentration focused on her. Each man struck a different pose, wide-eyed, smiling, or to her husband's greater disgust, with their mouths gaped open. She lifted her chin and dared to smile at him.

"She is my wife." John let that information register. "I know... you were going to offer your condolences."

"No indeed, my envious congratulations, General Rourke. And to you Mrs. Rourke, may I compliment your fine embroidery. I can say I have never witnessed such artistry. Why General Rourke, when General Lee hears of this, he will be attempted to rename your division to Virginia's hearts and flowers."

Catherine tossed her head and eyed John with cold triumph. "Hearts and flowers sounds romantic, Colonel Mosby. I must applaud you on your ingenious suggestion."

"Catherine, did you embroider all the uniforms like this?" Her husband's mouth set so tightly around his cigar she thought he would snap it in two.

She fanned her chest with her hand. "You mean the uniforms that were heaped in front of my doorstep?"

"The same," John said through gritted teeth.

Her evasion vexed him. Wonderful. "Those uniforms were in terrible condition. Dousing them with kerosene and setting them ablaze would have been an improvement. I walked on water to resurrect the miraculous condition you find them in now. You should be thankful." And then with feigned feminine confusion, she frowned, "Why on earth are you angry?"

"You already know the answer to that question." John snapped. "Why would you even ask?"

"I'm just making conversation." Catherine protested, pasting on her face, a picture of complete beguilement. "Conversation is one of the civilized arts, General Rourke. We can't all stump through life with sword and slaughter, beating our chests to the world. A few of us do try to preserve the dignities. Isn't that right, Colonel Mosby?" Then with one of her breathtaking smiles, she charmed the Colonel, and then glanced at her husband with smug delight.

"There!" Mosby smiled down on the two of them. "I do believe I could not have said it better." He bent over his horse's flanks and said to the general, "I can see why you are such an excellent strategist, General Rourke. Your wife hones her skills on you." Mosby then gave an audible sigh. "I wish I could have such a lovely creature for a tutor."

John muttered around his clamped cigar. "One such creature is sufficient indulgence for a dozen lifetimes."

Only Mosby was in hearing distance and threw back his head with laughter that made the leaves shake in the trees. "I can see my visit has been tedious for you, General Rourke. I must say, I have not laughed so hard in a very long time. Before I forget, your horse is tied to the rear wagon, courtesy of your brother, Colonel Ryan Rourke, who sends his best regards."

"Mrs. Rourke," Colonel Mosby addressed her in good humor, his gaze scanning over her. "I am hopeful to make your acquaintance sometime soon."

"I'm sure you won't," John bit out.

Mosby's mouth twitched with amusement. "How ungrateful you are, General Rourke, for the bounty I have presented to you?"

"It would be my pleasure, Colonel Mosby. We are thankful, aren't we John?" She was playing with fire.

"Perhaps she could assist your men with some of her craft with a needle," John said tersely. "Something appropriate, perhaps harps and cupids?"

"And what will she craft for you General," Mosby said, enjoying the sparring. "Horns and a pointed tail?"

John did not see the humor, especially when his wife dared to walk away without his dismissal.

Mosby offered his hand. "Enjoy the contraband General. It is not often our travels make us so lucky. Next time, the Yanks may not be as generous. There are a few prisoners in the rear wagon that need attending. I would take you up on your offer of a delicious meal this evening, but I do not want to leave the Valley unattended. These are tenuous times. Besides I can see you have other things on your mind." Mosby laughed, then rearing the animal on its two hind legs in a demonstration of showy horsemanship, spurred his horse out of the camp with the rest of his men following.

In the last of the wagons, Lieutenant Johnson had hauled out the captured Yanks, some frightened, others belligerent. John had seen it mirrored in their faces before. They were shipped off to prisoner of war camps until the conclusion of the war. A particular prisoner caught his attention. Even without the medical insignias braided on his coat, he would have recognized him. His memory seized the large proportions of the man with a full head of white hair, except now, he owned the world-weariness of a much older man.

"Lieutenant Johnson, bring that prisoner forward so I may speak to him."

The Yank rubbed his chin and shuffled forward with a cautious approach per the status of being singled out. When the older man finally stood in front of John, he garnered a look of calm resignation, his fate hanging in the Rebel Commander's hands.

John respected him. "Lieutenant Johnson, get Dr. Parks a drink of water."

The prisoner's blue-gray eyes lit from the general's knowledge of his name. "I apologize for any slight, but I am clearly at a loss, for I do not recall meeting you before——" said the doctor.

"We have met...under more unfortunate circumstances. Indeed, no slight is incurred or apology needed. It is I who thank you."

"When?" Dr. Parks searched his captor's face for clues.

"I am General John Rourke, Army of Northern Virginia, if that means anything to you, and I beg the honor of your presence at dinner this evening in my tent."

"I have heard a great deal, almost as much as General Lee. I do not understand?"

John held up his hand. "During the Battle of the Wilderness, a Confederate soldier, fatally wounded, met a Union doctor, presenting himself as a man of peace. The Union Doctor asked the injured Confederate why he thought a man of peace was in this war. The wounded man was in no state to reply. So the Union doctor shared his philosophy. Because fools make wars, and that he, the doctor, was the sad antidote to that reality. Then, the doctor, blind to the colors of blue and gray, gave the dying Confederate a drink of water, treating him only with courtesy and compassion. I remember that simple act of kindness as if it were yesterday."

The doctor shook his head. "There were so many casualties that day, and then the fires."

John nodded. From the artillery bursts, the forests had been set on fire. Men wounded or surrounded by a greater natural force were burned alive. "With so many wounded, I don't expect you to remember, but I do. You suggested we have dinner and talk things out like God fearing men are supposed to do."

The doctor nodded and Lieutenant Johnson appeared. John took the tin cup from his lieutenant and placed it in the doctor's shaking hands, both men understanding the extraordinary profoundness, bridging something far more tangible than a simple gift of water. "So will you do me the honor of having a long overdue dinner with my wife and I this evening?"

Dr. Park's voice choked. "I will look most forward to it."

John was in a better mood after leaving Dr. Parks. The good doctor had hinted at a significant inventory of needed medical supplies. Catherine would be happy. *She'd be happy for her sworn enemy?* John saddled his horse and clicked the equine into a gallop.

Mallory's taunts surfaced with a vengeance.

"She's our best. But don't be too down in the mouth, General Rourke. Miss Fitzgerald is our cleverest of agents. Her craft has been long practiced.

Likewise she's one of our most skilled, and may I add, treacherous strategists in intelligence gathering."

So many inconsistencies. When she had found him, he wasn't wearing a general's uniform and why would one of the North's clever agents be stuck in the countryside? Unless she knew who he was when she saved him.

Every night he resisted the urge to pull back the sheet and gaze at her slender white body beneath the sheerness of her gown. Every night he had to fight to suppress the almost overpowering desire to take her in his arms and let go inside of her, the violent flow of rage that swelled within him.

She was everywhere in the camp, the sight of her taking his men's breath away, taking his breath away. There had been thousands of women since the beginning of time, but he doubted any were as unforgettable as Catherine. Damn, he had enough trouble as it was without some golden-haired goddess to complicate things.

Danny boy had become more of an attendant than a guard. Catherine would walk arm in arm with him, laughing at his anecdotes. John's stomach hardened. He entertained cutting off Danny Boy's arm, yet there was nothing between them other than a brother and sister friendship. Still he did not like it.

At times, John could feel her watching him and he'd look up. She'd cast him a modest sidelong glance, a morsel to tempt him, to make him trail after her like a dog behind a butcher's cart. How he burned for her. How to stop the madness? He might as well command a river to curl back to its source.

Could she see the loneliness in his soul? Would she heal it? Or would she trample it with her dainty foot? No. He could not get hurt.

He stopped his horse at the crest of a hill. The animal pawed the earth and chomped at the bit. John dreamed of her, slept beside her, yet kept away from her, shunning her, daring not touch her. The pretense of hostility wove a safety net between them. Best to keep it that way.

He drove the horse hard, and then circled to camp. At a distance outside his tent, he dismounted and gave the horse to a soldier to feed and brush down. At full attention, Danny boy stood solid, refusing to allow John to take another step.

Did the boy dare to confront him? "Move aside, Danny. I've business with my wife."

"That's the point, General Rourke, Sir. She did her best to stitch those pants."

John crossed his arms. "I am aware she did *more* than her very best. You are to report to Brigid and have her prepare a special meal for three this evening—in my tent."

Danny refused to leave. "I would take exception if you were to do anything disciplinary with Mrs. Rourke."

Rourke sighed. "Are you countermanding my order, private?"

Danny lifted his chin.

"I appreciate your loyalty to my wife—"

"I must have your word, Sir, no harm will come to her," Danny demanded.

"My word?" A cold edge cracked in John's voice. "I hate to be bored, Danny Boy, so I am doing my best to assume you are amusing me. This will be the last and only time I'll explain myself, soldier, because I'm feeling charitable at the moment. I have never laid a hand on my wife despite the fact I'd like to wring her neck for insubordinate behavior. Right now, I wish to have a private conversation with *Mrs. Rourke*. If you are not out of here in one second, I will be forced to toss you across this camp."

"Just a conversation?"

"You heard me soldier. Get going!"

Mollified, Danny Boy dashed away, leaving John bemused.

Inside the tent, Catherine had fretted hours. What would John do to her? Whether he hated her or not, he would never hurt her, that much, she had learned already. But the embroidery? Then, embarrassing him in front of Colonel Mosby and his men? She bit her lip not even attempting to guess.

The tedium of waiting for John wore on her nerves. The longer she waited, the angrier she became. No doubt, he'd force her to wait until late at night. She leaned against his desk, opening and closing a wooden cigar box, inhaling the strong tobacco scent. The tent grew warm and humid, her clothing prickled against her skin. Releasing a ragged sigh, she took off her dress and loosened the stays of her corset, stripping down to her chemise and pantalets. Finding comfort, she threw herself across the bed, stuffing a pillow beneath her chin.

"A strange man you are, John," she said aloud, gazing at the blue-black gun barrels, gleaming, much the same color as his hair.

There is no trust.

She rolled onto her back and punched the pillow. He did not love her. How often had she turned to his sleeping form at night?

291

His warmth so close...her throat ached, and she had an unexpected powerful yearning to be held in someone's arms...John's arms. In Pleasant Valley, they were happy and in love, caught in a paradise immune from the horrors and intricacies of the outside world. Her mind drifted to his first wife where divorce was a disgrace, especially finding the woman with her lover. She shook her head, imagining the wound to John's pride, a lesion that blinded him to everything else. The dilemma twisted in her heart...but was there something more?

In the dark entrails of despair there still glimmered flashes of hope in the remembrance of what had been left unsaid between them, of distant echoes of emotion, of silent flashes in his tormented eyes, and that thin, tenuous filament between them that could not be denied.

His sword dangled from the center tent pole, a gorgeous piece of cutlery, with an ornamental hilt. Up on her knees, she drew the sword from its scabbard and a sharp play of light gleamed upon the blade. If she had to hold it upright for any length of time, her arms would ache. John came into the tent. She yelped, her mouth caught in a silent "O", and the sword's point dropped to his heart.

"Planning on killing some Rebs?" He challenged, moved to the bed where she knelt with the sword. "Why did you walk away from me without a dismissal?"

"Before your dismissal? Your treasure of genius forgets that it was you who ordered me here in the first place. Yet how can I forget that your every command is laced with a war whoop for the Confederacy and glorious cry of the South?" When he dared to take a step closer, she lifted the tip of the sword to his throat.

"You are my prisoner." His steel-blue eyes bored into hers, steel-ier than the pewter-cloaked clouds of an incoming storm, a menac-ing, vibrant, blade-sharp blue. He rubbed his knuckle against the scratch made on his throat. "The battle of North and South is a bad dance involving every kind of warfare, attack, defense, pursuit, eva-sion, parry, thrust, siege, with mutual respect and personal enmity."

Catherine raised an eyebrow. "How diverting. Is your sermon intended for our personal war?"

"My advice to you," John said calmly, "is to put the sword down before you get hurt."

She tossed her hair over her shoulders. "Advice worth nothing is given gratis. She brushed the tip lightly to his chin, "Charming, but I find your talent for observation, flawed, for it is I who hold the sword."

"If given the chance, would you truly harm me? Would you wish to see me dead? After all, I am your husband."

"I am sure you'd never let me forget, dragging me off by my hair, wielding your club like an ancient Neanderthal." Her eyes dipped to an inscription. "*Emeritus In Excelsis. One who has served with honor in the highest degree?*"

John felt like a man feels when his enemy's protective center and flanks were about to collapse. "A Latin scholar?" Her arms trem-bled beneath the sword's weight. Except—he dared not trust her. He wanted to—dared not. The fascination to her was folly, swing-ing from anger to desire in one wild second. John smashed the sword to one side. It clanged on the floor. He kicked the blade under the bed.

"I will have this out." His knees shifted on the bed, his arms placed on each side of her, and entrapping her against the pillows.

"You don't want any attachments. You want to be alone. Isn't that right, John?"

A dangerous pulse beat in his temple. "That's right."

"From the folly of your first wife, you carry a heavy weight, and that load gets kind of heavy doesn't it? You push me away before I get a chance to hurt you. Except I haven't hurt you and you know everything I've told you is the truth. My only sin was not telling you who I was. I was afraid and alone. Can you imagine my fears? Mallory was in control and even in the end his lies to you were for control. I am not a spy. I never betrayed you, but sought to protect you. Even your brother, Lucas believed me."

"Shut-up, Catherine. I don't want to hear anymore." He captured a frond of her hair and teased the end across the nipple of her breast, and his gut came ablaze with her throaty groan.

"You've thrown up a wall so high that you'll never climb over it. The real fear is that wall can be breached."

He would not allow her to breach that wall again.

With burning fire, his mouth came down on hers and she gave herself to the ravishment of his mouth. He unbuttoned his pants and his hand swept down, spreading the split in her pantalettes, the drugging scent of her woman's heat assailing him. Fully aroused, desire pulsed through his swollen rigid flesh and she pressed her groin against the thickness of his erection and the head of his cock bathed in her wet heat. No. He would not enter her, not yet. He toyed with her, spreading her moisture back and forth, biding his time until he filled her. He watched her writhe when his thumb flicked through the triangle of blond curls and at the sensitive piece of flesh at the core of her.

"John." She moaned and pulled him down into her embrace, her breathing ragged.

His breathing was ragged too, and then someone cleared their throat outside the tent. John ignored it, mesmerized by the flush on her cheeks, yet striving to draw himself from his passion-ridden lust, he struggled to focus on the reality around him, his primary thoughts, as his hardened loins dictated, on things he had to, must finish. "Who is it?" he gritted out at last.

"A courier," his adjutant said.

"I'll talk to him later," John rasped.

"He's from General Lee."

"Damn." John pulled Catherine to her feet. He assisted tying her corset and while she donned her dress, he buttoned his pants, straightened his shirt and waited for her to brush her hair. When he viewed the two of them in sufficient order, he threw open the tent flap.

"Salutations, General Rourke," greeted General Benson.

John groaned.

Catherine blushed not only from his intense perusal but for what they had been doing with an audience camped on their doorstep. Without invitation, Benson stepped into the tent and stood paralyzed. "Madam, you are the most stunning creature I have ever lain eyes upon. I came to see how marital bliss agrees with you, General Rourke. Now I can report to General Lee firsthand."

"Go ahead and try." With a curse, John removed his box of cigars from Benson's grasp. "Don't sit, you're not staying long."

Smiling and unaffected by her husband's rudeness, Benson took off his hat and bowed to her, "I'm General Benson. I have to introduce myself seeing how John is so flustered. Was it my untimely arrival?"

John bit the end of a cigar. "Next time, I'll have you cool your heels until you rot. Was this an actual assignment or purely voluntary? And when I get flustered, I have the urge to bury my fist in someone's face."

General Benson put his hands up and let out a hoot of laughter. "No need to take offense. I came on a mission for General Lee. Indeed, a pleasure to be welcomed by you, General Rourke, sharing in your genial mood and impeccable manners. You always were a clever rascal. Never could outwit you at West Point, which, by the way, calls me to reflect on our school days. Perhaps Mrs. Rourke would be entertained with some of our exploits?"

"Hardly," John growled. "Let's get down to business."

Benson pulled several rolled maps from waterproof casings. "Excuse me, Mrs. Rourke." General Benson addressed her and then turned to Rourke, speaking in Latin. *"Res circum Fredericksburgem gravis est cautione versimile, mox extraharis ut Richmondum defendas."*

Catherine translated Benson's words, *"The situation around Fredericksburg is serious. With all probable caution you may be pulled back soon to defend Richmond."*

John held up a hand for Benson to stop. "The information is too sensitive. My wife is a Latin scholar."

Benson clamped his hat to his chest. "Amazing. How did you and the general meet?"

Uncertain of what to say, Catherine glanced at John, his mouth twisted into a threat. Images flashed of what he had done to her before Benson appeared. John was selfish, arousing her carnal nature as a way to deny his love. Yet a crack yielded in his wall that he could no longer hide. She would chisel it apart, chink by chink.

Then she dredged up memories of his body thrown from the train...how she almost buried him alive. She bit her lip, the gruesome ordeal not a romantic way to meet one's spouse. But John's persistent warnings and stubbornness irked her. Inspiration struck. "He literally fell at my feet."

Her husband's expression became one of pained tolerance. "As I recall, my loving wife nearly buried me alive with her initial adoration."

Catherine narrowed her eyes. "Not to mention I should have hit him over the head with a shovel...would have saved me a lot of trouble."

"I believe you have some duties to perform," John interrupted her.

"General Rourke," General Benson protested, "Mrs. Rourke may stay. I am sure her duties can wait."

"Without question." Catherine breathed a most captivating smile for General Benson's benefit, as if her approval was the most important mission he could attain in life.

Out of the corner of her eye she saw John mutter a curse. He opened his mouth to argue with her but his gaze was drawn to her bosom. With certainty, he recalled where his hands had been moments before. He shifted in his chair. "Go to the kitchens and help, Brigid."

At first, Catherine gloated at her ability to rattle her husband. But for her duplicity, her body responded to the heat of his gaze with such a blazing fire, it could have burned down the tent. Heat rose to her breasts. She put her hands to her face, flushing, conscious of his scrutiny.

"Ahem!" General Benson cleared his throat, letting the two of them know of his forgotten presence. "I insist Mrs. Rourke stay. I am sure her duties can wait."

Like her, John was yanked back to reality. "Mrs. Rourke has pressing requirements that need her attention. She is quite handy with the needle and obliged to make mending repairs. Isn't that right, Catherine?"

John gave final notice. She glared at him, but when she turned to General Benson, she pasted on a look of angelic innocence, pleading and exaggerating the weakness of her sex. "Since my duties are overlong, I shall aspire to a fit of vapors that only hartshorn and hand-slapping will put into order."

"I must protest, General Rourke. It is not necessary for the wife of a general of the Southern States to work her fingers to the bone. You are a very harsh man, and I take exception to your insensitivity. Your wife is a delicate flower."

With her head held high, she sailed out the tent, slapping the flap down. She paused to smooth her skirts and heard the pinning down of maps to the table and imagined John hovering over the charts, laying out strategy that he would later concur with General Lee.

John blew out a loud breath and said, "I caution you, General Benson. She'll have your skull for a drinking cup before the sun sets, while roasting your entrails and drinking your blood with a toast to the moon."

John checked his watch. Catherine had dogged him as to who was their unexpected dinner guest. From General Lee to President Jefferson Davis, he let her guess, remaining mute. Catherine fussed with the silverware, glasses for wine on the table set with a white cloth and linen napkins. Brigid had cooked a sumptuous feast for the occasion and his mouth watered with the prospect of the rare treat ahead.

The candle flames wavered as she checked her image in the mirror and patted her hair in place. She didn't need to. Her hair was perfect. Brigid had swept it up in an elegant coiffure, secured with a tortoiseshell comb, and his hands itched to touch the ringlets cascading down her back. The fitted bodice of her iced-blue satin gown had an off shoulder neckline framed in ruffled beaded lace. Courtesy of Mrs. Briggs, the simple lines and rich detail of the gown made Catherine look like a fairy-tale princess. His chest swelled.

Ian appeared, escorting the Union doctor.

The doctor did a double take. "Miss Fitzgerald this is a surprise."

"Dr. Parks, is it really you?" She hugged the snowy white-haired doctor, and then stretched her arms out and shook her head.

"You know each other?" John moved off the platform and shook the doctor's hand, mystified from the revelation.

"Of course I do. Miss Fitzgerald is legendary, known for her work for the poor and destitute of New York. She has used her family's wealth and influence to build an orphanage, expending funds to house the orphans of soldiers lost in this terrible war. Then she worked with me at Mac Dougall Hospital in New York. Everyone knows of the tireless hours that she has devoted to working with the children and the soldiers, commendable for a woman of her stature."

"Thank you, Dr. Parks. But your praises are also to be recognized." The doctor drew out her chair and seated her. "Dr. Parks is a genius at modern surgical techniques. One of his techniques implemented during the war has been successful in saving men from losing their limbs, earning wide acclaim in the medical societies from Boston to Washington. He is amazing."

The doctor rubbed the back of his neck. "I am a little confused, but how is it you are so far south, Miss Fitzgerald?"

"I can answer your question," John said, "Catherine Fitzgerald is my wife."

"But how?" The doctor scratched his head, clearly perplexed on distant barriers and backgrounds. "I thought you were in Washington, Mrs. Rourke."

"It's a long story," John said, and then changing the subject to safer territory, he asked, "Have the two of you known each other for a long time?"

Dr. Parks warmed to the question. "The first occasion, *Mrs. Rourke* had hosted a party for her father in their home before the advent of the war. It was a lovely time and I made plenty of fine acquaintances, good friends of her family, and I remember it as if it were yesterday. If I recall, those in attendance were William Astor, General Winfield Scott, Horace Greeley and Colonel Ulysses S. Grant. The latter, I believe has since been promoted."

John ticked off the names, Astor, the richest man on the continent, General Winfield Scot, John had served under in the Texas-Mexican War, and Greeley was the editor of the New York Tribune. John turned to Catherine. "Why didn't you tell me you knew Grant?"

She gave a dainty shrug to her shoulders, and as if it was of no consequence. "You never asked. I know President Lincoln too." She turned to Dr. Parks. "Please call me Catherine. We are friends."

Conversation flowed through dinner on a wide range of philosophies. Catherine excelled as a hostess and had a flair for a multitude of topics, and at once, he imagined her, in her element at the top of the social whirl in New York. Catherine personified womanhood, quintessential femininity, and an air of mystery that at times seemed unfathomable.

Mallory's words slithered into his mind.

All wars are won with spies. However, the North's most prized possession or weapon is our beautiful seductress, Catherine…our most skilled intelligence operative.

"You should have seen how your wife worked with those orphans. She didn't worry about getting her hands dirty like other useless females of her society. Got right down on the floor and played with those children. Bathed them, fed them, nurtured them and gave them the love that they needed. Then she assisted me with surgeries, unusual for any woman. She was a quick learner and very efficient nurse. I found her indispensable. She is the most selfless person I have ever met. I cannot say enough about her fine character."

John finished his meal and lit a cigar, letting the doctor and Catherine monopolize the discussion. He threw back the remainder of his wine.

"Lovely is she not? You are not the first to be enticed. Many before you have confided and fallen prey to her charms."

"She has the poise and loveliness of a queen, but the heart of a saint. You are a lucky man to have such a woman," Dr. Parks said. "I would not be a doctor if not for the Fitzgerald's. I was an orphan with no money, but with plenty of talent and inclination for healing. Father Callahan cultivated my desire, and went to Mr. Fitzgerald, Catherine's father, asking him to finance my education. I owe the Fitzgerald's a great debt."

John poured more wine. "So you know Father Callahan?"

"Like a real father he was to me, a very good priest and quite pious. But boy can he work himself into a rage faster than a muddled up nest of hornets." Dr. Parks chuckled from his reflections.

"Must run in the family," John muttered.

"I left Mac Dougall Hospital feeling I'd be able to save more men by working on the front where injuries occurred. We were overrun by Colonel Mosby's men and deposited in your husband's camp.

John tilted back his chair. "I am in bad need of a doctor for my men. What do you suggest I do about it, Doctor Parks?"

"I do not know, General Rourke. As far as I know, I will be shipped to Andersonville."

"As a prisoner of war, you are under my command. As the general of this division, I command you to stay behind to be our Chief Surgeon."

Catherine threw down her napkin. "You have the diplomatic subtlety of cannon."

"I don't need to be a diplomat. I'm a general. I command diplomacy."

Before she began her tirade, Doctor Parks waylaid her. "Your husband is being very noble, Catherine. He knows that I have a sworn oath to the government of the United States. I believe he also knows that my sworn Hippocratic Oath as a physician comes first and foremost. I really do not care where I practice my skills. North or South makes no difference to me. I go wherever I am needed. Your husband is very generous in keeping me from facing the Confederate death pit of Andersonville. By commanding me as a prisoner of war, he also absolves me from going against my oath to the Union." Dr. Parks smiled at him. "Thank you and I accept. I hope your men will not mind a Yankee doctor attending them."

"I'm sure they will be most happy." John lifted his glass of wine and toasted Doctor Parks. "There is decency in men and goodness. I must never forget that."

"Thank you, again," said Dr. Parks. "The war is a changing paradox for me too."

"It is for us all." John said, and he knew Catherine felt his words were spoken about their connection. "In war, everything is simple. But the simple is difficult." John rose from the table. "It's late. I'll escort you to your new quarters. Perhaps you could look in on a few patients before you retire."

"Of course, I'd be most happy too." Dr. Park's turned to Catherine and bowed slightly. "It was a pleasure seeing you again."

With a smile on his face, John walked Dr. Parks to the hospital, walking over newly fallen acorns, observing his men over their cook fires, joyous with new rations from Colonel Mosby. He stepped over a fallen log, where pearl-like fungi, rioted its length, opalescent in the moonlight, like mussels on an ocean rock. Nothing could put him in a bad mood.

Chapter 25

When John left, Catherine could barely move, her body numb. Even her mind seemed static. She remembered the way John had touched her this afternoon, the way her body burned with longing. There was no denying that he had been affected as much as she. That deep down, he still loved her.

She pulled off her gown, chemise, corset and petticoat, folded the garments and placed them in the trunk. She slipped on her nightgown, pulled the pins from her hair, picked up a brush and glided the bristles through her tresses.

Oh yes, John was in layers, had built an impenetrable fortress. She had seen flickering emotions cross his face during dinner when Dr. Parks had sung her praises. His emotions held more a power over him than sword or poison. He was dying behind his wall, in sullen, taciturn silence, letting a horde of Trojan horses possessing hidden emotional poisons to circumvent the walls of rationalization.

Given a chance, she would pull down those walls and kill the Trojan horses. She could help him. She must draw him into her light and free the man behind the glacial steel-blue eyes.

She would confront him.

She dropped her brush on the bed in a thud. Alarm bells rang in her head, warning her of the danger. Like a deadly wind, her needs, her emotions threatened to drag her away where she would not know how to find a way back. It was a road she should not travel. Yet, however loud the warning bells rang around her, she would not adhere to them.

She wrapped her arms around her knees and sighed.

It was too late. Despite all that had happened to make her hate him, she was still in love with John Rourke.

He threw open the tent flap, letting it fall on his backside. Catherine sat on the bed, her feet tucked under her. Did her unnatural silence trouble him? He paused, hanging his hat.

"I used to think there was a future for us, John, but the bridge that would build our life together is too far to cross. I must find a place to nurture life and hope again, to heal from this insanity. But give me the courtesy of answering one question. Am I somehow mixed-up with your first wife's betrayal?"

"Don't you dare talk to me about her."

"I dare. I deserve the truth. It is not just about her infidelity, is it?"

"Don't go there, Catherine. Not one more word." He advanced on her, glaring down at her. His hands flexed as if he wanted to put his hands around her throat and strangle her. "You have no business."

"Oh how you fight to keep up those walls to camouflage your secrets, to keep them concealed. It is a game your mind plays, over and over again."

His jaw flexed. "Not one more word, I'm warning you."

"There is a cancer rotting your spirit, John."

His fists clenched, the muscles popped out on his neck. She saw something shattering inside of him, splintering his emotions from all rational control. A blind rage like fire swept over him. "Shut-up!"

"No."

He grabbed his head and grimaced as if in pain and then dropped his hands to his side. "When I came back from the Texas-Mexican War...I found her with her lover."

Loose ends dangled, puzzles cried out to be solved. "There's more."

He swept his hand across the table, sweeping the maps across the tent, his cigar box banged on the floor. "There's more. She laughed in my face, told me she hated me. But that was nothing compared to what she revealed."

Catherine saw how terribly he suffered, a deadly quiver, nothing more. She needed to goad him, to let him cleanse the infection, the cancer that chained his spirit, bracing herself and listening. "Go on."

His handsome jaw was taut, his mouth, drawn into a ruthless, forbidding line. "She had my son aborted. The witch killed my son."

"She gloated with her news, taunted me with it. Had gone to a backdoor slave shed with her lover to do the filthy deed, and then, glorying in triumph, smirking and exultant to not have brought my child into the world. Told me she had him killed well after the quickening. It took all my power and restraint not to kill her."

"Do you know how that feels, to know your innocent child was murdered?" His eyes clouded, wrestling with countless emotions—rage, hate, shame, bewilderment—all emotional deformities.

Pin-points of heat seared her inner eyelids. "I cannot imagine." Catherine searched his face, terrified of the growing aggression in him, a volcano ready to erupt. This was the demon that possessed him. Envisioning the events of John's history, she put herself in his shoes, thought about the irrevocable loss of a child and the accompanying grief.

"In my mind, I was there a million times, never to be able to protect my son."

"Listen to me, John. There is evil in this world. The war has its evil. There are people that are evil. But there is an overall good that supersedes this cancer."

John glowered at her as if she were some bizarre beast, an oddity, warped and repulsive to his sight.

Could she reach him? Could she release the demons he locked inside?

In two steps, his hand shot out, twisting the thin fabric of her nightgown at the neckline, drawing it taut. Her chest rising and falling in rapid, harsh breaths, she stared down at the strong, roughened hand at her breasts, the same hand that had once caressed her with gentle passion. Abruptly the hand tightened and with one quick jerk he plucked the thin garment over her head, flinging it away from her body.

In a blur of unreality, he stripped off his shirt, and she stared blindly at the rippling muscles of his powerful shoulders and arms. His hands went to the waistband of his pants.

She took a burning ember and blew it into a raging fire. "You put up walls of hostility and distrust, fostering a denial, to become a fugitive from life and love and healing. Love is like a dam. If you let a small crack form, a drop of water can pass, and before long, no one will be able to limit the power of the stream and the entire dam will be taken down. Because when those walls come down, then love takes over and it no longer matters. To love is to lose control."

The bed shifted beneath his weight as he stretched out on top of her naked body, his heavy weight covering her. Pain slashed across his features.

Panic trickled through her veins in icy dribbles. The tempest she had fostered was now a reality—an ugly, breathing reality. She shuddered, but pressed on. "John, you need to see through all of this." She stared at his cynical, ruthless face while her tormented mind superimposed other, tranquil remembrances of him. She saw him debating her on every topic, playing the piano in her parlor, and gobbling down peaches in her kitchen. She saw him gazing tenderly into her eyes when he made love to her up on the mountain. She remembered him reciting his vows to her with all the sincerity of the world mirrored in his eyes.

She was right. John did love her. She loved him. Love, hate—both were powerful enough to command the moments of their lives. Beneath the loss of his child, John maintained his rage and detachment. That he was punishing her was certain. He shifted between her legs, and Catherine's fear gave way to a deep, shattering sorrow. Her eyes ached with unshed tears for the proud man who had lost so much. She looked into his eyes and hesitantly laid her trembling fingers against his rigid jaw. "I—I'm sorry," she whispered, her throat clogging. "I'm so sorry."

"I don't want your apologies, and I don't need your pity."

His mouth came down on hers with savage brutality. He wedged his knee between her legs, grasped her hips, lifting them. Her eyes flew open. His harsh, bitter expression reeled above her just as he drew back and then rammed himself full length into her tight passage. A dry sob burned her throat as she offered her body as a vessel for his anguish. She wrapped her arms around his shoulders, taking it all in, anything to release him from the torment and anger.

With a violence bred of rage, he stamped out his rejection and hurt and pain into Catherine. Rock hard and fully aroused, he drove into her, again and again, desire pulsing through his swollen rigid flesh, his gut ablaze with a need for her so ferocious he could not stop the impulse if he wanted to. His head dipped toward her sweet breast and he suckled until she cried out, her breath hot upon his neck. He stroked, caressed, fanned the flames he'd created, anything to punish her for the past she threw in his face. He wanted to bury himself inside her as deeply as he could and not come out until he got his fill. His fingers stroked her in time with his thrusts, his hand swept down her body, slicked across the small, sensitive piece of flesh at the core of her, rewarded when she raised her hips to him and whimpered.

Except when her fingers raked through his hair, her tender touch inflamed him. The sweet offering of her body, the submission to his rage, her head thrown back, the adoration in her eyes, completely exposed in her trust of him. He plumbed the hot fire in her loins, a heat he never imagined, her body arched to meet his deep plunging thrusts.

"I love you, John," she gave way in a half-whisper, a half-cry, and it unraveled the last thread holding him together. Instantly John covered her mouth with his, taking all that she was giving and reacted to the spasmodic tightening of her muscles, pouring his seed into her womb.

Afraid his weight would crush her, John gathered her to him and rolled onto his side, taking her with him. Lying there, with Catherine cradled in his arms, his body still intimately joined to hers, he experienced a peace, unlike any he'd known in years. The blackness in his soul faded. He could feel it like the sun burning away the shadows, bringing light and warmth to a place that had known only darkness and ice for years. To see himself in his own reflection. He brushed back a wayward silky tress and cupped her chin in his hand until her blue eyes met his.

"Thank you, Catherine."

She curled her finger through his hair and kissed him gently before laying her cheek upon his chest. There he held her close, reveling in the feel of her as he cradled her with his body, her heart beating next to his.

"I am so sorry for not trusting you, Catherine, for every failure and every wrong and for the heartache and sorrow."

"There is nothing to forgive. You needed to figure things out. I pointed the way."

It was the very way she loved. How she cared for everyone around her as though they were *her* orphans. He saw her as she'd been in Pleasant Valley, courageous and beautiful and overflowing with innocent allure in his arms. He remembered how she laughed at his stories of his family...how she had saved his life. He saw her rebellious and frightened from the prospect of marrying a man, a virtual stranger and her enemy, a man who had seduced her, and who she had known only a week. He remembered her words as if they were yesterday. *What does a Rebel general's wife do? Will I have to knit sweaters for cannonballs or polish your rifle?*

With a surge of remorse, he remembered when he walked in on her bathing the week before and had said, *"You have ceased to be. You are my prisoner and my servant."* And despite the brutal way he had treated her, she demonstrated nothing other than bravery and determination. Scalding rage at his own blindness and stupidity seized John, the spectacles, the horrid bun, a disguise. She had been frightened, and in hiding, and he damned well should have known. She was an innocent and pure, that he knew too, yet he had believed the lies of one man against her. He deserved to be shot.

He had kidnapped her, taken her against her will, worked her like a common slave, and subjected her to humiliation in front of his men. How could one beautiful girl bear the weight of such cruelty without hating him?

"I have a lot of making up to do," John sighed.

"Now tell me from the start about Mallory and how was Lucas helping you?" He listened, asking questions, going back to where they had left off that terrible day in Pleasant Valley. He listened to her talk about her home, her brother, her parents, her uncle and Jimmy O'Hara. The floodgates opened.

On into the hours of darkness they talked of a myriad of topics. She drew circles on his chest and he was already hard for wanting her again. "I'm sorry, Catherine." His last words were smothered on her lips as she buried her hands into his hair.

Her hand moved from his cheek to his jaw. "Will you make love to me?"

John swallowed the poignancy of her words, a trusting caress across his soul. They shared an intense physical awareness of each other. John vowed he'd make her forget the misery he caused her. With a growl, he rolled her on her back and made delicious sweet love to her. Time passed slowly, for he made love to her again and again, and then held her while she slept. John exhaled and glanced at the pink light that slipped between the canvas flaps. He was overwhelmed by what had happened and never had he felt so content. That this beautiful woman had risked much, to taunt him, to suffer his wrath and to relieve him of his torments was more than he deserved. Without fear, she had reached into his soul and ripped out years of latent festering wounds, the liberation like a meteor exploding through the sky. That she did so proved without a doubt that she was far braver and wiser than any woman he had ever known.

That she loved him slammed into his chest.

Chapter 26

*J*ohn had ordered his adjutant that they were not to be disturbed, even if it were General Lee. For just once Rourke disregarded his responsibilities that included many points of consideration. The fact that there were four thousand men camped around them, his men, waiting for his command. The fact that a terrible war brewed like a tempest out there with a powerful enemy waiting to attack with hammer-like blows...and the fact that he had less than ninety hours to pull out and head wherever Lee decided. For once...for this one moment in time...he wanted freedom from strife and warfare.

All day they had made love and now Catherine took a lock of her hair and tickled his nose. He opened his eyes. He was already hard. "Wife, when will I satisfy your needs?"

She shrugged her tousled hair and, as far as he was concerned, he'd keep her in his bed looking just like that for the rest of his life.

"I'm the sole initiator?"

"You leave me thirsting and insatiable. If I had my way, I'd lock you in a tower and keep you hidden away so no man may feast his eyes upon you."

"That's an awful, overbearing, imperious thing to say, my husband." She pinched his chest and he grabbed her hand.

"I'm an awful, overbearing, imperious man."

"Tell me John, do husbands ever feel less than invincible?"

"No."

"But John if…"

He didn't let her finish her argument. His mouth covered hers hungrily—demanding the end of all conversation and with a low growl rolled her over and made swift, wonderful love.

They found a bottomless peace and satisfaction in the laziness of the day. They slept and made love over and over again. She dropped her cheek on his chest, snuggling as close as she possibly could. She sighed, caressing his neck and with an impish smile on her face, she asked, "Does your love include my embroidery talents?"

He laughed and nuzzled her hair. "Especially your embroidery talents. You are the most mulish, rebellious woman I have ever met. Big Samuel in red hearts?"

She giggled and moved slightly. John brought her back, holding her as if he let her go one inch she would vanish. "Hold still, my love," he commanded. "I want to see to the conception of our first child."

In the afternoon, Catherine went to the hospital to assist Dr. Parks. A jumble of leaden-billowing cloudlets tumbled against the rounded peaks of the Shenandoah. Across the hills they rumbled, lining up in parallel bands, deadly beasts against a dark lilac sky. The air hung heavy and the wind blew gusty swirls of fine dust in miniature tornadoes. The canvas tents strained against their moorings while soldiers eyed the angry firmament, preparing for the tempest to come.

Indifferent to the approaching storm, Catherine guarded a deepening peace growing inside of her. Since her parents' death and brother's disappearance, she had been detached and alone. Rourke made her feel connected, and happy, and part of something. She laid a hand over her heart feeling the profoundness of it all. As she wandered through the camp, the men nodded warmly. These were her men—men of the Northern Virginian Army and she loved them. How she hated war.

She had not seen her husband for an hour. She yawned, sapped from the night and day of passion they had shared together. John told her he did not want her to work anymore, in fact, he forbid it, wanting her rested and promising new activities at night. She had told him of the gratification she received from her tasks and he relented. To her disappointment, he had relieved Danny Boy as her guard, sending him off to needed picket duty.

She stooped to pick a bouquet of wildflowers to brighten the hospital and felt the heat of John's gaze upon her. Across the camp and underneath a knot of oaks, he watched her over the shoulders of two of his officers, but it was the intimate unguarded message his eyes conveyed. She swallowed. Her breasts prickled and loins throbbed. *How could he do this to her?* Her gut clenched and a distinct warmth flooded the area between her legs as if he were making love to her right there, his mouth, his callused hands gliding over her body. There was a dreamy intimacy to their shared awareness, flames burning within both of them, and his officers pivoted to see the cause of John's distraction. Swooning with mortification, she picked up her skirts and fled.

By the time she reached the hospital, the rain was spitting across the hilltops working its way down into the valley. Pattering hard against the muffled sound of canvas, streams of water channeled into rivulets where the water's weight grouped and poured into a large funnel. The wood smoke drifted about the camp as it searched for a way out of the beating rain. Rain hurled in through the tent flap, causing the candles to flicker. The camp would be difficult to traverse for the earth would be mired in mud.

Far off in the storm-shaken afternoon, there came the sound of thunder or was it a gunshot? Catherine looked to Dr. Parks but he seemed unaffected, used to the sounds of war.

"One shot means nothing." He allayed her fears. "A rain of shot would indicate a whole division marching down on us. Do not fear. Your husband keeps his camp well-guarded."

She wiped her damp hands on her apron. Something was wrong. She could sense it. She read to a wounded soldier and wrote letters for another. The rain did not stop. Nerves danced in her stomach with the increasing deluge.

Fidgety, Catherine opened the tent flap, receiving a wave of rain, and soaking her skirts. In the distance, John and Lieutenant Johnson carried a bundle through the cloudburst, coming straight toward her. Rourke shouldered his way into the tent.

"Dr. Parks." John commanded and laid a man on the table.

"Danny Boy?" She looked to John. "What happened?"

"Gut shot. His gun backfired. He'd seen movement, shot at it, but it was just a rabbit."

"Dr. Parks, can you help him?" Catherine begged. Tears rolled down her cheeks. The boy was as pale as a sun-bleached boulder.

317

Dr. Parks cut the boy's clothes off. Bile rose to her throat. She didn't need to ask.

Dr. Parks shook his head "I can make him more comfortable."

There was so much blood.

"Do what you can," John said.

Danny Boy's eyes fluttered open.

"How are you, Danny Boy?" John tried to smile.

"Intolerable, Sir."

"Everything's fine Danny. We have a real doctor this time," John encouraged.

Catherine's throat ached, moved by the depth of John's feelings, his love for this boy, and hatred for his useless death.

"Is Mrs. Rourke here?"

"I'm here Danny." She sat next to him, holding his cold hand while Dr. Parks did his best. The reality hit Catherine like a ton of bricks. He was bleeding to death and there was nothing anyone could humanly do.

Danny Boy started to cry. "Don't think me a coward for crying. The pains are terrible."

"Nonsense." Catherine smoothed his hair back from his forehead.

"I know I'm dying. Can I talk to you alone?"

Catherine looked to John. He nodded and everyone left.

"I was scared only once in my life, and I'm ashamed to tell of it," he choked out, his breathing rattling.

It was a confession. There was no priest, to empty his soul. "Go ahead. No one but me will ever hear what you tell."

"The screams were terrible. I can still smell the smoke. Feel the heat from the fire. My mother and sisters inside. I tried to get them out, but men sent by the landowners kept laughing at me. I burned my hands but the door wouldn't budge." He grew silent for a moment as his life ebbed away from him. His blood pooled to the ground.

"When did this happen?" she asked and stood, cradling his head in her arms.

"I was six. In Ireland. The landowners wanted the back rent and come to make an example to others that didn't pay. They nailed the windows and doors shut."

The famine was terrible. Thousands had flooded New York and Boston from Ireland.

"I tried to open the door. I cried. I was a coward. That's my sin."

"No it is not." she shouted from the injustice but before she could banish his guilt, his head fell sideways. He was dead. She cried for the darling Rebel boy in her arms. She hugged him and rocked him. What a horrible burden he carried. All the horrors of this war were nothing that matched the helplessness of a six-year-old's world. Catherine cried for a very long time. She resisted when John pried her arms from Danny Boy's body. Her dress was soaked in his blood. Her husband picked her up, cradled her head against his neck. Like soothing a young child, he whispered assurances to her. She put her arms around his neck and sobbed.

"Catherine you have an unaccountable need to save somebody. But it can't be everybody. Only God holds such power."

As John carried her across the camp, his men gathered in the slanting rain, a tribute to Danny boy who they mourned, and parted for them to pass. "Poor lass," they said. They had all lost their hearts to the general's wife.

Chapter 27

*J*ohn had risen early, reluctant to leave the warm arms of his wife, but was compelled to do reconnaissance work. He urged his horse ahead of his pickets, moving farther up the valley to scout the enemy. Although many farms had been stripped and torched by Yankees, many others escaped ruin. The land in the rich Shenandoah was heavy, like a woman ponderous with her approaching maternity. Peaches grew in groves waiting to ripen, hay was cut and laid in rows to dry, the wheat rose golden, ripening amber in the sun, and the corn was silking, growing so fast in the hot humid heat you could almost hear its thrust. Wooly lambs dotted the fields like so many clouds in the sky and up against the barns, weathered umbra red from lack of care, were snorting pigs, squawking fowl and cattle grazing in their yards. The mountains climbed high on either side, ancient sentinels, linearly endless in their protection of the Valley.

John missed home. Fairhaven. He missed the days of hard work, hams smoking in the sheds, baling hay high in the barns, training foals, and planting crops. He dreaded the continuation of the war. He was a farmer and destiny had made him a general.

Would Catherine like the life of a farmer's wife? She was far more suited for the tea and opera houses and other accompaniments New York society offered. Would she be content to raise a brood of children far from the glittering circles of New York? Would she be content to live in the isolation of a lone country farm?

John left the road, riding down an embankment, leading to a stream. He allowed his horse to drink, his other men following suit. The hackles rose on his neck, the war hyper-trained his senses to a well-honed edge. He was being watched, movement in front of him—in the shadows of the forest. He caught the barest glimpse of a man. Hand signaling to his men, they dismounted, taking defensive positions. How many? He waited for a round of gunfire. A lone man? When no volley took place, John concluded that the fellow had something to hide. A spy?

"Who goes there?" demanded John. "What company?"

"Third Division Calvary Corps, Army of the Potomac," said the man. "What Company are you?"

"Army of Northern Virginia."

"You're not Union Cavalry?"

"Nope." Big Samuel spit a tobacco stream.

"Come on out, slowly if you please," John commanded. Was this a ruse? Union Cavalry over the hill? A trap? He would have heard if Sheridan or Hunter were this far down in the Valley. Then again, communications didn't always get through.

The man trudged across the creek, his arms raised and not at all happy. "I am unarmed."

To John, he looked recognizable, but he had seen so many men during this damn war that everyone looked familiar. Still a nagging feeling gave him pause...the green of his eyes, color of his hair, and his defiant stance. John took an immediate dislike.

"You are now a guest of General Robert E. Lee." John informed him. "Where is your horse and where is the rest of your Calvary unit?"

"I have no idea," said the soldier which John doubted very much and his concern rose from the idiocy of the Yank's remark.

"You cannot take me prisoner," the Yank demanded. "I have to get home to New York. My sister is in great danger."

John's men laughed at the Yank. "Is she missing her parasol?"

"This is war, soldier, and your sister's perilous condition will have to wait. Big Sam, hold him here," John ordered. "The rest of us are going to take a little ride and circle the area to ferret out his comrades.

"Be my guest," retorted the Yank, "It will be a complete waste of your time."

John could not believe the arrogance or the glint of humor crossing the Yank's face. He had the sudden desire to smash his fist into his jaw. "You mean to tell me you are taking a stroll in Southern Virginia without a horse or gun, in a Union uniform, merely for pleasure, and you expect us to believe you?" John said.

The Yank chuckled, a dry, cynical sound. "Have a nice day."

For more than seven hours, John canvassed the Valley in search of the Yank's cavalry, expecting them to spring up at any time for a battle. No evidence was found. He gritted his teeth from the delay. John turned his men back to camp, his foremost thoughts were to see Catherine—alone. He fantasized of what he'd like to do, and grew warm in the saddle, thinking about the blush that rose to her cheeks. They met up with Big Samuel.

The Yank dared to stand there his arms folded in front of him. "I told you so."

John spurred his horse ahead eager to get to his wife so he could spend some private time before he questioned the Yank. Pulling into camp, he dismounted and with a welcome cry, Catherine threw herself into his arms.

"I've missed you," she beamed, skimming her hands up the border of his jacket and around his neck.

"How much did you miss me?"

In answer, she pressed her lips to his, caressing, teasing. John crushed her into his embrace, plunging into her mouth with savage intensity.

John's men rode in with the prisoner, breaking up their brief interlude. Catherine straightened, blushing from John's scrutiny, and the fact that his soldiers' had witnessed their indiscretion. "You better control yourself, my wife. My reputation is at stake." He jerked his head to where his men hooted with approval.

Catherine folded her arms in front of her. "I'm not going to share you with anyone at the moment." She took his hand and started drawing him toward their tent. "Business can wait. You've been gone all day and I have a million things to discuss."

"Just discuss?"

"You are incorrigible, General Rourke, but you catch on quick for a Reb. I was going to say you look a little dusty and need some dusting."

She peered up at him. He was lost.

"I happen to be a lot less distracted in our tent, John."

"I didn't know dusting required all that concentration."

"It doesn't. But other things do. First we have to remove those dusty clothes."

John threw back his head and let out a great peal of laughter that resonated across the camp. Ian called to him, asking what to do with the prisoner. John draped his arm around her shoulder and swerved to issue an order.

He felt Catherine stiffen, saw her face pale.

"It can't be true." She flipped off John's arm and started running in the direction of the captured soldier.

The Yank's mouth gaped open. He broke from his captors in a flat out run. "Catherine! Is it really you?"

Catherine fell into the Yank's arms, weeping aloud, kissing him all over his face. She held the prisoner in a death grip, refusing to let him go. "Is it really, you I'm not dreaming. You're not dead. You're alive and well?"

"Fit as I'll ever be, love. God, how I've missed you." He picked her up and swung her around.

John strode from behind, his men surrounding them in tight circle. "Yank, you'll take your hands off her. You forget your place or have you forgotten you're in the midst of a war?"

The Yank's eyes flashed a hostile green, full of sullen resentment. "Who the devil do you think you are?"

"I'm the commanding officer." Did the Yank have the insolence to look him up and down?

"I haven't forgotten my place. What the hell are you doing with her?" He pushed Catherine arm's length. "What are you doing

325

here?" Then the Yank turned his back, giving John a haughty cut-direct. "I've put up with a lot over the last seven months, and I'm not about to let some Reb deter me."

John put his hand on the hilt of his sword. To run him through had certain appeal. "I'm warning you, Yank, unless you want a good fight on your hands, you'll release her." He was through being polite.

"Do you want to finish him off, general?" His soldiers pointed their gun barrels at the Yank.

His wife stepped in front of the prisoner, shielding him with her body. "No. John, this is Shawn. My brother who has been missing all these months."

"What the Hell are you doing with my sister?" Shawn demanded. And then turning to Catherine he frowned. "You still haven't answered me. What are you doing in a Reb camp?"

"It's a long story, Shawn."

John saw she was trying to placate her brother and slow his temper. His men lowered their rifles, their mouths gaped open with interest. What's your name Yank?"

Shawn lifted his chin and annunciated his name with salute, "Lieutenant Colonel Shawn Callahan Fitzgerald."

John took a closer look. The green eyes and color of his hair. Of course, they were brother and sister. "I should have seen it from the start. I'm General John Daniel Rourke, the Army of Northern Virginia." He extended his hand.

Shawn's eyes spit like green fire. "If you don't mind telling me, General John Daniel Rourke of the Army of Northern Virginia," he mocked. "What the hell are you doing with my sister in your camp?

Have you perhaps taken it upon yourself to invade New York and kidnap young unprotected women from their dwellings? I'd like some answers, for my sister is a long way from home and I didn't care for the way you were mauling her when I entered this camp."

John raised an eyebrow as the Yank folded his arms in front of him, expecting answers as if he were the commander of the whole known world, and oblivious that more Rebels crowded around them.

"I'm waiting and I'm being very patient on the subject, for you see, the way I'd be thinking is that my sister has been compromised, and I want to know, General John Daniel Rourke, Emperor of plunder, rapine, destruction and infinite idiocy, what you plan on doing about it."

Catherine threw her hands up. "Shawn I'll remind you that you are not in your element and you are overstepping your bounds. If you need a geography lesson, I'll remind you that you reside in the heart of the Confederacy."

"Not where you are concerned, Catherine. I promised father when he died, I'd take care of you." Shawn pushed up his sleeves.

"And you are, Shawn," she admitted. "You've only come to blows with a general of the Confederacy, and one I might add who holds your fate in his hands. You may want to improve your manners and apologize."

"Apologize! The way he's manhandled and compromised you. Never."

"You will," Catherine avowed, digging in her Irish stubborn heels.

"I won't."

"You will," she said sharply.

"Pig-headedness must run in the family," John interrupted them. "Before this turns into a brother-sister brawl—"

"He'll apologize first." Catherine shrieked, determined to straighten the matter.

"Give me two good reasons," Shawn demanded.

"Number one," she told him with certainty in front of John's men, "I love him."

John straightened with her public declaration.

"She loves him." His men all nodded their heads. Someone in the back of the crowd yelled out, "I can't hear. What'd she say?"

His wife's temper flared, frustrated from Shawn's mulishness. "I said I love him!"

"Who does she love? The Yank or the Reb?"

"The Reb," she screeched.

"That's not good enough." Shawn shook his head. "You love him? But he's a—Reb."

"He's a Reb, and he's my husband which is reason number two, and don't tell me that's not good enough because I'll shoot you myself."

"She'll shoot him herself." John's soldiers muttered to one another, and then raised their guns again.

"He's really your husband. But how?"

"It was all very romantic, Shawn," she gushed, and missed the consternation on John's face. "He literally fell at my feet."

A louder murmur cascaded through his soldiers with nods of approval. "The general's very romantic, even fell at her feet."

John gritted his teeth. He needed a cigar.

She tapped her toe. "I'm waiting, Shawn."

Shawn wasn't about to give up.

With a grudge, her brother appraised John across the ringing silence. "So this is the man my sister has chosen for a husband. Your reputation reaches far, General. However, you must be quite a man to control my sister, knowing how headstrong she is."

"Yes," John admitted, thinking how much time it would take for the *'romantic'* part to reach General Lee's ears.

"You have my apology and my *pity*," Shawn said and extended his hand.

John shook his hand. "Thank you," he said. He was getting to like his Yank brother-in-law.

"I don't like the *pity* part, but I'm happy both of you have conceded to a mutual respect. "You can lower your guns gentlemen, this is a family affair," she ordered.

John nodded behind her and they lowered their guns. His wife was happy. She thought she had commanded them.

"We were just ready to take our coffee in the tent, Shawn," she slipped her arm through her brother's. "Weren't we, General?" She looked over her shoulder in that I'm-telling-you-husband look. "Really, Shawn, its ground chicory. Coffee is not as plentiful but chicory is very tasty once you grow accustomed to it. And where have you been for the past seven months?"

Chapter 28

𝓘nside his tent, John poured two glasses of Old Crow whiskey and shoved one across the table to Catherine's brother. Francis Mallory was at the core of the problem. John wished he could take Washington so he could strangle the bastard.

Shawn detailed his missing months. "Mallory orchestrated my kidnapping at The Battle of Brandy Station last October. During the melee, I had maneuvered off the road and through the woods. There were six Union soldiers in fast pursuit who I thought had my back. Surrounded, I was knocked unconscious. I awoke later, locked in a farmhouse in Virginia, guarded by the same soldiers who kidnapped me. The walls were thin and I soon gleaned that they were Mallory's thugs. They talked about how Mallory was circling Catherine and laughed about other crimes Mallory had committed. After a couple months passed, orders arrived from New York. Mallory in his perverted sense ordered me hanged and for it to look like a suicide."

Shawn drained his whiskey and John refilled his glass. "With the rope around my neck, the thugs slapped my horse from beneath me. Rebel sharpshooters had been watching and shot the rope in two before it snapped my neck, and then they chased off the thugs.

My head hit a rock. Unconscious again, and with a second head injury, I was in a very bad way. I roused from a dark fog and in a strange farmhouse owned by the seven Confederates, all brothers, who had rescued me. My life was a total blank. I had no recollection of any of prior events. The brothers assumed I was a spy for the Confederacy. To them, it didn't make any sense that Union officers would hang one of their own. What they didn't realize was that they were Mallory's thugs. The brothers' sister cared for me." Shawn cleared his throat and looked at Catherine. "We were married."

"What?"

Shawn nodded his head. "She is the love of my life and the finest woman I've ever met."

"Congratulations," John reached for his cigars and offered one to Shawn.

"For weeks, I had temporary flashbacks. Nothing was right. Then one day, everything came back all at once. The hardest thing for me to do was to leave Emma, my bride, but I had to get back to protect Catherine. I told her not to tell her brothers and that I would send for her. I had been moving north for a week, when you came upon me."

Ian brought dinner that Brigid had prepared. When his adjutant left, Shawn leaned forward. "I have to get back home and take care of Mallory. The monster has gone unchecked too long."

Catherine shoved half her portion on her brother's plate and waved his protest away. "Mallory has Father Callahan. John's brother, a Union Colonel in Washington and Jimmy O'Hara were to find him, but I've had no communication. I saw firsthand,

Mallory crushing Confederate soldiers that he had taken from Capitol Prison just for his sick pleasure." Catherine shuddered. "He also tried to kill John."

John kept his own counsel. The conundrum was a war within war.

"Mallory's destroying Fitzgerald Rifle Works," Catherine said. "He ordered his foundry-men to manufacture irregular-shaped gun-barrels. When the Fitzgerald rifles were fired, they exploded backward into the user. Mallory hoped to bankrupt us."

John pulled his cigar from his mouth when he heard that bit of information. "Danny Boy's death was from a Fitzgerald rifle."

Catherine's eyes filled with tears. "I tried Shawn. When the problem with the backfiring was discovered, it was too late. There were already many rifles in the field. After the report, I had our men test each barrel before assembly, then again after it was assembled. I made sure not one Fitzgerald rifle left the plant unless it had been tested, re-tested and perfect. I raised cash by selling the Fitzgerald jewels, and then gave the funds to our plant manager to secretly build another foundry in New Jersey so we would have our own barrels. Now Danny Boy has died because I didn't catch the error in time."

John rose and took her in his arms. She sobbed, her tears dampening his shirt. He was proud of her. No other woman he knew would have been so brave or been able to outwit her foe. But Mallory was too powerful and had to be stopped. He shuddered to think that Mallory had almost forced her into marriage. If John hadn't kidnapped her out of Washington—he hated to think what would have happened.

Shawn ran his fingers through his hair. "I realize I'm asking you to do something entirely against your principles, but if you could afford me a couple of hours and escort me to where the Union Army is positioned near Washington, then I can take care of Mallory. The situation is imperative."

John had no idea what to do as he glanced at his wife and her brother, waiting his decision. He needed time. He walked outside his tent. The last rays of the evening sun poked through the boughs of a hickory. A courier arrived, ordering him to Lee's headquarters. An order from Lee was an order from God. Would he have to pull his troops out and defend Grant's flanking movement or would he be asked to move his troops northward in the Valley? None of it mattered for now.

Marrying Catherine, John had a responsibility for her family. What she and her brother asked for was a lot. To commit treason? To take her brother, a prisoner of war, across lines? The dilemma was against his core beliefs and everything he fought for. He could be hanged for such an act against the Confederacy.

John made his decision.

"You do realize I could be executed for this," John said, reentering his tent.

"I know," Shawn admitted. "I appreciate what you are doing more than you realize. I'll owe you my life."

"I only want your sister." John made passes to get them through the pickets.

"You're a fine man, General Rourke. Odd this war..." Shawn shook his head. "Catherine and I have both married southerners."

"I'm risking being taken as a prisoner by the Union Army, that's if I'm successful moving you close enough without getting shot," John said.

"I have numerous political acquaintances and influences that would not allow that to happen," Shawn smiled.

John remembered the guest list Dr. Parks had mentioned. The Fitzgerald's were well connected but despite those connections, Mr. Lincoln would have a different opinion.

"We have exactly forty-eight hours. I'll have two horses saddled. Wear this over your uniform." John tossed Shawn his gray greatcoat. "Be ready in an hour...best to leave under cloak of darkness."

"Two horses? I'm going too," Catherine stated.

"No. You will not leave this camp. Under no uncertain terms will I subject you to danger." John looked to Shawn for support to halt the firestorm brewing.

"It would be easier to change the orbital velocity of the moon," Shawn said, and then spoke to his sister. "You need to listen, Catherine. Your husband wants you safe."

Catherine sniffed and reached inside her husband's jacket, trying to convince him in other ways the practicality of taking her.

John was no fool, and despite the erotic tenderness with which her hands stroked up and down his back, beckoning him, he wanted her out of harm's way. "There is only one thing that will quiet you." He kissed her long and hard and when he stopped, he turned her face up to his to see the rosy blush forming. That's the way he wanted to remember her.

Chapter 29

Catherine waited twenty minutes after John and her brother departed. Cloaked in a greatcoat, her hair tucked under a slouch hat and pulled low to hide her face, she presented a pass with her husband's forged signature and breezed through the pickets. She had to follow. She had to make sure both of them were kept safe. The idea was foolish but she would not let John risk his life. If the northern commanders captured him she would be there to help him.

The moon rose big and full, illuminating the landscape. She tapped her horse into a cantor. When John and her brother came into view, she slowed, keeping far enough behind to stay undetected. Her husband skirted towns and farms, anywhere they might be seen. Her back ached and her eyes drooped. To keep awake, she watched the brilliant July moon cast its long silvery shadows, waxing and waning in its journey across the night's sky. Dawn approached as well as noon with the sun torridly hot and reaching its zenith. When John and Shawn rested and watered their horses, she dismounted and pulled down the bridle, patting the horse's forehead. So far she had been unnoticed and wanted to keep it that way.

"You can come out, Catherine. We know you've been following us," said John.

Cringing, she led her horse by the reins down a steep slope until she stood in front of her husband. He had his arms folded in front of him.

"Your father should have worn out a hickory stick on you. As it is now, I'm half-attempted to perform the duty myself. I do remember giving you express orders to stay in camp. Is it too difficult for you to remember, or is it pure disobedience that compels you to go against my every wish?"

Her fingers clenched the reins. "If you think that I am going to let you endure any hardship because of me, then you have another think coming. You need my help."

John gave her a sardonic look. "Amazing how I've managed to make it through this war without *your* help. It's too late to take you back. Now I have the extra burden of your safety to consider." He grabbed her in his arms and kissed her fully and lingeringly. Her response was warm and eager, and it was a long, long moment before a polite clearing of her brother's throat interrupted them. John raised his head and her eyelids opened, her breath trembled from her parted lips. As if drawn away from a trance, she turned to see Shawn smiling.

"I believe you two need time off for a honeymoon, but I'd like to proceed." Shawn jerked his head in a northerly direction.

The ground beneath them thundered. A band of men coming out of the woods, rode at an unbreakable speed toward them. John and Shawn cursed.

"They have no uniforms," Shawn noted.

John grimaced. "This isn't good. I'll handle it. "They're probably home-guard militia. Catherine, take cover in the trees."

Ice ran through John's veins. He ambled up close enough to get a clear shot to kill several of the men at once. Shawn followed his lead, backing his horse around to use as a shield, a repeater rifle balanced in his arms. A small army. Twenty to two. Easy. Thirty feet in front, the men fanned around them. Eyes on him, blank and unwavering. Not the toughest, John had ever seen. Rough lives, and perpetual conflict in their ancestry. They weren't going to swoon if he shouted *Boo*. They didn't have the customary war-torn look of the home-guard. Every available man in Virginia was in the military or would have been home attending the family farm at this hour. Yet these dandified, young bucks were out joyriding. He glanced over his shoulder. Good. Catherine was well-concealed. He didn't want her caught in the crossfire.

"How can we help you gentlemen?" John said. No one answered. Not an encouraging sign. How many could he pick off in the first ten seconds?

"Mallory," Catherine screamed. John swung around. Mallory held a revolver to her head.

"I've missed you, Catherine." Mallory jerked her up in front of him. "Interesting our meeting. "General Rourke, I have particular hatred for your family. Your meddling brother, Colonel Lucas Rourke in Washington was going to arrest me, and has run me out of my country. I gave him the slip. And then dear sweet, Catherine Fitzgerald, I offered to marry her and make an honest woman of her. What repayment do I get? She runs run off with some Rebel scum. You Rourke's have destroyed my plans, but I vow I'll get everything back. I'll have it all. The Fitzgerald fortune will be mine. Without witnesses there can be no trial."

There were several trained guns on them, all Mallory's thugs. John relished a good fight. But Mallory had his gun on Catherine. "Don't lay a hand on her. I'll kill you."

"That's ungenerous of you. I'll take your guns for that." Mallory laughed, his black eyes alive. "No need for things to get messy with the young lady present."

His clothes were muddy and his horse was beat. He was on the run and a man on the run was desperate.

"Don't give up your guns," Catherine pleaded. Mallory twisted her arm behind her back.

John took a step toward Mallory. The bastard would pay. A rifle barrel jabbed in his midsection. Mallory's goons. He nodded to Shawn to lay down his gun. Two ropes were slung over the stoutest branch of an oak.

"I take pleasure from hanging men. To let your entrails become fodder for the crows."

John glared at him. "To have you digest twenty inches of my steel would give me pleasure."

"My only regret, General Rourke, is that I wish I could hang you twenty times over."

Shawn and John were mounted, their hands tied behind their back. The horses pranced nervously beneath. Nooses roped around their necks.

Like a cat with a mouse, Mallory toyed with his prey. "Shawn, you turn up like a bad penny. I had taken care of you before, but you escaped. This time I'll be sure to make it permanent."

"You'll meet your end, and I'll dance on your grave when you do," Shawn spat.

"Brave words from a man who is about to meet his maker," Mallory sneered.

"You are insane. You'll never get away with it. What have you done with my uncle?" Catherine stomped on his boot and bit his hand.

Mallory slapped her. Her head snapped back. "He's dead, and so is Agatha, your stepmother. It was a pleasure tightening my hands around her fat throat, her eyes bulging as she breathed her last breath. Remember my sweet. Do you still have the bruises?"

The bastard dared to lay his hand on his wife. Rage burst through John's veins and he curled his lips back in a snarl, "You won't get far. I have an army of four thousand camped over the hill and cavalry riding round to meet me any second," he bluffed. Mallory blanched then marched Catherine forward until they were ten paces.

"I love you," she mouthed.

"Touching," Mallory gloated in anticipation of the hanging. "We're all Robinson Crusoes. All on our own little islands. Do you wish to know what I intend to do with Catherine?" Mallory told John carelessly, and gestured toward his men. "After I have had my way with her and grow tired, my men will have a turn. Then I'll sail with her to the Indies, and sell her to the highest bidder. The prostitutes do not last long. Most meet with a premature death."

From far atop the crest of a hill, a whole host of Reb Cavalry bore down across the meadow. Mallory froze in terror. At once, his goons started shooting. Rabble compared to the experienced Rebels. A whole barrage of answering gunfire ensued. Most of

Mallory's men pitched forward in the dirt, the Reb sharpshooters meeting their mark.

Shawn and John's horses danced, the fear of gunfire frightening them. The rope whipsawed against his neck. He kneed his mount into submission.

Mallory screamed for his men to do the deed. The cowards who weren't shot fled. Mallory scrambled forward. Catherine clawed at him, ripped at his coat, trying to keep him from the horses. He backhanded her, sending her flying across the embankment. How John wished he could get free and wrap his fingers around Mallory's neck. Mallory slapped the horses' flanks.

"No!" Catherine's scream pierced the air.

Both horses reared and bolted. John felt the weight of his body draw on the noose. Shots fired. He and Shawn crashed to the ground. The sharpshooters had diced the ropes. Mallory flew into the woods. Catherine knelt beside John. A Rebel Cavalry officer pulled up. He threw a knife from his boot on the ground and Catherine cut them loose.

"I see your timing is impeccable," John smiled. "Almost too close, brother."

"Why is it I seem to be fishing you out of trouble, General Rourke?" Ryan asked.

"I've been pondering that thought myself." John rubbed his neck. "But there is a bigger fish I'm angling for, a dark haired dandy who disappeared in the woods. Make sure your men hunt him down. I want him alive."

Colonel Ryan Rourke gestured with his hand to his men. With a Rebel yell they plunged into the woods like hounds after a fox, and in a matter of seconds, found Mallory and the rest of his thugs.

John faced Mallory as he came out of the woods. His brother's men prodded him with their bayonets. A dead tree branch tripped him. He went sprawling face down in the dirt, his neatly curved mustache of which he was so vain, gone askew. The Rebel cavalrymen stood him up, his face mottled with rage and desperation.

Another band of men came galloping across the meadow, the colors of their flag evident of their allegiance—Union cavalry.

"Damn!" Rourke cursed. "Catherine, there's going to be a bloodbath here in seconds. You ride south. Get to my camp. You'll be protected. No argument and do not disobey me this time." He lifted her onto a horse and slapped the animal's rear.

Colonel Ryan Rourke rallied his Rebels into offensive position, ready to charge. Across the meadow, an older man with a shock of white hair flowing wildly in the wind like some ancient Irish warrior urged his mount far ahead of the Union soldiers. John smirked. Mallory had lied.

"Uncle Charlie," Catherine cried from behind him and plunged her horse into the center of the meadow before John could stop her.

"Halt," ordered Rourke. His jaw clenched, his wife in the center of two armies. "Hold your fire," he commanded. He ticked off seconds. Any moment there would be engagement.

Father Callahan held a white handkerchief high over his head and waved it for both sides to see.

John's stomach turned rock hard. "What on earth is that fool woman doing?"

Shawn answered for him. "Father Callahan and that foolish sister of mine are trying to prevent a battle."

He grabbed Ryan's binoculars. A whole Yank Cavalry spoiled for a fight.

"Doesn't look good," Ryan commented to his brother. "They're in range. I'm going to have to start firing to protect my men."

Without answering, John climbed up on a horse and galloped to the center of the field. Both sides had their firearms raised. There was a deafening silence marked with only a gentle wind that wafted and lifted through the field of wheat. Tenuous strands of wind. Rourke's heart hammered in his chest. Would Father Callahan's crude symbol of truce be respected? No way out. He reached Catherine and nodded to Father Callahan.

"What the hell do you propose to do to get us out of this mess?" John demanded.

"Leave that to me," Father Callahan said.

Leadership from the Yank Cavalry rode up, obliging Father Callahan's flag of truce. "Lucas?" John blinked.

"Couldn't miss all the fun," said Lucas. "Besides it's dull in Washington. Mrs. Rourke, it's so good to see you again." He nodded in her direction.

General Rourke was not in the mood for social pleasantries. He let Father Callahan take the lead. A Yank Captain joined them with a sour expression directed toward the priest. Ryan pulled up beside John. Both sides crowded nearer. Every soldier tensed, listening for battle to begin.

John prayed to a higher power, his hand on his revolver. Father Callahan better give the best sermon of his life.

"Gentlemen of the North and South," Father Callahan greeted, gesturing with his splayed hands to both parties. "We are here on a mission to arrest a single fiend who has escaped the north." His voice rose loud, clear, and booming, his Irish lilt mesmerizing.

"This is not a day for war but for settling a justice." He pointed to Mallory who was apprehended between two Rebels. "We have come for him and wish to retire without further bloodshed."

The Yank captain sat forward in his saddle and protested. "This is irregular. We have come face to face with the enemy and must engage unless they choose to surrender."

John heard rifles click behind him, saw the subtle gesture of his brother, Ryan, signaling for his men to wait. There would be no surrender on the Rebels part. The Yank Captain was either a greenhorn or a complete idiot, staring down the muzzles of seasoned Rebel sharpshooters. They outnumbered the Yank Cavalry.

"Captain O'Donnell," Father Callahan addressed the Yank Captain, "In this case, the rules of conduct are to be broken."

"That's traitorous behavior. We could be hung for such talk," said O'Donnell. "There's a Rebel general and a Rebel colonel at my disposal. They should surrender to me immediately."

The Yank Captain was not only stupid but insane. He wanted glory. To capture such a prize would guarantee promotion. So many times during the war he'd witnessed the vanity of leadership crumple like ruins into dust. Father Callahan had better do some fast-talking unless he wanted his whole family wiped out. Catherine was beside him. Her hands were folded over her saddle horn and she was swathed in his huge greatcoat. Her hair fell and rose with the summer breeze and even though the one side of her face was swelling, she lifted her head like a queen. Despite his annoyance with her consistent disobedience and the danger they were presently in, his heart swelled with pride for her selfless sacrifice to prevent bloodshed.

She must have felt his eyes upon her and she turned as her horse shifted beneath her. "What do you think about when you are in battle?" she whispered to him.

"Staying alive. Winning. In this case, keeping you alive so I can wring your neck."

She bestowed on him a dazzling smile and mouthed the words *"I love you."* There was no convincing her to ride to safety.

"Stay close to me. Very close," Rourke ordered beneath his breath.

"Yes, General Rourke," she said, bending a quelling look.

Father Callahan began a stunning if not cunning oration, pleading to the sensibilities and moral responsibilities of mankind. John had never heard him speak but imagined him in his marble pulpit, influencing the masses. Everyone around him was spellbound. He finished with a grand gesture demanding a proposition. For this, he turned on Captain O'Donnell.

"We have a situation that is beyond the moral circumstances of North and South. Since we have involved the Union and the Confederacy in this affair, we can remedy that without the required bloodshed." He took a deep breath and exhaled. "What I am proposing is very simple and can be solved with a boxing match between two men of Northern and Southern heritage. Not just any men—men with talent from both sides, so it will be considered a fair fight." He circled his horse, catching and controlling the interest of every man. His keen gray eyes missed nothing, and his stout body trembled as though shaken by some inner wind. His voice thundered now, commanding with a proper mixture of anger, arrogance and a touch of Gaelic charm. Father Callahan was a gifted showman, his performance affected without artifice or pretension. He could bow men to his strength of character merely by his words, soft and poetic one moment, then, in a split second, stirring like a storm-drenched sea. All of them were entranced, their eyes gleaming at the thought of a single fight. And like putty in his hands, they all nodded their heads in agreement, lusting for this new idea to unfold.

The sun had descended an hour from its zenith, casting small shadows on the ground as horses pranced with impatience, the metal on their bridles clinking together as they raised and lowered their heads. In the distance, glazes of heat drifted in hazy uncertainty, lifting and disappearing. The decision lied with the Yank Captain. With scorn, Father Callahan turned his keen gray eyes on the Captain, freezing him in his place like glacial ice.

"But it would be treason, and act against our sovereign nation." Captain O'Donnell objected.

"Bah!" Father Callahan said. "Who of the men here would not desire to see a real boxing match, pitting the best of North against South?"

"What happens if word of this gets back?" Captain O'Donnell blinked, afraid to make a decision against the rules of war.

"No man here will tell," Father Callahan challenged him. With efficiency he moved around, glaring each man in the eye. "Every man will swear an oath to that effect before me!" It was a command.

Every man nodded in agreement—except the Captain.

Captain O'Donnell withered under the priest's glare. No way did he want to go against the power of God. He nodded his head, giving his consent. John had the feeling that Father Callahan had known just what O'Donnell would do.

"Who's to fight?" asked one of the Yank soldiers.

Father Callahan shook his fist into the air. "I'll be deciding that notion."

"But who is good enough to represent the North?" persisted the same soldier.

"Not me," protested Father Callahan. "I'm too old and feeble. Beyond a shadow of a doubt I shall be dead soon." Everyone laughed.

What a clever use of levity to melt the hostilities. John considered Father Callahan. He was old, of course, but there was a spark of mischief in his eyes, and liveliness in his wizened face. With certainty, the old man was wily enough to court another hundred years.

"From the North," Father Callahan paused with skillful exhibition, "New York's finest boxer with a renowned reputation, the king of the ring, Francis Mallory. Bring him over boys," he motioned to the Rebels who held Mallory prisoner. "You Rebel boys should know we have been chasing this felon across half the state of Virginia. You did a fine job in catching him for us." He complimented them.

Catherine burst with Mallory's sins. "He took Rebel prisoners out of Capitol Prison and beat them without mercy. For his own profit, and with evil purpose, he sold misshapen barrels from his foundry to Fitzgerald Rifle Works. These guns exploded backward into the faces of innocent soldiers of both the North and South."

Both Rebs and Yanks spat in Mallory's direction. A fair fight was one thing, but corruption at the expense of personal gain was unforgiveable.

"Who'll fight for the South?" asked the same Yank soldier.

"We have a fighter in Mallory for I have even heard of him," admitted the captain. "But the South has no such man. None!" O' Donnell spoke, venom spit from his lips. "Need I remind you only the North has boxing parlors, while the South woos fighting with fowl in their barnyards with the stink of swine dung clinging to their feet?"

Father Callahan stared at Captain O'Donnell, his sharp eyes cutting him to pieces. He would not allow an idiot to destroy his attempt to preserve a separate peace.

"Is that a head wound you received in the war?" Father Callahan asked innocent enough, referring to the bruise on the Yank's head.

The Captain' face grew red, embarrassed and angered from the priest's question.

"I heard you were kicked by a horse." The old priest did not wait for an answer. The jerky head movements of the Yank confirmed the truth.

Father Callahan was in control.

"You should be grateful you weren't wounded anywhere crucial." Some of the Rebs laughed at the priest's slight, but before the insult registered on the Captain, he said quickly, "What do you think of a little wager to give it the right spice? I'm a gambling man. How about a few wagers between the men? Can't be any harm in that?" Father Callahan appealed to the Captain's greed.

"Who fights for the South?" yelled the same irritating Yank soldier.

Captain O'Donnell leaned down, looking over the lean Southerners, none of which had the massive arms and shoulders of Mallory. "Who fights for the South before I lay my wager?"

"A simple fighting man. But it must be fair for the sake of the wagers laid," Father Callahan said, taking him into his confidence. He turned. "General John Daniel Rourke!" He looked at John with a dominating eye that sanctioned no opposition. "It would be only fair to even the odds," he spoke over his shoulder for the benefit of the half-wit Captain.

Mallory, bolder now, threw off his jacket and began rolling up his sleeves. He stared at John. "Your lesson is not yet done." He started feinting in the air like a prizefighter, receiving hoots and hollers of approval from the Yanks.

Father Callahan rubbed his hands with glee. "General John Daniel Rourke." He turned his eyes on John. "Are you up for a good fight, my boy?"

"Agreed," said Rourke smiling.

"No," cried Catherine. "I won't allow it. I forbid it."

John looked to his wife. "Oh ye of little faith."

Her face turned ashen. "You don't know that beast. He's killed men. I've seen how's he's beaten them, crippled them."

Father Callahan glared at his niece. "You've more than humiliated an Officer of the Confederacy, girl. Keep your mouth shut, for you shame your husband. Jimmy, my boy, collect the wagers."

"You mean he's—General Rourke?" bellowed Captain O'Donnell. He took a deep breath out of fear and astonishment for his eyes beheld the true hero of the South.

"You're gambling over my husband's life. I won't have it. You must stop this madness." Catherine pleaded to anyone with sense that would listen. And then her eyes fell on a young boy. "Jimmy O'Hara," she shrieked in shock from his presence.

"Yes miss," said Jimmy, collecting the wagers from the men, he lifted his hands, palms up. "I have to do as I'm ordered. I'm working for the United States Military under Colonel Lucas Rourke."

"Father Callahan you should be ashamed of teaching a young child such vices. What kind of example are you showing him?"

Some of the Rebels were uneasy about their wagers. They knew General Rourke's reputation on the battlefield as a legendary fighter. In war, he had weapons, but boxing? Coins clinked. The men made their bets.

"Billy, bring me some water," condescended Captain O'Donnell. The Yank captain had acquiesced for the long haul.

Treated like his personal manservant, a gigantic black soldier dismounted his shoulders and arms bulging like a blacksmith. John let go a smirk. So this is where his old friend, Boxing Billy, the escaped slave had gone to. When Billy brushed past John on his trek to the creek to fill the captain's canteen, he lifted his left hand. John nodded with the signal from his old sparring partner.

Father Callahan moved to John out of earshot of the Yanks. "Greed is a terrible thing, but it works with half-wits like O'Donnell, doesn't it General? I see Boxing Billy sends his greetings. Remarkable lad. It's a pity our half-wit Captain doesn't understand what a prize he has right under his nose. Treats him like a dog."

John grunted.

"It would give me the greatest of pleasure to see you geld Mallory. It's a genuine gift I'm giving you." The priest boasted. "I'd do it myself but I abandoned boxing the day I took the vow of celibacy."

Rourke gave the priest a faint look of amusement. "You have a lot of faith in me."

"Good Lord, not faith, but common sense. If you need faith, I'll say a few Hail Mary's. Billy gives you his nod, so I'll take his word."

"Bloodthirsty aren't you, Father?" John reminded the priest, hinting at the sin of revenge.

"Not at all, General Rourke. Do you see the bruise on Catherine's face? I wonder how it got there."

A raw fury blazed into Rourke and with intent, Father Callahan had seized upon it.

"Should I make my wager for ten or twenty times?" the priest asked.

"A hundred," rasped John, his eyes glaring holes into the dancing Mallory.

"Good boy." Father Callahan rubbed his hands together. "I've spent enough time with the Southern side, and I must go back to the northern boys." He winked at John before he hobbled back. "Jimmy," he called. "Don't forget my wager."

If John could have seen through his rage, he would have seen the true genius in Father Callahan's tactful negotiations. But his mind was set on Mallory. John removed his coat and shirt, giving them to Ryan.

"Good Luck, John," Ryan said. "Are you sure you're up to this?"

His brother would call it off in a second, but then there would be full-scale bloodshed. John itched to get his hands on Mallory. He would not be cheated. "Does an elephant concern himself with a cricket?"

"I thought so." Ryan smiled. "I wonder why Lucas keeps rubbing his jaw."

"Fond memories." John smiled. "I assure you Mallory will have even fonder memories before this day is out."

Catherine appealed to Colonel Ryan Rourke. "You can't gamble over your brother's life."

"I don't care. This is the fight of the century. North versus South. This is the way the war should be settled anyway."

No one wanted to stop this fight.

John stepped forward into a square ring Billy had edged with a bayonet. Cheered by a chorus of Rebel yells, his blood began to race through his veins.

"You can beg for mercy now," Mallory told John, "if you want your death to be swift."

"You could quit now, Mallory, saving yourself a beating—" John countered, "—and the humiliation."

They waltzed a bizarre dance like two gamecocks circling each other. John gauged his opponent. Mallory came in hooking. Some of them were to hurt, though, and one of them was low. John broke and tried a short right for the jaw. It landed. It jolted Mallory and he took a step backward, his first of the fight. John followed, swinging with a wild overhand right. Mallory had the weight. John had the speed. John hit steadier, quicker punches. Half the blows Mallory initiated never landed. Rebs and Yanks circled tight around the boundaries of the ring, screaming.

Mallory continued the barrage. John put a left in his mustached face. In answer, Mallory punched at John's head hard with the pounding of a bull.

"I'm not even winded yet. I can waltz like this all day," Mallory taunted.

Most expected John to be the weaker of the two. Mallory slipped on wet earth then, and John beat down on him. His energy poured into just one thing, the lust for battle, even death, and he laid at Mallory with massive short jabs that drove Mallory back and back. The fists flew hard and both men cursed at one another before more blows were met. John punched, feinted, and taunted Mallory again and again, never giving Mallory a chance to recover from the throws of his fists. Finally, they pushed against one another breast to breast.

Men shouted at them, calling for blood, but John had no ears for them. He kept his gaze fixed on Mallory's cold, black, glittering eyes.

"I promise you," Mallory sneered. "You will kneel to me before the day is out."

"I'll live to see the stars fall before that happens." John pushed away from him.

Mallory came on him with the fierceness of a tiger and power of an ox. John blocked the blows, defending himself, letting Mallory exhaust his strength. John gave a massive cut to the right and twisted his wrist to come straight at Mallory's belly. Mallory quickly sidestepped and in an instant his arm came around and smashed him in the jaw. For a moment John saw only a haze of white as Mallory came at him again and again. He pushed away and shook his head, trying to clear his eyes, flicking the sweat-soaked hanks of hair from his forehead. It was hot in the July sun. He watched Mallory. The racket shook the meadow from the men shouting and could probably be heard all the way to Richmond.

Over Mallory's head John focused on Billy, his left hand punching the air. He knew John was a southpaw. Through the haze, his mind cleared, and John smiled at the black soldier. John pummeled Mallory, never letting up. Then Mallory ducked and pulled a revolver out of his belt, lifting it high over his head and smashed the butt end down on John's jaw. He turned just in time for the blow to glance off his mouth, but it still dropped him to his knees so fast, he didn't have the chance to taste the blood.

Catherine screamed and was pulled back by her brother.

"Let him finish," Shawn bellowed.

John whipped his leg around and tripped Mallory, bringing him down to his level, finishing him off with a crack to the jaw. But the fight wasn't over. Mallory pulled a knife from his boot and only the sharp glitter of it brought John to attention. He narrowed his eyes, never leaving Mallory's eyes. Mallory took a slash toward him, then another. Rourke, despite his size, was on his feet, dodging every attempt, leaving Mallory frustrated.

In his fury, Mallory charged. "You're one dead Rebel!"

Ducking, but not quite enough, the knife glanced off his forehead and blood poured down. It burned like the fires of purgatory. With one glancing blow to the wrist, John knocked the knife from Mallory's hand, the weapon sailing on the ground between them. Mallory dove for the knife, but a rifle shot from the Rebel quarter spit up the ground in front of them spinning the knife out of his reach. With the shot going off would there be a free for all?

"Hold your fire, boys!" shouted Father Callahan. "He shot the knife out of the way."

John started punching, his knuckles bleeding from landing on bone and anything else he could reach, his strikes coming at Mallory with the speed of a cobra striking. In desperation, Mallory fought just as hard, his fists finding well-aimed targets into John's face and ribs and stomach. John tried to stave off the soreness, aching in every part of his body.

John faked a feint with his right and with a left hook powerful enough to disembowel an ox he smashed his fist into Mallory's face, knocking him out cold. Disgusted he stepped over Mallory's prone lifeless form. John didn't look back. He hoped that when he died, he wouldn't wind up in the same circle of hell as Mallory. It would be tiresome to have to fight him all over again.

Catherine ran to him and threw her arms around him, cooing to him over his bruises. "Careful woman, remember I'm immune to pain, I'm a general."

"I'm taking care of you now," she ordered him.

The Yanks dragged away Mallory's body and tied up his thugs.

"That was an amazing fight, General Rourke," Captain Joseph O'Donnell admitted. "Even though I lost a hefty chunk of gold, it was worth every cent of it." He looked at the old priest gloating in the sunshine. "I have a funny feeling Father Callahan knew the outcome of this match before it started.

"I could say, of course to that notion, if you consider yourself a half-wit, but I know you wouldn't find that idea agreeable. Instead, I'll introduce you to Boxing Billy of the South."

The captain frowned, and then glanced to John. "You're the famous Boxing Billy? The South's boxing champion, the greatest legend in boxing history, even the world?"

John shook his head. "He was my tutor. Great boxer though, left both painful and powerful impressions on me as a lad. To tell you the truth, Boxing Billy was a slave on a plantation neighboring mine. We sparred often. I consider him the greatest of friends. He disappeared when the war started. I haven't seen him until he popped up recently."

"Remarkable. I didn't know he was a black man. You actually knew and sparred with Boxing Billy? You are very lucky to have met such a man. I would be down on my knees paying homage to meet someone like him."

John half-grinned. "You can start kneeling now."

"What do you mean?" asked the bewildered captain.

John inclined his head. "He's standing next to you."

The captain turned, studying the large black Union soldier he treated as his manservant. "You're Boxing Billy! Why haven't you ever said so?"

Billy flexed his hands. "You never asked."

Colonel Ryan Rourke spoke up. "It would be nice to continue our conversation, but if we are caught like this, we'll all feel the noose over our heads. Better to disband now."

Colonel Lucas Rourke nodded in agreement. "I'll make sure Mallory is locked up for a long time. I've have a long list of his crimes. One of his thugs was so kind to confess. And then there is the murder of Agatha Fitzgerald as witnessed by one of the servants."

Before Catherine could say anything, Shawn held his hand up to quell her. He discarded John's greatcoat, revealing his Union uniform. "I'm going with you to make sure Mallory pays for his corruptions."

"Who the hell are you, and what are you doing with a Reb general?" Captain O'Donnell snapped.

Shawn lifted himself up into full stature, looking him square in the eye. "I'm Lieutenant Colonel Shawn Callahan Fitzgerald."

"Of the Fitzgerald's of New York—the family that owns Fitzgerald Rifles?" Captain O'Donnell gaped like a beached trout.

"The same and I suggest you rethink your attitude, Captain, or I'll give you over to the general."

"Yes, Sir. My apologies, Sir." Sweat beaded on the Captain's forehead, apparently realizing just how close he was coming to court-martial. He moved to the side of the men.

"It's good to have you back," Colonel Lucas Rourke said.

"Any relation to General Rourke?" asked Shawn, confusion swirling in his eyes.

"We're brothers—" Lucas smiled. "A regrettable occurrence that derives from different opinions on the war. We need to cut this reunion short. Ryan is right. We've taken long enough and dare not dally any further."

"Son of a bitch," roared Captain O'Donnell, searching through his pockets. "Where's my wallet. I had it here two seconds ago."

"Jimmy!" Colonel Lucas Rourke shouted.

Catherine stood next to Jimmy and took the wallet from him, pretending to pick it up off the ground. "You must have dropped it, Captain O'Donnell," she said, eyeing the smiling Jimmy O'Hara with a warning glance. After returning the wallet, she whispered to Jimmy. "I see Colonel Lucas is wise to your tricks."

"He appreciates my talents. That's why I work for him."

Before Catherine could answer, John pulled her aside. "Do you wish to return with your brother? I'm concerned for your safety. There are no guarantees with the war on Virginia soil."

"I'm staying with you, John. I am not fearful and you'll never drag me away. I love you too much."

"Then I insist on taking you to my family's farm to live. I will not risk you near the lines of war. Do I make myself clear? There will be no disobedience this time. Do I have your word or do I send you back with your brother?"

"You have my word," she said and laced her arms around his neck, pulling his swollen face down to hers for a kiss.

Chapter 30

*E*ven in February, Fairhaven was beautiful. Catherine chuckled, remembering how she had called John's home *a little farm*. Why his family's property took a day and half's ride to circle the boundaries, and even more surprised to learn his family's wealth equaled hers.

She had grown to love everything about John's ancestral home. The house was majestically confident in its affluence, a magnificent elegant structure with everything that a hundred and more years of unlimited prosperity could accumulate. The living quarters were large and airy in the summer, and warm and inviting in the winter. The foyer hosted one of the South's finest double staircases that curved upward with a gallery of former ancestors staring down, each with their own separate tale. Large windows let in a host of light and there was a large porch that wrapped endlessly around the entire house, lending a charm and grace caught in a time warp and, so far, devoid of war.

There were servants to do what was needed and Catherine enjoyed every one of them, including Old Cyrus who warned her to take care when she left the house for her walk. She took a westerly route, taking care not to travel far and admired the rich beauty of the landscape nestled in the Shenandoah. The air had the bite of late winter and with the dawn, the swollen sun hung low and pale in the frosty mist. Black starlings flocked on brown and fallow fields, and the barnyards were frozen muddy by the hooves of livestock penned for winter slaughter. A few rust-colored shriveled apples clung to the higher branches of a tree, shaking when an icy wind blew. Catherine wrapped her scarf and coat tighter. Molly with the long legs, John's dog, nudged her hand, waiting to be petted. Catherine lifted her eyes to the horizon. A formless and heavy gray horizontal mass of cloud, released a veil of snow. She plodded through its silent beauty, incredibly lonely. Of late, she had not heard from John, understanding the Confederacy's position to be very grave. As far as she knew, the siege continued around Petersburg, Grant pounding and tightening his noose as supplies and will dwindled for the South.

Catherine had grown ponderous with child, a secret she kept from John. He had enough on his mind. There was no need to give him additional worries. After the baby was born, she would tell him.

The stark browns and blacks of oak, hawthorn and ash were dusted white with snow. The cattle were lowing near the barns, their music making her melancholy escalate. How she missed her husband. The last few months had been agony. He had written her every day, the letters arriving grouped in packets. But of late she had heard little at all, and her preoccupation with John's survival grew.

She did not share her anxiety with John's parents although she discerned they shared the same fears for all of their sons. She loved his mother and father. They treated her with the deference of a daughter they never had, welcoming her when John dropped her unannounced on their doorstep. That had been several months ago and she had not seen her husband once. Christmas arrived and still, no John.

John's parents had tried to fill the gaps as best as they could. Mother Rourke clucked over her, excited about the prospect of her first grandchild. Catherine basked in the love John's parents shared and looked forward to having a large family of her own, something she had missed growing up in New York. They insisted she not work and showered her with gifts. She spent hours sewing clothing items for the baby with John's mother, and was touched when John's father presented a cradle made of black walnut, carved by his hands. As her time approached, she grew more jealous of the Cause that kept her husband away, praying daily for his safe return and a quick end to the war.

Her brother, Shawn, received an honorable discharge by President Lincoln to return home and take control of the company. Shawn had secured the Fitzgerald fortunes and used his power to put Mallory behind bars, not that it was difficult when his thugs started stating his crimes to lessen their own sentences. The foundry had been finished and now the rifle company used good barrels. And as far as she knew, his bride still waited until the war finished and it was safe enough for her to travel north. Catherine sympathized with her brother's longing.

Her uncle was back in Pleasant Valley, taking care of his parishioners. Jimmy O'Hara worked with Colonel Lucas Rourke in Washington and she had Shawn forward funds to Washington for Jimmy's tutors and living expenses. It was the least she could do for the orphan boy who done so much for her. She had learned from Lucas that Boxing Billy was treated like royalty by Captain O'Donnell and there had been boxing events, attended well in the Yank camps. And not one word of that day in Virginia, where an obscure but extraordinary boxing event had occurred between North and South had ever been whispered.

She paused to catch her breath, and the baby gave a whopping kick. "Stubborn like your father." She laughed and then smoothed her hands over her swollen stomach. She waddled like a goose, her breasts were sore, and her legs and back ached. She entered the barns and moved to the stall to brush her thoroughbred, a gift from John. Not able to ride her mare yet, Catherine built up a steady friendship with the beautiful equine by grooming and singing to the animal in a daily ritual.

The front doors of the barn opened and she peered over the ledge of the stall. John? A solitary figure led a horse through the barn. He dusted fallen snow from his head and broad shoulders. About to cry out for sheer joy of her husband's return, she stopped cold. The visitor possessed the same height and same dark hair. He turned, startled by her presence. His eyes were a different color. Her shoulders drooped.

He smiled then, that same jaunty, confident smile of John's, and tipped his hat. "This is a pleasure ma'am and might I add, a boon to my homecoming."

Was he flirting with her? With certainty, this was John's youngest brother, Zachary. Feeling a little mischievous, she decided to play along and mocked him with a slight curtsy.

He led his horse into the stall next to hers. "Do beg pardon, ma'am. I have been gone long from Fairhaven, my home. Are you perhaps a new serving girl?"

Catherine smiled, her enormous middle hidden by the partition. "Perhaps? Would that be agreeable to you Mr.—"

He grinned. "Mr. Zachary Rourke. Zachary would be fine, and yes—I'd find it mighty agreeable. In fact, I have never seen a serving girl as pretty as you. To tell you the truth, I don't want to just meet you. I'd like to know more of you," he said, but the implications were obvious to Catherine. He unbuckled the girth and yanked the saddle off his horse.

"I do not think that will occur," she told him. "However, there is charm in what you say." Pulling back a length of her long hair, she dropped the currycomb into his stall.

Limping, Zachary bent to retrieve it, then handed her the comb. "I stand guilty as charged but beg the honor of learning everything I can about you."

"What of your wound, Zachary?"

"Just a scratch with an Indian I encountered in the Plains. The Indian was fierce to have my scalp and I was fierce to keep it."

Catherine laughed.

"But the pain is nothing compared to the wound of Cupid's arrow at the moment my eyes fell upon your incomparable beauty."

"Perhaps you should be more circumspect," Catherine offered.

"If my manners are boorish, I apologize for them. It has been long since I've been home and tasted the refinement of proper etiquette."

"How long will you be staying home from your travels?"

"As long as it takes."

Catherine pretended not to understand. "As long as what takes?"

"As long as it takes to have you accept my proposal of marriage for I have fallen in love."

"I see," Catherine frowned, pretending to give his proposal some thought. "But there might be a problem."

"Does my mother work you overlong?" Then looking at her with the currycomb in her hand he became appalled. "We have hired men to do the stable work."

"Oh that. I enjoy being busy."

He opened the stall door and took her hand, leading her around the gate. When he caught sight of her huge and extended abdomen his eyes grew big.

"I would say you have been quite busy."

Catherine smothered a smile. "I'm your new sister-in-law. I married your brother, John." She extended her hand and introduced herself. "Catherine Rourke, a pleasure and honor to meet you at last."

He jerked his head back. "John married? That's a revelation. When? Never mine. Is he here or is he still in that stupid war?"

Catherine swallowed a sudden lump of sadness in her throat. "He's still in the stupid war."

"Fool should be here for the birth of his child."

Oh, John, how I miss being kissed and touched and held in your arms. "You can't blame him for I've chosen to keep it a secret."

"A secret! Good lord woman, you're ready to hatch. What are you doing out here with the horses? You could get kicked or fall on ice. I insist you go inside and go to bed."

"I'm not ill, Zachary, I'm expecting a child." Zachary was as bossy as his older brother. At the thought of John, her mind set to worrying again.

"I'll wait for you to feed your horse, and then you can escort me inside, so I won't slip on the ice," she said to placate him. She didn't tell him she had already walked two miles.

When he finished feeding his horse, they strolled arm in arm toward the house. A sudden violent wind roared down from the tops of the Shenandoah and Catherine paused, grateful for Zachary's steady strength. The snow bit hard at her nose and cheeks and the tempest did not seem to cease. Winter was letting them know it still had its edge. Catherine watched, fascinated, the wind twisting and coiling the snow, obscuring the distant mountains and landscape. Suddenly the wind parted the snow in two separate veils and where it parted, Catherine noticed a horse drawn cart approach.

"Who in the world could be visiting?" Zachary asked.

Her heart sank. She dropped Zachary's arm and started running. The snow-covered canvas on the back of the cart spoke louder than words. That was how they brought dead men home to their families. John would be riding his horse, no matter what condition he was in. Wouldn't he? She stumbled on her skirts. *Oh God, please don't let it be John.*

She stopped, stared at the shroud with an unfocused gaze. Her hand went to her mouth. She couldn't breathe. Cold. No movement. *It's not true! It's not true!* He promised her, he'd come back. He promised to keep her warm at night, to love her over and over again. He promised to grow old with her.

Her world slowed. They argued about everything, but that was what made them stronger. John had planted a fire in her heart and awakened her soul. To have him ripped from her? How could she go on?

The baby moved sharply but she ignored the pain. Why had she never told him about the baby? John would never know he would have the child he so dearly wanted. He deserved a child. He deserved to take joy in the flesh of his flesh—and death was his reward?

She swallowed. "Is he——" She couldn't say the words.

"No Ma'am. But he's hurt real bad and need to get him where it's warm real quick," shouted, Lieutenant Johnson above the wind's fury.

She snapped to attention, recognizing Rourke's lieutenant for the first time. Zachary and Lieutenant Johnson lifted John upstairs. Mother Rourke had a bed prepared and ordered a blazing fire in the fireplace. More quilts were added. John's parents and Old Cyrus stood beside the bed.

Catherine's stomach knotted. The ashen color of John's skin was that of a dying man, like many she'd seen working in the hospital. A cold, stark fear ratcheted through her.

"John," she called to him, closing her hand around his.

His steel-blue eyes fluttered open for the barest of seconds. "Catherine?" He breathed, and then, his eyes closed, and his head fell to the side.

"No...John..." she screamed. "No...no..." she placed her hands on his cheeks. "Stay awake...please don't die...please, please, please..."

"Got him here as fast as possible. He was shot real bad in the leg when Grant made a move to break the siege barriers. One doctor wanted to take his leg, but I put my gun on him and ordered for Dr. Parks to be brought forward. If not for Dr. Parks, his leg would have been amputated."

Catherine and Mother Rourke breathed a sigh of relief.

"After General Rourke was stabilized, we received special permission from General Lee to bring him home, but I'm sworn to return as soon as possible," said the lieutenant.

Catherine removed the bandage. His skin was hot to the touch. "I'll need boiled water and a salve to draw out the poison. And fresh bandages." A piercing pain compressed her lower stomach and she closed her eyes until it passed. *Not now, little one. You must wait until I have your papa attended to.*

"I'll get a salve I brewed to draw out the infection and make some willow bark tea to bring down the fever." Old Cyrus hobbled from the room.

Mother Rourke nodded to one of the maids, hovering in the hall. "Boil water and get the bandages out of the linen closet."

Catherine swallowed her fears and panic. She had to keep a clear head and take care of her husband. John was burning up with fever...so pale and worn. *Would he make it?* Of course he would. He had to see his child born. With Mother Rourke's help she rolled the quilts off John. For several hours, Catherine used her nursing skills. She cleansed his wound and put on the salve. Zachary helped lift John, so she could force him to drink the willow bark tea. He burned with fever. John thrashed. He sweated. He screamed. What horrible horrors he relived.

Mother Rourke took the men downstairs and had a hot dinner served to them. Then she ordered a room prepared for the lieutenant to rest before he returned, but he refused until he knew the general was better.

Again and again, Catherine bathed her husband with water, to cool him down. She pulled off the bandage, mopped the infection and put on more salve. She wound on new bandages and placed a thin sheet to cover him. Time would tell.

Hours passed. John quit thrashing, quieted. She checked the bandage and his wound lost the unhealthy dark color, finally turning pinkish. She placed the palm of her hand on his forehead. He had lost his fever. He'd make it.

The pains in Catherine's back increased, she supposed from being on her feet so long. The pains suddenly wrapped around her front, knifing into her abdomen. She sank to her knees and clutched her abdomen.

Mother Rourke returned from downstairs and knelt beside Catherine. "I think I'm about to be a grandmother." She helped Catherine rise. "You are going straight to bed." She clapped her hands. "Cyrus, go get the midwife. Maybelle, boil more water and bring fresh linens. Sara, pull down the blankets in the room next to John's. Hurry." She performed her tasks with the logistical calculations of a general. Catherine could see where her husband earned his stripes.

John's father, Robert ran up the stairs. Catherine screamed. Robert put her arm around his shoulder and helped her to the bed.

She reeled with another pain and she collapsed on the pillows. Mother Rourke shooed him from the room, then helped Catherine undress and put on a soft cotton gown. The pains were faster now. She couldn't catch her breath. She clutched Mother Rourke's hand.

"I don't think the midwife will be here in time. Don't worry. I've given birth four times and assisted in numerous deliveries. I'll help you," Mother Rourke soothed, but Catherine screamed from the top of her lungs.

From the fog of fever, John woke. His body felt like he'd been hammered with a railroad tie. He stretched. His leg burned. He opened his eyes. Zachary, his father, old Cyrus and Ian were there. Nothing made sense. He was conscious enough to know it wasn't him who was doing the screaming. "Where am I?"

Another ear-splitting scream pierced the air. John snapped his head around. "What in the hell is that?"

"That is your wife," his father smiled, running his hands through his hair. "Welcome to the land of the living."

John did not smile. What was the matter with them? His wife needed help. He tried to get up, but Lieutenant Johnson and Zachary flew to the bedside to keep him down. "What's wrong?" he demanded when he heard Catherine scream again.

"Your wife is having a baby." Zachary smiled.

"A baby?"

"It's a usual course of nature when two people get married." His father assured him. "She didn't want you to worry. She felt you had enough pressing things on your mind with the war. Mother sent a maid in a few seconds ago and told us all is going well."

Another bloodcurdling scream came from the other room and his father went to check.

"Well it doesn't sound like things are going well to me. Take me in to see my wife. Now." John demanded.

"I'll knock you out if you don't keep still," Zachary said.

Then John heard the healthy cry of his child being born, the sweetest music under the sun.

"Thank you God," John said. "How's Catherine?" he demanded when his father came into the room and he tried to get up again.

"Mother and child are doing fine. Congratulations son. It's the beginning of another Rourke generation that the eyes of this old house will see raised and nurtured. How's your injury?"

"I don't care about my injury. I'm getting up to see my wife and child, and I don't give a damn what anyone says even if I have to fight you all."

"Your mother delivered the baby and she has given strict orders for you to wait until she tidies your wife and child."

Zachary and Ian lifted John on a stretcher, making sure there was no movement to his leg. They settled him on the bed next to Catherine and everyone left to give the new family privacy. As the baby suckled at her breast, John picked up the tiny infant's hand, letting the baby's fingers curl over his callused finger. He ran his other hand over the infant's downy head of black hair and marveled at the miracle that brought this new life into the world. Catherine was tired but glowing with a special love that touched his soul.

A great wind hurled itself around the house, lifting shingles and slamming shutters, and then slowly, softly settled quietly as the two gazed at one another.

"We have a son, John, a beautiful baby boy. Thank you for this blessed gift." She bent over and kissed him. "I have demands on your convalescence. You will be still so that leg can mend. And you are staying home."

"There's not much left of the war, and my leg will keep me out of action."

With tears in her eyes, Catherine whispered, "That makes two blessed gifts."

Author's Note

$\mathcal{W}$inston Churchill once claimed that the **Great American Civil War** was, "...considered the noblest and least avoidable of all the great mass conflicts of which till then there was record."

Preceding *Surrender the Wind* was the second **Battle of the Wilderness**. Fought on May 5-6, 1864. The opening engagement of the Overland Campaign has gone down in the annals of American History as one of the bloodiest battles, and the turning point in the war in the Eastern Theatre. As a fresh appointment to the General-in-Chief to the Union Armies, Ulysses S. Grant led the Army of the Potomac south in what he anticipated to be a rapid ploy to outflank the right of Confederate General Robert E. Lee and his Army of Northern Virginia. Chaos exploded in the lines, and tangled in the monstrous undergrowth of the Wilderness, many men perished in uncoordinated fighting and, a terrible fire that swept through the forests. Grant almost succeeded in breaking the Confederate lines. For Lee, the battle was a tactical victory.

Five Points District was a neighborhood in lower Manhattan, New York City, New York. In the Five Points District, large numbers of Irish Catholics fleeing the Irish Potato Famine suffered extreme population density, disease, infant and child mortality rates, unemployment, prostitution, political corruption, violent crime, and other archetypal ills of the city's deprived. Inhabited by gangsters and other criminals, Five Points bore the highest murder rate of any slum in the world at that time.

Elmira Prison was a prisoner-of-war camp constructed by the Union Army in Elmira, New York during the American Civil War. Twelve thousand Confederate soldiers were imprisoned with twenty-five percent, dying from malnutrition, exposure to harsh winter weather, overcrowded conditions, disease, poor sanitary facilities and lack of medical care. Despite the excellent harvest that year, the Confederates were given little or rancid food to eat. Dubbed "Hellmira" by its inmates, many charges were alleged that the camp was not a prison but a death camp and consequently, the North's brutal answer to the South's Andersonville.

General Jubal Early's raid on Washington: To lessen Ulysses S. Grant's pounding blows to Petersburg, Virginia, General Robert E. Lee sent General Jubal Early and his Army of the Valley up the Shenandoah to make a daring raid on the northern capital of Washington, D.C. With ten thousand Confederate firebrands breathing down the Capitol's neck, reinforcements were led by General Lew Wallace (author of Ben Hur) to help hold them off. The real skirmishing began at Fort Stevens outside the Union capitol. President Abraham Lincoln walked the parapets to view the action, his height, making him easy pickings for Rebel sharpshooters. Captain Oliver Wendell Holmes concealed below chastised the President. "Get down, you fool." (He later became a Supreme Court Justice.). General Early realized the strength of

Union reinforcements and withdrew across the Potomac, ending his attack on Washington D.C.

Boxing during the War Between the States took on a life of its own. Cultivated by the Irish masses in New York City, the sport soon stretched to the farmlands of the South. Bare-knuckled boxing seized the day and was a popular pastime with soldiers between long marches and battles to amuse themselves. Of course, gambling accompanied the sport. It is rumored that, when officers were not present, sometimes Yanks and Rebs would cross picket lines and secretly assemble for a bare-knuckled boxing event. Two men with nowhere to go and with only their fists to determine their fate, endured as a symbol for good against evil, mental power versus brute strength. North against South. If caught, the men would face execution for this treasonous act. With irony, it is sad to disclose that they would be shooting at each other again the next day.

I always say that I'm a storyteller, not a historian, and as a storyteller, I'm more concerned with the what-ifs than the why-nots. I so enjoy taking a bit of license in order to bring you the most exciting, sensual, love story that my what-if imagination can create.

About the Author

Elizabeth St. Michel is the award-winning and bestselling author of *The Winds of Fate*, for which she was a quarter-finalist for the Amazon Breakthrough Novel Award and was a number-one hit on the Amazon bestseller lists.

Her second novel, *Surrender the Wind*, won "the Catherine" and "the Marlene," the respective Romance Writer's Awards of Toronto and Washington, DC. She is also the recipient of the Holt Medallion Award in honor of literary excellence in romance writing. Born and raised in western New York, she is the mother of five wonderful children.

Acknowledgements

M ost books wouldn't be written without the help of some special people. I would like to acknowledge Caroline Tolley, my developmental editor and Linda Styles, my copy/line editor. Their insight and expertise were indispensable. Hugs also to my spouse, Edward, five children, eight grandchildren, Dr. Marcianna Dollard, and posthumously, Loretta Bysiek—your love and comfort surround me.

Many thanks to the gracious support of Nancy Crawford, Linda Bysiek, Brenda Kosinski, Paula Ursoy and Western New York Romance Writers Group.

Finally, a special note of gratitude to my readers. You will never know how much your enthusiasm and support enrich my work and my life. You are the best.

Dear Readers,

It has given me particular pleasure to write, *Surrender the Wind* for you. There is no greater compliment to me as an author than for my readers to become so involved with the characters that you want me to write more. That said, I'm happily immersed in a series, with the powerful Rourke family of Virginia and their three strong-willed sons. As you know, my first installment detailed the journey of legendary Confederate General John Daniel Rourke, the eldest son and his providential meeting of Catherine Fitzgerald from New York during the American Civil War.

My second installment acquaints us with John's younger brother, Lucas Rourke. Of a different sentiment than his family, Colonel Lucas Rourke is honor bound to uphold the Union and is responsible for a vast network of spies. But when Confederates abduct him, his only hope is the enigmatic spy, Rachel Pierce. How unfortunate, for Lucas to have his orderly world turned upside down by the stubborn Rachel, even worse that he has to depend on her to navigate him through enemy territory.

Although I can't tell you much more I can promise you this: like my last novel, it is written with one goal in mind—to make you experience the laughter, the love, and all the other myriad emotions of its characters. And when it's over to leave you smiling…

Warmly,
Elizabeth St. Michel

P.S. If you would like to receive an emailed newsletter from me, which will keep you informed about my books-in-progress as well as answer some of the questions I'm frequently asked about publishing, please contact me on my Facebook, Twitter or webpage at www.elizabethstmichel.com. I would be thrilled to hear from you!